C000228235

REVIEWS FOR EM]

"In this fast paced, twisty action packed sequel, ... much more, and in desperate need for book 3!"
        - Anat Eliraz, author of Jewels of Smoky Quartz

"David Green has become an insta-buy for absolutely any and EVERY thing he releases. Brilliant, BRILLIANT author."
    - Rachel Rener, author of The Lightning Conjurer Series

"The work of a fantasy writer who knows his craft."
            - JMD Reid, author of the Illumination Cycle

"For any epic fantasy fans out there - this one is for you. Just trust me on this."
    - Catrin Russell, author of The Light Of Darkness series

"There's no mercy shown outside of a few, and even that mercy buys time not clemency... I can't wait to see where this series goes next."
        - Rachael Boucker, author of The Night Order Series

"David Green continues his epic fantasy with diverse and flawed characters, battles to blow your mind, and a story that makes jaws drop and profanities fall from lips."
            - Neen Cohen, author of Cold as Hell

"Hands down one of the best books I've read this year"
            - The Magic Book Corner

PATH OF WAR

Eerie River Publishing
www.EerieRiverPublishing.com
Hamilton, Ontario Canada

Paperback ISBN: 978-1-990245-67-1
Hardcover ISBN: 978-1-990245-68-8

Edited by S.O. Green & Michelle River
Cover Design Grady Earls

PATH OF WAR

DAVID GREEN

Also By David Green

In Solitude's Shadow (2021)

Dead Man Walking (2020)

Devil Walks In Blood (2021)

Coming Soon to the Empire of Ruin Series

"Before the Shadow: A Short Story of Tilo"
"Beyond Sundered Seas" Book 3
"At Eternity's Gates" Book 4

Never miss a new release!
Follow David on social media
and sign up for his newsletter.

https://linktr.ee/davidgreenwriter

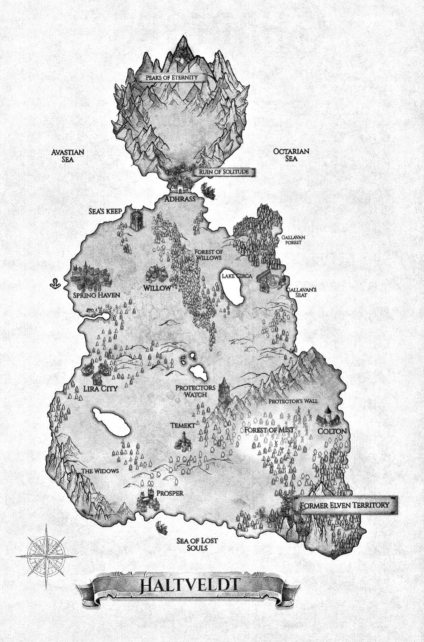

PEAKS OF ETERNITY

AVASTIAN
SEA

OCTARIAN
SEA

RUIN OF SOLITUDE

ADHRASS

SEA'S KEEP

GALLAVAN
FOREST

FOREST OF
WILLOWS

LAKE CIRCA

WILLOW

SPRING HAVEN

GALLAVAN'S
SEAT

LIRA CITY

PROTECTORS
WATCH

PROTECTOR'S WALL

TEMEKT

FOREST OF MIST

COLTON

THE WIDOWS

PROSPER

FORMER ELVEN TERRITORY

SEA OF LOST
SOULS

HALTVELDT

CHAPTERS

*Please be advised this book contains trigger warnings for self-harm,
violence, death, mention of drug use, deadly magic and violence.*

**Note the self-harm is in chapter 25 and may be skipped or
skimmed without detriment to the storyline.*

For Ollie, You inspire me every day.

PROLOGUE

THE FIRST STEPS

Faye du Gerran twitched one of the purple curtains aside and glanced out of the window. The emperor's people had chased her from Spring Haven, back to Temekt city, the place of her birth, a culture well-known for protecting their own against outsiders, even if they were now part of Haltveldt, and had been for centuries. Some traits died hard.

Still, Faye didn't feel safe. The Emperor's Hands—inquisitors, assassins, spies and Raas knew what else—searched everywhere, and more often than not found their quarry.

A mass of bodies squeezed by each other on the street below. Faye had wanted to hide in the country, maybe even in the foothills near Protector's Wall, but her companions—Dredrico Fern and Sara Fairgrass, Sparkers like her—had argued to stay in the city and count on the Empire's unwillingness to act in such a crowded place.

Ex-Sparkers now, I suppose. There's no going back. We're enemies of Haltveldt.

"People are saying Kade Besem got away. Others say he fell to his death. I heard Nexes himself threw him from a droking window. Of all the ways to die."

Faye turned at the voice. Dedrico looked to have aged a decade during their race from Spring Haven, when his spies had tipped them off about the Hand. Even here, in the safety of the Golden Sparrow's top floor room, both he and Sara appeared haggard, haunted and lost.

"What about Bertrand?" Faye asked, glancing out at the street again.

A cloud crossed the sun, casting a shadow over the people who went about their business, unaware of the treachery planned by their emperor. She frowned. It wasn't a plan anymore; Solitude would lie in ruins by now, all the Sparkers there dead. That included her mentor, Salazar, father of the High Sparker, Balz du Regar. Her closest companion.

Well, *former* closest companion. He'd thrown his lot in with Emperor Locke, as had most of Spring Haven's aristocracy, her own family included. How had it come to this?

"Dead." Sara scowled down at her fingertips. She'd gone into town that morning to receive word from her 'wee helpers'. "But not before giving that droking bastard Nexes every one of our names. For what it's worth, my people saw Kade boarding a ship north, bleeding and broken but alive."

"Doesn't matter. They found him and Bertrand with droking ease, and they'll come for us next. Mark my words." Dedrico shook his head. "Kade's as good as dead now if he went north. Agents of the Empire would have his name on their blades the moment he escaped Nexes' clutches, and if they didn't do him in, there's too many ways to perish in

Haltveldt these days. We won't hear from him again. We were fools to listen to either of them."

"Fools to try and stop the emperor murdering the two hundred Sparkers defending Solitude?" Faye snapped, throwing a baleful stare Dedrico's way.

"Fools for thinking we could make a difference," Sara murmured, laying a hand on Dedrico's forearm. She always had a calming influence on him. "A handful of Sparkers led by a disgraced spice-addict, and a tired, old nobleman who enjoyed the sound of his own voice too much. What chance did we have? Really?"

Faye swallowed her retort and clutched at her crimson robes instead. The others had dumped the clothes that marked them as members of the Order. Though she resisted wearing them in public, she changed back into them in the safety of the inn's room. They reminded her of who she was, what she represented. Sparkers were meant to inspire people, help them, and to leave a better world than the one they were born into. Raas and Janna, the gods, had said so, and the gift of magic came from them. So the scriptures said.

Tears stung her eyes, and she scrubbed them away before they dripped down her cheeks. The world she'd clung to had died, if it ever existed at all.

"What will we do then?" she asked, turning to the window again, not wanting her companions to see the red rings lining her eyes, the unshed tears shining in them.

The shadows had made the streets their domain now, and rain drizzled against the glass. The people of Temekt hurried away from the deluge, formless blobs of ink as she studied them through the window.

"Dedrico and I are heading to Prosper. We have a boat waiting to take us on to Avastia. We know other Sparkers who've fled there." Sara glanced at her husband. "You could come too."

"Avastia?" Faye barked out a volley of mirthless laughter. "I'm sure the elves there *love* watching Sparkers appear on their shores!"

"They know we don't all share the Empire's views," Dedrico muttered, "though no doubt we'll have much to prove. Better than here, anyway."

"Why not Octaria then? Or Velen? *Anywhere* else."

Faye asked questions. If she asked questions, it stopped her from having to make a decision herself. Her own spies had given her a sliver of information, a chance to strike a blow against the Empire. They claimed to have a source deep inside the emperor's circle, an influential figure sympathetic to opponents of Haltveldt's war machine. She still wanted to make a difference.

Deep down, she knew it wiser to flee, but she couldn't. Not when an opportunity loomed before her to strike back against the monsters smothering *her* Haltveldt, corrupting *her* Order.

"Our daughter is there." Sara smiled. "We haven't seen her in so long. She fled years ago, after she refused to take her place on the frontlines against the elves."

"Yuon?" Faye gasped, shooting forward in her chair. "I thought she'd died!"

"We all have our secrets," Dedrico offered, spreading his hands. "So, what are you going to do?"

They're really leaving... Well, there's no point in keeping this to myself. Maybe they'll help. Janna knows I'll need it.

"I can't leave." Faye shook her head and filled her lungs. "I received a tip... There's a hidden place the emperor created about a decade ago, not far from Spring Haven. They call it a school, but it's worse than that. *Much* worse."

"Go on." Sara nodded, glancing at Dedrico. The two shared a Link, so no doubt they conversed in private. If one of them spoke, they often did for both of them.

Faye suppressed a shiver. "I'm told it's a place where they teach these Shadow Sparkers. If I can do something about it, destroy it somehow, I can delay the Empire's plans."

Shadow Sparkers. They'd appeared at the Order of Sparkers university in the days after the Law of Engagement's abolishment. The holy rules had always kept them from using their power to attack unless threatened, and for years Emperor Locke had put Sparkers in the front lines of battle where they'd come under constant attack instead of letting them focus on defence and healing. Some Sparkers had chafed against the Laws and wanted to see them brought to an end.

The emperor, in his infinite wisdom, obliged.

Overnight, the Shadow Sparkers appeared, hooded mages in black, shadows clinging to them. Silent, withdrawn, obsidian eyed...

"They come from somewhere," Faye whispered, when her companions failed to speak. "The emperor didn't just abolish the Laws and these...things sprang out of the shadows, fully formed. They've planned this for years."

"And you aim to take them down?" Dedrico frowned at her, thick eyebrows pushed together like a stern and hairy caterpillar. "Alone?"

Faye looked through the window, the clouds so dark

and thick it appeared as though night had fallen, even though the day had just passed noon. She shivered, pulling her robes closer. They'd have to light a fire.

"I've done enough running," she replied, giving her friends a tight smile. "It's time to fight. It's time to—"

A sudden swell of magical energy cut her off. Behind her companions, the door leading to the corridor outside ripped from its hinges and flew across the room, heading straight for them.

Faye flung herself from her chair, calling on her Spark and drawing on her own energy to throw a gust of air at the wood hurtling towards them. It lifted over their heads and crashed into the wall, shattering the windows. Wind and rain howled through from outside.

Dedrico and Sara shot to their feet, spinning, summoning their magic.

Too late.

Two black-robed figures slithered through the doorless opening, jets of black oozing from their raised palms, ebony eyes glittering beneath their heavy hoods.

Fear wormed its way into Faye's gut at the sight of the monstrosities, insults to Raas and Janna, but she shoved it deep down. She didn't have time for fear.

Faye summoned her Spark, but it refused to respond. Instead, she reached for the sword on her hip, but her arms stuck to her side. She couldn't move, couldn't reach the magic inside her. All she could do was stare as a third black-robed figure entered the room. It severed her from the Spark, restricted her movements, and forced her down to the ground with a gesture.

Faye screamed as her friends dropped to their knees too, flesh turning grey, hair shedding from their scalps.

The Shadow Sparkers Eviscerated them. A forbidden spell for so long, now thrust into the acceptable conduct of war. It stripped away the life essence of a target, turning them to dust and bones. Dedrico and Sara would never get to Prosper. They would never see their daughter again.

No one escaped the Empire. No one.

Sara's eyes, filled with abject terror, rolled in Faye's direction, one of them drooping onto her cheek as her flesh lost its firmness. Black tendrils of magic plunged into her and her husband's bodies, devouring them, sucking away their essence. It appeared like a living creature, a writhing, black worm with many heads, plunging into her friends, feasting on their bones, their flesh, their magic. Dedrico and Sara melted before her eyes, their cries of anguish and despair turning to wet gurgles as their mouths deformed and their organs liquefied.

Faye whimpered, tears falling now, until nothing remained of her friends but an oozing pile of slime atop some discarded travelling clothes.

"What are you waiting for?" Faye cried at the Shadow Sparker who pinned her, glaring at the others who'd murdered Dedrico and Sara. "If you're going to do it, do it!"

The figures didn't answer. The two who'd disintegrated her friends stood in rapture, eyes closed, licking their lips as though they could taste the life they'd stolen. The other cocked its head as it stared down at Faye, impassive.

"No doubt you'll get your just desserts soon." A woman in plain clothes entered the room, glancing at the steaming mess on the floor and raising an eyebrow like she'd seen it all before. Perhaps she had. "We have questions for you."

Faye glared at her. The woman appeared utterly nondescript, unremarkable in every way. Average in looks, build and height, with a plain face beneath mousy-brown hair and dull eyes. But Faye knew the woman possessed a sharp mind, superior fighting skills and an unshakeable faith in Haltveldt. For people like her, the pride she felt in her nation verged on religious frenzy.

For members of the Hand, Emperor Locke, First of His Name, was a god.

"I'll never answer you!" Faye spat, struggling against her invisible bonds in vain, the cords in her neck tight, the muscles in her arms and legs rippling.

She grabbed at her Spark, begged it to answer. It lay just beyond her reach. So close. Raas, her magic might as well have waited for her in Sea's Keep for all the good it would do her.

"You might as well kill me now," Faye snarled, spittle flying from her lips.

The Emperor's Hand smiled.

"Names, Faye du Gerran. Places. Rumours and facts. You have all I seek. You'll be coming with us to Spring Haven, and you'll tell us what we want to know once we're done with you. Well..." She glanced at the Shadow Sparkers. "Once my *friends* are done with you."

A black bag pulled over her head stifled Faye's screams as magic lifted her from the ground.

No one escaped the Empire.

No one.

CHAPTER One

UNLEASHED

'There are no rules in war. Anyone who says otherwise is a fool. A dead one.' - From the journals of Spring Haven's Master of War, Retor, architect of many atrocities, who never suffered defeat on the battlefield.

Master of War Nexes Almor surveyed the elven ranks from the sloping hill where he stood. Despite the morning's heat—thick and oppressive this far south with the bright, glowing sun bold in the sky even at this early hour—he tightened the black leather gloves he wore. When his army charged, he would lead it, wade into the thick of it. A blood-slick grip would betray him, let his weapon slip from his hand, and nothing escaped Nexes.

He licked his lips, relishing the thought. Though he preferred battle with honest weaponry over magical means, he longed to see Emperor Locke's Shadow Sparkers unleashed, despite the nagging thoughts they awakened, those memories that wouldn't stay buried.

The fear he resented with every fibre of his being.

He kept it squashed at the pit of his stomach, like a terrorised dog, hiding in the corner with its tail between its legs. Like any cur, it made its presence known, and a kicking wouldn't send it away forever.

Nexes' second-in-command—a towering, personality-free brute of a man named Martinez Rogo—cleared his throat, a deep, phlegmy rumble that made Nexes' lip curl in disgust. His silence no doubt put Rogo off-balance. It often did that.

Still, he couldn't fault the Drum Major's loyalty to the emperor, to Haltveldt, or his talent in following orders, assuming they were spelled out to the letter. The only virtues he had, though they proved a double-edged sword.

Rogo had commanded the legions harrying the elves before Nexes' arrival and the Master of War had soon realised he carried out his commands so well only because he possessed so little imagination he couldn't do otherwise. He couldn't react to the intricacies of battle.

The man represented a problem within the empire. Those from noble houses gained too much influence and power when they didn't deserve it. They revelled in their trumped up, decorative ranks and looked so fine on the parade ground, but when it came time to make war, they were ill-prepared. If only the emperor would...

No. Scars under Nexes' sleeves itched. *No. We do not talk that way about our emperor, do we? No, we don't.*

He shoved the doubts, the criticisms, the lurking fear

of the Shadow Sparkers aside, buried them deep down. If he couldn't rid himself of them, he'd smother them under layer upon layer of control.

"Do the Shadow Sparkers stand ready?" Nexes demanded.

"They do, my lord. Twenty of them. I expected more."

Nexes turned to face him, staring into the man's beady, wide-set eyes. "How do you feel when you look at them? When you try to peer beneath their hoods? I know you try, despite yourself."

Nexes did too, but he wouldn't admit it. He exposed weaknesses in others, preyed upon it, used it to his advantage. He'd give no one the pleasure of doing the same to him, though Emperor Locke appeared to have the knack for it.

Rogo blinked, frowned, then glanced at the ground and the mud beneath his boots. His olive complexion turned red. Shame, Nexes surmised.

"My skin feels like it wants to shed and flee, sir. And when their hoods turn my way, and I know they're looking right at me... God's Teeth, I feel like pissing myself. Sir."

Nexes nodded, somewhat surprised at the dullard's insight and clarity, and resumed his study of the elven horde.

"Twenty will do. Go, prepare the troops. We charge within the hour; riders with a small Sparker presence at the front, Fighter's Guild and infantry with regular Sparker support at the rear, the emperor's new weapons in the centre."

Rogo hesitated. Nexes expected it. His orders lacked the meticulous tactics the soldiers knew him for, and the type the dull-brained fool longed to receive.

"Questions?"

"We don't flank them? Or at least send the Sparkers with their shields to provide cover first? Those tactics have been sufficient until now."

Nexes drew one of his shortswords. The morning sun caught its steel, causing the light to dance across Rogo's face. He pointed it down the slope, towards the scum.

"For controlling them. I want to wipe them out. The aim is to punch a hole through the centre. Sow confusion and panic. We've harried the beasts to this basin for a reason. We hold the high ground, and we'll use it. They've prepared as best they can—see, they've harvested from the forest and built a stake line—but our horses will smash through their defence. Our speed will prove decisive."

"Sir... It'll be a massacre. Chaos. I'm happy to deliver the day for the might of the Empire, but your orders aren't usually so imprecise. Begging your pardon, sir, but am I missing something?"

Nexes slammed his sword into its sheath. He stood toe-to-toe with Rogo and stared up into the man's simple face. Gods, how he despised looking up at someone, never mind a Raas-forsaken fool like Rogo.

Suffer the fools, Nexes. It's all for Haltveldt. All for the emperor.

"Yes, you are 'missing something', Rogo." He fed ice into his voice, let his lip curl with the contempt he felt. "Believe me, those twenty, the Shadow Sparkers you fear so much? They feed on death. It makes their magic more potent. It's our job to serve it to them on a plate, and when we do, the elven scum won't see the sunset. Now leave me, before I give you another reason to piss your pants."

"Hail the Empire's glorious day, sir!" Rogo cried, well-trained at hiding his embarrassment. Snapping off a smart salute, he turned on his heel.

Nexes breathed through his nose as he watched the man depart to the Haltveldt army's staging area. Twelve thousand fighters against the gods knew how many elves. The horde crowded behind their crude defences, grouped together, undisciplined. Desperate. They numbered more than Nexes' troops, but his scouts couldn't assign a fixed amount. They'd speculated between twenty and thirty thousand.

There had been more human soldiers, but he'd sent them north already, as the emperor demanded. With the Shadow Sparkers, he wouldn't need them, Locke said, and the Empire had other battles to win.

If the Shadow Sparkers work as promised...

He scowled and turned, snarling, back to the horde. Nexes trained his mind against doubts that surfaced about the emperor. They'd come often on his journey south after their encounter in the Cradle, the hidden place that contained Haltveldt's forgotten memories, known only to Nexes, Emperor Locke and High Sparker Balz. Whenever inklings of worry rose, his arms itched.

But we both know slaves serve a master.

The emperor's words. His friend since childhood, but his master nonetheless. He'd smirked when he'd spoken, as if he knew Nexes would ponder the meaning. A man like him existed above worrying about slighted feelings.

Nexes gripped the hilt of one of his shortswords, squeezing until his fingers protested. Did the emperor see him as a slave? A tool, a useful one, but no better than a gutter elf from the Spring Haven slums when it boiled down to it?

Nexes relaxed his grip, burying his rage deep in his stomach alongside the fear, shame and suspicion. He'd bring it all out on the battlefield, unleash it on the scum. He knew others saw the iron control he had on his emotions, the way he lived his life with cold detachment; many envied it. Nexes had fought for that control, and the violent vices he indulged in helped keep that prized exterior.

"I've taken a gamble here, following the emperor's orders to the letter. Twelve thousand plus a handful of the dark mages against the horde are not great odds." He took one last look at the elven filth in the valley below, cowering behind their defences, ignoring the itching that throbbed into a pain beneath his sleeves. "But he holds an absolute belief in the Shadow Sparkers, and his word is law. So must I believe, and what better way to send a message to the rest of the Sparkers than to use this twenty as an example?"

The emperor, along with Nexes and their close friend, Balz du Regar, leader of the Order of Sparkers, had long studied the limits the mages placed on themselves. They clung to dogmatic scripture like the Laws of Engagement—rules set by the Gods themselves, the fools screamed—of how a Sparker should use their gift. Countless emperors had exploited loopholes in their attempts to use the magi as weapons, and none more than Emperor Locke and his friends.

They'd made use of those Sparkers who'd pushed past those limits themselves too. In fact, sometimes, they'd forced the issue.

Together, they'd experimented on Sparkers, ones the Council believed exiled to Solitude or perished in battle. Balz told them how the life of a Sparker resembled a constant struggle; how much power is too much?

"The sweetest nectar," Balz once said, as the trio reclined in the emperor's quarters, not long after Emperor Locke had ascended the throne by stepping over his father's corpse. "Each time I embrace the Spark, I feel it making me more, drinking in life surrounding me, holding all that power in the palms of my hands... My friends, I struggle to let go. Every Sparker does."

Nexes had watched the emperor then. He drank wine from a golden goblet, a shrewd cast to his face.

"Say we 'indulge' this lust. The way we turn a puppy into a feral fighter. An army of Sparkers, free of the Laws." He winked at Nexes then. "Some weapon, that."

Through Balz's teachings, and their subjects, they knew Sparkers had an innate power, their own energies to draw on, but they drew from their surroundings too—the wind, water, earth, even life itself. Then, through their experiments, and the work of a disgraced and conveniently dead Sparker by the name of Ricken Alpenwood, they discovered more.

Sparkers could draw on death.

Using the power of death came with consequences. It twisted them. Nexes knew this from experience but couldn't prove it as succinctly as Alpenwood's journals did. As a child, he'd stood mute in Spring Haven's Tallan Square as a rogue Sparker, hunted by her brethren, laid waste to all without discrimination against men, women or children. He'd watched his grandparents melt before his eyes—Eviscerated, he later learned—as the Sparker laughed. Tears of madness running down her face, hands thrust out before her, leeching from the innocent folk who tried in vain to escape.

It had taken five Sparkers, arriving in their gleaming, bright-coloured robes like saviours from above, to take her down. Her screams had invaded young Nexes' dreams for months.

These were the secret fears in the soul of the Master of War, the dread that drove him on. The Sparkers were necessary, yes, but they were abominations, every single one harbouring insanity, chaos and evil. He'd learned it that day, and as he grew into adulthood, into a position of power and influence, he came to understand only a nudge would send the Sparkers down the dark path.

They hid behind their veneer of wisdom, generosity, piety and the Laws of Engagement their order preached at every turn, but if they indulged their inherent lust for power and destruction, with no one to halt their descent? They stopped being human, let alone Sparkers. They became shadows filled with corruption, their true selves revealed to the light.

The emperor and Balz purred as they trained that first crop of Shadow Sparkers, watching them Eviscerate elves and criminals. Other Sparkers too. They congratulated themselves as their new weapons shed their body hair, as angry, red cracks appeared across their skin, as their eyes turned black.

Nexes didn't join in his friends' jubilation. That cold, detached demeanour benefited him once more. The Emperor and Balz wouldn't have expected much by way of response from him other than icy calculation. He noticed Balz held himself back from Evisceration, ordering others to do it instead.

Nexes appreciated the Shadow Sparkers as assets, crucial in the war effort. They would wipe out the scum once and for all before Haltveldt turned to the Banished and whatever threat Avastia, Octaria and the rest of the world posed. But that didn't mean the Shadow Sparkers didn't sicken him. Sickened him good and proper, even more than the regular magi.

He hated catching glimpses of the Shadow Sparkers, despised it when he thought they peered back from under their black hoods. Nexes remembered that day in Tallan Square all too well. His grandparents, throwing themselves in front of him, sparing his life.

His lip curled again as he turned away from the basin and headed back towards Haltveldt's staging area.

"Parasites," he spat, letting a scowl form on his face. "All of them. Any who can use the Spark, feeding on everything around them. God's teeth, let the Raas-blind fools annihilate each other for all I care. But the elves first. All in good time, Nexes. Remember that. For Haltveldt. It's all for Haltveldt."

His hands fell to his blades. The feel of metal in his gloved hands chased his white-hot anger away, as it often did. But the rage would return. It always did, building, forever building, unless he unleashed it.

The battle couldn't come soon enough.

Nexes warhorse neighed as it stamped its hooves with impatience, no doubt sensing his torrent of emotions. The Master of War would join the charge, as he always did. The emperor had called it a reckless habit but didn't talk him out of it.

Because your death wouldn't spoil his breakfast. He'd replace you as soon as he decided how he'd like his omelette.

"No," he growled, wrapping the reins around his fists.

"Sorry, my lord?"

Nexes blinked. Rogo watched him from the ground, eyes narrowed, brow furrowed. Nexes ignored him. The man wouldn't join the charge; he'd stay behind to co-ordinate the attack. Only Nexes had left nothing for the oaf to do.

Coward. We both know why he won't join the fray.

He sniffed, the stench of horseshit and piss thick in his nostrils. His mount stomped again, eager to gallop. He hated waiting, but knew they had to. Defending soldiers could wait all day behind their fortifications, hoping the assault would never come. Those tasked with breaking them had to work themselves into the mad frenzy required.

So, the fighting men and women of Haltveldt, the mercenaries of the Fighter's Guild, even the Sparkers, drank themselves senseless, screamed each other's blood hot, pushed, cajoled, and fought where necessary. There came a tipping point, where that fake, alcohol-fuelled courage reached its peak, before an army collectively lost its bottle.

Nexes could smell that time approaching.

A desperate edge had crept into the cries filled with false bravado, the slurs aimed at the elven scum waiting at the bottom of the slope. He nodded. Time to act.

His blood surged as he gave his weapons one last check. Nexes had fitted his saddle with a sheath for a longsword designed for mounted combat. He'd use that for the charge, then abandon his mount. Up close and personal, that's how he preferred it.

For a second, he allowed his thoughts to drift back to the room in the Auntie's Blessing, where he'd kept the traitorous fool Bertrand alive, and in exquisite pain, long enough to give him the names of every conspirator he and that elf-droker Kade Besem had brought to their side.

Their plotting, all for naught. Kade may have escaped him in Spring Haven, but not for long. They'd caught up to him in Adhraas, stuck a knife in his ribs and pitched his corpse into the harbour. And that morning, Nexes had received word. Solitude had fallen overnight. Sparkers loyal to the Empire had scouted the area at a safe distance, and what they'd reported... Nexes wished he could have laid eyes on the carnage. Just as the emperor had envisioned.

The fortress and its washed-up Sparkers, useful at last. When word reaches the people of Haltveldt of the massacre, they'll want vengeance against the Banished. And I'll deliver it.

A week had passed since he'd last seen Locke. A week of travel, of thought, of stewing and grating at inaction. Too long since Nexes' blades had tasted blood.

"Rogo!" Nexes called, rolling his head in a tight circle, a ritual of his before joining battle. It hadn't failed him yet. "Where's your mount?"

The man's mouth dropped open. "Sir?"

Nexes had grown tired of the man's idiotic, droking

face. It said much about the state of Haltveldt's armies that a craven such as Martinez Rogo had climbed the ranks, a problem Nexes would attend to once he'd crushed the elves and dealt with the Banished in the north.

Nexes came from good stock, but he deserved his position. Too many in power held rank only by their families' name or riches. Haltveldt required a purge.

"Your horse, man. Where is it? You can't charge without one."

"My h—"

Arm a blur, Nexes unsheathed the longsword from his saddle and pressed the point to Rogo's throat. "Get on your Raas-forsaken horse, you pitiful, pathetic excuse for a man. You shit. You're almost as worthless as an elf. Mount up before I kill you myself."

With a trembling hand and a gulp, the man pressed his knuckles to his temple in salute. "Yes, my lord."

"Herald?" Nexes cried, sawing the reins of his horse as it gathered to leap. The animal knew the time had come. He raised his blade. "Signal the charge."

The horn blew. Two solid blasts echoed through the basin, sending adrenaline shooting into Nexes' fingertips and toes. A roar answered; a swelling, incoherent cry as twelve thousand Haltveldtian voices snarled as one. The elves replied, a distant din from a greater number. Nexes didn't fear them. Battle clarity set in, chasing the doubts away.

He'd own the day's victory. He always did.

After that day in Tallan Square, after surviving the mad Sparker's rampage, he'd understood, even at eight years old. He had a purpose. Something grand to achieve. He'd accomplished many impressive feats in his time but hadn't yet written his name across Haltveldt's history books. He wouldn't allow himself to die until he did.

Nexes' gut told him today was the day they'd remember him for.

"No mercy!" he cried, his mount rearing. "We wipe the scourge from Haltveldt's face today! Charge!"

He gave the horse its head. No point trying to control it yet, surrounded by so much flesh, energy and emotion. Nexes felt the air vibrant with it and wondered how the Sparkers could control themselves with so much power at their call. Not that they had to worry now that the emperor had abolished the Laws of Engagement. And the Shadow Sparkers... For them, a battle would resemble a feeding frenzy.

The ground trembled as six hundred horses charged in a wedge down the slope. Cries filled with bloodlust saturated the air as the reckless charge made the riders take leave of their senses. They lived in the moment. But not Nexes. No, not him. Though he rode with them, though his heart thundered, his blood pumped, his soul sang with the promise of battle, he kept himself apart. In control.

He'd lose it at just the right time.

Nexes glanced to his right and saw Rogo cowering low against his horse's neck, no weapon in his hand.

Cur.

Ahead, the wooden stakes drew close, the elves behind them. Arrows flitted through the air, most falling short but some striking home. Strangled screams from his soldiers and panicked whinnies from their mounts proved that.

"Faster!" Nexes commanded, cords in his neck taut as he yelled above the din. The next volley would strike home.

He threw a look over his shoulder. The rest of the army followed on foot. A space drew his eye, a crowd of black-robed warriors no one wished to approach. The Shadow Sparkers.

Let's see what you can do.

Nexes dug his heels into his mount's side and steadied himself. After the charge, confusion would reign. He'd need that control. After that... He'd indulge himself.

"Steady!" he shouted, as he saw the whites of the elven archer's eyes.

They wouldn't manage that second volley. They'd run out of time. Their entire race had. Nexes aimed his horse for the gaps between the palisades and prepared his mount to leap.

Screams tore through the basin as horseflesh crashed into wooden stakes and elven bodies alike, the explosion of noise like a thunderclap. Nexes glanced to his right as his horse soared through the air. Rogo's mount had impaled itself through the shoulder and chest, sending the man hurtling through the air and into the midst of the enemy.

Nexes swung left and right with his longsword. No rhythmic dance of battle, no tactics for now, he just dealt out carnage as he worked to create space. The elven line dissolved into a confused rabble. Six hundred horses slamming against a front line will do that. He snarled a smile as his arm vibrated, his blade cleaving deep. Blood soaked his forearm, spurted across his face.

He licked it from his lips, savoured the taste.

Even so, he kept control, leaving the monster locked inside. Nexes' lust for blood pulsed as his blade cut through flesh, as the stench of gore filled his nostrils, and his body ached to descend into the rage-haze of battle. His deep-seated, bottled-up reservoirs of rage, shame and doubt screamed for release. But he wouldn't let them go. It wasn't time, though the beast grew with each drop of blood spilt, each organ pierced.

Nexes glanced about the press. Enough horses had levelled the stakes, more than enough for the foot soldiers to pass through. He blocked out the cries of the dying animals—a hateful, pitiful squeal, as if their lives meant so much—and spun his mount in a tight circle, aiming his blade at any elf unfortunate to get close. His horse bucked, just a touch, then its frenzied breathing morphed into a scream.

An arrow stuck out of its eye, and another thudded into its throat.

Nexes let his longsword fall and leapt before the animal took him down. He'd seen soldiers crushed that way before. He hit the blood-soaked ground in a roll, flowing to his feet and drawing his dual shortswords in one graceful, terrible move.

Elves pressed about him, his own people too. Nexes didn't care. Now he could let the monster free.

Time slowed as he studied the hateful faces looking his way, killing and being killed without a second thought. He drew on the events that had fed his frustration, let them build his rage to fever pitch. The traitors his inquisitors hadn't yet found. Kade Besem's escape. The Fighters Guild bartering with him to extract a better price instead of doing their job for the empire they served. The emperor's sneering words when he compared him to a droking elven slave. Rogo's gormless face—oh, how Nexes wished he could see his trampled, mutilated corpse now—and the elven scum screaming in their Raas-forsaken tongue.

But most of all, Nexes drew upon the fear of the Shadow Sparkers, the emperor's new toy, the weapon designed to supplant men like him. He remembered the fear he felt as a child in Tallan Square, as his grandparents gave their lives for him. He pulled on all of this and grinned a cold droking grin.

Nexes Almor let the bottle burst. It shattered into thousands of pieces and spread across the battlefield.

Teeth bared, screaming Raas-knew-what, he threw himself at the closest elf—at least, the part of him still aware of anything other than malice and death thought it *looked* like one—sweeping one blade high and one low. The shock on the corpse's face registered with Nexes for a second before the severed head toppled from its neck. With a growl, Nexes pulled the other blade from the body's hip, letting it topple into the blood-thickened muck, and spun away, swords dancing, a whirlwind of death.

He laughed. Well, almost a laugh; the sound lived somewhere between mirth and despair as his head swam and the rancid stench of battle drove him on. The screams—sobs of the dying, begging for the mercy of a quick end, or wishing to see their loved ones once more—faded into the background. Nexes' breathing filled his ears. Sweat dripped from his golden-hair into his eyes—gods' rotten teeth, the heat of battle!—and he revelled in the carnage around him. The madness of war.

A face appeared before him; Nexes jammed his blade into it, forcing it through the nose until it punched out the other side, his fist clutching the hilt disappearing into the ruined cranium. He pulled it out, gloves and forearm caked in gore, cartilage and grey matter, and snarling, sought his next target. Anything would do.

Anyone.

More featureless faces appeared from the press of flesh. They died before him, a storm of violence as he spun and hacked, graceful yet wrathful, muscled arms vibrating when his blades hit home and sunk into flesh. Nexes moved, always flowing to the next target, using shoulder, fist, foot and steel. Someone got too close inside his defence. He lowered his head back and butted the soldier in the face—human, elf, he didn't give a drok—felt cartilage crunch against his skull from his assault, blood and mucus fiery on his skin. His swords followed, cutting the leg at the knee. The other sank through the neck as the body toppled into the filth.

From the corner of his eye, Nexes saw an arrow slicing through the air towards him. He raised his blade to cut it out of the air—the mad arrogance of the battle frenzy gripped him—but it pinged off an invisible barrier before it struck home and ricocheted into an elf who fought a Haltveldtian soldier, driving through the scum's ear and sending him sprawling amongst the corpses.

Nexes glanced around, eyes furious, and discovered a Sparker in bright blue robes staring at him. They nodded as if to say, 'You're welcome'. The mage had thrown a shield around the Master of War, protecting him from the lucky, errant shot of a panicked archer.

How droking dare they?

The rage surged, feeding the frenzy smothering Nexes' mind. That day in Tallan Square bloomed in his mind. A Sparker, surrounded by death. A parasite feeding on life, squashing the normal folk under their heel like droking bugs.

Glowering, blood-smeared, frenzied, Nexes levelled his blades and charged. Drok them all!

The Sparker's eyes flew wide, and they had no time to react before Nexes buried the swords in their chest. He let the weight of his charge carry them into the muck, pulled his weapons free and plunged again.

And again.

And again.

More. Droking more and more and more, Raas and Janna, damn them both. And damn the other gods too. Damn their droking rotten teeth!

Blood covered Nexes, slid down his throat as he screamed his fury dry, his blades quivering as he hacked at the ruined Sparker. Around him, bodies pressed and swayed, the haze of battle and bloodshed driving men and women into unspeakable acts of violence and frenzy. Humans slew elves, massacring their oppressors. Sparkers, unleashed at last, battled their elven counterparts, bright-robed mages giggling, drunk on mad power.

And still, Nexes hacked away. His blades sank into the gore-fed mud. The Sparker's chest disintegrated by his fury, his lust. Flesh, tendon, muscle and blood covered his gloves, his arms, his throat and face. Nexes' weapons had turned to crimson.

"What are you doing?" an unfamiliar voice yelled, a lilting, musical accent, thick with revulsion and disbelief. "He's one of yours."

No mean feat to elicit that response on a battlefield. The voice made Nexes pause mid-plunge. An elf's voice, cutting through the haze.

Nexes looked up. The scum took a step back when their eyes locked. He drank in the details; light, gore-stained golden chainmail, a necklace of trinkets arounds its neck. One of their leaders, so shocked it stood rooted to the spot. The press of bodies lessened, as if the soldiers on both sides knew to avoid the Master of War.

Not this elf though; ill fate had brought it Nexes' way.

He surged to his feet, boots slipping in the mud, when a shadow crossed the morning sun, so sudden it brought a lull to the battle. Rain tore from the sky, the deluge sticking Nexes' blond hair to his skull. One moment, a hot southern morning, warmer from the fire of death; now, dark as the grave. Thunder rumbled and lightning answered, lancing across the sky.

Nexes wiped a gore-slick backhand across his brow, swiping the moisture from his eyes, and bore down on the elf.

Until it exploded.

It burst from the inside, a shower of giblets that flew in all directions, hitting Nexes like a thrown bucket of pig guts from a butcher's window into the street below. It smelled worse.

Wet squelches filled the air as the yells of battle-fury turned to cries of fear and shock. Nexes spun around. More elves turned to red bursts of air, and through the crimson mist he saw the reason.

The Shadow Sparkers had arrived.

They strode in a pack, the air oppressive around them, as if the darkness in the sky lent them its gloom and they turned it blacker. They'd cast their hoods back, their scarred faces twisted in sick, rapturous glee, hands thrust in front of them as they turned Haltveldt's foes into paste.

One broke off from the pack, bearing down on an elf who'd sunk to its knees, eyes wide and tongue lolling. A bright-robed Sparker—even under the dirt and blood, Nexes recognised Mara Jura, one of the few mages he cared to associate with—paused to watch, head cocked, as the Shadow Sparker's black eyes rolled into the back of her head.

The elf jerked, a strangled cry the only noise it made. Its neck bulged as if some entity had entered its throat. Its eyeballs popped as its hair turned from raven to white. Its olive skin turned to chalk, then melted. The bones too. Within seconds, only a puddle remained on the corpse-filled mud.

Evisceration.

The Shadow Sparker turned, red scars pulsating. She nodded to Mara, who smiled in return. A hungry, lustful smile. She spun and thrust a hand towards a retreating elf. It sunk to its knees and screamed.

Unburdened from the Laws of Engagement that had restricted them so long, the Sparkers indulged their darkest desires, just as the emperor had foreseen. Twenty Shadow Sparkers had seemed a gamble, but others of the Order would soon swell their ranks.

It had already begun.

Horns sounded. Signals for retreat. The elves routed. Nexes should have smiled, should have felt satisfaction. Instead, he threw up all over his boots. He let his swords fall to the ground as the Shadow Sparkers swept by him. There'd be no mercy for the elves. They didn't deserve it, but a death from steel, a warrior's death. Surely, they deserved that?

Didn't they?

Numb, Nexes stumbled through the mud, not noticing the dead at his feet, through the elves' pitiful, broken defences, and up the slope he'd so valiantly, in his mind, galloped down, back towards his tent. The battle had lasted less than thirty minutes and would go on for hours yet as his forces harried their retreating foes, but he knew, deep in his gut, no one needed him.

A black victory on a red day. One for the history books. A slaughter with the name of Nexes Almor attached to it. The day he'd unleashed the Shadow Sparkers on Haltveldt and its enemies.

They'd remember him, alright.

One day, the entire world would.

CHAPTER TWO

DECISIONS

'The path to war was ever laden with mistakes, and one above all: failing to learn from our past.' - From the diaries of Zanna Alpenwood, written for her daughter before her exile, and discovered by the Emperor's Hand.

From the treeline, Calene stared down on Solitude. On where it *used* to stand. Now a canyon separated the Peaks of Eternity, and created a divide between Haltveldt and Banished lands.

Because of her mother's sacrifice.

On the other side, Banished worked, turning their demolished siege weapons into bridges. She'd spent the day since the battle on the walls watching them, her anger coming in waves, regret invading when it ebbed away.

Mother. I wish... No, I wanted to make things right between us. Better. Why do I have to be so droking stubborn? Why?

Her hands balled into fists at her side, the rage coming back strong.

"Calene…" Vettigan coughed, drawing his cloak tight around thin shoulders, thinner than they used to be.

Much about her old friend had changed since his encounter with the Shadow Sparker in the Forest of Mists. Since it had near-Eviscerated him and implanted some parasitic evil in his body.

"How long are we going to stay here? We've done nothing but stand on this hill for hours."

Calene almost spat the words that crept up her gullet. Instead, she let them loose in her mind.

Drok off. My mother's dead because of you.

The heat left her blood as soon as she thought it. Zanna's sacrifice had saved countless lives. Even if Vettigan hadn't lost control and released the dark thing inside, without Zanna's heroism, the Banished would have overwhelmed them. Instead of building rope bridges and preparing to cross the great canyon that lay where Solitude once stood, they'd have already poured into Haltveldt.

Not that she thought the Banished wanted war. The time she'd spent with the strange Banished warrior, Tilo, the events on the road to Solitude, and what she'd seen on the battlements of the fortress, had convinced her they had other motives.

But they wouldn't escape war when they crossed into Haltveldt. Emperor Locke wouldn't allow it. With the Laws of Engagement abolished and the Shadow Sparkers at his disposal, the Banished wouldn't stand a chance.

"Vettigan." A touch of heat remained in her voice. She

left it there. She had the right. "My mother just died. Right here. Somehow, she wiped an entire droking fortress from existence, just to buy us time. She lifted us from Solitude, probably saved us all. I didn't even know someone could push the Spark that far. I know we need to leave, but...I can't. I... I don't know what to do, and whatever direction I go in, I leave my mother behind. So, for Raas' sake, give me a break, just for a moment, will you?"

"You said we'd move south. You said you'd tell everyone what Zanna did here. Has something changed?"

"I know what I droking said, Vettigan. But it's not that simple, is it? Teeth of the gods, give me strength."

Vettigan's eyes narrowed, suspicion lurking behind those faded, orange eyes. Calene sighed. They used to shine so bright, but nothing about Vettigan Baralart rang true anymore.

What did? Not much in Haltveldt made sense these days.

She prodded the part of her mind that once housed the Link with her mother. Nothing of it remained, and that puzzled her. She'd heard stories of the profound grief Sparkers felt when their Link partner died—sadness worse than anything imaginable. They said they felt the loss in their bones, in their minds, and the echo of that passing lived on inside them for years.

Grief threatened to unbalance Calene. Loss too. Regret? Oh, yes. So much of that.

But it all felt normal after losing her mother, not the bone-deep hollowing threatening to destroy her that she'd heard about. She hadn't felt Zanna go, hadn't felt her die, ripped away like the old, lonely Sparkers spoke of. Instead, an almost overwhelming feeling of love, of complete pride, had flooded her Link before it vanished.

She didn't feel empty. More like she'd lost limb, but the space still itched at her, a maddening nag that demanded her attention.

She shared a Link with Vettigan too. Calene didn't want to brush against that again, even if an urge to feel some comfort, some familiarity, pushed her that way.

Vettigan bore physical changes from the failed Evisceration that her magic couldn't heal; always a slim, short man, the magic had sucked away what meagre fat covered his bones. His skin had turned to pockmarked parchment, and his thick, silver hair had become patchy, lank, and white.

Inside, her old friend, the man she'd turned to after her mother's exile, had suffered even more. The darkness remained in his body, eating away at him, corrupting his Spark and soul. It had taken control of Vettigan during the battle of Solitude, the death of thousands calling to it, feeding it.

Their Link might still have been active, but the explosion of dark power from within Vettigan had burned away his Spark. He'd lived with his magic for almost one hundred years, and the Shadow Sparker had taken everything from him.

And it could have been worse.

If it hadn't been for Zanna, the loss at Solitude would have been incomprehensible. Her mother had done what Calene had always wanted from her. She'd found another way. Dealt with an impossible situation with compassion and love, not using the talent for violence that ran in their blood.

"I couldn't even tell her I loved her. Not until it was too late."

She hadn't meant to give words to the thought, but now she had. Vettigan shrugged, like she'd made him uncomfortable. Drok his feelings!

Calene stared at her fingers, at the ring she wore, the one her mother had given her on her sixteenth birthday. Zanna had worn it once, and Zanna's mother before her. Besides her family home, the one Calene had sworn never to return to, she had nothing else of her family. An idea wormed itself into her head.

Home.

Vettigan shifted beside her as they gazed across the fresh ravine, staring at the Banished and the towering Peaks of Eternity. A luminous column of green reached into the heavens after Zanna's astonishing act. In the distance, a white column touched the highest peak and rose into the sky. The sun climbed behind it, lending the gathering clouds a red hue. A promise of blood on the horizon.

Calene shivered. She'd spent most of her time in the south and didn't often journey further north than Spring Haven. The cold could drok itself.

"Zanna didn't need to hear you say it," Vettigan whispered, voice hoarse. "I'm sure she knew, Calene. A mother knows."

She spat on the floor. "A mother I'd spoken to once in ten years? Raas' teeth, so much love in that, isn't there?"

She closed her eyes, snapped her jaw shut. *I'm acting like a brat. He's lost a friend. Lost a whole droking lot more too.*

"Sorry. How are you? Still feel nothing?"

Vettigan didn't have the tell-tale signs of a burned-out Sparker. Another curiosity. He'd survived the impossible amount of magic he'd wielded unharmed. It should have killed him, and their Link should have died with him. Burnouts ranged from popped eyeballs to charred skeletal remains, depending on how far beyond the Sparker had pushed themselves, and Vettigan had gone miles past his threshold.

Now, the Spark simply didn't exist in his soul. Their Link remained, and so did the shadow, even without the Spark to feed on. Just a sliver of it existed, oozing thin tendrils around Vettigan's mind. She could see it with her Second Sight, felt it calling to her through their Link. It wanted something else to feed on. All the while, it would warp Vettigan into something...other.

She saw its shadow cross Vettigan's face as he scowled for a split-second, before he forced a smile at her question. "Feel like a new man. While you're staring across at where that damned fortress used to be, why don't you tell me what you can see?"

Calene knew he meant with her Second Sight. They'd both commanded that ability hours before. Now, only she could wield it.

"There are a handful of Sparkers on this side of the ravine. Less than fifty. All that survived Solitude, I reckon. They're moving south. The boy, Arlo, he's moving north and east, on the other side. Tilo's with him."

"I thought you said the Banished had no Spark?"

A dark look crossed his face again. Without thinking, Calene took his hand. He tried his best to be the old Vettigan, but she knew he'd died out on the road before they'd even arrived at Solitude. Even so, she couldn't give up on him. She had no one else.

Well, maybe not no one.

Calene pushed Brina out of her mind. She didn't want to dwell on her elven friend too much. They'd met days before and had fought together, journeyed together. She hoped the elf still lived. Her gut told her she did, but she wanted to consider their next move with her head, not her heart and loins.

Calene entwined her fingers in Vettigan's. His felt clammy, cold and gnarled, like withered tree roots caught in the rain.

"He doesn't. Next to Arlo, I sense...life. Pure life. I see it with all the Banished now I study them, but with Tilo it's stronger. He's different from the others, and Arlo has the Spark. It's easy to make them out. They're apart from the rest. It seems purposeful, like they don't want to meet with them or they're watching, waiting for their moment. Whatever that might droking be."

"Well, Tilo's not our problem now. The boy either. South, remember? You said we'd go south."

Calene let his slack grip fall and spun to face him. "I know what I said!" she snarled. "Whatever all this is about, Tilo and Arlo are at the centre. *Liesh*. Purpose. That's what Tilo kept droking saying, over and over. I'm not letting them take off on their own now. Those other Sparkers, *they'll* spread the word."

Vettigan laughed, a bitter, twisted retch that made Calene's toes curl. "Like the emperor will allow those fools to tell their story. And what do you propose we do? Run across one of these bridges they're building into the midst of an entire army? An army who just stormed one of the oldest and largest fortresses in Haltveldt? With what? One Sparker, no matter how powerful and talented she is, and me? A bitter old man with thoughts of pushing a sword into his guts popping into his head every damned second? And let me tell you girl, the more my soul aches, the more this droking voice whispers in my mind. I'm just as likely to run at the first Raas-forsaken Banished we meet and beg him to relieve me of my head!"

He finished with a yell, his body trembling. Calene glanced at his hands; his fingers curled into claws.

He wants death? Really? Oh, Vettigan...

Echoes drifted across the canyon. The Banished sang as they worked. Tilo's song always calmed her, made her feel strong. Its own unique magic. She missed it.

"What do you reckon, then?" she asked.

She couldn't meet Vettigan's eyes. An alien presence lurked behind them, staring through them, terrifying her. Not just for what it had done to her friend, but because Haltveldt had more Shadow Sparkers, *more* agents of this evil. And they'd continue to create them now they'd done away with the Laws.

Calene had smelled the rot standing atop the walls of Solitude, the stench of dark magic. Sparkers throughout history had lost control, succumbed to the temptation. The Order of Sparkers had long been a religious one, built for study, learning, defence. Hope. Over the years, the Empire had eroded that, bent on using the magi as weapons. Many

Sparkers embraced it and fell from the old ways. Emperor Locke had trodden all over their ancient traditions for his own ends.

Calene ground her teeth. Zanna had believed in Raas and the gods. That's where her mother's name came from— her parents so devout they'd named her just a short-step from Janna—and Calene had studied the teachings too. Now, the thought of having the Spark powering her soul terrified her.

The darkness came from it too. How could something pure and holy allow that *thing* to fester and grow? How?

More droking questions.

Vettigan hadn't answered. She glanced at him to find her old friend glowering at the spot where the fortress had stood. Calene stared past him, into the woods and down the road to Adhraas, the dock town some ten miles from Solitude. She didn't want more arguments. She didn't want to feel more alone.

Vettigan breathed through his nose, then rubbed at his temples.

"We have friends on this side." Vettigan lent too much patience to his voice, like he explained a particularly vexing matter to a three-year-old who had no intention of listening. "We find them and head to Adhraas, help with the evacuation. Try to get word out about what happened. Or..."

He eyed her, then clenched his jaw.

"Or what, Vettigan?"

He took a step closer to her. "We get a ship to Avastia. Leave this place forever. Let Haltveldt consume itself in endless war. Please? A fresh start for us both."

Friends.

Calene blinked. Wrapped up as she'd been with her mother, and with Arlo and the Banished across the canyon, she'd almost forgotten Kade Besem, Arlo's father. Not Brina, though. Calene couldn't forget about her. The elf had carved out a permanent place in her mind.

She knew her feelings would sway the decision, that she'd look for the beggar elf who'd saved them from the Shadow Sparker ambush. They'd grown close as they'd journeyed together, and Calene felt a pang of shame for discounting those feelings. Why shouldn't she do something for herself for once?

"We don't know they're alive," she muttered, but the words rang hollow.

Zanna had saved everyone.

"Look," Vettigan replied, pulling the hood of his cloak up. He'd enjoyed his appearance, his hair especially, despite the over-sized robes he often wore. He called them 'roomy'. On their boat north, he'd smashed the cabin's only mirror and kept his face hidden as much as he could. Calene shuddered at the memory, the murderous stare he'd turned on her before she'd fled to the safety of the deck. "There's only one place to go from here, and that's Adhraas. If Brina and Kade go there, we need to find them. It isn't safe for an elf. You know that. Do you think Kade can protect her? You healed him, but I saw him sweating, his hands shaking. The man's coming off a spice fix the hard way. Brave, but foolish. Makes him a liability. And after recent events, I know all about those."

Calene bit her lip. Vettigan, for once since the ambush,

spoke sense. She knew it, couldn't argue with it. So why did she wait?

The answer stared back at her.

Each time she looked across at where Solitude stood, she didn't study the Banished or look for Arlo and Tilo. She watched the green column of light, the last reminder of her mother.

"I can't just—"

Before she could finish, the light faded, as if it knew Calene would stay there until Eternity's Gates swung open as long as it remained.

A fat tear escaped her eye, running down her dark skin, and dropped onto the ground. The time to leave Solitude had arrived.

"I'm sorry, Calene."

She turned to Vettigan, hooded and bowed. His voice sounded like it had before the Shadow Sparker just then. Maybe the man he used to be could emerge with her help. Their Link might still have existed for a reason.

Calene barely understood any of it. Evisceration, Shadow Sparkers, the Spark ripped from someone's soul but still they lived. If anyone knew, if anyone could make sense of it all, Calene had a fair idea of where she could start.

"There's a third option," Calene muttered, kicking at rocks on the ground. "Instead of leaving Haltveldt or leading a doomed crusade in Spring Haven."

Vettigan's eyes narrowed. "And what's that?"

"We heal you."

"Just how do you propose we do that?" he whispered, hope bleeding through his harsh voice.

Calene bit her lip. Home. They'd go to her home. Another place, like Spring Haven, she'd rather avoid. The estate she'd grown up on, first learned to harness her Spark. The place her mother had Eviscerated her father, after he'd taken the darkest path.

Ricken Alpenwood had fought in wars all his life, always within the Laws of Engagement, but his mind broke. No one noticed at first. Her father had begun his experiments into the darker side of the Spark in his study and had spent weeks there. He'd explore the Spark's potential, for good and ill.

Then, he'd overpowered Calene, taken her captive, planning Raas-knew-what. If Zanna hadn't intervened...

But she'd gone too far, hadn't she? Eviscerating Ricken had caused her exile and led to their estrangement. She had gone too far.

There's always another way. Right?

Other than marching to Spring Haven and forcing her way into the Order of the Sparkers—Calene doubted they'd break out their finest vintage for the occasion after the emperor had sent a death squad after her—she couldn't imagine anywhere else would hold the answers about Vettigan's condition. If there *were* answers.

They'd abandoned the place, even if it still belonged to Calene. She'd stayed on the road since, or in Spring Haven, but it was hers. Plus, it lay close to Haltveldt's capital, in case they had to visit the Order, even if she'd rather they never set foot in the city again.

"We'll talk about it on the road. Let's go. Keep an eye and ear out for horses. I'm droked if I'm walking the entire way."

Calene left without a backwards glance, though she offered a silent goodbye to her mother. The site of Solitude would always hold her memory, her sacrifice.

As Calene strode away, it still cast too long a shadow.

"Arlo!"

Kade lurched upwards, head spinning, stomach cramping, a hundred twinges of pain clamouring for attention from within his body. *Am I alive? Is this Eternity's Gates? No, the gods wouldn't let us take our pain with us, would they?*

He glanced around, too quick for his guts. Bile erupted from his mouth, splashing onto the grass around him. Kade wiped his mouth with the back of his hand. The taste on his tongue caused him to heave, but nothing else came. From the sudden throb of hunger, he reckoned his stomach empty now he'd voided it.

Wait, grass?

Closing his eyes and taking a slow, deep breath, Kade ran his fingers across the ground, avoiding the vomit. Fresh morning dew kissed his skin. He cast his mind back through the fog, through the droking haze of spice withdrawal. Jumping from the window of the Auntie's Blessing, his leg crumpling beneath him on the cobbled street, before he lost his box of Octarian spice. The fever dreams that had assailed him in his cabin on the ship headed north. The hatchet job on his injured leg, and his first days without spice in over a decade. That Raas-forsaken blade plunging into his body, tearing his flesh apart before he toppled into the water.

Calene's healing. He remembered that too.

Arlo. On Solitude's ramparts. So small, framed against the backdrop of battle—smoke, blood, ash—as a Banished bore down on him. Kade, hurling the sword he'd found, saving his son. Then...madness.

The Sparker they'd travelled with, Vettigan. The other magi, Calene and Zanna, screaming at him as he howled with frenzied laughter. Tilo throwing himself at Arlo as a wind tore into them, almost tossing Kade from the ramparts to certain death. He remembered strong fingers clutching at him, an explosion of light, and nothing more.

Kade's head throbbed, either from withdrawal or dehydration, he didn't know. The entry points in his torso where the sailor had stabbed him—Nexes' man, paid off to take care of Kade after his escape—ached. Calene's healing had worked, but now the pain returned with the fatigue.

And his thirst for the spice.

Kade had been an addict since his wife's death. Rune, an elf in his family's service—a nice way of saying slave—had died in childbirth. He'd promised to smuggle Rune to the free elves in the south, but he hadn't, and he bore the blame for that. He always would. Instead, he'd shouldered the burden of scandal and raised his son, Arlo, alone.

Rumour in Spring Haven's upper echelons spoke of some great shame—a fateful night at the brothel, an illicit affair with a cousin—but the renowned and powerful Besem clan kept Arlo's true heritage secret. Kade paid for their displeasure. Besems had held influential positions on Spring Haven's council, chairs such as Master of Coin, Master of Trade, even Master of War, over the years. Kade became Liaison to Solitude, a role with no honour, shepherd to a forgotten fortress and two hundred Sparkers no one gave a drok about.

The spice made his shame easier to carry. The shame of his secrets, including the one he kept buried in his guts. He'd told himself Rune had loved him, that they shared some great romance, but his father had said it.

You forced yourself on that slave, fool, and she allowed it for an easier life. She didn't love you, and now what have you to show for it? A bastard. A disgrace. An elf for a son.

Kade argued against it then, and against himself now, but deep down, he couldn't deny it. The power in their relationship had been his, and the visions of Rune he'd suffered on the boat north had laid bare his inner turmoil.

Hence the spice.

Arlo had seemed like any other boy as he grew; a son Kade loved more than anything else, even through the spice haze. Only a young man himself, he'd devoted every moment to Arlo, though his parents distanced themselves from their grandchild. As the boy approached puberty, his elven heritage crept into his features, something Kade tried to dismiss. Many children in Spring Haven boasted fair-hair, high cheekbones and wide, curious eyes, and Kade kept his son out of the public eye as much as he could, despite how lonely it made the boy.

Then Arlo Sparked.

Spark magic proved hereditary in most cases. The vast majority, in fact. It didn't run in Kade's blood, or Rune's. That made Arlo one of the few who Sparked at random, a fraction of the population, and those magi proved amongst the most powerful. Kade would have had to send his son to the University, where his heritage couldn't hope to stay hidden.

So, he'd sent him to Solitude, to prentice with Zanna Alpenwood, a talented but exiled Sparker. A parent herself, and one who opposed the Empire's hatemongering towards the elves, he decided the far-flung fortress his son's best option.

"Instead of keeping him by my side." Kade groaned as speaking aloud made his head thunder. "A coward. I've always been one. Always will be."

"You seemed brave enough to me. Stupid, sure, but you didn't piss your pants. That's something."

Kade goggled as a figure appeared from the smoke billowing between the trees in the forest where he found himself. A tall woman, dressed in dark leathers beneath a dirty green cloak. Redheaded, olive-skinned. He gasped as a blast of wind revealed her pointed, elven ears.

"Rune?"

Just like his fever dreams back in the cabin, his dead wife visited him. Back then, she'd taunted him, snarled his worst fears, gave voice to his deepest doubts. Nightmares, brought on by the spice withdrawal. He thought he'd passed through the worst, but now Rune strode through the trees, bearing down on him with steel at her hip and a face like murder.

"How do you know that name?" she snarled, eyes blazing.

Kade blinked as she drew close, the fog in his mind still heavy. Faint, white scars crisscrossed her face. Rune never had those, but this woman looked so similar.

Memories flashed in his mind. The elf with Calene. The one who clung to him on Solitude's walls, saving him from plummeting to his death. Brina?

Yes, she's real. I saw her, spoke to her. Get a grip, Janna damn you!

"Sorry. A name from the past. I'm...confused."

The elf wore a question on her lips, but with a scowl and a shake of her head, she dismissed it. Instead, she crouched before Kade, staring at him, the pure green of her eyes making his head swim. Without the scars, and the grim, stone-like cast to her face, she could have been Rune.

"Confused's one word for it. I've seen my share of fools going cold turkey from spice in my time. Could have picked a better time for it. Staging a daring rescue and all that isn't the best time to shake off a vice."

She held out a hand. Kade took it and she hoisted him to his feet, like he weighed no more than a rag doll. He wobbled, the ground shifting beneath his unsteady legs. Brina let him lean on her and for that she had his eternal gratitude.

"Gods, it's hot," Kade gasped, blinking the sunlight out of his eyes.

"You're worse than I thought," Brina replied, clasping his head in a vice-like grip and studying his face. "It's as cold as Sea's Keep in winter. Perhaps we'll find you a physician in Adhraas, unless they've all evacuated already."

She kept him propped up with one firm hand and pulled a waterskin free from under her cloak, holding it out for him. Kade took it, guzzled from it like a suckling calf.

"Adhrass?" he asked, licking the moisture from his lips. "Rune, we need to find Arlo."

Fire blazed in Brina's emerald eyes. Kade flinched, anticipating a blow that didn't come, but it looked like the elf tried her damned hardest not to strike him.

"Why do you keep calling me that? Who is Rune to you?"

Kade hesitated, taking another mouthful of water and glancing around. He heard singing on the wind, drifting through the smoke of battle. Something tickled the back of his mind. Something missing. Then it struck him. He turned in a circle, slow enough that his stomach didn't expel the water he'd just put there. He scanned the horizon, just in case he'd got his bearings wrong.

"Where's Solitude?"

He saw the Peaks of Eternity, circling until they almost touched, but the fortress that kept them apart had vanished. Instead, a yawning chasm took its place, like a smile that had lost its two front teeth, top and bottom.

"Gone." The elf's voice sounded like a lioness' growl. "The Banished prepare to cross, and we need to leave. But not until you tell me about Rune. That's an elven name. Who is she? Your slave?"

Kade looked away. He knew he needed to answer. Brina might tear him limb from limb if he didn't, but Solitude? Gone? How in the Underworld had that happened, and where did that leave Arlo? He'd come all this way to bring his son home, and now he'd lost him again.

"She's Arlo's mother." Kade could count on one hand the number of people he'd shared that secret with, and the words came thick. "We married in secret, but she died in childbirth. She... Well, she looked very much like you."

Brina's eyes narrowed, but Kade thought she stared through him, to another time, another place. Her face turned cold, emotionless, like winter's heart.

"Rune was your family's slave? You married her in secret after you put a babe in her stomach?" Her sneer caused Kade to look away. "Typical human, always taking what you want and making excuses for it."

"No!" Kade gasped, the elf's words too much like his father's. "I loved her, and she loved me."

"I've heard this story too many times before." Brina's lip curled. "Maybe you did love her, truly, and perhaps she felt something too, eventually. But don't fool yourself into thinking she had any choice in it. Slaves know better than to say no."

His stomach lurched, the urge to vomit rising again. His thoughts, and his family's, reflected back on him from one of Rune's own kind.

"Please." Kade took her hand, felt the calluses on her fingers. He couldn't focus on the past now. He'd pay for his crimes when he reached the Underworld. "Do you remember what happened at Solitude? Did you see Arlo?"

She blinked, as if just remembering Kade stood with her. "You're planning on going after him, aren't you? Fool, but an honourable one, to a point. Following your loved ones into the maw... I've done the same. I wish you better luck than me. A wind swept us from Solitude's walls, but a gentle hand laid us on the ground. Your son and Tilo are in Banished lands. Sure you don't want to change your mind? If I were you, in your condition, I'd turn tail and flee to Gallavan's Seat. Or, better yet, Octaria, and start a new life.

No shortage of spice there, eh?"

Kade shook his head. He couldn't—wouldn't—leave his son again. His decision to send Arlo away was the reason the boy now found himself in Banished lands.

"Come with me. I could use your help."

"And have you look at me like your long-lost love the entire time?" Brina snarled, then sighed. She pulled a dagger from her belt and pressed it into Kade's hands. "Keep the waterskin. I'd refill before you cross over. The Banished are building bridges. If you wait for them to pass, the coast is clear. Or you could scale the mountains. An army couldn't cross them, but one man might. I'd try the lower points, where Solitude stood."

She strode away without a goodbye, cloak flapping by her ankles and disturbing the lingering smoke as she reached into it.

"Wait," Kade cried, raising an arm toward her. She paused without turning. "Where are you going?"

For a second, he thought she wouldn't answer, but then her shoulders sagged. Just a touch.

"My war with Haltveldt stretches back years, and I've ignored it for longer than I should. I've lost much, Kade, and you've just reminded me. What happened here is a part of the never-ending cycle of poison flowing from Spring Haven." Brina glanced over her shoulder, her tan skin pale with white-hot fury. She drew two fingers down her face, from forehead to cheek through her eye. Black paint trailed from her fingers. "There's only one way to end it. I'm going to kill the emperor and anyone who stands with him."

Kade let his arm fall as he watched Brina walk away. The elf embarked on a suicide mission. How could one person hope to assassinate the most powerful man in Haltveldt?

Run after her. Convince her to change her mind.

"No," Kade muttered, turning to face the Peaks of Eternity, his fingers clutching the dagger Brina had given him. "She has her mission; I have mine."

Chapter Three

LIESH

'What's beyond Solitude? Nay, you ask the wrong question. What's behind those bloody peaks? That's the right one. Folk laugh at me, but mark my words, it ain't just more mountains.' – The ravings of Hewitt, Prosper's fabled adventurer, who spent his last years addled by the spice.

Arlo. Come to me.

He almost tipped over in shock. The voice, older than Arlo could comprehend, reverberated in his mind, nearly knocking him senseless. His small hands reached out to press against the boulder he slumped against on the ridge of the Peaks of Eternity, near where Solitude used to lay. Jolts of panic stabbed in his chest.

Voices in his head, no matter how wise they sounded, were the last thing he needed to hear right now.

Lights flashed in his eyes, and even though he hadn't slept since being swept off Solitude's walls, Arlo felt thrust into a waking dream. Or a nightmare.

The voice lingered in his mind, its echo fading into a whisper that tugged on the edges of his mind, begging him to focus on it.

He crouched behind an outcropping of stone near where Solitude had stood. His companion, if Arlo could call him that, a large Banished who'd pointed to himself with a smile and called himself 'Tilo', watched the others of his kind swarm below as they salvaged wood to build bridges. He'd been doing the same thing for at least four hours. Maybe more. Arlo found it hard to tell.

He'd woken up close to where he hid, when the sun crested the distant mountains. Tilo had awoken with a jerk and carried Arlo into the boulder's shadow. They hadn't moved, or attempted to speak, since.

Arlo had no idea if Tilo had kidnapped or saved him. True, the man had sheltered him on the ramparts of Solitude when madness turned into chaos, but he hadn't tried to reunite him with the others, with his father.

The Banished must be his captor, but that didn't make sense either.

Curiosity, worry and doubt remained and gnawed at Arlo as they crouched in silence. He couldn't outrun the Banished, and where would he even go? Tilo hadn't marched him straight to the army below, so that counted for something.

Since Solitude had disappeared, along with Zanna and his father—how he'd even come to be there, Arlo couldn't begin to understand—Arlo had focused on staying silent and small, not wanting to annoy Tilo and spark him into fury, though the smile he offered each time they locked eyes suggested thoughts of aggression hadn't entered his mind.

Still, Arlo couldn't trust him. He didn't know him.

Tilo had cocked his head when the voice boomed in Arlo's mind, a wide smile on his face, as if he heard it too. But if he did, he didn't say. Tilo's Haltveldtian left a lot to be desired. He enjoyed saying 'liesh'; Arlo knew that.

Arlo. The journey shall be difficult, but you must come to me.

He leaned against the stone again, his vision blurred, ears ringing, stomach lurching as the ancient, cracked voice commanded.

Leave me alone! Arlo gritted his teeth, failing to squash the fear rising in his gut. *Father, I wish you were here! Please take me home!*

A presence watched him, the weight of its attention pressing down on Arlo, making his chest tight. It came from the horizon, from the distant mountains. Arlo lifted his reluctant eyes to stare at the tallest point of the Peaks of Eternity, and the white column of light connecting it to the heavens, when the distance shifted.

Rooted to the spot, Arlo tried to scream, but his jaw locked. He tried to cover his eyes, but his arms wouldn't move. The miles between where he stood and the distant peak sped past, like the world moved under his feet while he stood still. Arlo's stomach lurched with the motion; his heart thudded in his chest until, with a jolt, he reached the foot of the peak.

Then he ascended.

Faster than before, leaving his guts in his boots, his

bladder flipping, his lungs trying to escape through his mouth, Arlo shuttled into the sky until he stopped, opposite the tallest peak.

He fought the urge to look down, to glance over his shoulder, but he couldn't, even if he wanted to. The summit held his attention. The presence he'd felt since the Banished moved against Solitude came from there, the one he'd tried to explain to Zanna but didn't have the words, the one he'd dreamed of. The peak glowed with a faint, green light that pulsated and grew stronger.

"What do you want with me?" Arlo screamed in his mind, his tongue refusing to work.

Come meet your purpose, Arlo. I await you here. Trust in me.

The tight strings holding Arlo in place, suspended in mid-air, snapped and he fell back to the stone ground on the ridge with a cry, gasping and casting around. He still lay in the shadow of the boulder, Tilo beside him, a scowl on his pale face.

In the distance, the peaks loomed, watching him. Arlo tore his eyes away.

"Noise." Tilo pressed a finger to his lips. "No. Bad child."

Arlo bristled, climbing to his feet, avoiding glancing at the mountains in the distance.

"Bad child? What, you expect me to act all happy about you kidnapping me? What does it matter, anyway?" He thrust a finger at the Banished below. "They're your people! What are you waiting for? I might have the Spark, but it's not like I'm going to cause trouble against that lot, am I?"

Tilo pulled him back down into a crouch, stare focused on the Banished again. "Talk much. My people, yes. You have purpose. Me also."

Arlo's blood ran cold. Purpose. Just what the voice had said.

Yes. Tilo is part of your journey too. It is all meant to be, you might say...

"Go away!" Arlo snarled, feeling the Spark building inside him. "Leave me alone!"

The swirling emotions trapped inside his chest grew and, without wanting to, Arlo pulled on any energy he could find, his anger powering his Spark into action. It fed on the earth beneath the mountains, the water running through the towering slopes, birds in the sky, the lingering of grief and death, the residues of magic. The singing coming from the Banished tickled the edges of his hearing, and a part of his mind—a cold, calculating part—told him to *feel* it instead. On instinct, Arlo reached out to it, felt its energy, and drew on it.

The Spark inside him lit up, a blazing sun, and made his blood run with fire and ice, made him feel like a giant amongst ants, yet insignificant surrounded by so much life. He realised all the good he could do with such power, and all the evil. He held it all within his grasp, but he understood he could draw more.

And more. More, more, more. He rose from the ground and on to his feet, without even thinking of how he did it.

The Spark whispered to him, its voice honey and sunlight, though black clouds hung on the horizon, lending a bitter edge to the sweetness. He hadn't just pulled on the essence of life and nature, along the Banished's singing. He'd fed his magic with the memories of death and grief swirling around the place Solitude had stood. Arlo's eyes widened. The Spark didn't care how someone used it. Good, evil—it didn't matter to it. The magic inside him desired to be called on. To be used. To be fed.

Too much, Arlo!

That droking voice again. It drove sense from the young boy's mind, and petulance replaced it.

Arlo spun around, drawing on sudden fear from the presence that watched him, adding it to the conflicting energies in his soul. His limbs trembling, his bones vibrating, Arlo's feet lifted from the rocks, dust swirling beneath his boots. Mouth hanging open, overcome by the power inside, he turned his face to the sky in a wordless cry. Tilo grabbed him, trying to pull him down, but Arlo ignored him. He couldn't have done anything else if he'd tried.

The Spark had him in its grasp.

The heavens above pulsated with light, like when they'd torn themselves apart before the Battle of Solitude. Red, green, yellow and purple danced across the cloudless skies, lightning lancing across them. Thunder rumbled and wind stirred, tugging at Arlo's cloak.

So be it! the ancient voice thundered. *If you will not listen to me, perhaps you will listen to her.*

"Go away!" Arlo screamed. He thought his voice would echo through the mountains, shatter them, but it only sounded in his mind.

His teeth rattled, his blonde hair stood on end, light shone through his skin, but still he drank life. Energy. The song. Fear. Anger. Death. Above all that, Arlo channelled his own sorrow—the death of his master, the loss of his father.

The musical voices swept over all. *Why are they still singing down there? Can't they see me? Aren't they afraid?*

Because they can't see what you're doing, Arlo, but others might, and you need to stop! The Banished don't have the Spark, not anymore. They have their Song.

Zanna. Arlo would recognise her voice anywhere. His master spoke to him!

Tears filled his eyes. His Spark wavered, and his feet thumped down onto hard stone again. The wind died. The bright blue skies stretched away in all directions.

Emptiness made his limbs weak, but excitement powered his mind. Zanna spoke to him!

What happened, Master? Where are you? You're still alive, aren't you? He grinned, almost laughing. Tilo shot him a confused look. *I knew it!*

I died, Arlo, Zanna answered, an odd echo to her voice. *But please, don't be sad for me. I'm still with you.*

He couldn't do as she asked. Tears ran down his cheeks and he sobbed, and even let Tilo place a meaty arm around his small shoulders. The man must have thought him mad with his sudden change of emotions.

Dead. He remembered the battle, and seeing Zanna float above the ramparts as the black miasma and wind threatened to kill them all. His master had done something to save them all; Arlo knew it, but he hadn't realised the cost.

Is my father dead, too? he asked. *I saw him on the ramparts. He couldn't have gotten away, could he? I'm amazed we did.*

Maybe his mind played tricks, but he fancied the presence smiled at him, almost like it cupped his chin in its hand.

Kade Besem lives still, but you have a purpose, Arlo. We all do. You must travel to the tallest peak, into the Throat of the Gods, and you can't let anything stop you. Do you understand?

Arlo nodded, wiped at his face, and glanced around. If he had to reach those mountains, he needed to shake off the Banished below, and the one with him. They fled from the Peaks of Eternity, and Tilo wouldn't let him just wander back that way, would he?

His...whatever he was...still had an arm wrapped around his shoulders, so he leaned into Tilo's embrace then drove his elbow deep into his ribs. Breath exploded out of the warrior in a whoosh, and Arlo aimed a kick at his face as he dropped to the ground for good measure, before running down the slope and into Banished land as fast as he could.

Arlo scrambled and slipped on the craggy, uneven ground as he fled. He stumbled away, realising what an idiotic 'plan' he'd come up with; he had no idea of where to go other than straight ahead, and no clue what awaited him. He was under no illusion that Tilo could run faster than him. For a moment, Arlo forgot that, unlike Tilo, he could use the Spark.

That would stop Tilo from following him.

He heard the stomping of footsteps behind and spun, arms raised. The Banished's singing drifted upwards from where the army toiled and Arlo pulled on it, adding it to his own energy as he called on the Spark.

Too late.

Tilo crashed into him, just like he had on Solitude's ramparts, and brought him down in a roll, the warrior cushioning the fall with his own body. Arlo grabbed at his hands. Without thinking, he sent the mixture of Spark magic and the Banished's song into Tilo's body.

His mind exploded with light, images flooding his vision. He saw the Lodestone through Tilo's eyes, the glowing green rock with the magnificent, gnarled tree growing from its centre, white and pink blossoms filling its branches. Fear and confusion bloomed at the strange presence inside it, speaking to him, directing him. It had always been a stray, distracted whisper before. Tilo strode through a meadow, hand-in-hand with his wife—Arlo couldn't say how he knew that—as they watched their three young girls run ahead of them, two yapping dogs darting between them, tails wagging. Drada, Tilo's wife, smiled as she told him they expected a new baby boy.

He understood the words like he'd spoken them his entire life. A surge of emotions jolted Arlo alongside the images too. Pride, love, longing. Purpose. Tilo missed his family, he thought of them every second he spent apart from them. They mattered most to him. His liesh. Everything he did—finding and protecting Arlo, gathering the others at Solitude so he could bring him across the mountains—he did to protect them.

From something far more terrible than the Banished, or the Haltveldtian Empire.

Good. The voice he didn't know again, ancient and purring. Arlo sensed Zanna's presence though, lurking behind it. *You have Linked. Your Sparkers would call that impossible, but you are a special case, Arlo, and they understand less than they pretend to. Tilo is special too, in his way. Besides, no one ever tried Linking between your kinds, did they? Anyway, this makes things much easier. For everyone.*

Arlo's vision expanded again, towering into the sky like before. By the way Tilo grunted in surprise, the boy reckoned they shared this experience.

Tilo knows where to bring you, my boy. But you need to know what stands in your path to the Lodestone and the Throat of the Gods.

The clouds hurtled by as they flew through the sky. This time, Arlo did look down as they sped beyond the Peaks of Eternity, gasping as he saw behind them. Grass and trees spread out as far as his eyes could see, and filling it, a massive army. A gateway stood open in a meadow, one made of shimmering, white light like the one in the sky, and more people poured out of it. Arlo remembered looking down at the Banished from Solitude, their number almost overwhelming his mind.

A rabble compared to the black-clad soldiers that amassed here. He sent a silent prayer Raas' way, hoping they hadn't seen his use of Spark magic on the ridgeline.

Without warning, the white column of light blinked out, as did the portal down in the meadow.

The Return, the voice told him.

Arlo wanted to scream. He screwed his eyes tight, so he didn't have to look at that army, those towering mountains, the dark clouds gathering. He wanted nothing more than to sit in Zanna's study, or in Solitude's library, or better yet home in Spring Haven, playing chess with his father.

His father, who Zanna said lived still. Hope rushed into his chest, battling with the overwhelming fear, beating it back. His father lived, but that army would crush him. They'd crush everyone!

Water splashed on his face. He opened his eyes to find himself still in the foothills, Tilo crouching over him, hands on his shoulders as rain dripped from the now-grey skies.

"Are you okay?" Tilo asked.

He didn't know if he spoke Haltveldtian or the Banished's language. It really didn't matter anymore. Through the Link, Arlo could feel Tilo's determination, his absolute belief that he did this all for his family. Bringing Arlo to the Lodestone would stop the Return and save everyone from certain annihilation.

"You know they're down there." The boy pointed to the Banished—the Children, as they called themselves; he knew that now, through Tilo's thoughts—and turned as a look of pain flashed across Tilo's face. He felt it in their Link too. Heartache. "We could just go to them, get someone else to bring me to the Lodestone, right? You can be with them."

Tilo shook his head, a sad smile on his face. "There is no time, and I am the only one who can lead you. You saw what approaches. We must do as he inside the Lodestone asks. If we don't, my family won't have long to live. No one will. I trust it. Every vision it revealed to me has proved true."

"'He inside the Lodestone'? It isn't the Lodestone talking? You seem confused about it."

Tilo shook his head. "No. It's...complicated. I don't understand it myself, you are right, but whatever that voice is, it isn't the Lodestone. It's helping us."

And Zanna is with it. Arlo gazed out at the tallest point of the Peaks of Eternity, miles in the distance.

Miles!

"There's so many of these Returned," Arlo whispered, sinking to the floor, wondering if he could convince Tilo to head the other way and find his father instead. He could always use his Spark on him if he said no. "How are we meant to find our way through?"

Tilo climbed to his feet and held out his hand. Arlo took it, and the warrior helped him up. "Together."

"You heard Zanna too, didn't you?"

Tilo nodded in response.

"I miss her. So much. She says my father's out there, somewhere. But we don't have time to look for him either, do we?"

Worth a try.

The warrior placed an arm around his shoulders again. "No. Gods willing, you shall see him again. This is your purpose. You are the one, Arlo. The person who can end all of this."

They walked away, finding a winding path that led across a mountain ridge, high above the pass where Solitude once stood, as the spitting rain turned into a deluge. Arlo glanced over his shoulder, looking back across the peaks, towards Adhraas and the rest of Haltveldt. Towards where his father would be, if Zanna spoke the truth, and why wouldn't she?

"I hope so, Tilo. Teeth of the gods, I hope so."

CHAPTER FOUR

A MEETING OF MINDS

"Attachments? Those we can work with. Gives us a target, a weakness to exploit. We're better off without them." - The Temekt City Guild of Assassins takes a dim view of love and friendship...unless they make a job easier.

W et, miserable and bone-tired, Calene drew her cloak tighter and ignored the rain dripping into her eyes.

"I'm pretty sure..." Calene panted, hands on her hips. "No, I'm certain, I said I wouldn't walk all the way to Adhraas. Who droking knew, eh?"

Using the Spark to draw a watertight bubble around her made little sense; not with the Emperor's Shadow Sparkers loose. The Hand too, and they could turn up droking anywhere without warning. At least she could sense another magi from a distance. Right then, not an ounce of Spark leapt out at Calene, but she knew it meant little with Haltveldt's inquisition in play.

Channelling her Spark would make her stand out like an Eru Day bonfire at nightfall. Anyone searching for

Sparkers would keep their magic under control and scan with their Second Sight, until they found their quarry.

Vettigan had trailed behind all the way since they'd moved south, trudging through the thick mud with slumped shoulders. They hadn't travelled by road, instead taking a winding route through the forests. He'd argued with each step at first, pointing out that any Shadow Sparkers in the region would have already made their presence known, the battle with the Banished too rich a temptation for them to pass up. That they'd embarked on a fool's errand. He couldn't be healed. Couldn't be saved.

Calene ignored him, just like the droking rain—well, she tried at least—and let his complaints fade into the background.

Hard to do. The forests lay silent, like all the wildlife had fled, as if they knew what approached.

War.

"Anyone with half a brain would run for miles," Calene muttered.

They lurked on the outskirts of Adhraas, the gigantic stone statue of Raas looming over them, dominating the dock town. Before they entered the settlement, Calene had studied the place from the trees. No ships swayed in the harbour; the place seemed abandoned. They'd risked approaching in the hope of finding supplies, judging their need worth the peril.

Vettigan nudged her, shoulder banging into hers with a little too much force for her liking. "And here we are, wandering through the hinterlands with the horde on our backs, lurking in alleyways like a pair of beggars."

"What do you want me to do?" He didn't meet her eyes

as she turned to glare at him, the thick sheet of grey drizzle falling on Adhraas almost swallowing him. "Make us magically appear at another place. A bit beyond the Spark, that."

Calene bit her lip when Vettigan scowled in response. Frustrated tears stung her violet eyes. Nothing pleased Vettigan anymore. He hadn't wanted to travel north into Banished territory, and he'd made fair points why, but her old friend despised journeying south just as much, despite what it meant to him.

It's like he wants to curl up in a ditch and die.

No. Vettigan wanted to leave Haltveldt, and Calene understood that. During his many grumbles on their ten-mile trek, he'd brought up Avastia. Octaria. Velen even. The call of adventure and a fresh start whispered in her ear as she replayed the events of the last week in her mind. Why shouldn't she escape this Empire bent on ruin? Listen to her heart and go the way it wanted? Nothing tied her to Haltveldt, no matter how much she'd hoped to see Brina striding through the trees on the journey.

Her only tie, her mother, had died. Whatever remained of Vettigan, if anything did, wanted to flee.

"Her sacrifice keeps me here." Calene gripped her sword hilt, hidden beneath the folds of her cloak. The steel added strength to her resolve. "It can't all be for nothing. It won't."

Healing Vettigan mattered too. She'd sworn she'd never return home, to the place her life changed forever, and for the worse. But her oldest friend needed saving, and she believed her father's work might hold the answers.

The Battle of Solitude—the events leading up to it and its aftermath—had robbed Calene of everything. Her new friends, her oldest, and Zanna. It had brought another war to Haltveldt's doorstep. Running made sense, yes. Of course it did.

But running with Vettigan in his present condition? She might as well journey to a land ruled by sheep with a wolf by her side.

The hairs on her arm prickled. Calene's breath caught in her chest. Magic swelled in the streets of Adhraas. Someone used the Spark, lighting a signal for any magi in the vicinity. Calene closed her eyes and reached out, breathing long, deep breaths. The Spark whispered to her, urging her to use it. It always did; the magic often felt like a living entity inside her, but since the battle of Solitude, its insistence had grown. A Sparker's life went hand-in-hand with struggle, with knowing when the threshold of too much approached and having the strength to let go, to give back. They all faced a choice between using their gift for good and following Raas and Janna's teachings, or embracing the power Sparking their souls and forcing the world to conform to their desires.

Now, the Spark's whisper repulsed her when she'd once revelled in its sweet caress. As a support soldier in the elven wars, and in hunting rogue Sparkers, the Spark's evils held no surprises for her. Not to mention her mother's actions all those years before, when her father's Eviscerated remains oozed on the floor. But her experiences couldn't compare to what had thrived inside Vettigan after the Shadow Sparker's attack, what had unleashed itself on Solitude's ramparts.

It had writhed and fed like a living entity, begging, urging, cajoling anyone with the Spark to set it free, to use it and sink into corruption and filth.

Just like the Spark inside her did now.

It went against Raas' teachings—her mother's beliefs, and her own —but she couldn't ignore the thought bubbling to the surface of her troubled mind.

The Spark wasn't a tool for the betterment of humankind as the scriptures taught. Not a benign power, as she'd believed all her life. No, the Spark didn't care about good or evil; it desired *use*, no matter the end. The Spark lived in her soul, urged her to embrace it, to experience life like a mere human couldn't. It wanted her to taste the sweetness on the wind, let the rain's rich flavour quench her thirst, let the vibrant colours of the grass, sky and trees dispel the grey murk sucking the joy from nature.

Calene forced her soul into stone, her heart too, and opened her eyes. She couldn't let emotion lead her on this journey. She always had and look what it delivered to her door. Letting out a shuddering breath, she set aside her magic and turned her gaze to the sky, to the towering monolith above them.

Sparkers gathered at the feet of Raas' statue. Survivors of Solitude.

"Come on," Calene called, not waiting to see if Vettigan followed as she broke into a jog, the cobblestones echoing beneath her boots.

"What is it?" Vettigan called, with more than a little frustration in his voice. He couldn't feel the swell of magic in the air.

"Sparkers. Follow me."

"Why not leave town?" Vettigan breathed, as they pounded through quiet, darkened streets. Calene picked side streets and poked her head around corners before sprinting into alleyways. "We don't know who they are!"

"They're survivors," Calene hissed over her shoulder, the statue of Raas drawing closer.

"How do you know?" Vettigan snapped.

Her Second Sight revealed it. The Spark gathered just ahead, pure magic without a hint of darkness. Calene came to a stop, the town square opening up before them, and pointed.

"I just do, Vee. Look, see? You recognise any of them?"

A group of bedraggled Sparkers argued beneath the statue, pointing and waving hands, until one pointed to his throat, and his voice smothered the rest.

"Heran. He's the one blowing hot air." Vettigan shook his head as they lurked in the darkness between two buildings, the walls slanting together so their roofs almost touched. The night drew late and cast long shadows across the town square. "Look at him, using the Spark to amplify his voice to a handful of frightened nobodies. Pompous fool. Needs putting in his place."

"Vettigan, you're acting the rasclart, and I'm sick of it. To my back teeth."

Calene grabbed him by the cloak and pulled him around so their eyes met. His expression flickered with anger, lips locked in a half-snarl. She stared him down like she would a feral dog, jaw set in determination, refusing to back down. Her old friend blinked; his face sagged, the tightness flooding from it, and broke the deadlock.

"Pull yourself together, for Raas' sake."

She let go with a half-shove, pushing him against the

building's wall. Vettigan slumped against it, shaking his head. His hood had slipped, revealing his patchy, grey hair and pockmarked, yellowed skin. Calene's heart went out to him, compassion overriding the anger, and the stone she sought to encase it in.

He's lost so much and wears it for all to see. At least I can keep my hurt inside.

"I'm sorry, Calene. For—"

"Wait." She held a finger up, cutting him off. A scraping sound came from behind. Calene spun, a glint catching her eye. Moonlight on steel. "We're not alone."

Their hands fell to their swords, Vettigan hissing as he inched his free of its scabbard. Calene grabbed his forearm, a silent warning to wait and watch. Whoever lurked in the darkness had the drop on them. If they'd wanted them dead, they'd have acted already. Still, Calene's blood surged, pumping adrenaline through her body.

She welcomed the chance for a good fight, steel on steel. A proper way to work through some issues, that.

A shape formed from the shadows, tall, graceful and flowing towards them. The Spark nagged at Calene, begging for use.

What if I'm wrong? What if it's a Shadow Sparker, and I'm standing here like a lamb on Eru Day?

Calene bared her teeth, indecision paralysing her.

Soft. You'd have just acted before Solitude, an accusing voice whispered in her mind. Her own voice. *Before you watched your mother die, and you did nothing.*

A snarl thick with anger built in her throat—she didn't know if the malice surging through her came at her own expense, or at the figure approaching them, maybe both—but before she could act, the stranger lowered their hood.

A scarred, tanned face—now with two, thick lines of black paste passing over her eye from forehead to cheek—framed by red, braided hair. Bright emerald eyes flashing as the moonlight struck them, and a half-smile touching her lips.

"Brina, for drok's sake," Calene cursed, letting go of her sword hilt. She went to reach out, to embrace the elf or maybe strangle her, but caught herself, wanting to keep the relief she felt at seeing the woman to herself. For now. "What in the Underworld are you playing at, sneaking up on us? We're Sparkers, remember?"

Well, one of us is, but she doesn't know Vettigan's lost his power.

The elf's green eyes flickered across their faces, then down to Vettigan's sword. He still had the weapon half-drawn.

Calene thumped him on the shoulder.

"So are they," Brina said, ignoring Vettigan as he slammed the steel back into its scabbard. Instead, she fixed her focus on the group of Sparkers remonstrating at the feet of Raas. "Why are you hiding?"

"We're not," Calene bristled, heat rising in her cheeks. "I'm surveying. Who knows where their loyalties lie? I saw plenty of Sparkers losing the run of themselves up at Solitude, and there might be—"

Brina held up a hand. "Shadow Sparkers. I get it. Wise, can't fault you there. Your mother, did you pull her out?"

"Dead." Vettigan growled, but the heat in his words

evaporated as they left his mouth. He sagged against the wall again. "My fault... All my fault."

Every time she heard that word, a fist hammered into Calene's gut, twisting and driving deep. A part of her wanted to reach out to her old friend—an ally through wars fought, inns drank dry, tears shed until no more would come—but a greater impulse agreed with him, discounting all the facts. What the Shadow Sparker had done to him, how the parasite had taken control. If only Vettigan had listened to her and not touched his Spark...

No. If only Calene had left him behind, Zanna might live still.

She couldn't blame Vettigan. He'd lost a battle. An internal war no one should have had to wage. No shame in that.

Calene blamed herself. She'd brought her old friend into the battle, even though she sensed his struggle. She'd blocked Zanna out for a decade, refusing to find middle-ground. She hadn't even been able to shout 'I love you too' fast enough for her mother to hear. Zanna sacrificed herself, not knowing how her daughter felt.

Calloused fingers brushed the back of Calene's hand and saved her from her thoughts. She blinked herself back into the present. Brina stared into her eyes, concern swimming beneath her hard exterior.

"I'm sorry—"

"Where's Kade?" Calene interrupted, as she rebuilt those walls in her mind. She'd strengthen them further this time. Make them unassailable, even if she'd done a piss-poor job of it so far.

"Chasing his son into Banished lands. The *thiemea* fool! He'll get himself killed." Brina scowled and muttered like she spoke to herself. "Shaking like a new-born lamb, thinking me someone I'm not, tempting me with..."

Another crack appeared in Calene's walls. A small one, but there nonetheless. Drok. Calene needed a better mason than herself.

"Well, we can't help him. What are you doing here, and what's with the makeup?"

"Considered sailing across the Sundered Sea," Brina replied, raising an eyebrow, "but where's the fun in that? Picked up your trail a while back. We're heading in the same direction. Thought you'd come here to find transport south."

Brina didn't mention the black paste running from forehead to cheek, and Calene knew better than to press.

Vettigan grunted. "Or away from here. No such luck. This one has a fool notion in her head to heal me."

Brina gave him a level look when he fell silent. "Are you going to expand on that? I thought she and Tilo did that already?"

Vettigan bared his teeth. "Do I look droking healed to you? The Spark's gone... Just...gone."

Brina met Calene's eyes, face unreadable. Calene took the elf in; the black paint on her face, the set of her stone-like jaw, her complete non-answer before.

"South, eh? Why not flee, or find some pockets of your own kind? What are you planning?"

Brina's scowl deepened, but as she opened her mouth to answer, shouts from the Sparkers snatched Calene's attention, as did a surge in Spark. The old magi by the statue of

Raas embraced his magic as they argued.

"What is it?" Vettigan hissed like a spitting, toothless viper, all venom and no bite. She tried to understand his suffering, experiencing the world without the Spark.

Must be like losing your eyes. Worse—smell, touch, hearing too. Drok it all, Vettigan; maybe I should have let you die. More mistakes.

"This could get messy. They need to leave." Calene strode from the shadows, Vettigan following. "If the Empire has Sparkers around here, they might as well set the droking statue on fire and draw them right to us."

Brina stayed in the shadows. For the best. An elf appearing might start another fight. Calene glanced over her shoulder; the woman held her sword by her side, ready to charge if needed. More cracks in the wall.

She ground her teeth. *I have to be stronger. It's the only way to survive, to stop others getting hurt. Why is it so hard? I shut them out for years about Mother.*

A lie. She'd blocked the contact, but her anger, regret and shame had driven her for the decade, had led her down every path she'd walked. She just hadn't wanted to admit it to herself. Remaining detached had never been easy for her.

"What in the Underworld are you all doing?" Calene bellowed, without using the Spark. The magic inside her responded to the residue in the air, the charge of built-up energy just waiting for someone to grasp it. She didn't trust it, or herself.

The old Sparkers spun around. Dirty, panicked faces with wide eyes—the whites stark in the fading light—stared her way. It struck her then. These old men and women wouldn't know about the Shadow Sparkers, or Emperor Locke turning his back on Solitude. Despite the Laws being abolished, and more than one of them indulging themselves in the Battle of Solitude, the group in front of her comprised old, weary, forgotten Sparkers, many of them devout followers of the old ways. Survivors of a fight thrust upon them they were ill-equipped to deal with.

Like Vettigan—drok, like so many!—they'd suffered profound loss. Their home, their way of life, their faith. In the space of a week, it had all come crashing down, leaving them abandoned, scared and filthy, sheltering at the feet of their god. Calene scowled up at his chiselled features. The uncaring rasclart.

"Who are you?" the one called Heran asked, his voice still amplified. "What are you doing here?"

"Release your Spark, for Raas' sake," Vettigan snarled beneath his hood. "If anyone's looking for survivors to finish the job, you're sticking a magical arrow in the sky pointing right down on Adhraas!"

A Sparker near the edge of the crowd peered at him, eyes narrowed, before a smile broke out across her face.

"Vettigan! It's Vettigan Baralart. You were at Solitude?"

He didn't answer.

"That makes you Calene Alpenwood," Heran called, still using his Spark. "Your mother spoke of you often, and of your friendship with Vettigan. I can see you favour her. Where is she? We could use her wisdom."

"If you respected my mother," Calene grated, "you'd do as Vettigan asked and release your droking Spark. Now, or teeth of the gods, I'll rip it from you. Zanna died protecting you all. She sacrificed herself to spare more bloodshed. There's more going on here than you realise. We're all in danger."

"What are you talking about?" Heran gasped. Unsparked, this time.

"Zanna's dead?" someone cried. "How?"

"Listen!" Calene strode to stand beside Heran. "You know the emperor abolished the laws, but that's not all. He abandoned Solitude. He wanted to see you all die. The emperor demands war! The elves are on their last legs, and the next target is the Banished. He planned to sacrifice you, and Solitude, as the first act of war. A travesty to unite the people of Haltveldt against a new enemy."

"Preposterous," Heran said. "How could you possibly know what the emperor planned?"

"Because I came here with Kade Besem, Liaison to Solitude. He told me everything, but there's more. As if the massacre at Solitude wasn't enough! Vettigan? Come here, please."

Vettigan slunk forward, his heavy travelling cloak still covering him from head to foot. Splashes of mud licked the bottom of the sodden, frayed material. Glancing around, Calene took in the sorry lot huddling together. They all resembled beggars—harried, exhausted, dirty, and lost. But they watched, they listened. They held their breath for what she would say next.

"Don't make me do this, Calene," Vettigan begged by her elbow, voice low and harsh. "I know what you want. Spare me."

"I know, but help me save these people." Stooping a little, Calene peered into the murk of his hood. Vettigan's wary, dull eyes peered back at her, pleading. "They *must* understand what the Empire has become. Words won't do it."

Beneath the cloak, Vettigan's shoulders twisted, like he wanted to flee, but he nodded. Calene turned back to the crowd, filled her lungs, and breathed out slowly.

"On the road north, Sparkers attacked us. Ones not loyal to the Order, but to the emperor himself. They had a weapon. A Shadow Sparker, they called it."

She nodded at Vettigan, who let his cloak fall to the ground. Her heart tried to escape her mouth as her oldest friend flinched at the gasps of the other Sparkers. The wall she'd built to hem in her emotions and attachments would lie in ruins before long. Another failure.

Vettigan shivered from the cold but stared back at the group. His chin tilted once their cries of disbelief died down. He stood there—shrunken body, yellowed skin, lank, patchy hair—and let the Sparkers take in every detail.

"He has no Spark!" someone cried from the group. "This Shadow Sparker did this to you?"

"It attacked us," Vettigan growled. "Tried to Eviscerate me."

Heran took a step toward him, squinting. "There's something inside you... Some residue. Dark, evil. That was you, up on the walls, wasn't it? That miasma that threatened to destroy us all. I felt it, even though I fought far from there. It called to me, wanted me to embrace it."

"That's enough, Vettigan." Calene stepped in front of Heran as the wounded old man hid himself in the deep folds of his cloak again. Pride welled in her chest.

Maybe there's hope for him yet, and this isn't a fool's errand.

She eyed Heran but raised her voice for the other Sparkers.

"The emperor's new soldier didn't just try; it Eviscerated him. The magic only touched him for seconds before I stopped it, but it transferred some essence into Vettigan. It craved death, chaos, destruction. We did our best to contain it, but the battle caused it to grow, to take control. You saw the rest."

The crowd fell silent. Brina, across the square, at the edge of the shadows, shrank back. Calene frowned but pushed thoughts of the elf from her mind. She had a job to do.

"This Shadow Sparker didn't appear in Haltveldt the moment the emperor abolished the Laws; it's existed for years. Trust me, I've seen nothing like it. I killed the droker, or thought I had, but it wouldn't die. Not until its head left its droking shoulders. That's Haltveldt's future. That's what the emperor desires the Order to be. Weapons. No, monsters. Nothing more, and nothing less."

Silence. Some of the old Sparkers glanced at one another, some stared at the cobblestones. One or two glared up at the statue of Raas, as if the god had caused all the treachery in Haltveldt.

"What would you have us do, Calene?" Heran whispered at last, his voice carrying to all the souls crowded in the silent square. The old Sparkers sent her their own quiet pleas, etched across their weary faces. They needed guidance like a baby required milk.

Drok it all anyway. When did I become a leader? When there wasn't anyone else, I guess.

Calene set her jaw and nodded. Right then, they needed her, and she needed to matter. Craved a purpose. The thought almost made her smile. Almost.

"For all the emperor knows, no one survived Solitude. I'm travelling to the capital, to tell anyone who'll listen what happened here, what the Empire did and what Zanna Alpenwood did to stop a massacre." She didn't see the need to tell them of her real mission. The one to save Vettigan. "I'm heading for the heart of our Order, to make them see what the emperor and his cronies are doing to us. But you don't need to. You've given your lives to an order and empire that have abandoned you, that wanted you to die so they could wage another war and tried to pervert you into corrupt weapons. Teeth of the gods, go. Anywhere. Find boats and travel to Octaria, Avastia or Velen; disappear amongst the millions at Sea's Keep or Prosper. Go anywhere that isn't here or Spring Haven. You deserve better. We all do."

She met Heran's bright blue eyes, luminous the way the Unsparked could never be. They flicked to the hooded Vettigan, then back to Calene, before he nodded. Reaching up to the emblem of the Order sewed to his dirtied, red cloak, he dug his fingers beneath it and channelled a touch of fire, tearing the badge off and tossing it into the mud.

"You're your mother's daughter, Calene Alpenwood. And I couldn't think of a worthier thing to say to you. Be well."

Other Sparkers followed his lead, throwing the mark of the Order at Raas' feet. Calene tried not to wince at the small spurts of Spark and craned her neck to stare up at the statue's face, looking across Adhraas forty feet above. The noble features appeared smug, a slight sneer on their lips.

You can keep your droking opinions to yourself.

A thought occurred to her. "Heran? A word."

The Sparker looked back, frowning. "You've said enough. We're convinced. In truth, many of us have been for years but we ignored it."

"It isn't about that." Calene grimaced, glancing around. Vettigan hung back, a rare show of wisdom on his part of late. "You knew my mother. Did you know Ricken too? Did she ever talk about him?"

Heran eyed Vettigan, a speculative look on his shrewd face. "No. She rarely spoke of her past, and when she did, she talked only of you." A dagger in Calene's heart. Another crack in the droking useless wall she'd constructed. "I knew of your father. His experiments. I see your mind. You seek to help your friend, but some things are best left in the past. If we ever meet again, I hope it's under better circumstances, but I fear happy times have abandoned Haltveldt. Farewell, Calene Alpenwood."

He turned and left without another word, shoulders hunched. Defeated, but at least with a future without the Empire. A fresh start.

"Nice speech," Vettigan muttered, as the Sparkers followed Heran from the square. She understood their reluctance to go their own ways—Solitude had been their home, and the other Sparkers their family—but Calene hoped they'd run far and enjoy the rest of their lives, however and wherever they could. "Really think you should follow your own advice. A boat to Avastia appeals, don't you think?"

"I'm going south, Vettigan."

"Why? You can't save me and you know it! You've had your mind set on going south since Solitude fell. What is it? Suicide? Is that what you want? Listen to yourself! You owe the Empire and the Order not a jot. Remember what they tried to do to you. What they did to me."

"I'm not doing this for the droking Empire," Calene snarled. Across the square, Brina appeared from the shadows at a jog. "I'm doing it for my mother. I won't let her sacrifice go unnoticed. How long before the emperor's agents blame her and those sorry sods up there for the massacre? I won't let it happen, Vettigan. Rotten teeth of the gods, I won't! And I can save you. I will. I'm not losing you too!"

Calene's eyes flew wide as Vettigan's hand dropped to his sword, but a shout brought them about.

"Sorry to interrupt," Brina gasped, skidding to a halt. "Four Banished are scouting the town. Might want to do something about them if you want to avoid a fight with those Sparkers wandering about the place."

Chapter Five

SCOUTS ON THE ROAD

'Folk who've never fought in a battle before will tell you there's something romantic about a warrior with nothing to fear. One who'll throw themselves into harm's way without a thought. Utter drok. Let me tell you, there's nothing worse. They always get themselves, and the ones next to them, killed. Every time.' - Among the infantry, there's always something to be said for unity.

Calene followed Brina's finger as they hid in the thicket. The town's main road ran through its centre, and there they lurked, waiting. Night had fallen on the abandoned town. Stars twinkled like diamonds across the vast sky, the moon glowing like a beacon above them. So picturesque. Calene could have appreciated it if she hadn't been fleeing from a battle with a rogue elf and a friend who seemed intent on doing her harm.

The echo of hooves drifted her way, and she squinted, peering through the moonlight. In the distance, the Banished emerged from the gloom. Four of them travelled together, one mounted at the head of the party, the others leading their animals as they scanned the road, just like Brina had said.

"Drok," Calene spat, throwing a baleful glare Vettigan's way. His hand hadn't moved from his blade since they left the alleyway, fingers caressing the bastard thing. "Let's head them off. Maybe we can talk? Worked for Tilo."

"He's one of them." Brina rolled her eyes, but she tilted her head to the side as if considering. "You don't even know their language."

"Well, you might help there," Calene replied. Elves and Banished shared some common words, and Brina had helped Tilo learn the common tongue on the journey north. Perhaps she'd picked up a smattering.

"Think you're overestimating my skills. Still, I appreciate the vote of confidence. Did I tell you it's nice to see you again?"

Calene smirked, despite their situation. Her stomach flipped at the elf's words. "You left that bit out."

Nice to see me, eh?

"There's no talking to them," Vettigan growled, interrupting the unexpected turn of pleasantness. He sat rigid, like a lion about to pounce. "You saw what they did at Solitude. You want those Sparkers back there to start a new life? Start by ending theirs."

"Shut up, for Raas' sake. Keep quiet and stay hidden until your bloodlust settles, will you?" Calene turned to Brina. "We'll wait for them on the road there, heads uncovered, hands free. You and me, we'll talk to them, nice and polite, yeah?"

She grabbed Brina's forearm and led her off a little, so Vettigan wouldn't overhear their whispers.

"It's good to see you too. Really good." Calene forced the heat from her cheeks, hoping the night would hide her blush from the elf's keen eyes, then blew a stray hair away from her face. The wind moved it back. "But we've got a problem with Vettigan. He isn't the same. That droking Shadow Sparker did a number on him, then the battle at Solitude pushed him over the edge. He wants death, and I can't let him find it."

"So, you're saying we need to avoid a fight?" Brina asked, reaching out and brushing the hair out of Calene's face. "Be bastions of peace and tranquillity?"

"Something like that," Calene murmured, staring into Brina's emerald eyes. The elf's fingertip had brushed against her skin. "He's not going to be easy to get along with, but please try. That's if you're coming with—"

A yell interrupted them.

"Change of plans, I think." Brina almost choked. "Your friend has other ideas. Come on!"

Vettigan had torn from his hiding place and ran down the road, straight at the Banished party, sword swinging as he ran.

Drok! Forget what I just said, I'll kill him myself when I get my hands on him!

She chased him down, Brina on her heels. Vettigan didn't stand a chance against four horsemen, not in his condition. And judging by how she'd seen the Banished fight, not before either, even with Vettigan's skill. Not without the Spark.

He charged at the Banished leading the party, a hulking, pale man wearing leather and furs. The warrior sat with his head cocked, a puzzled look on his face as Vettigan bore down on him.

"Vettigan, stop!" Calene yelled, drawing the attention of the Banished.

"*Huar!*" the white-haired scout cried. "*Sa fera huar!*"

The other horses whinnied, and the stamping of hooves filled the air. They tasted the coming bloodshed before their masters did.

Vettigan closed the gap and swung at the Banished's mount, aiming for a leg to bring it and its rider down. The warrior danced out of the way, manoeuvring the animal with his thighs and quick jerks of the reins.

"*Huar!*" the Banished roared, the horse moving sideways from Vettigan's unrelenting attack.

Calene stumbled, falling to her knees, the palms of her hands stinging as she grazed them on the stones. "Stop, Vettigan! For Raas' sake! They don't want to fight, can't you see that?"

Vettigan didn't listen. Maybe he *couldn't* listen. The parasite trapped inside him, cut off from his Spark, drove him on. It wanted to taste death on Vettigan's soul. The evil within controlled him, just as it had at Solitude. Her Second Sight told her as much. It writhed within him, its tendrils in his heart, mind and soul.

Let him die, a voice in Calene's mind whispered. *Like you should have done before. Let him die before it's too late, and he gets you or Brina killed. Or turns on you.*

The Banished drew his sword, ready to fight back.

Vettigan had boasted unparalleled prowess with the blade before the Shadow Sparker attack, but his best days lay behind him. Now he faced a Banished warrior with the advantage of horseback, in the prime of life.

Vettigan didn't stand a chance.

"No," Calene whispered. To the voice in her head, or her old companion's death, she couldn't say. She could only feel dread swelling in her chest as she knelt on the road.

The Banished danced his horse away, raised his sword, then darted forward, dwarfing the small, thin, cloaked figure in the darkness.

A flicker of silver in the moonlight flew by Calene's face, then a sickening thud rang out. The Banished's horse screamed as its rider swayed in its seat, the hilt of a dagger sticking out of his forehead, blood turning his pale face crimson.

"Come on," Brina growled, pulling Calene from the floor and producing a second dagger from her belt. "Vettigan needs us. If it wasn't clear before, it is now!"

The Banished fell to the ground, his horse bolting. Vettigan had already moved on. The dismounted warriors further up the road rushed to meet him.

"Drok it anyway." Calene raced to join the melee, pulling her sword free. "A fool to think anything in Haltveldt could end without blood."

There's always another way. Right?

The Spark whispered to her, seducing her with its sweet power. She could end the fight now; subdue the Banished without violence, or scrub them from existence, burn them to ash. Calene had the means to act flowing through her veins, coursing in her blood. The power lay there in her grasp. The potential to do anything she wanted. Death, life, punishment, mercy. Anything.

But she couldn't trust the Spark. Not anymore, and what's more, she didn't trust herself *with* it.

Before her journey north, the Spark rested inside her, waiting for her command. Now it raged and swelled, more potent than before. It had changed, she'd changed, and anyone could be watching to see it used. Anyone.

"There's no other way," Calene snarled, baring her teeth, tears stinging her eyes as a Banished woman moved to head her off. "Damn it, but there isn't."

The warrior dwarfed her, all height and muscle, but she hesitated as Calene threw off her cloak, letting it fall to the ground to free her arms. Ahead, Brina's sword clanged against a Banished's, her travel cloak already discarded, and Vettigan faced off against another woman. Calene brought her focus under control. She'd need it.

Her opponent shrugged off the hesitation, darting forward with more speed than her bulk should allow. Gasping, Calene hopped back, blocking a low attack with her blade, vibrations rattling into her shoulders. Sword a blur, the Banished kept up her attacks, overarm flurries following low slashes. Sweat beaded on Calene's forehead despite the night's chill as she did all she could to defend herself. The torrent of emotions and doubts assaulting her had stolen her edge, her clarity.

I need to attack or I'm dead.

Calene met a swipe and rolled with it, moving to the Banished's side. She feinted forwards, hoping the warrior would fall for it, then darted the other way, searching for a hole in the woman's defence.

Too slow.

The Banished caught the attack and flicked out a backhand, catching Calene on the jaw. Pain filled her skull, and the iron tang of blood flooded her mouth as her head snapped back. A stinging burn bloomed in her thigh as the warrior sliced her sword across it.

Crying out, Calene fell back onto the road, head ringing, thigh screaming. Blood trickled into the dirt as the Banished pressed her, sensing the kill.

The Spark, coiled within her, pulsed. For a moment, she thought it tried to take control of her, to defend the body carrying it.

Tricks of a weary mind, Raas let it be that.

Gritting her teeth, Calene pushed herself to one knee, free hand scrabbling amongst the stones on the road. She grabbed what she could and flung it into the other woman's eyes.

The Banished stumbled as dust filled her vision. From her kneeling position, Calene drove forward, two hands on the hilt, and thrust her sword into her opponent's belly, pushing through the resistance the warrior's innards gave until the blade burst from her back.

Sagging against it, the Banished met Calene's eyes. Pale yellow, filled with sadness. Crimson trickled from her lips as tears ran down Calene's cheeks.

"*Sa fera huar...*" the Banished warrior breathed. Her last.

She toppled to the ground. Calene pulled her sword

free, the road quiet save for the braying of horses.

"Drok, I'm sorry," Calene whispered. "I really am."

Brina had retrieved her cloak, looking no worse for wear, like she hadn't even killed the warrior at her feet. Vettigan stood over a body, sword dripping crimson in his hand, staring at the corpse as if committing the woman's face to memory.

Calene spun, her neck muscles tight, black rage filling her.

"Vettigan! Look at what the drok you've done?"

He kept his back to her. She stalked across to him, spun him around with such violence his hood fell back. Tears streamed from his dull eyes down his haggard, blood-smeared face.

"You should have let me die," he whispered, letting his sword fall to the ground with a clang, his words echoing the voice in her mind. "All I bring is death. Look at them! I couldn't help myself. I saw them, the weapons by their sides, and rage exploded inside me. *Huar,* they screamed. I don't know how, but I understand it. 'Peace'. That's what they said, and yet I attacked. Only the taste of blood on my blade mattered."

Calene left a hand on her old friend's shoulder, memories of their years together flickering through her mind; he'd comforted her after her mother's hearing and exile, had visited their family home when she collected her belongings, unable to go in there alone and revisit the horrors. They'd laughed, drank, cried, killed and sang together. Spent hours in comfortable silence as they travelled Haltveldt's four corners.

That Vettigan had died during the Shadow Sparker ambush. He wanted to leave, to escape Haltveldt. Why did she keep him around? For some wretched, haggard reminder of her old life? Selfish.

"Go, Vettigan," she muttered, her injured leg trembling as pain bloomed in it. Her jaw didn't hurt much less. "I can't let you die, but I won't stop you from leaving."

"No, Calene." He shook his emaciated head, lank hair swirling in the wind. "I can't. You're all I've got left too. I need saving, even if the darkness inside me pushes any help away."

She wanted to pull him closer, to embrace him and smile. Laugh. Tell him she *would* save him, that she wouldn't rest until she found her answer. Instead, she nodded.

All she could do.

"Fetch us three horses and any supplies they have. I'd say bury the bodies, but we're out of time. The Banished are coming and we need to leave."

Vettigan covered his head and retrieved his sword, cleaning it on the dead Banished's furs before moving away. Calene staggered, the wound in her leg bleeding and angry.

"Sit down before you fall down," Brina commanded. "Let me look at that cut."

"Whatever you say," Calene muttered, almost sighing the words.

She let the elf lower her to the ground, studying her face as she worked. Another puzzle. The woman made her loins stir, no doubt, and they'd grown close in a way since they'd met in the Forest of Mists. But Brina had told her little of herself, and from the scars running across her face and hands, the haunted look in her eyes, the fresh black paint on her cheek, Calene understood the elf kept volumes of secrets.

"The more things change, eh?" Brina smiled as she looked up from the wound. "You're always needing my help, aren't you? The mighty Sparker, requiring assistance from the lowly elf."

"Lowly." Calene barked out a laugh, then winced as Brina prodded the gash in her leg. "I wouldn't call you that."

The elf paused, fingers pressed against Calene's leg. She fought against the urge to wiggle lower in an effort to make Brina move up her thigh.

"And what *would* you call me?" she asked, gazing at her from under her red hair, the strange black paint running through her eye making the emerald pop.

Calene swallowed, then cleared her throat. *Change. The droking. Subject.*

"Why are you going south? Why don't you disappear too? Go back to what you were doing?"

"I have a mission." Brina glanced down at the wound, the moment passed, and pulled a small bottle from her belt, pouring a drop onto Calene's leg and rubbing it in. It soothed the stinging, and Calene continued to enjoy the touch of her fingers. "The cut isn't bad. Just a flesh wound."

"What mission?" Calene stared at her until Brina met her eyes. "Tell me."

Brina glanced over her shoulder. Vettigan returned, leading three horses.

"Not here. Not now. But let me tell you this; Vettigan spells trouble. For all of us. You need to see that, and you have to send him away. Forget about saving him. He's beyond it.

Trust me. What he said is true. They shouted 'peace'. They haven't come to fight, Calene, but with Vettigan around, we'll drown in blood."

Sighing, Brina got to her feet and pulled Calene from the ground before stalking away up the road, no doubt searching for any sign of more Banished. Flies bothered the corpses, the bugs already summoned by the stench of death. They hovered around Vettigan as he stared at the warriors he'd killed.

Calene shivered and went to retrieve her cloak.

I wish your words didn't ring so true, Brina, but I can't abandon Vettigan. I can't. Please understand that.

Chapter Six

PRESSURES OF STATE

'The Order of Sparkers? Their tower used to shine like a jewel in the centre of Spring Haven's crown. Now? I hear some of them have gone missing, and the gleam of their university is a little duller when the sun sets.' - The citizens of Spring Haven rumour about the Order of Sparkers, and with good reason.

"Emperor! We've expected you."

High Sparker Balz grinned and bowed at the foot of the steps leading to the university and grounds of the Order of Sparkers. His smile appeared tight and forced. Nerves, or something else?

Locke decided against rolling his eyes. He detested any signs of weakness in Spring Haven's supposed leaders and rolling his eyes wouldn't go unnoticed by the watching crowds. Instead, he returned the smile, showing a few too many teeth for it to be called warm.

Of course you've expected me. Everywhere I go, I'm expected, fool.

Still, Balz had carried out his duty for a state visit. He couldn't exactly let the emperor's arrival go by without a bit of pomp, even if Locke wished that once, just once, he could go somewhere unnoticed.

But that would mean I wouldn't be Emperor, and I can't have that. This forced smile though... He's hiding something.

As a child, Locke had read many a tale of reluctant kings or heroes full of doubt, striving against their inner turmoil as they took on the mantle of leader, inspiring the people below them to greatness. Not that he believed the stories. Who didn't desire power?

He'd taken them for what they were—stories for peasants, to make them believe the old kings of duchies gone weren't any different from them. Full of drok to boot. After this epiphany, he studied his own father, then the Emperor of Haltveldt. He'd been born into it, and the young Locke surmised the old man could only inspire a pimp to provide his finest whores by paying the correct price, but everyone seemed to enjoy life under an uninspiring monarch just fine.

Anyone who mattered, at least.

His father enjoyed being the richest and most powerful man in Haltveldt. The war efforts continued as they always had, the propaganda woven and whispered in all the correct places, and the wealth flowed.

As he grew older, he saw his father in a different light. A troubling one. For years, Locke surmised that Emperor Edum Dazel, first of his name, glorious figurehead—and a distant and uncaring father—had done his job well. Haltveldt's losses against the elven scum to the south didn't bear mentioning, relations with Velen, Avastia and Octaria wouldn't sour in his lifetime, and the rich grew all the richer.

On a tour of the nation for Locke's fourteenth birthday, the young man, his close friends Balz and Nexes in tow, discovered the startling truth.

Haltveldt grew lazy. Even seditious. The war of attrition with the scourge to the south seemed destined to last centuries more and, worse, the citizens furthest from Spring Haven, especially those close to the elven borders, tired of war, thinking it cruel and unnecessary. Those to the north, like the city of Willow, grumbled about throwing off the Empire's grip and regaining their independence.

The Empire wouldn't fail in a decade. Not even two or three. But fail it would, if change didn't occur. Locke had never been one to put much stock in tradition.

"...Nexes moves north."

Locke blinked, Balz's monotone drawl pulling him out of his thoughts.

"What?" he asked, gazing around. He didn't even remember taking the steps down from his carriage.

Pressures of state. Yes, let's put it down to that and not being bored out of my mind by these needless, petty processions. I should do away with them.

Balz gave him a level look, followed by a smile suggesting he knew he'd almost overstepped his bounds. The High Sparker wasn't a man who enjoyed repeating himself, but as far as it concerned Locke, he'd continue saying the same sentences standing on his head if it pleased the emperor.

"I received word that Nexes moves north, Emperor."

"You know, Balz, I tire of having to rely on second hand information to hear of what's happening in my Order of Sparkers."

Time to move onto business. Small talk achieved nothing but wasted time.

"Yes, my emperor." Balz stuttered the words, eyes shifting, skin grey-hued. Locke frowned a little. As far as reprimands went, he hadn't set too much of a fire under the man's feet. "Preparing for the new ways now the Laws don't stand in our ways has taken much of my attention."

Locke gripped the shorter man's shoulder and squeezed. Balz's height pleased him; the emperor could never be described as tall, no matter the lifts he wore in his boots. Looking up at people, Nexes included, vexed him. Staring down at a sorry fool pleased him for more than one reason, and Balz seemed smaller than usual. More hunched.

The man hid something, but he would shirk and dodge if accused head on. Locke cooled his rising impatience. It wouldn't do here. Not now.

"Understandable, Balz, but make sure you keep me abreast, yes? Nexes moves north. The elves will no longer be a nuisance. The Banished, however... A looming threat, and word will spread of their barbarity quicker than cock rot in the dockside bars. After I'm done here, I'll return to the Cradle and see what else I can find. Nothing can be left to chance. Nothing."

"The stone door again? Emperor, I'm beginning to think nothing will shift it."

Locke breathed through his nose and sucked on his teeth. Better that than backhand the man across the jaw. "Something will shift it. It's a door, made of stone. We just haven't found the key."

"Never saw stone like it," Balz muttered, and the emperor turned away, refusing to be drawn into a conversation about the Cradle's most vexing secret. It had gifted them so much over the years, but this last mystery refused to reveal itself.

"Are my quarters ready?" he asked. Of course they would be, but he wanted to change the subject, and whatever the emperor of Haltveldt desired...

"Yes, my emperor." Balz gulped, a sickly smile on his face. "How long do you plan to stay, if I might ask?"

Locke raised an eyebrow as he climbed the stairs. "I don't see how that's any business of yours, Balz."

Cheers erupted from around the square, and Locke turned, storing his ire at Balz for the moment. He hadn't paid any mind to anyone watching his arrival, aside from displaying the appropriate decorum when dealing with his underlings. A procession meant a crowd and a welcoming party, and he'd granted them both the attention he thought they warranted.

None whatsoever.

The emperor gazed around now. The Order of Sparkers lay in Spring Haven's commercial centre, more central than the palace, and it always drew onlookers who gawped at the powerful Sparkers coming and going. Many a koff house nestled amid the rows of buildings near the grounds, popular haunts for the citizens partaking in the warm, bitter drink, smoking from flavoured pipes and eating olives mixed with cheese.

Locke had enjoyed frequenting them himself in his youth, before his face became so well-known that even the poorest farmer in Velen would recognise it. He'd never acquired a taste for koff, but he enjoyed a lungful of smoke and a pot of spiced green olives and feta as much as the next man, and Sparkers had always fascinated him. They held so much power, commanding the elements. Technically, they should bow to no one, but they allowed dogmatic scripture to turn them into nothing more than servants, acting like common infantry, tutoring fools and healing the unworthy.

Religion. The emperor would certainly roll his eyes at that.

He raised a hand in thanks at the crowds lining the streets, gauging a gesture of humility and strength, and put on his best smile. Being emperor meant it didn't matter that his 'best smile' made his lips too thin and hooked his nose more than was desirable. He'd long come to terms with the fact he'd win no beauty contests, especially spending so much time with Nexes, the handsome bastard, but power held its own allure. He'd learned as much early on in life.

The Sparkers waiting on the top of the steps didn't clap, didn't cheer. Not that Locke expected them to; it wouldn't be proper. Over his shoulder, he gazed at them in their bright robes, some smiling—those who backed him and his progressive ways—some wearing shrewd, calculating looks as they peered at him, heads bowed in a manner both respectful and yet not sycophantic. Those were the ones who sat on the fence about his decree.

Some Sparkers didn't agree with Locke's judgement at all, and those? Well, they were part of the reason for his visit to the Order.

The other reason? They stood away and to the side. A stain of darkness, bold in the midday sun; black clouds defiant in a rainbow-filled sky.

His Shadow Sparkers, no longer a secret. Haltveldt's latest and best weapon. With them, Locke would make his nation safe from the rest of the world. An enemy would think twice about attacking them, and Haltveldt would lay the foreign nations to waste before they ever discovered how to create their own.

Avastia, for example. Elves lived there, and many from Haltveldt had fled to those shores, swelled their numbers. They were a threat. Locke would turn to them after they'd dealt with the Banished.

"Have the Sparkers here spoken of the events at Solitude yet?" Locke asked, glancing at Balz as the crowds continued to cheer.

"I've heard whispers, Emperor," Balz murmured, gazing over his shoulder at his fellow Sparkers but avoiding those of the shadow. Despite being instrumental in their creation and having delved deep into Ricken Alpenwood's studies himself, the High Sparker seemed bothered by their presence, even though he tried to pretend otherwise.

The emperor had learned to read a citizen's body language before he even knew his numbers.

Balz possessed a weak stomach when swallowing the necessary and that, Locke surmised, wouldn't do. It wouldn't do at all. As much as it pained him to admit, he'd erred when elevating his friend to the position of High Sparker. He'd helped weed out the weak and traitorous in the Order, but Balz hadn't acquired the steel Locke hoped he would.

"They say Solitude has vanished, that the barbarians used an ancient and unknown magic to level the fortress," Balz finished, licking his lips.

"Good," Locke smiled, "I suggested that rumour myself. Quite evocative, wouldn't you say?"

"Better than the truth," Balz replied, holding back as Locke moved toward the university. No one walked in step with the emperor. No one. "If anyone knew..."

Locke stopped and spun around, not giving a single drok to those watching. He didn't care for the hint of warning in the High Sparker's tone. Balz took a step back.

Good.

"If anyone knew, what? What would they do?" He took another step toward Balz, who paled, despite the might flowing in his soul. His Spark. It made a poisonous rage coil in Locke's gut that a man so spineless as Balz commanded the power to destroy the entire university without breaking sweat. "I've worked for years to build Haltveldt's majesty and all the power in this continent is mine. All of it. Would they announce that I defeated the elven scum in the south, a feat no other emperor achieved, with the might of the Shadow Sparkers I'd created? Would they thank me, shouting from the rooftops, for lifting centuries old restrictions on our magi to better defend ourselves? Or would they dare speak of treason and attempt a coup? How did it work out for Kade Besem and that fat, old sow Bertrand de Reyes?"

Locke's eyes flicked to the street, back to his retinue and the crimson-clad guards, to the crowd beyond. It didn't take him long to find what he searched for. He knew the signs. Balz followed his stare and the last drops of colour drained from his face. The High Sparker knew what lay out there, if he didn't know exactly who.

A small figure with olive skin stood beside an androgynous beauty that would draw the eye of any man, woman or anyone in between, sipping at a koff cup. An unremarkable fellow in every way; average height, indistinguishable features neither ugly nor handsome, and a medium build that hinted at either muscle or flab. The crowd contained many more like him, men and women sworn to Locke and only Locke, and they existed within the Order of Sparkers too.

They existed everywhere.

Other than the Shadow Sparkers, they were the most dangerous people congregating outside of the university. The Emperor's Hand. Sometimes inquisitors and assassins, other times protectors and spies. But, most importantly, always his.

The one in the crowd made a small motion, a thumb to his throat, index finger against his nose. The Hand had an urgent message, one the emperor needed to hear without delay.

"Do you think anything happens in Spring Haven without me hearing about it?" Locke breathed, meeting the High Sparker's fear-filled eyes. "Do you believe a single droking subject is spoken about in this damned Order without me knowing, Balz?"

"No, Emperor."

Locke smelled the uncertainty coming from his old friend in waves. His instincts told him whatever this Hand needed to tell him concerned the Order. "Good. I'd hate to have to disabuse you of that notion."

Locke swept his gaze across the waiting Sparkers, looking for a subtle shift, a small sign of acknowledgement, and found it. A woman in crimson robes thumbed at her ear as she met his eyes. Raising an eyebrow at Balz, Locke headed over to the row of mages, hands behind his back.

"Ah, do you require something, Emperor?" Balz muttered, scurrying to keep pace with him.

"No," Locke replied, "and you can wait here. I wish to inspect these Sparkers alone. They're soldiers of the Empire now, in every sense of the word. I want to see their mettle for myself."

Giving himself a mental pat on the shoulder for his quick thinking, Locke left Balz behind and approached the Sparkers, staring each one in the eye and nodding. Really, he paid them little attention. The one he wanted stood near the middle and he wanted to get her alone. Balz wasn't a complete fool. He must have known the Order contained members of the Hand, but no one could know who. Reaching her, he gave her the once-over, just like he'd done with everyone else, and moved on, before seemingly changing his mind.

"You," he barked, pointing at her, then crooking his finger. "Come here. Now!"

"Me, Emperor?" she replied, eyes wide and doing a fabulous impression of a deer caught before charging cavalry.

"Yes. You. Did you see me point at anyone else?" Locke held a hand up towards Balz, telling him to remain where he stood. The crimson-robed Sparker came forward, striding clear of the pack. Locke circled her, studying her in silence.

"There's a Sparker due in the Turning Room, Emperor," she breathed, lips barely moving. "Tomorrow or the day after. The Hand is bringing her up from Temekt. She worked with Kade Besem and Bertrand de Reyes. Her capture has unsettled the High Sparker."

Taking a step back, Locke met her eyes.

"How long have you served the Order?" Locke asked, raising his voice. He needed to give some reason for singling her out with Balz watching.

"Since my Spark bloomed, Emperor," she replied, voice shaking. A fine actor, like most of the Hand. "It's my pleasure to serve."

"And how do you feel about the abolishment of the Laws of Engagement?"

"It's about time, if you don't mind me speaking freely, Emperor." A grin spread across her lips. "The old ways restrained us too much."

Locke bowed his head a touch, a gracious lord, and pointed for her to return.

"She speaks sense!" he cried, spreading his hands. Many of the Sparkers laughed but, Locke noticed, a sizeable number didn't. More than a few watched him with narrowed eyes.

Turning on his heel, Locke grinned across at the Shadow Sparkers clinging to the dark corners of the Order's walls—they were his too, wholly and without question—and glanced up at the hulking statues standing guard by the doors. Byar, the old non-Sparker war hero, and Cicero, the building's founder, their faces noble and solemn. One day, when Locke had achieved his goals, he fancied Spring Haven's people would demand statues with his likeness be raised alongside them. Demands he'd gracefully agree to, once he'd weeded out any and all signs of weakness.

Between his own instincts and the work of his Hand,

he'd detected a thick vein right in the heart of his Empire at the Order of the Sparkers, and in his old friend, Balz.

"I'll bring you up to speed with Nexes and the war later," Locke smiled, joining the High Sparker, "but first, I feel the need to freshen up before my appointments."

No need to tell the exact truth and tip Balz off. He wanted to watch the High Sparker sweat.

"Take me to my quarters. I believe I will spend the next few days here. Word reached me this morning; a rogue Sparker is in custody and is on their way." He paused, studying Balz. The corners of his eyes tightened and he gulped. "I want to see the Order's progress in the Turning Room, Balz, and I want you by my side when our new subject arrives."

The High Sparker bobbed his head as he hurried after Locke, up the stairs and into the towering building. The tall doors swung open and revealed the shadow inside.

CHAPTER SEVEN

INTO THE TREES

"My great-grandaddy told me stories when I was a young 'un about them elves. Told me, years ago, they lived in forests, made merry, helped folk with their magic. Godsrot. I fought 'em, lost a leg and an arm to 'em, and I can tell you this... Ain't nothin' fiercer than an elf. If they ever had goodness in 'em, I'm Janna herself." - To some of Haltveldt's citizens, the war with the elves is justified.

The road through the Forest of Willows stood quiet as Brina and her companions made their way through, and that proved no bad thing at all.

Though the skies decided to tip a month's worth of rain on their heads since the fight in Adhraas two days before, Brina found the journey pleasant, even with her mission to kill the emperor in mind, and Vettigan's continuing sourness.

Calene hadn't left her side.

"I'm thinking avoiding Sea's Keep altogether was the

best decision, Brina." The woman smiled at her, strands of blue hair poking from beneath her dark hood, violet eyes twinkling. Then they fell on Vettigan's back and lost some of their brightness. The old man had argued long and hard to go to the city, and anywhere that wasn't south. "Is it always so quiet around here?"

"Most of the time," Brina replied. "It's a great place for people who want to keep to themselves when travelling."

"And you'd know all about that, wouldn't you?" Calene laughed, raising an eyebrow. The sound brought a smile to the elf's face. "What with you and your secret life and all that."

Brina spread her hands. "I've lived a long life, what can I say?"

"A life you still haven't droking told me about." Calene sighed and pursed her lips. "Long journey south. Even if we're parting ways at some point down the line, it still gives us plenty of time for stories, no?"

Parting ways. Brina still hadn't told Calene her reason for travelling south, but she reckoned there might not be a reason to go off on their own paths once Calene reached her own home. It wasn't too far from Spring Haven, after all.

"We'll see," Brina replied with a smile. "I wouldn't want to bore you."

"I don't think you could ever bore me," Calene muttered under her breath, heat rising in her cheeks. The words weren't meant for Brina, but she heard them anyway. Elven hearing and all that.

"Still, the Forest of Willows might be quiet, but it doesn't mean they're empty." Brina studied the thicket around them. "Don't want to run into anything unexpected, eh?"

She dismounted, wringing out her red braid and tucking it into her hood. Rain oozed from it and dripped down the back of her neck. The north and a bone-deep, soggy damp went hand-in-hand. "I'll scout ahead. Stay on the road, remain together, and Vettigan? Try not to kill anyone."

Brina didn't joke. The glare she shot Vettigan told him what would happen if he did. For once, the old man didn't snap back.

Since the fight at Adhraas, she'd racked her head, wondering why Calene, the *thiemea* fool woman, kept him around. Wondered why she wanted to save him, but deep down, Brina knew. She understood it all too well, in fact.

Calene and Vettigan were family, and she had nothing but the broken old man left. No one in her position would give up too easily, and the woman was nothing if not determined.

"Don't be too long," Calene whispered, taking the reins of Brina's horse and eyeing Vettigan's back. "I'll do my best to get him in a pleasant mood when you return. Just don't go too far, you hear?"

Warmth heated her words, enough Brina could have soothed her cold hands on them.

She drew in a breath and opened her mouth. Vettigan scowled across at her from beneath his soaking fringe, fingers twitching as they itched towards the pommel of his sword. She sneered at him and swallowed the friendly words on the tip of her tongue.

"Just making sure we're not heading into another ambush, or worse." Brina nodded and offered Calene a small smile. "See you soon."

Brina moved off the dirt road and into the cover of the Forest of Willows. They'd made decent progress, and at least two of them wanted that good pace to continue.

"Not a simple task with the old man complaining every step of the way," Brina muttered, kicking at a particularly offensive shrub that should have been minding its own business. Kept under wraps for so long, her frustration spiked. "That Vettigan. *Thiemea!*"

She slammed a fist into a tree trunk that really asked for it and Brina thought it should have been looking to avoid trouble like any other kind of tree. She closed her eyes, let the pain in her gloved fist bloom and shoot up her arm. Sometimes, pain soothed her. She'd given up wondering at the weirdness of that a long time ago. Anger proved a balm most of the time, though letting it go around Vettigan only led to bickering. She didn't want to put Calene through that. Scouting let her blow off some steam.

Really, Brina couldn't blame Vettigan, but she barely knew the man from before the Shadow Sparker attack. He'd treated her with kindness when they'd met on the road, but that man had vanished into darkness.

Calene, on the other hand... Well, she liked the woman. More than liked. The way she'd leave no one behind, the way she'd followed Brina into battle without hesitation when they came across the slavers, the quiet moments they shared on the road. How their eyes met. The tingle in Brina's stomach when their fingers brushed—

"No, no, no!" she snarled, forearms shaking from balling her fists so tight. "What's happening to me?"

Connections made her weak. Relationships brought mistakes into her life. Friends caused her pain when they died. Lovers became easy targets. Brina had lived it all before, had made those mistakes more than once, and she'd sworn to never repeat them again each time.

So why hadn't she left? Why had she tracked Calene and Vettigan—well, not him—and caught up with them when she could have been miles down the road to Spring Haven already?

Droking because. That's why. *Thiemea!* When she rode beside Calene, when they spoke, it drove doubts from her mind. Chief among them the fact that Calene was a human.

Brina thought herself cursed. Doomed to repeat the same mistakes throughout her entire pitiful existence. Fate forced her into solitude time and time again, so why did she rebel against it? Why did she seek out even more sorry souls to travel with, to lend aid? To love?

Because you're a good person, Brina. You'll find your way.

Her sister's last words always came to her when she didn't want to hear them. No, not just a sister. Her *twin*.

Anger. Brina let it build from her gut. Anger made her think clearer. Better than self-pity. Better than doubting herself. Anger had kept her alive for centuries, and through fiery anger came vengeance.

Brina had discovered years ago, vengeance wouldn't rescue anyone from the Underworld, but Godsrot did it satisfy her in the moment. She'd revel in it when she took a blade to Emperor Locke's throat. Getting to him presented a problem. He'd have Sparkers around him. Guards. Shadow Sparkers too.

"That's why I need Calene," she breathed through gritted teeth, leaning her forehead against the abused tree she had no doubt had asked for it. "She can handle them. It's why I need to convince her to come with me."

But the words rang hollow. Her mission to kill the emperor wasn't the only thing she wanted the Sparker for.

If you can be honest with yourself, maybe, one day, you will be with her?

"Drok off."

Brina scowled, ready to join the others again, anger vented. A mark in the muck caught her eye.

A faint imprint, an impression most would miss. Just one. Half of one, really.

A footprint in the mud.

Brina knelt closer to it, casting about. She hadn't left any herself. She'd made her footprints light as any elf worth their salt would, and she discovered no more. It appeared light, not caused by a heavy boot.

Just one half-footstep, made by mistake by someone journeying with care not to leave tracks. Maybe when they heard angry mutterings, or violence against an innocent tree.

An elf walked through these woods. Had stood in this spot just minutes before.

A twig snapped, and Brina spun, a blur of movement between the trees. She took a step forward, then staggered, confused.

Pain bloomed in the back of her neck. Reaching, her fingers found something hard sticking from her skin.

Another staggering, slow step, and the blur of movement ahead of her merged into two cloaked figures, striding through the trees.

"Why...?" Brina slurred, dropping to her knees.

Her face met the clammy mud, and darkness swallowed her.

Brina's eyes flew open, head snapping back, vision blurred.

A slap? Did someone—?

"Strike her again," a voice commanded. "She's not with us yet."

A gloved hand rattled her jaw, stinging her flesh.

"Give her one—"

"Slap me again," Brina growled through gritted teeth, "and you won't live past the hour. I promise you."

A bitter chuckle came in response. Blinking, the world came into view. The forest surrounded her, along with two elves, one male, the other female. They stared at her with stony faces, wariness in their eyes, a look she'd long associated with her people. They didn't trust anymore, didn't smile. And why should they when every human in their land wanted them dead?

Not just dead. Exterminated.

Still, that didn't temper the anger swirling in Brina's chest. They'd attacked one of their own kind!

"*Thiemea!*" she snarled, testing her limbs. They'd tied her arms behind her back, then fastened the ropes to her ankles and forced her into a kneeling position. The rough cord sliced her hands, blood tacky between her fingers. Trussed up like a hog. "Let me go! I'm one of you."

The male knelt, out of head-butting range, much to Brina's chagrin. Grey dusted his red hair at the temples, marking his age to be at least five hundred. Hazel swam in the green of his eyes; angry red scars stood out on his pale skin.

"The only one of me," he sneered, "is me and Rae here. There is nobody else, understand? What are you doing in my forest?"

"*Your* forest?" Brina bared her teeth. "Mighty fine elf you are, Lord of the Woods. I'd salute you, but some fool's tied my hands together."

The woman, Rae, sighed and pulled the king of trees, mud trails and grass to his feet. "Mela, do you have to? No wonder we're standing on the edge of extinction. Other elves aren't the enemy."

"No, you're right," Mela replied, kissing two fingers and placing them on Rae's lips. "Humans are. And this vagabond elf travels with them. Care to explain that, traitor?"

"I don't have to explain anything to you," Brina snapped, testing her bonds.

Useless. Powerless. Trapped. Her heart hammered against her ribs, blood pounding in her ears. She couldn't be captured. An image popped into her head. Herself, but younger, surrounded by captured elves and leering slavers. Her family weeping. Pleading. She gave her head a frenzied shake, clearing it.

No. Not again. Never again.

Her breath came fast, panting like a hound left out in the scorching sun, but she didn't care. Brina had to gain her freedom. She had to fight!

"Mela…" Rae began, but Brina couldn't hear the words. Her vision lurched. Her muscles tightened, coiled, begging for action. Flight or fight… Something. Anything but this. Tied up. Helpless. Waiting for others to determine her fate.

Brina's fingers scratched at her stinging palms, opening the wounds from the rope. The warm trickle of blood grounded her a little, brought colour back to her clouding vision. Her darting eyes took in the elves talking, their mouths moving as they stared at her, brows furrowed in puzzlement, but Brina had left comprehension behind.

Mela took a step toward her, and Brina acted. She did the only thing she could.

Throwing herself on her side, she scrabbled through the mud, kicking her legs as she inched herself away. Brina's wrists and ankles screamed at her, each pitiful movement driving knives through her joints, but she had to keep moving. Gritting her teeth, she shuffled. A strangled whimper filled her ears, and she realised it came from her, but she kept struggling, kept pushing herself through the fallen leaves and thick mud. A lame horse whose legs had long given out, but its spirit needed to run one last time.

She couldn't be a prisoner. Not again. The screams of her family filled her ears. Screams for mercy, wails of fear, centuries behind her. Begging. Pleading. No, no, no! She had to move. Had to. Had to. Move. Move. Move.

Brina's body urged her, pulled at her, to escape. She could find Calene. The Sparker would break her bonds, heal her, tell her everything would work out. Whisper to her, tell her she'd be safe. Calene would…

A hand pressed against her cheek. Soft, warm skin. Brina blinked, limbs stilling, heart slowing, the torrent of blood in her ears easing.

Rae's eyes looked into hers, a sad smile on her face. "You'll hurt yourself. Please, let me free you. We just want to talk. You're safe. I promise. Mela... Trust doesn't come easy to him. Not anymore."

Tears stung Brina's eyes and she couldn't stop them from falling. Her limbs shook as adrenaline deserted her. Cold bit deep, but the chill came from inside. Nodding through the sobs wracking her body, Brina searched for Mela. He watched, a few steps away, looking but not seeing. She recognised the look. The elf's mind had wandered to the horrors of his past, to another lifetime, to the experiences that had eroded his trust.

War.

War had made them this way. They weren't elves anymore, not really living creatures. They were survivors, bags of flesh, blood and memories with only one purpose. To run. To flee. To keep their pitiful breath in their lungs for...

One.

More.

Moment.

Just one. And then the next. And then the next.

A pitiful existence for pitiful creatures.

Brina's stomach lurched. Her throat burned, and she vomited into the muck as Rae cut her free. Pain bloomed in her arms, her legs, her back. She cried out.

"Can't you help her?" Rae's pleading voice cut through

the haze of pain and panic. "She's going to hurt herself!"

"I'm sorry," Mela muttered. Footsteps boomed beside her, and his fist crashed into the side of her head.

Brina flopped onto her back, the sun twinkling through the foliage above her, a slither of light before the darkness swallowed her once more.

Chapter Eight

A Different Point of View

'Aye, I saw them, those Shadow Sparkers, and I ain't afraid to tell you this; laying eyes on them made me piss meself. And after I saw what they could do on the battlefield? I'm never fighting again. I'm not afraid of much, but them? Yeah, they scare me.' – A Fighter's Guild mercenary, upon resigning his position after the infamous Battle of the Black Sun.

Brina sat upright as an ice-cold wave struck her. Dripping with water, blinking it out of her eyes, she started to cast about when another hit her.

"Calene!"

The name escaped her mouth before she could stop herself.

"Enough, Mela! She's awake."

Brina focused on the direction, and almost fell backwards when she lifted her arms on instinct. They weren't bound. She wiped the water from her eyes and brow, glaring around at her surroundings. Rae and Mela stood over her, the latter with a bucket sloshing with water in his hands.

"Where am I?" Brina grumbled. The world spun when she forced herself to her knees, her stomach roiling. The taste of vomit in her mouth helped her decide to stay where she knelt.

"Who's Calene?" Mela asked, his shadow stretching over her. "The savage you're sworn to kill? A human's name, yes?"

"Kill?" Brina replied, squinting.

Her head throbbed. Bits and pieces of before she'd passed out returned to her. The panic. The urge to flee or go down fighting. The pressing need to do anything but lie there, trussed up like a pig.

Or a slave.

She rubbed at her wrists, anger helping her focus, like it always did. The elves had brought her to a secluded alcove cut into the ledge of a cliff, looking out over the forest. The sun set above the trees reaching up into the sky, and in the distance, she saw smoke. No doubt the city of Willow. The road she, Calene and Vettigan travelled on led there.

The road. Scanning her surroundings, she found where she fancied it lay and cursed. Calene walked it alone with a madman. A road far too open and exposed, despite how quiet it had proven so far. Things changed. She'd advised them to travel this way for haste, all so she could have her vengeance. *Thiemea!*

"Yes, kill." Mela knelt. A thick, red scar ran across his neck. A mark of hanging. "You wore the black paint."

"No, not her." Brina would have to reapply the mark when she could. The death mark couldn't leave her face until her quarry fed the worms. "There's a man who's caused me much pain. My family and our kind too. He's my target, and you've waylaid me enough."

"You're not going anywhere until I get some answers," Mela snapped. "You swear vengeance against a human but travel with two of them? Yes, we saw you. Not to mention crying out the woman's name when you wake." His lip curled. "Human lover. Makes me sick."

"Come now." Rae laid a hand on his shoulder. He sagged at her touch, a marionette laid to rest, the anger in his face fading. Absolute love could do that. "We don't know her situation. She's one of us."

"There's only me and you, Rae," he grumbled, getting to his feet. "I don't trust her. Maybe she serves her humans, betraying her own kind. We've seen that before. Or she could have come from the south. Refugees to take our home. This place is ours."

"The south?" Brina asked. She staggered as she got to her feet. Rae rushed forward and steadied her. "You've word from the south?"

Rae pointed to the back of the alcove. Another elf lay there in the shadows, eyes shining in the gloom. Brina mouthed a silent curse after failing to notice the bedraggled, dirty elf huddled up right behind her.

"We found him about six hours ago." Rae's soft voice carried through the cave. "He flogged a horse to death, then took to rambling through the forest, wandering alone. If we hadn't found him, some human surely would have, and they might have discovered us."

"And that only means one thing," Mela muttered. "He'd be better off dead. Not that I have to tell you that."

"What do you mean?" Brina snapped. She had no time for idle talk. Each second took Calene further away and into the path of gods-knew-what.

"You've spent time as a slave, no? Your reaction to the bonds tells me as much." He pointed at the wrists she didn't realise she rubbed. "How'd you escape?"

"Might ask you the same thing."

Brina didn't want to think about it, and didn't really care about Mela's experience. Recent events, like finding herself bound again and that idiot Kade calling her Rune—of all names; she most certainly didn't want to dwell on that—brought the memories flooding back. The gods sported the sickest of humours.

Over two centuries had passed since a slave train happened upon Brina and her family. They'd killed her father without a second thought, removing his head from his body mid-sentence while he screamed for mercy for his wife and girls. His head had come to a rest at Brina's feet, glassy eyes staring at her, tongue hanging over broken lips.

The slavers laughed as they put her in chains, taking cruel delight in the promises Spring Haven held in store for 'such a pretty elven whore'. They bound her mother too, and her sisters. Her twin.

She'd grown up knowing a run-in with a human meant slavery or death, and that for a young woman like her, death would spare her the horrors of a life in servitude to some human lord with a heavy fist and rampant libido.

Funny, she often thought, how humans claimed elves repulsed them. It didn't stop them raping them. Sating their gods-forsaken appetites whenever the mood struck.

"I got this from trusting a human." Mela's rough voice cut into Brina's thoughts. He pointed to the scar on his neck, eyes hard.

"Mela saved a human babe from a pack of wolves in the wilderness, decades ago," Rae murmured, taking Mela's hand. "He heard it crying, alone in the snow near Sea's Keep. He nursed the child back to health and tracked down where his family had fled to."

Mela cleared his throat. "They accused me of stealing the baby for my 'perverse elven dark magic'. They spat at me. Beat me. Laughed when I begged for mercy. Then they hung me. The fall didn't break my neck, but it knocked me out. The crowd thought they were leaving just another dead elf swinging in the breeze."

"I'd followed him, even though he told me to stay away." Rae wiped away a tear. "I cut the rope, though I thought I came too late. Gods be praised."

"No, not gods. We make our own luck. And that, elf, is why you never trust a human. Any of them. This 'Calene' you're so attached to, she'll betray you. Mark my words."

"Brina," she growled, sick of the way Mela's lips twisted when he called her 'elf', tired of his assumptions about Calene. She wouldn't betray her. She wouldn't. Not after killing the slavers. Not after Solitude. "My name's Brina. I'm talking to the stranger back there, these tales of the old days are riveting, but I've heard them all before."

"Haven't we all? Fine, talk to him." Mela met her eyes.

"Then I want you gone. I've no quarrel with you, but I can't have an elf with the stink of human near me. And you reek of it. No offence."

Baring her teeth, Brina turned, then glanced over her shoulder, a question gnawing at her. "Did you ever see the child again? The one you helped?"

Rae and Mela looked at each other. A long stare, one filled with hurtful, conflicting feelings that had never healed, only scabbed over. Rae shook her head and moved away, sitting on the precipice.

"I did." Mela tilted his chin. "Years later, on a battlefield. Him and his father crossed my path. The father recognised me. He whispered to his boy, and the human's face twisted with rage before he charged at me, sword held high. I don't know what his father told him, but I killed them both, and watched the light die in their eyes. I got my vengeance, in a way."

Brina turned away. Elves and vengeance had become well-acquainted over the centuries, and now she sought more. It all came back to war and the human thirst for blood. It drove them feral, exterminating every elf they could find. In her gut, Brina believed killing Locke would change matters. It had to, and if Calene walked the path with her then all the better.

"You," Brina snapped, kneeling to look the elven refugee in the face. "You came from the south?"

The stench of the road hit her, a mixture of dried blood, sweat and waste, but she swallowed the retch bubbling in her throat. He met her eyes and looked away. They almost rolled with fear.

She regretted her sharp tongue when he flinched. She'd seen the broken before—had caused their breaking more than once, in fact—but this pitiful figure had gone far beyond that. The free elves who lived in the forests and wild places of Haltveldt owned souls of fire, a will to fight until their dying moment. They owed their lives to it.

The stranger reminded Brina of a slum elf, but one with a key ingredient missing. The elves locked away in Haltveldt's slave quarters lived without their fire, the flames long snuffed out from torture and servitude, a long-lost war of attrition. But while their hearts still beat, they had the embers of hope. Dying embers, but they burned still. One day, they might rise up, overthrow their human captors. Or a saviour might throw down the iron gates and let them flood the streets like water gushing from a burst dam.

This elf, afraid to make eye contact, twitching in the shadows, whimpering like a dog kicked too many times by a cruel master, had left hope far behind him.

Brina reached out, inching her fingers towards his face. He closed his eyes, lips trembling, fearful of her touch but not able to move away. A dog, trained to obey, even if it pissed itself at its master's feet.

"What's your name?" she asked, her voice soft. A wisp of wind. She laid her palm against his cheek. He leaned against it, tears leaking from his eyes wetting her fingers. "Can you tell me? Please."

He let out a shuddering breath. Sunlight flooded into the alcove, covering the stranger in light. Brina gasped. Filth covered his skin; dirt and dried blood with sweat tracks running through them. Mud and gods-knew-what stuck to his clothes. He'd come from a battle. Run from it, if Brina judged right.

"F-Ferran," he half-stammered, half-sobbed.

"You're safe here, Ferran," she murmured, glancing at the other elves. Rae watched, leaning on her longbow. Mela stared out at the forest, his mind miles and years away. "You're amongst friends."

His hand shot up, pressing hers harder against his face, and he closed his eyes.

Picturing someone he's lost. A loved one touching him one last time. Savouring it. A gift I'll gladly give. What else can I do?

Deep inside, the fires of her anger raged. She could do nothing for the broken elf before, but she would have her droking vengeance. For her. For him. For all the elves.

"We're finished," Ferran sobbed. "Finished. The humans... What they've done... What they can *do*..."

"What happened?" Brina urged, grabbing his shoulder.

His eyes shot open. Ferran stared at her, seeing her for the first time. Confusion flitted across his face. She wasn't the elf he thought he'd touched. His hand dropped from hers, and he shifted his head away. But he didn't tremble. He didn't sob. Ferran met her stare, and what Brina saw there made her stomach twist.

Terror. Pure, undiluted horror. A mind broken beyond all comprehension. Beyond all reason. An elf with nothing left to live for.

"They met us in battle. We outnumbered them. A rare thing, but they amassed with pretence, let us draw more of our fighters close." Ferran's words came out in a rush, emotionless. Flat. Rehearsed, like he'd thought them so many times, run them through his head over and over on his journey north. "They smashed a hole in our defence, but we fought them, could have held against them, pushed them back. Then... They came."

"Who?" Brina asked. His eyes slid away, his stare unblinking and wide. She grabbed his head, snapping his attention back on her. "*Who* came?"

"The Sparkers in black."

Ferran grinned. Blood stained his teeth. His tongue flicked across his lips, revealing the sores where he'd chewed them raw.

"They brought a storm with them. Lightning from the sky. Explosions from the earth. They pointed at Trian. Sweet Trian, she stood there, sword in hand, a proud warrior. Then...gone. Just a mess in the mud."

"They brought their new mages," Brina breathed, settling back on her haunches.

"They're not mages," Ferran snapped, jerking his head away and grabbing her hands. "Demons! Demons in black from the shadows of the Underworld. They massacred us. The elves, they're gone. I heard the screams for miles as I fled. I rode as fast as I could and didn't stop. Three horses I rode into the ground trying to escape their screams!" A shrill laugh escaped his lips. "But I can't. I can still hear them! Me, you, those two. We're the last free elves in Haltveldt! Oh, Trian..."

Brina caught him as he sagged, trailing off into giggles, whimpers and mumbling. She lowered him to the ground and covered him with blankets, jaw cracking with the force of gritting her teeth.

The Shadow Sparkers. The emperor had unleashed them. No doubt some scattered remnants still lived, but the days of free elves were finished.

"You've heard his tale?" she asked Rae, standing beside her. Mela still studied the horizon.

"Not quite as eloquently as that," she replied, with a grimace, "but, yes. We pieced it together. The elven war with the Empire is over. They've won. We think the massacre happened three days ago. Four at the most. If he hadn't ridden his horses to death, I think he'd have kept going until he rode into the sea."

"Not yet," Brina snarled, her hand falling to her pommel. The feel of metal focused her anger. "They haven't won yet. Not while I draw breath."

"Give it up," Mela sneered, looking over his shoulder. "Flee to Avastia with the rest of the cowards."

"Coward?" Brina snapped, grief and rage battling to see which spilled over first. "I won't give up, *thiemea!*"

"Because of the human?" Mela snarled, climbing to his feet, pale with anger. "You heard what they've done. You've *seen* what they've done! Yet you'll stay here in these gods-forsaken lands for one of them?"

"No!" Brina snarled. A lie, and she knew it, but it didn't diminish her other reasons. "There's something I must do first."

"Vengeance," Rae whispered, coming to stand between her and Mela. "The black paint you wore speaks to it. I've seen that look in your eyes before. It's personal for you, isn't it? Beyond what the Empire has done to us all."

Personal? Aye. As personal as it gets.

"The Empire took my mother, sisters and me." Brina sniffed and ran her tongue across her teeth. "I swore never to be powerless again. And I swore to free my family."

Her thoughts flicked to Kade Besem and the boy Arlo as she spoke. He looked like he'd seen a ghost when he spoke to her, and Brina didn't believe in coincidences. Wasn't she abandoning a part of her family by coming south?

She turned the shame and doubt into anger instead and added the blame to the emperor's ledger. He'd pay for that too.

Mela cocked his head. "So what? You plan to free every elven slave in the Empire, hoping you'll find your family along the way?"

"A better plan than yours, hiding away in the Forest of Willows. Godsrot, why don't you listen to your own advice and flee?"

Mela eyed Rae and shook his head. "We won't leave. Haltveldt is our home. Our people's home. Elves built their lives in these lands before the humans crept out of the dark corners of the world. We walked beneath the stars and sang our songs, free. Happy. This is our home, Brina. Why should we leave?"

"You'll stay even if it means death?" Brina whispered, meeting his eyes.

His words struck her. Haltveldt belonged to them, and the elves belonged to Haltveldt. The elders preached that they'd once lived in peace, at the dawn of time, but they'd lost themselves to war and vengeance. Forgotten what they were, and what they could be. The humans had taken so much from them.

Too much.

"I'd rather die here in the lands of my ancestors than on some faraway shore," Rae answered, taking Mela's hand. "Haltveldt drowns in blood, Brina. But it's our blood, and our land. We won't run. We can't."

"Why don't you stay with us?" Mela asked, taking a step forward. "Our life isn't so bad. We hunt. We laugh sometimes. We prey on scum from the Empire who stray too close to our home. With you, there's four of us—"

A strangled laugh echoed from the back of the cave.

"Four of us?" Ferran cried, staggering to his feet. He swayed and leaned against the alcove wall, voice shrill, eyes wide and unseeing. "Four against a nation. All the nations! Why can't you see it? We don't live! We exist, waiting to die. Bugs under the heels of the Empire, and by the gods have they crushed us!"

"Calm yourself," Brina murmured, holding her palms up and taking a step towards him, like approaching a wild, skittering horse. "You need your rest."

Ferran spat on the floor, took a wobbling step forward, and laughed. "Rest? What do I need to rest for? You don't know what I've seen, what they did to my Trian." He howled with laughter. It echoed through the alcove, disturbing a nest of nearby birds. They took to the sky, startled. "You're all *thiemea*. Fools! All of you. Run! Flee while you can!"

"Ferran," Mela warned, his hand dropping to his sword. "Careful now. You've been through a lot—"

"Don't you pity me!" he shrieked, shambling forward. "I don't want it. I don't need it."

"What do you want?" Brina asked, taking a step toward him, hands wide.

He eyed her, face slackening. Tears shone in his eyes. Light flooded the alcove as clouds moved from in front of it. Ferran laughed, sniffed, and drew the back of his hand across his mouth.

"Freedom..." he whispered.

Ferran shot forward, his speed catching Brina unawares. He knocked her to the side, barrelling past her to the alcove's edge. She spun on the ground, throwing out her hands, hoping the other elves had their wits about them.

They didn't. Ferran acted too fast for Mela and Rae. They watched, aghast, as the refugee from the south, the elf who ran from the Empire's massacre, the soldier who'd stood by powerless as a Shadow Sparker ripped his lover apart, threw himself from the cliff and plummeted to the forest below.

The elves looked at each other. They had no words. Another elf dead. Another soul to lie at the feet of an Empire bent on their ruin. Brina forced the tears in her eyes, the sobs in her chest, back to where they came from.

Killing Emperor Locke might not stop anything. It might make matters worse. But it would feel like standing before the droking Gates of Eternity themselves. She'd end his life and make him look into her eyes as she did it, so he knew a filthy, Raas-forsaken elf had finished him.

Climbing to her feet, the muscles around her mouth straining to let out her grief, she breathed in deep through her nose. She'd kill the emperor, and anyone else who got in her way.

"I'm leaving," she muttered, refusing to look at Mela and Rae. "Going back to my friends. We're done here."

"Back to your human?" Mela asked, his voice thick. For once, Rae didn't try to stop his words. "They did this to him. They've done it to us all, and they'll do it again."

Fists balled at her side, Brina stalked away, his words ringing in her mind.

Calene paused at a fork in the road and dismounted, staring left and right, not sure which way to go, then glanced behind, biting her lip.

"The Sea of Storms," Vettigan whispered. "We could go there."

Calene rolled her eyes. She hadn't engaged him on his plans to travel since Brina had disappeared into the trees, but it didn't stop him from mumbling about places they could run to. This latest suggestion proved the most outlandish of the lot.

"The Sea of droking Storms?" she snapped, slapping at a bug that had the cheek to land on her face. "And what? Sail around on a boat for the rest of our lives?"

"There's a tower out there, in the middle of the sea. A banished Sparker built it, a long time ago."

"Brilliant plan, Vettigan." She shook her head, hands on hips. "And they didn't banish him. I've heard that story too. Wasn't he crazy? Went there to conduct some experiments, and not the kind that'll help us, unless you want an extra arm or leg?"

"Perhaps he wasn't so mad," Vettigan breathed, almost to himself.

Calene sighed. "Maybe not. How can anyone tell?"

"She isn't coming back," Vettigan grumbled, kicking a stone across the dirt road. "It's time to decide on a direction."

His words hung in the air.

Calene didn't have to ask who he meant, and she feared her old friend spoke the truth.

"I don't know which way to go, Vee," she whispered, clinging to the reason for her delay. Every moment she spent deciding granted Brina more time to return. No doubt the elf could track them either way, but the decision had become symbolic in her mind.

Vettigan glanced around. "You could climb a tree? Magnificent views up there."

Her eyes narrowed. The lava inside bubbled. Her mouth twisted as it threatened to spill. Then Vettigan grinned. A joke. A droking joke. Not the best one she'd ever heard, but considering the circumstances...

How she missed their Link. Vettigan had changed, no doubt. No reason to try to hide it, but if they'd still been able to use their Link, Calene could have anticipated it, read his mind. Helped the man who'd aided her so much over the years when no one else could or would. She just couldn't bring herself to brush that part of her mind. Every time she did, she felt the shadow lurking, poisonous and vile, on the other side.

Without the ease of their connection, she had to learn their friendship all over again. Sparkers used their abilities, the Link included, like a crutch and, with it taken away, they stumbled and staggered.

And social skills had never ranked high on Calene's list of talents.

All her problems came back to the Spark. Vettigan's too, and she'd looked at it as a gift from the gods her entire life. Now, it resembled a curse.

"Haven't scampered up a tree in years," she grumbled, wiping her hands on her tunic, and pushing sour thoughts from her mind. "Probably like riding a horse. You never forget."

"I think plenty of folk forget how to ride a horse, Calene," Vettigan laughed. That shred of hope sparkled when he did. Maybe there was more of her old friend in there than she realised. "And if I remember correctly, the last time you tried to climb a tree, you'd have fallen on your arse if I hadn't called on the air to catch you."

Calene's cheeks reddened. She could file shoddy climbing alongside her lack of social graces.

"Well, can't rely on you this time, can I?" Calene muttered, wincing when she heard the edge in her voice. "Sorry. It's just that…"

"What?"

She met his eyes, faded and dull without their Spark. This conversation, just a few words about a droking tree, had been the longest they'd had without the darkness oozing from Vettigan's pores since Solitude.

"I really thought Brina wouldn't leave us," she breathed, shoulders sagging.

"And I haven't," a voice called.

Brina pushed her way through the foliage, her face like thunder. The black paint running through her eye had faded and smudged in places. The elf stalked to her horse and mounted it in one swift movement.

"Are we going then? We'll hit Willow soon."

Calene almost ran to her, but the clipped tones gave her pause.

"Everything alright?" Calene asked, climbing onto her horse and studying the woman.

Red ringed her eyes and her olive skin appeared pale as snow. Her jaw muscles bunched so tight they looked like they might pop through her skin. Brina dipped her hands into her saddle bags, refusing to meet Calene's eyes.

Calene wanted to say she looked sad. Wanted to walk her horse over to hers and reach out to offer any comfort she could. The elf had shed tears, but she couldn't let the words pass her lips, and her limbs refused to move.

Brina withdrew a small box and dipped her fingers inside it, covering them with black paint. She drew them down her forehead, through her eye and onto her cheek as she stared into the distance. Calene followed her gaze. A mountain peak poked above the trees.

"I'm fine," Brina snapped. "Let's move. The south awaits."

Calene's body responded. Moving her horse on, she reached over and grabbed Brina's arm. She expected the elf to shrug her away, but she leaned into Calene a little before catching herself and sitting as still as a statue.

"What happened out there? You were gone for ages."

"It doesn't matter now," Brina snarled, turning to stare at Calene.

She gasped. Raw loss and grief swam in the elf's eyes, made them shine, but anger underpinned them. Sharp and hot.

"The Empire's army moves, and we need to get out of its way."

Pulling her arm away, Brina drove her heels into her mount's sides and trotted away. Vettigan glanced at Calene, raised an eyebrow, and followed.

Calene sat there, the rain falling again. Brina had returned, but she wasn't the same person who'd left.

"What happened?" she whispered, nudging her horse forward, gut aching like Brina had driven her fist there.

Craving some kind of connection, some kind of comfort, she nudged against the part of her brain that housed her Link to Vettigan and shivered away from the corruption she found there. When she turned to her Link to her mother, she sighed. She'd have better luck catching smoke.

Calene followed, Vettigan behind her, the party silent as the rain continued to fall.

CHAPTER NINE

BEYOND THE MOUNTAINS

'Haltveldt is ours, and one day, we'll take back what belongs to us...' - Elven refugees in Avastia haven't forgotten their roots, and as some beyond the Sundered Sea whisper, they never will.

"What am I doing up here?" Kade muttered. "It's madness. Complete and utter madness."

He'd followed Brina's advice. Well, to a point. Kade had ignored the part where she told him to run in the opposite direction and had instead made his way up into the craggy mountains alone. Now, he huddled behind a rock in the upper reaches of the Peaks of Eternity, above where Solitude once stood

The elf had been right. A single person could cross, and even had recently. He'd come across scuffed footprints in the dirt where it looked like a couple of people had come to some disagreement. It would have taken an army months.

He'd tried to picture Solitude still nestled in the pass. The Sparkers there would have swatted any force attempting the winding, craggy passes off the mountain at their leisure.

At first, he'd made decent progress. The effects of his spice withdrawal wore off and Calene's healing bedded in, but then his lack of experience outside of a city reared its head. Hunger became the main reason for weak limbs and stumbling feet. Pausing to rest proved a huge mistake; Brina had likened the temperature to Sea's Keep in winter and she hadn't lied. Once Kade's fever had cooled and his legs stopped moving, the icy winds caught up to him, chilling the sheen of sweat on his skin.

He hadn't come dressed to scale a mountainside and thrust into enemy territory to rescue his son, any more than he'd prepared himself to storm north and rescue Arlo from Solitude and the Banished.

"I'm a fool," he breathed, teeth chattering, hands thrust under his armpits to keep him warm. His clothes lent little protection. "I'll die before I reach Arlo, and Janna knows it."

He craned his neck to gaze beyond the rock. The Banished had finished their bridges two days ago and crossed in earnest, rushing with as much speed as an entire people could muster to traverse the narrow pathways. At first, from his position at the top of a descent into Banished territory, he'd tried to estimate how many flooded the plains, and had given up.

Even on Eru Day, in Spring Haven's Tallan Square, he'd never seen so many people gathered in one place, and he reckoned that vast plaza could hold 300,000 souls with ease.

Arlo had landed on that side of the Peaks of Eternity

after the Battle of Solitude. One Haltveldtian boy, alone amongst enemies. The sight of so many Banished almost stopped Kade's heart. His chest burned with such ferocity he thought he'd gone beyond heart failure and existed in some half-dead, pain-ridden coma. A state between life and death where he would pay for his failures over and over again.

Kade couldn't say it. He didn't even want to think about it, but the thought—a solid, bone-deep belief lurking in the corner of his mind and on the tip of his tongue—wouldn't give him peace.

Arlo couldn't have survived. His son was dead, and Kade embarked on a fool's errand that would end only one way.

"No," he growled, shoving the taunting notion aside with such force he hoped to knock it from his head altogether. "He's alive, and I'll find him. Gods' teeth I will!"

The words tasted like lies in his dry mouth but lies would nourish his famished stomach.

His limbs grew stiffer the longer he sat huddled behind his rock, his hunger deeper, his thirst greater. Kade had to act, had to do something unless he wanted to die there, alone in a craggy pass on the Peaks of Eternity. Idly, he pictured a group of explorers coming across his skeleton in years to come, wondering just how the corpse found itself where it did. A fool, no doubt, caught up in the mountains without a plan, without a notion, without a will to live. A craven who succumbed to the inevitable and laid down to die.

No. That wouldn't be him. Kade wouldn't allow it. *Couldn't* allow it. Not while his son needed him.

Arlo does *live. Teeth of the gods, he does!*

Groaning, he twisted around, gripping the rock as he peered over it and blinking at what confronted him. The rear of the Banished horde! He could see the godsrotting rear of the Banished horde! Behind them, the plains lay empty. Pushing aside his weariness and rubbing his eyes, Kade scanned the vista.

Around the edges of the mountains lay sparse foliage and trees, places that offered a little protection in case of stragglers.

And forests meant wildlife. He fingered the pommel of the blade he'd acquired at Solitude. Kade could kill an animal if he discovered one. Couldn't he?

"As long as it's slow-moving and lame, like me," he muttered, pushing himself into a low crouch. "I'm not exactly in fighting form. Time to move. I need food. And it's got to be a little warmer down there. Gods, it's colder than Raas' balls up here."

Making himself small—his gnawing hunger helped, since it forced him to walk almost doubled-over anyway—Kade lunged away from the rock, staggering and stumbling as he did, his frozen, weak limbs as sturdy as water. The summit of the Peaks of Eternity loomed in the distance, an impossible peak, a black stain on a grey horizon. It lay quiet now, the strange column of light and colours dancing above it disappeared, but still it drew his eye. Its sheer size sent an unsettling fear creeping up his spine.

"Think it's big now?" he muttered, shaking his head. Talking to himself helped bring order to his thoughts. "Hope to the gods you don't have to stand at its feet."

He approached the edge of the crest he'd rested at.

'Resting' sounded finer 'almost giving up and dying next to a rock', though it would have proven more accurate. The mountains sloped from this point, and Kade scanned the decline, looking for a path that wouldn't break his neck when he attempted to descend. He glanced to his left, where the canyon yawned, and studied the Banished.

"They'll have crossed within the hour. An army that size... The main force will have breezed by Adhraas by now. Gods save Willow if they keep moving south, the militia and the Patriarch's army won't stand a chance."

An hour. It'd take him longer to descend, and he really didn't have time to wait. Not if he wanted to find food and warmer clothes. He grabbed his waterskin, the one Brina had given him. He'd refilled it before climbing. Now, he sucked up the last drops of liquid it held.

"Let's add water to the list," he croaked, glancing at the Banished again. "They won't notice me. I'm one man, a speck amongst the rocks. If I'm going to do this, now's the time."

Kade took one last look over his shoulder, staring into Haltveldt, wondering if he'd ever walk there again, and scowled. "That place gave me nothing but pain, anyway. Except Arlo, and he isn't there. Good riddance."

If he could have worked up enough saliva, Kade would have spat on the ground. Instead, he filled his lungs and descended into Banished lands.

"God's teeth, what I wouldn't do for just a sniff of spice right now," Kade gasped, lying on his back and staring up at the startling blue sky. He couldn't see a single cloud blocking the cold, pale sun. "Just enough to cover my little finger. To give me a kick. That's all."

But it would never be all; Kade knew that. A little bit of spice never proved enough. One fingertip of orange dust on waking turned into a fistful by lunch, the rest of the day lost in a haze of listless apathy until it came to feed his habit again. No, he had to get by without it.

Not that he had a choice. He'd lost his spice box back at Spring Haven docks, the precious container falling on to the decking, boots kicking it this way and that. For a moment, he wondered what journey his spice had embarked on, then gave himself a mental shake.

"I think I'm getting delirious," he laughed, rolling onto his front and pushing up from the loose shale. "The Great Journey of a Spice Box! An Addict's Tale. I could see that selling out for months at the Spring Haven Theatre. God's teeth, Kade, get a grip."

His body ached, his muscles alternating between too stiff and the consistency of water. His skin stung from a thousand tiny cuts, and his shirt clung to him where the blood congealed beneath his clothes, but he lived. Glancing over his shoulder, he stared up at the mountain he'd clambered, shuffled, slipped and slid down, and glanced away, a spike of panic jolting him.

"Raas, they're so...huge," he gasped, staring at the ground until he quelled the anxiety pulsating in his chest. "And this is the smallest part of the range!"

Closing his eyes and turning around, he faced the path

he'd descended from, and breathed deep through his nose. Starting at his feet, he raised his eyes, an inch at a time, taking in every step of the journey he'd just made, until his gaze reached the peak. He stood straight, head tipped fully back, but he didn't look away, even when his bladder threatened to relieve itself.

"A small victory," he breathed, smiling through gritted teeth.

He looked to the right, past the yawning gap where Solitude had stood only days before, and kept turning, running his eyes across the towering mountains, building in height, until his gaze settled on the summit of the Peaks of Eternity on the far horizon. Even though the ground built in a slow rise before him, the awe-inspiring mountain stood above it, peering over the plateau. He couldn't judge the distance between where he stood and the range dominating the horizon, and Kade hoped he'd never have to walk it.

He lowered his eyes, and a mound caught his attention.

Frowning, swaying on the spot from exertion and hunger, he wiped a hand across his face. He'd planned to keep to the edges of the range until he came to the forest's edge, but the small hill captured his focus.

Other than shale, nothing stood out on the plain now the Banished had left. Odd, he thought, since a battle had just raged here. Zanna had performed her magic, spared so many lives, but people had died by the score. The scorched ground paid testament to that, the rock and sparse grass blackened in so many places, but Kade saw no bodies, no discarded weapons, no broken siege engines.

Kade staggered forward, his steps taking him towards

the strange rise in the middle of the plain. It lay opposite the bridges the Banished had created, a thousand paces or so away from the mountain wall. His frown deepened as he inched forward. The hill grew larger than he'd anticipated. Kade recalled little of what he'd seen of the Banished lands when he stood atop Solitude's walls, but he couldn't picture the horde swarming by such a rise, and he'd fixed his focus on the warriors clearing the bridge when he'd crested the mountain.

With about a quarter of the distance left, Kade gasped and came to a halt, hands covering his mouth.

It wasn't a hill.

The Banished had piled their dead atop one another in a massive burial mound, a slope of corpses, a lasting reminder of the battle and lives lost at Solitude. Falling to his knees, strength deserting his legs at last, Kade crawled closer, tears stinging his eyes.

"How could they leave them like this?" he croaked, coughing as the stench of rot swam into his nostrils. "Don't they care?"

Heathens. That's what mothers whispered to their children about the strange Banished living beyond Solitude. Monsters, grandfathers would murmur, eyes narrow and leaning in close, terrors who'd steal misbehaving youngsters away in the dead of night, though the common folk of Haltveldt saw them as simple shepherds, an isolated race forgotten by time.

Kade had discovered a little truth in all the old assumptions; the Banished's prowess in warfare made them dangerous, and the cold disregard for their dead, leaving them in a heaped mountain of carrion food in an uncaring wasteland, increased the peril in Kade's mind.

Not even the bastard Nexes would do this to his fallen, and that Raas-forsaken fool would kill his own grandmother if the emperor commanded it.

Kade couldn't tear his eyes from the mound, additional details becoming clear as he inched closer. Unseeing stares gazing into the vast sky, charred skin, faces twisted in terror or pain, while some appeared to sleep in peace, a smile on their lips. Men and women, of fighting age and beyond, lay one atop the other. And, the sight that brought Kade to a full stop, children.

His empty stomach heaved, forcing a retch from his throat. Kade had nothing to bring up, but his body fought to do it anyway. Now he'd discovered one, he found more. Children of all ages, scattered in the mound, tiny fingers stretched toward him for mercy. So many, their blood-crusted faces peering at him, searing into his mind.

He didn't understand. Who brought children into battle? Who brought the old and infirm?

"Why?" he whispered, as he stared up at the hill of death. A foul wind stirred the tendrils of smoke still lingering on the plain, whipping up the dust and stench of death.

It's too much. It's all too much. God's teeth, it is. All I want is my son! To find him, hold him again, and take him...

Where? Kade couldn't return to Spring Haven, not after his failed uprising. With Bertrand dead and Nexes out for his blood, they'd be hunted. Not to mention Arlo's budding spark and half-elven nature. He slammed his fist into his palm, but he had little strength left.

"I haven't thought any of this through. Any of it."

He stared up at the sky, tears stinging his eyes. Raas. He always beseeched Raas in times of need, but where had his prayers gotten him? A dead wife, a disgraced legacy, a drug addiction and a son lost in Banished lands. His lips curled, showing his teeth. A beaten dog who'd taken too much, now backed into a corner, snarling its warning that one more blow would send it over the edge.

"Damn you. You've taken everything from me. Everything!"

But a small voice whispered to him from the depths of his soul, a voice he knew too well, one dripping with self-loathing and doubt. *You've no one to blame but yourself. You chose the path you walk; the failures are yours.*

Snarling, he shoved the words out of his mind, hands flailing like he warded off physical blows, but his limbs flopped, vigour almost spent. Dehydration and hunger had caught up with him. His empty stomach gnawed at his insides. Swallowing felt like trying to force razor blades down his throat. His head pounded, the pale light of the Banished lands burning his eyes.

"Janna, please. Show me the way." He'd placed his faith in Raas so long; why not try a different god? Maybe this one would take pity on him, before he lay down before a mound of corpses and died, a final body to add to the pile. "Spare me, I only want my son to... What's that?"

A sound tickled his ears, interrupted his words. He gazed around, wide-eyed, staring into the heavens.

Singing. He heard singing. A sweet voice, lilting and melodious but sad, though hope underpinned it. The music spoke to him, and he sobbed, images of Rune's dying moments replaying in his mind, mixing with his first glimpse of Arlo's tiny, pink face. Death and birth—that's what it reminded him of, and the beauty and fear they both held. It rose and fell, growing stronger as Kade strained to listen. His jaw dropped.

Before him, at the bottom of the mound of corpses, a bright green stem wound its way between the bodies, and others joined it, pushing their way towards the sun. White flowers sprouted from them, unfurling and covering the dead, turning the bottom of the mound into a real hill, green and white. New life in the midst of grey stone and destruction. Hope where none lay before.

"Janna?" Kade stammered, tears mixing with the stubble on his cheeks. "It can't be. Can it?"

The singing grew louder, echoing through the silent plain, and other voices joined it, voices lower and higher in pitch. Kade blinked. Emerging from the haze beyond the mound of dead, slowly reclaimed by nature, figures emerged.

Banished.

Chapter Ten

meeting the others

'They say some Sparkers up in Solitude, bored with life and exile, would go live with the Banished. I think not. No one checks on them. More likely they find passage across the seas to Octaria. Imagine how many of them are over there, waiting. Plotting...' - Protector Garet on the Sparkers of Solitude, before his assignment there.

Five Banished emerged from the haze, an ancient, bearded man with hair the colour of pure snow at their lead, inspecting the mound as he stumbled forward. Two others followed, a man and a woman—old, but nowhere near his advanced years—helping him forward. Two others trailed behind, arms stretched at their sides, singing with the elder. As one, they fell silent as their stares found Kade, the hill blooming on its own behind them, the song taking root.

Kade studied them, weak fingers twitching as they itched to pull his sword free. The Banished carried no weapons, wore no armour for battle. They dressed in fur and simple robes, creased faces filled with sadness. One wept.

"Priests," Kade whispered, pointing at them, meeting the ancient man's eyes. "You're priests, aren't you? Seeing to your dead."

The old Banished man pointed behind Kade, to where Solitude had loomed. "*Il Renuish. Tu ra. Tu ra!*"

Il Renuish... Tilo said the same thing. What does it mean?

Flowers continued to bloom, covering the entire bottom third of the mound now. In years to come, Kade realised, people would just see the beauty of it, unaware of the atrocities beneath the surface. If anyone ever came to the Banished lands again.

"How did you do this?" Kade asked, raising a trembling hand at the hill. "Your singing?"

"*Il Renuish,*" the old man repeated, his speaking voice the exact opposite of his singing, like the creaking of old leather. "*Tu ra, renuish la Haltveldt.*"

Renuish, that word again. What does it mean? Halt-veldt...

Kade glanced over his shoulder. Nothing but scorched shale and dust between him and the crossing into Haltveldt. His body jerked when his eyes swept by the towering mountain range, a sudden weight pressing down on him, conflicting impulses urging him to run, or stay and fight, conspiring against each other to cause paralysis. Gritting his teeth, he focused on the Banished and pushed himself to his feet.

And promptly fell on his face.

"God's teeth," he croaked, fingers making tracks in the dirt.

His memories toppled. His mind floundered. Arlo at birth. The last moment he saw him before leaving Spring Haven, a teary-eyed boy on the verge of puberty. Rune, a quiet servant, fading into the background of his family home, then his bright-eyed lover, his radiant, secret wife. The frown on her face, the hurt in her sad smile, her hand reaching out to him, falling, lifeless, when her spirit left her body. Nexes, gloating, piercing eyes seeing his secrets. Bertrand, stomach and chest ripped open, organs spilling from pulled back ribs. Hanging from the walls of Solitude. Brina, who looked so much like Rune, holding him, refusing to let go. Arlo and Tilo spilling over the far side, out of Kade's reach…

Darkness surrounded him, flooded his vision. His lungs ached as he sucked in a wheezing breath through cracked lips.

Arlo. I've failed you again, for the last time.

Squinting, his eyes fell on those of a dead child pressed amidst the crush of corpses. Flowers sprang up around him, swallowing him from sight, hiding an ugly image the world should never see.

It won't be you. It can't be. Gods, please, don't let it happen. Arlo.

Pressed against the ground, the beating of his heart—a slow, weak flutter—reverberated against him. One beat, then another, a longer gap until the third. And then?

The moment stretched. Kade waited for his heart to

give another weak rattle or give up completely. He couldn't even raise his head anymore, strength gone, vision almost black, a single white flower surrounded by darkness all he could see. His fingers twitched in the dirt, his leg kicked, limbs realising what approached and trying in vain to fight back. But he had no fight left in him.

Kade closed his eyes, or thought he did. It didn't matter; he couldn't tell the difference anymore. He waited for that final heartbeat, to find himself before the Gates of Eternity or on the shores of the Underworld. Slipping, floating into oblivion. No pain. Cold, so cold...

Singing in his ear. A soft murmur he could cling to as his mind reeled, his body failed.

Thump.

A heartbeat.

Thump.

Another. Stronger.

Hands touched him, rolled him onto his back. The Banished stared down at him, concern etched in their faces as the ancient one sang, hands pressed against Kade's chest.

The melody quickened, and Kade's heart beat faster to catch up, pumping blood through him. Pain flooded his limbs, the agony of life, his mind and body in sync once more as they became aware of one another, a hundred cuts and scrapes, the lingering ache in his ankle that Calene had healed as well as she could, the stabbing reminder of metal thrust into his flesh.

And still the ancient Banished sang. As Kade listened, his body reacted. Saliva wetted his mouth, and he almost gagged on it. The searing pain subsided. He raised a hand to his face and gasped. The scrapes there faded before his eyes, fresh skin taking its place.

A Banished took his hand and eased him up from the ground. Kade expected the world to spin, but it didn't. He sat there, the Banished's song now a hum, and glanced around. For the first time in a long time, he felt steady, the tremor in his hands gone, the fog lingering at the edges of his mind clear. He met the ancient man's pale eyes and smiled.

"Thank you."

The Banished nodded, and fished a waterskin from his pack, passing it to Kade along with a handful of berries and three strips of meat. "*Ret. Ret.*"

He mimicked eating with his hands, and Kade set to it with relish.

"*Il Renuish.*" Kade pointed toward Haltveldt, then at the Banished, one at a time, "That's what you're doing, isn't it?"

The old man shook his head, worry creating even deeper lines in his aged face. He pointed toward the summit of the Peaks of Eternity. "*Sa renuish.*" He pointed at himself and his people. "*Ui etra.*"

Swallowing his food down with a mouthful of water, Kade opened his mouth to speak, but the Banished jumped to their feet.

"*Etra,*" one of the women whispered with palpable urgency. "*Etra!*"

Grabbing the older man, the elders moved away, hobbling with as much speed as they could muster without a backward glance, leaving a confused Kade with the waterskin. He glanced around, at a loss as to why the Banished had departed so abruptly. Only one thing seemed clear now; the strange people beyond Solitude weren't the monsters of legend.

They helped me, an enemy, when I lay before the very Gates of Eternity. They're not evil.

Kade rolled his shoulders. Vitality had returned. Confidence, too, in himself and his body. The mountains no longer daunted him, nor the vast, empty sky above his head. He studied the hill again. It continued to bloom, white flowers and grass covering half the mound of dead now.

And this isn't an invasion, it's a migration. Why?

A thought prodded at him, his mind sharper than it had been in years. The sky. No birds flew in it, like they'd left these lands too.

No, not a migration. They're fleeing from something.

The ground rumbled. A rider approached, fast-moving, the clatter of hooves growing louder. The Banished hobbled away, refusing to leave the ancient healer, the one responsible for the new life on the burial hill and his own salvation. They fled from the rider, and they couldn't escape. They had little chance of fighting back either.

If the Banished run from this rider, who in the Underworld could it be? Haltveldtian? Out in the wastelands?

Narrowing his eyes, Kade pressed himself against the bottom of the blooming hill, training his mind to forget the corpses beneath it, and inched his sword clear of its sheath.

I have to take a stand so the Banished can flee. It's the least I can do.

A black horse thundered past, a crimson-cloaked rider on its back, shining sword in hand.

Kade reacted.

"Hey!" he yelled, jumping away from the blossoming hill and drawing his blade. "Over here!"

The beast reared, surprise getting the better of it. Sawing his reins, the rider twisted in his seat, hate-filled eyes meeting Kade's. The horse stumbled on the uneven shale and tipped, crashing to the ground, screaming as a snap echoed, its leg broken.

Snarling, the rider hurled himself from the saddle, hitting the ground in a roll, dust exploding from the ground. He came to his feet as his mount writhed on the floor, squealing, snorting. Kade almost covered his ears, the noise piercing his soul.

The horse kicked out from the ground, hooves flashing wide of the rider who danced out of their way, then surged forward and plunged his sword deep into the animal's neck. Blood spurted, covering the man's face, gushing into his mouth. He spat it back on the animal, kicking it in the guts and ignoring the frenzied wails from the stricken animal as he pulled his blade free and hacked at it again.

Anger coiled like a viper in Kade's chest. The fall had made the animal lame, and putting it down would relieve the animal of its misery, but the hacking, the kicking? It wasn't humane.

In the distance, the party of Banished had turned, waiting and watching.

"*Run,*" Kade breathed. He bared his teeth as the rider struck the horse again, cutting off its head and its screams. "What are you waiting for? I jumped out here to give you a chance to get away!"

They didn't move. Not that they could hear him anyway, but the old Banished stood there, dust blowing around them, framed by the yawning gap between the Peaks of Eternity.

"You!"

Kade switched his attention to the rider.

He speaks Haltveldtian? How?

Blood dripped from the point of the stranger's sword, matted fur and sinew sticking to the blade as he approached. He wore no helmet and, to Kade's eyes, little armour. Instead, a suit of crimson leather covered him from chest to boots.

Then again, I'm not exactly wearing full plate.

The rider flowed forward and closed the gap to Kade with stunning speed.

Still the Banished watched.

The stranger gripped his sword in one hand, flicking his wrist and spinning the blade over his head as he made the final steps to meet Kade, bringing his weapon slashing down in a diagonal arc. Kade's arm vibrated as he parried the blow, adjusting his grip so the steel scraped together, sparks flying as their hilts touched. Hatred made the rider's brown eyes shine in a too pale, drawn face. Pure, unfiltered rage had driven the man into butchering his horse when it failed him. Now it pushed him to attack Kade after a single word.

"Who are you?" Kade breathed, his attention moving to the rider's hand. It dropped to a belt holding a knife as long as his forearm.

Grunting, Kade pushed with all his might, thanking the gods the Banished party had healed him so well, and dropped, swiping low with his blade. The crimson warrior dodged backward and hurled the knife in one movement. Kade rolled sideways through the dirt, coming to his feet with his sword held before him. The dagger thudded into the hill behind him.

The rider's eyes flicked to the mound, scowling at what he saw, not at all surprised by the miracle unfolding.

He's seen the Banished before, knows their magic. But he clearly isn't one of them. He speaks my language.

The stranger glanced over his shoulder, taking in the elders watching in the distance, then back at Kade. He smirked. His eyes still flashed with desire for the kill.

"You're not of their kind," he breathed, his accent smooth and hard to place. He dropped into a defensive stance, having taken Kade's measure and ruling out an easy win. "Why fight for them? If you hadn't called out, I'd have run them down and headed on to the mainland without seeing you."

"They're old. Defenceless. I couldn't stand by and watch you butcher them."

The rider laughed. "The First People aren't defenceless, fool."

"First Peo—"

The warrior attacked, taking advantage of Kade's confusion. He scrambled, feet moving with hard-earned intuition from the training yard, adjusting for his poor stance and giving Kade a better platform for defence. His opponent moved with such speed, flowing from one attack to the next that Kade could only parry, deflecting his enemy's blade and absorbing the shock into his arms, using the adrenaline to keep moving. Their grunts broke the scraping and clanging of their blades, the gore from the butchered horse splashing onto Kade's face when their swords met.

Backwards, backwards, backwards. Kade's only move, his arms growing heavy from the constant weight of impact, his mind slower from anticipating the rider's attacks. Sweat beaded across his forehead, as it did on his enemy's, the perspiration adding to Kade's resolve. An unending attack could tax limbs just as much as a resolute defence, though one mistake, one failed parry, would spell the end for Kade.

Their swords met again, blades skittering against each other. Twisting his wrist, Kade sliced down, faster than the steel's movement, catching the rider's fingers. One fell to the ground, blood spurting from the wound, oozing from the digit alone in the dust.

Grimacing, the stranger threw back his head then smashed it into Kade's nose.

Kade staggered backward, dropping to the ground, pain lancing through his head, blinding him. Hot liquid covered his face, dripped into his mouth.

Blood. I need to act. Need to...

Footsteps crunched in the shale, his attacker approaching. Kade acted on instinct, groping fingers gathering a fist-full of rocks and debris, and hurled them, at his attacker.

Cries of pain and rage rang in his ears.

Blinking, Kade struggled to his feet, backing away, but stumbled when he met the burial mound. The rider materialised out of the white light spoiling his vision, scrubbing dirt out of his eyes, smearing blood across his face from the wound where his finger had been. With a snarl, Kade attacked. His nose ached, but he threw the pain aside. He'd deal with it later. He had the advantage now, his dirty trick paying dividends.

Kade snaked his arm out, a low thrust, but planned for his foe to block it. He did, a touch too slow. The rider's blade rattled, his wrist too weak. Kade used the momentum and spun, slicing through the air as he came back around.

The resistance of steel cutting through flesh filled him with satisfaction. The crimson warrior bent over, a hand pressed against his midriff, a thin slice in his strange armour leaking blood. Kade's heart sank. Just a flesh wound, one that'd slow the man down, but his clothing had absorbed most of the blow. If the rider had caught Kade the same way, he'd have spilled his guts across the shale.

"Not bad." The warrior grimaced, flicking his hand in Kade's direction. Blood splattered on him. "What's your name?"

His head spun from his broken nose; his vision flickered. He welcomed the respite, but kept his focus, watching for any sign of attack. "Besem. Kade Besem."

The rider laughed. "A Besem! Yes, I've heard of your family. Never thought you'd have the fight in you."

Faint singing drifted across the wasteland. Kade's eyes flicked to the Banished. It came from them, the eldest on his knees, arms spread wide.

"Enough talking," Kade growled, hefting his blade. "Let's finish this."

Grinning, the rider stepped forward, then stumbled, confusion flickering across his face. He glanced down at his leg, eyes wide with shock. "What? No!"

Kade followed his stare and gasped. Roots shot from the ground and wrapped around the rider's foot, holding him to the spot. Snarling, he hacked at them with his sword, but fresh vines replaced the ones he severed, the roots growing faster than he could hack.

"Damn you," the rider cried, throwing a glance over his shoulder. "Damn you all to the Underworld!"

The singing grew in Kade's ears as he watched nature cover the warrior, shoots of life blooming around him, pinning him to the spot. Like the hill, flowers sprouted from the vines, but these white petals sported flecks of crimson. The rider struggled as the vines reached his waist, then snatched out, pulling his arms, sword and all, to his side. He flexed, snarled, but nothing made a difference.

Breathing hard, he stared at Kade, eyes filled with hate and more than a little fear. "You can't stop the Return, Kade Besem. No one can."

The Return... Il Reniush. Could it be?

The vines covered his chest now, snaking up to his shoulders and throat.

"Who are you?" Kade asked, sword loose in his hand, the pain in his face forgotten.

The rider laughed, then choked. Roots erupted from his mouth and bent, arrowing for his eyes, plunging through them. The sound of splintering bone echoed as they broke through the back of his skull. Within moments, a grotesque statue made of roots, vines and flowers stood before Kade, nature's figure before a flowery hill, alone in a wasteland of barren rock. Life where no other bloomed.

In the distance, the elder raised a hand toward Kade,

and the singing stopped. The party helped the ancient one to his feet, and they turned, heading towards Haltveldt.

Kade dropped to the ground, staring up at the warrior encased in flowers.

"The Banished are fleeing from them, and Arlo heads in their direction. I must find him before it's too late."

The encased rider didn't answer, and never would again. His secrets died with him. Kade drank from the waterskin and splashed more on his face, scrubbing away the blood and ignoring the blooming pain. Forcing himself to his feet, he left the hill behind. Life created from death. Nature nourished from spilled blood. The Banished helping him, a new foe, with strange and incredible magic.

Kade didn't care. He just wanted to find his son and take him far from this place, away from Haltveldt.

Like the fleeing Banished, he'd never look back.

Chapter Eleven

THE BEST OF BOTH WORLDS

'The elf parades? Bad for business. Godsrot, they are. Folk crowding in doorways, not spending a penny... But seeing the filth marched out of the city to their deaths? Never fails to brighten my day. I can lose a bit of coin for that.' - Spring Haven's business owners hate to miss out on money, but the spectacle of the hunt more than makes up for it.

"Do all you Banished just eat leaves and rocks?" Arlo grumbled. He kicked at a stone as he and Tilo crouched on an outcropping in the lower passes of the Peaks of Eternity.

Stomach rumbling and calves burning, aching feet for good measure, and the boy's lower back attempted to outdo them all by sending shooting pains through his legs whenever he moved them. Arlo had never walked so much in his life. Mountain passes and rocky ledges were a far cry from the paved roads of Spring Haven, or the steady, even parks in the city, not to mention all the sneaking and creeping around.

Arlo glanced at Tilo. The Banished warrior's clear eyes gazed at the sparse forest below them, taking it all in. Looking for signs of life, no doubt. They'd spoken little over the last day or so, the man keeping watch while Arlo slept, never resting himself. It didn't appear to bother him, and the boy knew it for truth. He'd prodded the strange connection he shared with the Banished in his mind and discovered no sign of tiredness, no resentment. It appeared Tilo had no need for sleep.

Tilo had noticed when Arlo first pressed against their connection, telling him to stop and leave him some privacy. His words had been short and harsh, but that hadn't deterred him. Instead, Arlo had approached with stealth and delicacy, learning from his first attempt when he'd booted open the door and rummaged through the drawers of Tilo's mind without a care.

Arlo learned to inch closer, recalling the time his father had taken him to see wild horses galloping through the Medero Plains outside Spring Haven. His father had waited in the same spot, steady and calm, a hand raised and eyes down, warning Arlo that any sudden movement or noise would make the beasts flee. He let an animal approach him, inching closer, snorting less. When it did, his father had replied in kind, taking slow steps and slight movements until his hand touched the horse's nose. Its muscles trembled until it understood his father's intent, his calm air settling the beast.

Arlo had done the same with Tilo's mind, though recalling the time spent with his father filled him with deep sorrow. He'd never see him again, Arlo knew. The boy wondered what his father would do, how he'd cope.

He'll blame himself. That's what he always does.

Throughout his life, right up until Solitude, his father had been there for him, and then Zanna had picked up the mantle. Now he'd lost them both.

"We eat meat, vegetables, fruit, bread," Tilo murmured. Arlo blinked. He'd forgotten he'd even asked a question. "Sometimes leaves. Never rocks. Too tough."

Arlo glanced around, frowning. "Where do you get those things from then? Other than other Banished fleeing into Haltveldt, I haven't seen any sign of life here. Not even a bird."

He didn't mention the vast army his vision had shown him, filling the wastelands. He didn't need to speak about them. Didn't *want* to. Being scared all the time made him tired.

Tilo pointed into the distance, towards the highest point of the Peaks of Eternity. Dark clouds hovered above them now, thick and writhing. Arlo shuddered when he looked that way, remembering the lights shooting from it, the colours shredding the sky. Each time he stared that way, a sensation tugged at him, urging him to walk faster, to forget sleep and run if he had to.

"It's different beyond the Peaks. Fertile land, lush forests…" The faint smile Tilo wore faded. "Not ours anymore."

"Who are these people?" Arlo blurted the question out. Tilo had avoided the conversation any time the strangers came up, and that had suited them both fine, but they had to talk. Questions filled Arlo's mind from morning till night, despite his reluctance to acknowledge they existed, but what would ignoring them achieve? "Do they come from a different land? Are they from beyond the mountains?"

"I don't know," Tilo muttered. Fear flooded the connection now, an anxiety so potent it made Arlo want to curl up on the ground and whimper. "The Return, that's all it is. From what or where? The Lodestone didn't tell me. I just know we—you and I—must reach the peak."

Return? That means they were here once before.

"And then what?"

"I'll see my family again. But who knows, we may never get there if we don't eat." The warrior rose into a crouch, "I see something below us. Stay behind me."

Arlo jumped. Movement in the woods, rustling drifting from below. He glanced at Tilo, eyes wide, but the man wore a satisfied smile without a hint of worry.

"What if it's one of them?" Arlo hissed. Tilo moved to the edge of the mountain shelf they hid upon, a drop the height of two men.

He raised a finger to his lips. "It isn't. When you hear my call, follow, but not before. Understand?"

"How am I meant to—?"

Drawing his sword, Tilo turned, readied himself, then dropped from the edge. Gasping, Arlo ran, throwing himself on his belly, and peered over. A high-pitched squeal of pain and rage destroyed the silence, the sound of thrashing through the thicket below him, and a grunt from Tilo. Then...

Silence.

It stretched as the leaves and bushes steadied, the un-natural quiet of the Banished lands falling once more. Arlo scrambled to his knees, wringing his hands together.

"Tilo?" he whisper-shouted, his voice hoarse. "Are you okay?"

Please let nothing have happened to you.

He peered around, breaths coming fast. The mountains surrounding him loomed higher, the sky vaster, emptier.

I can't be alone. Not here. Please.

He wanted to call out again but couldn't trust that a scream wouldn't tear from his throat. Instead, he leaned forward, staring into the thicket.

Please...

The bushes rustled.

"Arlo." Tilo's voice almost brought tears to the boy's eyes. "Come down; it's safe."

He glanced around, the relief flooding him short-lived, looking for a way down. All of a sudden, the drop appeared higher than before. No problem for a full-grown warrior like Tilo, but for him? A skinny boy used to city life? Visions of his body flipping mid-air, only to land on a broken neck, flooded Arlo's mind. The promised purpose over, unfulfilled and forgotten.

"How?" he hissed, seeing no option but to jump. He crouched on the lowest part of the mountain range in sight. "If I jump, will you catch me?"

"Jump?" Tilo laughed, amusement and a touch of exas-peration flooding their connection. "Can't you use magic?"

Heat warmed Arlo's cheeks. The *Spark*. He could use

the Spark! It all sounded so simple, except he'd never used his gift for anything more than simple tricks. If he didn't count the time he'd almost Eviscerated an apple, which he didn't. Zanna had stopped him, and he tried not to think about it, how he'd wanted to keep going until the fruit had turned to mush, how his skin tingled as he withered the apple to its core.

The memory sullied his time spent with his mentor, made his skin itch. Had it only been two weeks ago? A little more? It felt like a lifetime since he'd sat in Solitude's hall with his master, practising his talent.

When his master still lived.

It still hadn't sunk in. Not really. A month ago, he'd never imagined that he'd be roaming the wastelands beyond Solitude with a Banished warrior, the fortress gone, his teacher, Zanna, dead alongside so many others.

Arlo shook his head. The world beyond Spring Haven's walls wasn't what he'd expected. Now wasn't the time for feeling sorry for himself but thinking of his master put an idea in his head. She'd stepped off the top of Solitude's tallest tower and floated down to the bottom. Before Protector Garet had lost his mind and unleashed the Underworld on the Banished people massing before the fortress walls.

She used air, and so could he.

Closing his eyes, Arlo reached out with his senses. The element he needed surrounded him. Of course it did. He stood on the outcroppings of a mountain, the vast, blue sky stretching out above him. The Spark surged within him, making the air taste sweeter on his tongue, smell richer in his nostrils. It all came easy. Too easy.

Other scents reached him—pine from the trees, the iron inside blood, salt and sweat, dirt from his own body. It would have made him gag if he hadn't submerged himself in his Spark, like the rest of the world couldn't bother him. His awareness of it existed but sinking into his magic had removed him from it.

The presence watching him swam into his awareness. Arlo let it wash over him, letting his mind become aware of it without focusing on it. The summit of the Peaks of Eternity. It came from there, from the voice who'd spoken to Arlo in his mind.

It hadn't whispered to him again since it showed him the foreign army, the one the Banished fled from, but it watched now. Did Zanna too?

Arlo had resisted embracing his Spark since then, since he'd almost lost control of it as he absorbed the swirling maelstrom of energies lingering above the mountains near Solitude. It felt greater within him, terrible and sweet at the same time. Vast and unknowable, the core of his being expanded beyond his comprehension, but it still existed within him. Part of him. Just as much as his arms or legs or the blood running in his veins. The Spark flowed through his core.

Ice rushed through his body as he pulled the air around him into his core. Arlo didn't know how much he'd need, so he kept pulling, but with care, sucking it in until his feet left the ground, fists by his side, and judged that enough. He didn't want too much, not again.

Opening his eyes, Arlo spread his arms, palms up and pictured the air inside him surrounding him in a bubble, and his Spark made it so. It worked with him, making the vision in his head possible. He felt protected, safe, bolstered.

Smiling, he stepped off the ledge.

The air caught him. Pointing with his finger—Arlo didn't know if he needed to or if his Spark would just work alongside the need he felt inside—he lowered through the foliage, leaves moving out of his way as the solid bubble of air brushed them to the side.

Tilo stood below the treeline, staring up, blood-covered sword in hand and a skewered boar at his feet.

"Food," he grinned, nonplussed by the boy's feat and without a mention of Arlo's magic. The boy fought against the irritation welling inside him; Zanna would have commented on his amazing act, boosted his confidence. Tilo didn't seem to care.

The Banished knelt and wiped his blade on the sparse grass then let it fall to the ground.

"I hope you know how to skin that thing," Arlo muttered, eyeing the massive boar. It matched him in length and boasted much more bulk. Tilo seemed to have dispatched it with a minimum of fuss. He studied the man again, taking in his size, his physique, the well-used blade on the ground beside him. "Aren't you supposed to be some kind of monk, and here you are, plunging through the trees and hunting wild boar?"

Tilo laughed, then bowed his head, hands pressed against the animal's carcass. Arlo frowned when he sang, cocking his head when he understood the words.

'For this, we thank you,
For this, we regret.
Life that is not ours,
We take to survive.
Our lives we give back,
When our last breath leaves our throat.
Life for life,
Blood for blood,
Until the last day.'

Tilo sang in a low, steady voice, a hypnotic chant tinged with both hope and sadness. Arlo closed his eyes as the Banished repeated the words, his thoughts turning to his father. He'd always appeared sad, even when he laughed, like it would never leave him no matter what he did. His father wore sorrow like he did clothes. No, deeper than that. It flowed in his blood, pumped from his heart.

Arlo wiped at his eyes, not wanting Tilo to see him cry.

"There's no need to hide your sadness," the Banished whispered, still bowed over the boar. He raised a finger to the side of his head. "I feel it here, in this thing we share. Your father loved you, and still does. I could sense it in him when we met."

"You know my father?" Arlo asked, kneeling next to Tilo.

"We travelled together for a time." He frowned, then turned to Arlo, their eyes meeting. "I think I can show you."

"How?"

"I don't know. It's just a feeling. Come, close your eyes and do as I do."

He closed his eyes and reached out, taking Arlo's head and pulling him close so their foreheads touched.

Dubious, Arlo copied him, fingers sinking into the Banished's curly hair.

"Empty your mind," Tilo whispered, "and keep your hands on me."

Arlo held his breath, waiting. For what, he didn't know. He knelt there, head stuck against Tilo's sweaty skin, wondering what someone would think if they happened by them, kneeling together in some kind of silent prayer.

Why can't he just tell me instead? This is stupid. What in the Underw—?

Lights flashed in Arlo's mind. Bright blues and dark greys swirling, until images formed from the mixing colours. A massive statue of Raas appeared, looming above him as it gazed with pride above a harbour town. Arlo remembered the settlement from his journey to Solitude. Adhraas, with its bustling streets and deep joy in being the so-called birthplace of Raas. He stood on the deck of a boat as it cut through the water, the shore zooming by, and gasped.

He saw Tilo's memories! No, he *lived* them.

Arlo tried to glance around, to look for his father—why else would Tilo bring him to this place if his father wasn't close?—but couldn't move.

I can't do anything but look where Tilo did. It's like I'm sitting behind his eyes, watching the world go by as he remembers it.

The Banished's attention latched onto the harbour, his vision flicking as a woman and a hooded figure brushed by. Arlo almost shouted but realised he couldn't do that either.

The woman looked so much like Zanna he wanted nothing more than to run to her, hold tight and never let go.

Calene, it must be Calene!

Tilo's memories locked onto another ship as they sailed by. A man stood by the side, talking to a large fellow. Arlo recognised the smaller figure, even at this distance, even with his back turned.

Father. What? No!

The other man stabbed him. Stabbed him again, pulling the bloody blade free and plunging it into his flesh over and over. His father reached for his sword to defend himself but his attacker threw him overboard, blood streaming into the water, turning it crimson. Arlo tried to look away, fought in vain to close his eyes. He didn't want to see this, his father struck by a blade and tossed aside like a ragdoll. He tried to scream, but no sounds came from his mouth.

Why are you showing me this?

His vision lurched, spun. Shouts erupted around Arlo, screams, the splashing of water, then a strange, muted half-silence as the world turned murky. It hit him. Tilo had dived into the bay. A darker colour bloomed ahead as the Banished surged forward, cutting through the water, then collided with his father's body, grappling with him, pulling him upright so his head would break the surface first. His father didn't notice. His eyes were shut, blood leaking from his wounds.

The memories moved faster. Tilo watched Calene heal Kade's wounds as he sang in his melodious voice, somehow bolstering her Spark. Arlo tucked that information away for later. The Banished gazed at his father as he awoke on the back of a cart heading to Solitude, listening as he spoke about Arlo, and his desire to see him one more time.

Through the vision, Arlo stared into his father's eyes as he spoke about him and recognised the same look that Zanna had whenever she mentioned Calene. Love, regret, hope and longing. The need to do more, to do *better*.

Lights flashed, the figures losing form, dissolving into a mixture of colours and formless shapes, until the vision faded. Arlo's head moved backwards, Tilo's fingers slipping from his scalp.

Silence hung between them, weaving through the sparse forest in the upper reaches of the world. Arlo breathed in, a ragged, wet, shuddering sound as he tried to compose himself.

"He didn't need to do better," he whispered, meeting Tilo's strange eyes. The Banished blinked back, listening. "He did what he had to, to keep me safe."

"He loved you." Tilo smiled. "He still does."

"Do you think he's alive?" Arlo's voice cracked and wobbled.

Grabbing the boar, the Banished got to his feet and, with a grunt, flipped the carcass onto his shoulders as if it weighed the same as a sack of grapes. Remembering how Tilo had lifted his water-logged father from the water, Arlo quashed his surprise. The man commanded a great well of strength.

If he's a monk, I wonder what their warriors are like.

"I do," Tilo replied, gazing around, ignoring the blood

leaking from the dead boar. "Come, a wild animal means there's a cave nearby. Let's find it. We'll need a fire if we're to feast on this meat, and I don't want anyone to see the smoke."

"How do you know?" Arlo asked, stopping him in his tracks. "That my father's alive?"

Tilo looked over his shoulder. "Because I would not allow myself to die if my children still needed me, and Kade Besem is the same. Those wounds you saw, his near-drowning, all the rest? They'd have killed a lesser man. Your father will live until you're safe. I know this because I have taken the measure of him, and I found a worthy soul, one riddled with guilt and pain, but one who would do anything for his son." Tilo looked away, and muttered, almost to himself, "As a man should."

Arlo's feet wouldn't move as his companion moved away, because they understood his sudden need for solitude. Even for a moment. Wiping at his cheeks, he took a deep breath before following Tilo.

I hope you're right. The gods make it so.

CHAPTER TWELVE

LOST

'You ever hear about Sparkers whose Link slips? Their minds merge as one. Thoughts, emotions, memories swimming together in an ocean choppier than the Sea of Storms. And easier to lose yourself in to boot. Nasty stuff, let me tell you...' - Brius, a Sparker famed for his madness, on the risks of Links.

"You've never skinned a boar before?" Tilo asked, voice thick with disbelief.

Arlo laughed at the look on the warrior-monk's face. Eyebrows climbing his forehead, jaw slack, he looked like the boy had just told him he couldn't read. Like the thought of a child never skinning an animal wasn't one that existed in his head.

"No! And not just a boar, any animal." Busy as Tilo was, Arlo reckoned it the perfect time to discover more about his strange people. It wasn't like he had anything else to do. "Listen, do your people read? Like, do they have books and all that?"

They'd found a cave close by without much effort. Arlo had been dubious, expecting to stumble upon another boar—or worse, a bear—but Tilo pronounced it safe, insisting the claw marks and excrement belonged only to the dead creature. Still, Arlo wasn't certain nothing else lurked in the shadows.

Tilo waved a bloodied knife, one Arlo had been doing his damned best to avoid looking at. On cue, his eyes sought out the half-prepared carcass, taking in the giblets, blood, matted fur and organs spilling from it. He had no idea what to call any of it. He'd never laid eyes on an animal's insides before. His stomach protested, and he shifted his gaze before he retched all over the cave floor.

Why do I keep looking at it? What's wrong with me?

"Don't change the subject." Tilo acted like he wasn't bloody to the elbow, that the carcass hadn't dripped all over his clothes on the hike to the beast's den. "How have you reached this age without skinning an animal? Next you'll tell me you've never even hunted one."

"I've never hunted one."

The Banished's knife clattered to the cave floor. Arlo couldn't help himself. A laugh escaped his mouth at Tilo's dumbfounded expression, his look of pure disbelief. His bloody hand remained raised, like Arlo's confession had turned him into a living statue. The boy nudged their connection and the tumult of conflicting emotions rolling around in Tilo's mind hit him—amusement, curiosity, confusion, swirling atop a sea of others hidden underneath. Fear, anxiety, shame. Regret.

Arlo pulled away, cutting his laughter short.

I shouldn't keep pushing against it, but I can't help it. How did Zanna resist living in Calene's mind whenever she could?

"You've never hunted?" Tilo asked, oblivious to Arlo's mini-moral dilemma.

"No, never." Arlo gazed around the snug cave. Tilo had told him a whole warren of them existed in the peaks. "Life's quite different down in Spring Haven, you know? Some of the nobles hunted for sport, but it never appealed to father."

"Sport?" Tilo asked, as he reached for the knife. He stopped himself and eyed Arlo instead. "How do you mean?"

"Members of the Conclave, the rich, friends of the emperor—they'd all go out together on horseback, fancy weapons all shiny and clean. People would line the streets and watch them leave."

One time, on a rare occasion when his father had been invited, Arlo had watched the party leave through Tallan Square. They'd looked so grand until Arlo studied the finer details. The nobles swayed in their saddles, drunk before the sun had reached its midway point. They'd looked so grand from afar, as their kind often did.

He'd waved at his father, who hung back as the party left, then turned away, abandoning the hunt. They spent the day in their apartments instead, playing squares and reading stories. A few days later, Arlo's grandfather visited, raging at Kade for sullying the Besem name once again, for embarrassing himself and his family.

His father didn't seem to care and took the verbal barrage staring into the middle distance with the look of a man who'd heard it all before.

"Never really interested me much. I prefer reading. Do your people read? You didn't answer before. Do they have books?"

"Why do you answer my questions with questions of your own?" Tilo asked.

"Because I'm twelve," Arlo replied, with a smile.

"You will get your turn. This is important. These nobles, they only killed when necessary, yes?" Tilo asked, his stare intense. "They thanked the gods for the trade?"

The song the Banished had sung after slaying the boar returned to Arlo. It wasn't just the custom of a strange people; Tilo had meant every word.

"No. They just did it for fun, and killing animals wasn't the worst of it."

Arlo glanced around out of habit, something everyone did when speaking ill of the Empire. His father's servants whispered about the Emperor's Hands, his elite personal army who listened at each and every one of Haltveldt's dark corners, hunting secrets and traitors. They wouldn't reach him up there, would they? He suppressed a sudden shiver.

"They say the emperor and his friends round up elves from the slums, or slaves who displease their masters, and set them loose in the countryside, then ride them down. Father and me never went to the parades, so I never really believed it. But after Solitude... I just don't know anymore. I don't know anything."

Tilo bared his teeth. "And my people—my family—journey south into a pit of snakes! Worse even! At least a serpent doesn't kill for its own amusement!"

"The north isn't so bad," Arlo replied, recalling what

his father had always said whenever he'd plan to move from Spring Haven, even if he never followed through on it. "Tilo, I think after what happened at Solitude, your people wouldn't get a warm welcome anyway."

"We didn't want to fight," the Banished growled, cutting into the carcass. "We don't walk the path of war."

"But how do you know that? Really?"

Arlo eyed the knife, the blood oozing across the ground. His stomach flipped, memories of the battle on the walls flickering through his mind. They came to him disjointed, like he didn't really remember them, and Arlo realised he didn't. He peered at the days leading up to the fall of Solitude through a haze filled with nightmares and sleepless nights, but he couldn't shake the image of a Banished charging at him, mace slick with gore, anger writ plain across the man's face.

"You weren't there."

"I know my people! You stood there and watched as they approached the fortress. Who made the first move when the battle started? Who? I can tell you it wasn't us!" Tilo's shout echoed around the cave, bouncing from ceiling to side. Regret flooded through their connection, and the Banished sighed. "I'm sorry... I shouldn't take my anger out on you. My fear. It's just difficult. I feel your emotions in my head and it's getting hard to separate them from my own."

Heat turned Arlo's cheeks red. He reckoned he'd been subtle, watching Tilo's thoughts from a safe distance, but he'd flooded the man's mind with his emotions.

"Ah..."

Words didn't come tumbling from his mouth like they

always did. A rarity for him.

"See!" Tilo muttered, returning to the boar. "Embarrassment. Confusion. Shame, building with each of my words."

"So, maybe stop talking about it?" Arlo squeaked, looking everywhere but at his companion.

Tilo grunted. "Come here. You need to learn. It'll empty that head of yours. And mine too, I hope."

Filling his lungs with air, Arlo nodded. He didn't like blood. Never had. The sight of it made his head spin, and his father had once told him how he'd cry as a young boy whenever he picked up the smallest scrape or scratch, that he'd talk about the injury for weeks after.

One time, before the fireplace in their apartments, Arlo listened, mortified, as his father recalled a time when he'd fallen on some stones. Fearing a cut, Arlo had refused to lift his trouser legs, wailing all the way through Spring Haven as he carried him home, making his father promise he wouldn't look at it. Once Arlo had fallen asleep, his father had taken great care in rolling up the trouser leg and discovered nothing.

The next morning, Arlo woke, amazed at his bare, unmarked skin, asking if the Sparkers had used their magic to take it away, or maybe the elves and their secret sorcery.

Bracing himself, Arlo got to his feet and approached Tilo, pinching his nose. The Banished glanced at him and, with a shake of his head, smiled. "I remember the first time my father took me hunting and taught me to skin my kill."

Arlo's stomach lurched, the thick blood pooling beneath the staring carcass. He covered his mouth and gagged, muttering through his fingers, "Go well?"

"I vomited all over it the moment I made the first incision."

A laugh escaped Arlo's mouth before he could stop it, and he kept going. Giggling until his body lost its strength, and he fell on his back, staring at the cave's ceiling through tear-filled eyes, even harder when Tilo's chuckles reached his ears, the man's amusement flooding their connection and spreading through Arlo's mind. The boy's stomach hurt but he didn't care; he couldn't remember the last time he'd laughed. It swept through their connection both ways, amusement building, rising to new heights. Tilo thumped to the ground, wheezing, wiping at his eyes, body shaking with each peal of laughter.

"Stop laughing!" Arlo squealed, struggling to breathe. "Please, stop!"

Tilo nodded, eyes wild, incapable of speech. Panic seeped through their connection, anxiety's edge making their laughter frantic.

"Breathe," Tilo managed, laying a hand on Arlo's chest. "Clear. Your. Mind... Breathe!"

Clear my mind? Easier to please Fen in the Underworld!

Amusement kept coming in waves, along with a heady mixture of emotions—panic, fear, shame, confusion. Arlo didn't know which ones came from him and which belonged to Tilo, but he had to control them somehow, separate them before the torrent of feelings overwhelmed and consumed him. His breathing came fast now, quick bursts of air failing to fill his lungs, his heart hammering against his ribcage. Tilo had removed his hand to clutch his own chest, long legs kicking against the boar.

Arlo closed his eyes, but he refused to surrender. He knew that meant disaster. Their emotions, thoughts, memories merged. Instead, he shoved the feelings aside, resolving to pick them apart later to see what belonged where, and focused on the one thing he could always count on to calm him down. The one memory Arlo retreated to when his father's grief, and the addictions he tried to pretend didn't exist, overwhelmed him.

Arlo went back to a day spent on a riverboat, alone with his father, where they fished, played squares, read stories, and planned for a future he now knew they'd never see.

Sadness flooded his mind, but at least he knew it belonged to him. That wasn't the real reason Arlo recalled the memory. Until he arrived in Solitude, it had never made him sad. They'd talked about travelling around Haltveldt and beyond, of what Arlo wanted to be when he grew—a historian—and it became clear that everything his father spoke of had Arlo at its centre.

When his father called him special, he believed it.

Arlo wrapped himself in that day, and let the memories separate him from Tilo. His eyes still closed, Arlo drew a deep breath and let it ooze out. *One. Two. Three...* He breathed between each count and, as he reached ten, he turned his head.

Tilo watched him, face calm, sweat beading on his forehead.

"I thought we were gone," he whispered, reaching out to place a finger against Arlo's head. "I found myself in here, swimming against a raging tide, lost. Then, I saw your memory with your father, and I knew who I was again. I'm sorry I saw it, but I'm grateful I did just the same."

Arlo let his head drop against the stone ground and exhaled. They both lay for a moment, the boy staring but not seeing, listening to his heart thump in his chest, the blood rushing in his ears. The knot of emotions in his head pulsated, but Arlo didn't approach it. He wasn't ready.

For now, he just wanted to lie there and thank the gods he still lived, but the silence needed breaking. He and Tilo had shared a joining—one neither of them had been prepared for—and it couldn't happen again. Arlo turned onto his side and studied the warrior-monk's profile. Tilo blinked up at the ceiling, the muscles around his eyes tight, hand still covering his heart.

"This connection we share. Zanna, my master, called it a Link."

Tilo turned his head and listened in silence.

"She told me Sparkers who trusted one another would join their minds so they could talk over great distances, reach out to each other, know how the other felt. But I never knew people who weren't Sparkers could do it. Can you…? Do you have the Spark, Tilo? Is your magic the same as ours, but you sing to channel it?"

The Banished sat up and stared at the discarded boar leaking by his feet. The sight of blood oozing from the carcass didn't bother Arlo as much now.

"No. We don't have the Spark." He glanced at the boy, then ran a hand through his almost white hair. "Our magic is different now. A gift from the Lodestone after it took the Spark from us, a long time ago."

"So, you used to have the Spark?" Arlo asked, frowning.

"Yes, thousands of years ago."

"And you say the Lodestone took it away? They say the elves used to use a unique magic too, in stories. I wonder if what you have now is theirs, and maybe this Link isn't from the Spark at all."

Tilo shook his head and retrieved his bloody knife. "I can see its uses, but to have someone living in your head all the time? No. Not for me."

"Not even your wife?"

The pocket of emotions, the Link, pulsated in Arlo's head. He shrank away from it, not wanting to get anywhere near the torrent of empathy.

"I would give anything to hear her voice, true," Tilo muttered, studying the boar, but Arlo knew the man peered elsewhere, back into the past. Back to his family and the son in Drada's belly. "But that's different. People's ideas, how they feel, belong to them. Not that I have much of a choice now. Our minds are Linked regardless of my thoughts."

"That's just it!" Arlo scrambled to his knees. "Zanna laughed, drank, brooded, and I guess Calene did too. And she fought in battle; her emotions would have raged then!"

"So?"

"So, neither of them were overwhelmed by the other's emotions. We don't have to let this happen again!" Arlo spoke before Tilo could object, knowing what he'd say. "Not that we chose it! But now we know better."

"You have any suggestions?"

"Zanna said her daughter built a wall around their Link, how she had to barge through to get her attention.

Maybe we could do that?"

"Maybe." Tilo pointed the knife at him and smiled. "You work on that, and I'll work on our friend here, but observe and learn. I'm not carving up every meal we come across until we reach the Lodestone. And no laughing."

"Deal," the boy grinned, huddling closer to the Banished as the temperature in the cave plummeted. Not for the first time, he rued their lack of blankets. "How about a fire? We need to cook the meat too."

Tilo nodded, gazing around. "This cave will hide the glow and smoke, but we need wood. Go find some after I'm done, but don't stray from the entrance. I'm going to assume you've never kindled a fire before either."

Smiling, Arlo held out his hand and closed his eyes, drawing his body heat to mix with his Spark. Orange flames erupted from his fingers. "Don't worry about that. I'm a Sparker, remember."

Tilo returned the smile as he plunged his blade into the carcass, the sound of separating meat and squelching blood combining to make Arlo queasy. But he kept watching, as the Banished had asked.

As he did, his mind worked, examining the Link pulsating in his brain and worrying about building his walls high. He had to.

The next time their minds merged like that could be their last.

Chapter Thirteen

The Turning Room

'The Spark. What do we know of it, really? We think of it as a gift from the gods, from Raas and Janna themselves. A tool to create harmony and a better world. If you walk my path, you'll see it clearer. The Spark is alive.' - Notes recovered from the journals of Ricken Alpenwood.

The screams reached Locke's ears before the doors even opened.

Darkness swirled in the forgotten corridors of the university's lower reaches, blacker than night, despite the gas lamps hanging from the walls, like the shadows knew what happened behind the stone walls and grew thicker and more potent with every cry.

Perhaps they do. There's still so much we don't know about the Spark. Hence, the experiments.

Locke glanced at Balz and frowned. He'd avoided Locke as much as possible during the emperor's stay and spoke little. Great darkness fell on Balz with each step, and the man shrank inside it. They said a person could get used to anything, but clearly not the High Sparker. To his credit, Balz had led the creation of the Shadow Sparkers, building on the findings and experiments of many a disgraced Sparker like Ricken Alpenwood and others, spending hours in the Turning Room. Now, he quailed.

I think we need a High Sparker with more... teeth. The Shadow Sparkers are lions. Can't have a pussy cat sitting above them for Haltveldt's new dawn.

"We need more Shadow Sparkers, Balz. Nexes says they performed well on the battlefield."

An understatement. The Master of War's report detailed the utter ruination of the elven ranks, that the scourge melted away after Nexes' charge. Even more encouraging, other Sparkers gave in to the surrounding darkness and Eviscerated without control.

Balz hadn't answered. His eyes darted in their sockets, and he winced at every scream echoing from the darkness.

"High Sparker Balz?" Locke barked, coming to a halt.

They stood alone in the corridor, or so it seemed. In the darkness, Shadow Sparkers lurked, and no doubt so did a few of his Hands. Locke never truly went anywhere alone.

The High Sparker blinked and gazed up at him, the gas lamp's blue light flickering across his too-pale face. Gaunt and shrunken, Balz's robes hung from his shoulders, thin wrists and bony fingers protruding from his sleeves. Locke hadn't noticed the man's decline, but then again, when had he last really studied him?

"My apologies, Emperor," Balz whispered, voice flat

and hushed like he thought anything more than a murmur would disturb the heavy shadows. "My mind wandered. It often does down here. You asked me a question?"

White-hot annoyance flared within Locke. He wasn't a patient man. Emperors never were. He didn't care for waiting, or excuses, and tolerated them even less. Balz had pushed him to his limit with both since he'd arrived.

A creeping doubt stayed Locke's wrath. The tiniest of slithers. Even though he possessed not an ounce of the Spark, oppressive watchfulness weighed on his shoulders since descending to the lower levels.

This place had become the Shadow Sparkers' lair.

"How do you feel when you're down here?" Locke asked, narrowing his eyes.

Balz appeared to shrink further into his rich purple robes, and the tendrils of the shadows creeping from the corners of the walls seemed to tug at the hems. Blinking, Locke looked again.

Nothing.

Godsrot. Even my mind plays tricks down here.

"You wouldn't understand, Emperor."

Locke's eyebrows climbed his forehead. Such insolence, and so unlike Balz. A lifelong friend but a craven through and through. His left hand bunched into a fist, but Locke forced his fingers to relax before he beat the snivelling worm to the ground and spat on his corpse.

"Remember your place," he breathed instead, taking a step closer.

Over Balz's shoulder, Locke spotted a Shadow Sparker watching. It'd unhooded itself, obsidian eyes blazing like the high, black sun on Eru day, crimson cracks and fissures running along their grey skin, angry and bright.

Breathing in through his nose, Locke tilted his head back, and met the living horror's black eyes. *I created you. Me. You are mine!*

"It's my Spark," Balz stammered, right eye twitching. "I barely trust it down here. Can you understand that? Not wanting to use a thing that's been part of you since you were born? Could you stop believing your memories, or keep your lips from saying the words you want to say? That's how I feel down here. What we've created *speaks* to me. No. No, no, no. It speaks to my *Spark*. The darkness. It wants me to join it."

Balz looked away, shoulders shuddering like he held back sobs. Locke reached out with a finger, and lifted his chin, forcing him to stare into his emperor's eyes. They wouldn't focus, and the muscles surrounding them twitched. Understanding dawned on Locke.

"And why don't you?" he asked, voice light as a feather, heavy as the continent itself.

"Because I want it all! Everything! Death, life, creation, chaos. I won't stop, Emperor, and I fear my Spark won't let me. Once it's unleashed... Oh, Raas, the Spark... A gift..."

Balz's face twitched again, fingers trembling, feet shuffling. His mind had broken under the weight of their task. Locke's lip curled. Weakness stood before him. Wearing the face of a friend, but weakness all the same.

"Enough," Locke snarled, turning away from the High Sparker, hiding the disgust from his face. "Take me to my Turning Room, then we'll discuss your future."

How disappointing. He'd had high hopes for the man. Nexes had vouched for him too. A pity if it meant he'd need to examine his judgement in the Master of War as well.

"I have other uses for you, Balz."

After a moment's hesitation, the High Sparker moved away and Locke followed, picturing the silent retinue following in their wake.

They wouldn't enter the Turning Room though. Not without an invitation. The 'room Raas doesn't see', Nexes had coined it, with a cold smirk on his face, and Locke reckoned he had it right. Most never saw it, and if they did, they were never the same after. For years, Locke and his closest allies had examined the Spark, looking for ways to weaponize the Order and remove many obstacles in their path along the way.

"Remember those first Sparkers who helped us, Balz?"

Locke gazed around, nostalgic, an emotion alien to him at the best of times. They'd worked long and hard to create the Shadow Sparkers, to massage Haltveldt into the position of welcoming such abominations. When he'd read Nexes' report of their prowess, he'd drank a whole bottle of red wine in celebration.

"How could I forget?" Balz replied, steady steps echoing, but falling flat when they reached the shadows oozing from the walls.

"Yes, I get what you mean," Locke replied, rubbing his chin. "They attacked the situation with such gusto. Who knew the great Zanna Alpenwood's husband had inspired such disciples to his cause? I wonder if it would please him to know he'd begun a revolution."

"Pity he wasn't one of the first," Balz muttered, turning a corner. He and Locke knew where the Turning Room lay with their eyes closed; they'd spent so much time there over the years. Balz kept his pace slow and ponderous. He desired to be anywhere other than the Turning Room. "A fine Sparker, such power. Only his wife and daughter outstripped him."

"Now they would have been fine additions to our ranks, no?"

"Calene especially. I shudder to think what she would be capable of as a Shadow Sparker. Dead now, I suppose, along with her parents."

Locke nodded. He'd sent a retinue of Sparkers to kill the girl when she'd discovered the Banished in the south. He expected their arrival any day now with great interest. To actually lay eyes on one of the First People! To see how long they'd last under the knife.

Zanna Alpenwood had been at Solitude since she'd Eviscerated her husband. A shame, Locke had thought, but the High Sparker at the time wouldn't budge on the matter. Locke had pushed for a private execution—really a spell in the Turning Room—but the High Sparker and Zanna had been friends, and he decided on banishment.

"Still, we've done well. Those first Sparkers who went over to the shadow, we have much to thank them for. Pity they're all dead."

"A necessity," Balz replied, shaking his head. "They knew too much and hungered for control."

In those early days, rumours spread of Sparkers being

exiled to Solitude, or killed on the frontlines in great numbers, but in reality, those men and women found themselves here, the emperor's first allies cutting them off from their Spark through shielding and carrying on the work of Ricken Alpenwood under Balz's watchful eye. They'd explored just what the Spark could do, what it could achieve, if unleashed. They all knew of Evisceration, a technique banned by the Laws, but they sought to push the very nature of magic.

Could they alter the amount of magic a Sparker could use? Would taking a Sparker's blood and injecting it into the unborn create a Sparker? Did two Sparker parents *always* create a magic-using child?

Nothing went unexplored.

The surviving children were taken away and moved to a location only Locke, Nexes and Balz knew of, to be taught the ways of warfare. The oldest would be approaching eleven now, and Locke often wondered when he'd get the chance to bring them onto the battlefield.

Shadow Sparkers from birth. Imagine their capabilities. Pity we have to wait for their Spark to bloom.

Their major breakthrough had come when Balz himself successfully changed the essence of a Sparker, turning them to the shadow. Something he hadn't done since and refused to even contemplate. Now, he ordered others to do the deed. More weakness.

Ever since, if a powerful Sparker became a nuisance, instead of killing or banishing them, the Order locked them away beneath the university. Those Sparkers who resisted most became their subjects, and thus the Turning Room had been created.

Locke and Balz came to a halt before a nondescript set of double doors. The High Sparker reached out, gripping the handles, hands trembling, and hesitated.

And now we come to the matter at hand. The Turning Room's new guest. It isn't just fear Balz feels, is it?

"Who's in there today?" Locke demanded, when Balz didn't open the door. "Well?"

"Faye du Gerran." Balz didn't turn, didn't open the door. He stood there, stock-still, shoulders hunched. "Your Hands discovered her working with Kade Besem and Bertrand as they plotted against you, Emperor."

"Ah." Locke smiled, the pieces falling into place. Faye du Gerran. It all made sense. "You still hold a flame for her, don't you? Just goes to show, you can't trust anyone in Haltveldt." Locke gripped Balz's shoulder and turned him around. "Anyone can be a traitor in this nation. Anyone. Now, open the doors. I want to see her Turned myself."

Balz's face spasmed, shoulders drooping. The man had clearly hoped to avoid witnessing the Turning, just as he'd desired Locke's visit to be a briefing rather than a prolonged stay.

No such luck. Not with such weakness on display.

Haltveldt needed no fragility, and Locke would hammer it out and reforge wherever he found it. He'd done it with his own droking father, and he could do it with Balz du Regar without losing a second's sleep. He'd do the same to Nexes the next morning before breakfast without spoiling his appetite.

You had to have mettle to be the emperor, and Locke

had enough for three or four of the old bastards.

He glanced at the darkness in human form looming behind him. "Shadow Sparker, come with us."

The doors swung open, silent and smooth, and the emperor strode in, Shadow Sparker at heel. They left Balz behind.

A Sparker in crimson robes spun around, bowing low when he saw who entered the room. He stood beside a vertical slab where they'd bound the woman, Faye, by wrists and ankles, a gag in her mouth to stifle the screams.

Of all the places under the university where the shadows lay, they clung thicker here. They oozed like slime, dripping off the walls and creeping across the marble floor, tendrils of darkness reaching out to the Sparkers, striving to touch the imprisoned woman with her wide, staring eyes and sweat-covered brow.

Glowing glyphs stood out against the polished obsidian slab. They covered it, ancient runes long-forgotten, another gift from the annals of the Cradle. These etchings limited a Sparker's power, cut them off from the magic inside. It meant victims no longer needed to be shielded when Turned. They could still sense their power, no doubt, and stretch for it with all their might, but it lay just out of their grasp.

"Your name?" Locke demanded, glancing at the male Sparker who would Turn du Gerran.

The man's eyes darkened, the light of the Spark replaced by the void. He hadn't become one of the Shadow yet—his head still boasted hair and few of the red cracks and fissures, though his skin looked greyer than it should—but Turning other Sparkers meant it wouldn't be long before he did. The darkness within would corrupt him.

"Ludin," the Sparker whispered, bowing again, taking in Balz and smiling.

Locke studied the woman, eyebrow raised. "Have you begun?"

She glared back, teeth biting down on her gag. Her eyes narrowed when she spotted Balz.

"No, my emperor. She arrived shortly before you did. May I begin now?"

Locke frowned. The man's voice never raised above a hush. Quite annoying really.

"No, leave us." Ludin bowed and swept from the room. Locke appreciated the man's ability to follow orders, even despite his grating voice. "Balz, do it. Now."

Silence. The double doors clicked shut, and yet the High Sparker hadn't moved.

Locke glanced over his shoulder, meeting his old friend's eyes. Hatred lurked behind those bright irises. The Shadow Sparker loomed behind him.

"Do I need to ask again?"

The Shadow Sparkers had given Locke an extra measure of control. A way to cow the Order. Doctrine and dogma tied the mages to the Empire, rather than allow them to seek their own fortunes, but faith could be undermined. Faith could falter. At any time, a High Sparker could decide Locke had pushed the Order too far and usurp him. They had the power, as all of their ilk did.

The Shadow Sparkers limited that possibility.

They belonged to him. No other. The Turning included Spark magic that bound them to Locke. That, combined with the ways he allowed them to indulge their depraved passions, meant they could never betray him.

"Balz..."

Locke took a step forward, and flicked his head over the High Sparker's shoulder, letting him know what lurked in the shadows. Balz followed his stare and paled. His attention snapped back to the emperor, bottom lip trembling. Locke took a breath, then backhanded the pathetic slug.

"You're a mess. Strung out. Unfocused. Making excuses. Because of this *woman*? You knew, since the morning I arrived here, that she was coming here. You'd place her above your nation, your duty? Your *emperor*? Need I remind you what we're attempting here? We're an island, beset by enemies, surrounded by vultures waiting for any sign of weakness, ready to pick our bones clean if we fail. Balz, I cannot allow a moment's hesitation, even a second's doubt. You loved this woman; perhaps you still do. But this is duty. She is a traitor. It doesn't matter if you droked her or you loved her, or even if she bore your bastard child, your loyalty is to me. Understand?"

Balz faltered, fear leeching the colour from his already pale skin, eyes wide in the face of his emperor's cold fury. Being childhood friends wouldn't stop him from seeing Balz Turned like any other Sparker who stepped out of line.

Haltveldt couldn't afford weakness. Not in its Emperor. Not in *anyone* who mattered.

"Yes, Emperor."

Balz raised his shaking fist to his lips, kissed his knuckles then pressed his hand against his heart. To the man's credit, he didn't glance over his shoulder at the looming Shadow Sparker, but the rigid straightness of his posture told Locke he fought against every fibre of his being to keep from doing just that.

"It isn't just her. It's..." He cleared his throat, letting the excuses fall away. "Your word is law."

"Yes." Locke grinned. A cat with all the cream in the world, and an extra dollop to spare. "It is."

"My apologies. It's just that—"

"Actions, Balz. Actions. That's what matter." A lie. Thoughts running through a citizen's head mattered just as much, as did whispered words his Hands always heard. "To think, your childhood sweetheart will be your first, true Turning. No experimental accidents this time. Faye du Gerran your first in all the things that matter. Now, there's irony for you, eh?"

The shadow of a scowl flashed across Balz's face, but he nodded with a gulp, clearly in no mood for gallows' humour. A pity. Locke enjoyed it more than most.

The High Sparker took a heavy step forward, the sound of it like a sepulchre falling closed. Locke moved aside, studying Faye du Gerran's face. Her wide eyes implored Balz, begged him as she sobbed around her gag, limbs straining against their bonds. She shook her head, tears running down her cheeks, but Balz refused to look at her. He stared at the floor beneath her dangling feet. Remembering better times, perhaps, or training his mind to see someone else there, a different Sparker ready for Turning. Some other traitor.

Locke smiled as anger filled the tears falling from Faye's eyes. The shaking of her head grew more defiant as Balz took another slow step forward. Tendons stood rigid on the woman's wrists as she fought in vain, sobs turning to snarls that tore from her throat. The High Sparker raised his head and met Faye's eyes. The thrashing stopped as they stared at each other in silence, a conversation flowing between their stares.

They're Linked! Locke gasped, and his smile deepened. *Oh, this explains everything! Did he know her plans? How could he not, being Linked the way they are...?*

Locke raised a hand, a signal to the Shadow Sparker looming at the rear of the room to stand ready. This could go south. He'd wage his empire on the Shadow Sparker taking down Balz and Faye without too much trouble, but Locke might be caught in the crossfire.

The emperor took a step back, to the edge of the room. He wasn't afraid, just prudent.

Balz's shoulders dropped and the glyphs on the slab glowed so bright they forced back the tendrils of shadow reaching out to grasp Faye. She'd attempted to summon her Spark, thrown everything she had into the action.

And failed.

"I'm sorry," Balz whispered, and raised his hands.

Locke had seen many Turnings over the years; the early failures, the crushing deaths, to the resounding successes. They all involved screaming. Locke recalled each one, so vivid, so delicious, but he wanted more. How he resented that Balz and other Sparkers could *feel* a Turning, not just bear witness. Locke drank in the writhing, the wailing, the jets of coal black magic, but the Sparkers felt it inside them. The curse of his non-magical blood meant a whole world remained closed to him, and it infuriated him to his core.

Despite the gag, Faye's cries filled the room, the muscles in her neck taut, her fingers clawed and her toes curled. The restraints spilled blood as they sawed into her wrists and ankles. The shadows surrounding the room surged, hungry, attracted by the summoning of Balz's Spark. Black devoured the whites of his eyes and he bared his teeth in a rictus grin, his pallor shining through the darkness.

He took another step forward, and Faye slammed against the slab, head twisting this way and that, trying to get away, to somehow escape the Turning.

She wouldn't. They never did.

Glancing over his shoulder, Locke met the gaze of the Shadow Sparker, its blazing black eyes glowing through the miasma surrounding them. He motioned toward it and stood in morbid fascination as it slid forward, utterly inhuman.

They belong to me. No one else.

The Shadow Sparker and the heavy darkness appeared as one, hovering before him. Locke peered up at them, the angry fissures across the Shadow Sparker's skin becoming clear.

"Yes, Emperor?" it croaked, voice like gravel spilling from a sack.

Locke turned away, focusing on Balz and the struggling Faye. "Tell me what you see. Describe it all to me."

The Shadow Sparker licked its lips. "Gladly. You'll see it yourself, Emperor, soon enough, but you won't feel it. Such a pity..."

Faye's muffled screams spoke to some feral instinct inside Locke, exacerbating his annoyance at the Shadow Sparker evading his question. Certain noises had that effect. Before the birth of his son, he'd heard babies wailing as they made their maddening racket, and he'd had no inkling to help, to pick up the child and comfort it. Smothering it with a pillow to cease its crying appealed more, but the first time Locke heard his son, his own flesh and blood, call for help in the way only a child could? The sound compelled him to come to its aid, to do anything in his not-inconsiderable power to make the poor child's tiny world better again.

This soul-splitting scream told him to run.

Locke ignored it, forcing himself to watch the invisible battle raging between Balz and Faye, lovers no more.

"Tell me!" he snapped, thrusting a finger in the Shadow Sparker's face. They belonged to him!

"The colours, the energy inside his body. So terrible, so beautiful." Longing filled the Shadow Sparker's voice, like it wanted to reach out with its Spark and join the battle. Locke always referred to them as 'it' and never learned their names. They weren't human anymore. They were weapons. "The High Sparker has revealed his Spark, and the darkness within. Oh, how sweet it is, how different your world would be if you could taste just a drop of it."

For a moment, Locke forgot one of his subjects spoke to him with such frankness, with such a lack of humility.

"Darkness within. You talk about the Spark as if it's a living thing."

A hiss of a laugh escaped from its emaciated lips. "It is. Pure. Good. Evil. The Spark is all of these things and none, Emperor. A tool for using, some say; does the blade of a knife choose if it's used for cutting bread or flesh? But the Spark, oh, it isn't some creation of ours, is it?"

The screaming continued, and Balz took a staggering step forward.

"What's happening?" Locke asked, his heart hammering with such ferocity in his chest he worried it might burst through his ribcage. He had to know!

"You feel it, don't you? The energy in this room." The Shadow Sparker closed its eyes, shoulders trembling. "Yes, how could you not? A trickle compared to the torrent flooding me, urging me to succumb and let it wash me away. White light shines from the High Sparker's hands, Emperor, and it connects to Faye's Spark. Darkness spreads through the luminosity, and it grows as the High Sparker twists."

A ragged gasp tore from Balz's throat, and he sank to his knees, hands still outstretched. Locke took a half-step forward.

The Shadow Sparker chuckled.

"What is it?" Locke asked, frowning at the monster lurking in the darkness.

"High Sparker Balz feels what he's doing to her." The Shadow Sparker raised a pale, gnarled finger to its temple. "They're Linked, Emperor. The pain I felt on my Turning, I won't ever forget it, and when I use my Spark, I want to feel it again. Cause it. Feed it to the darkness inside me. My Spark appreciates it. After the first taste of corruption? It thirsts for it."

The screaming stopped. Faye leaned forward with such tension that only her restraints stopped her from flopping to the ground. Blood oozed from the angry welts at her wrists and ankles, pooling below her feet. It hissed as steam rose from it, the tendrils snaking their way into Balz.

"He draws on more energy," the Shadow Sparker murmured. "He drinks it in. He pulls on her, on me, but my Spark swats his away. This one is strong. She'll make a fine addition to your army, Emperor. A fine addition."

Crimson tears leaked from Balz's eyes and a pregnant silence fell upon the room. Locke held his breath, afraid to break it, worried that even a sigh would turn the tide of this war between the Sparkers the wrong way. Because of the silence, he heard the whisper, just above the level of hearing, fall from Balz's lips.

"Forgive me..."

Tendrils of black shot from Balz's hands, pulsating and writhing, driving into Faye, slamming her back against the slab. The High Sparker bared his teeth, crawled forward, forcing himself back onto his feet as white lightning forked inside the obsidian thread delving into the stricken woman's vibrating body.

The gas lamps flickered. The room trembled. The Shadow Sparker took an eager step forward, its face tilted back, eyes rolling.

Balz and Faye cried in unison, and the darkness filling the room flooded forward, smothering Locke's vision, swallowing any illumination the lamps offered. Blinded by the shadows, Locke moved backward, sweat dripping down his face, ragged breath pumping his lungs into a frenzy, until he pressed against the too-cold wall. His fingers spread across the clammy bricks. Even they seemed to sweat.

He'd seen Sparkers Turned. He'd watched so many, but the intensity of this one, the heaviness of it, outweighed every one he'd had the pleasure to witness.

A hiss came from somewhere in the darkness. One of satisfaction.

The air popped, and the darkness streamed back, the blue-green light of the gas lamps forcing the shadows away. But they didn't return to the room's corners. They surrounded Balz, who knelt once more, staring with unseeing eyes, and Faye.

She hung limp in her restraints, eyes closed, head lolling. The shadows circled her, pressed against her. Then, they disappeared into her core, seeping under her skin.

Her eyes snapped open, onyx and glowing with malice. The glyphs on the slab pulsated, and the hiss from the Shadow Sparker grew louder.

Shaking, Balz forced himself to his feet, muttering beneath his breath, pointing at the newly created Shadow Sparker.

It wasn't done yet.

A dark miasma formed at the High Sparker's fingertips, growing until it stood at a similar height and width as Faye, then flowed toward her. Snarling, she fought against her restraints, blood streaming from behind the gag where she'd chewed through the material, her lips, gums and tongue like a rabid dog.

The miasma settled over her and throbbed as it settled on her skin like a shroud, covering her from head to toe.

"The Binding," the Shadow Sparker whispered, a mocking smile on its lips. "My favourite part."

Locke didn't expect them to like it. The spell, another of the Cradle's gifts, assured compliance. Unbreakable compliance. It even worked on the non-magical, the reason he trusted the members of his Hand implicitly. He had no doubt the Shadow Sparkers worked to undo the Binding, but no one ever could.

"Faye du Gerran," Balz barked, getting to his feet again and staring up at the woman with black eyes. Clumps of brown hair fell from her head, mixing with the blood on the floor. "With this Binding, do you swear to obey Emperor Locke Dazel, first of his name, placing his bloodline and the needs of Haltveldt above all else?"

A formality. Sparkers liked these kinds of ceremonies and meaningless words. Balz could have told the woman that her actions belonged to the moon for all it mattered. Her agreement meant nothing. The Binding ensured her loyalty.

Faye snarled in response.

"Do you swear to protect Emperor Locke Dazel, first of his name, and his bloodline at all costs, and never do them harm?"

Another snarl.

"With this Binding, it is so." Balz raised his hands, and the miasma settled into Faye's skin, disappearing from sight. "With this Binding, you belong to our Emperor and to Haltveldt." With a ragged sigh, Balz turned, the darkness fading from his eyes, and bowed his head. "It is done."

"The Binding settles on her soul," the Shadow Sparker murmured, making a fist and covering it with its other hand. "Traps it with no escape."

The Shadow Sparker and Balz stared at one another. What passed between them, Locke didn't know. For once, he didn't want to know.

"Balz, get her down and you can start her training today. In fact, you can take her with you. Your time at the Order is at an end."

CHAPTER FOURTEEN

UPRISING

*'Only four of Haltveldt's emperors have suffered assassination,
five if you give credence to the outrageous rumours concerning
our glorious Emperor Locke I's father, which we do not. Still,
it's four too many, and we can never rule out further attempts.'*
- From a debate during the Meeting of Historians. Emperors
killed in the line of 'duty' prove you can't please everyone.

L ocke left High Sparker Balz stewing for a full day
after the events in the Turning Room. He'd already
decided the man's fate, but it amused the emperor
to think of his old friend sweating on his future. He'd ordered Balz to spend time acclimatising Faye du Gerran to
her new role as a weapon of the emperor, and had assigned
the Shadow Sparker present at the Turning to his personal
guard while at the university. The monster had taken to
tracking Balz's movements.

"Where is he now?" Locke asked, ignoring the Sparkers

bowing as he swept through the corridors.

"The Turning Room, Emperor," the Shadow Sparker hissed. "He has spent much of his time there with the woman, du Gerran, since her Turning."

Locke paused, and rounded on the shadow following him, holding up a hand so his retinue stayed away. He stared down the abomination, refusing to let its glittering obsidian eyes cow him.

"Except for when he met the others you spoke of?"

"Yes, Emperor." The Shadow Sparker bowed its head. "They entered the study one by one. Nervous. They did not want to be seen."

Locke resumed his march, making for the lower levels. The time had come to deal with Balz. The Emperor's Hand confirmed what his nose told him. Something stank in the Order of Sparkers, and that stink threatened to spread across his empire.

Insurrections and cells of resistance were nothing new. He'd dealt with them before, but the discovery of treason in the Conclave itself, led by Kade Besem, had exposed evidence of more. The trail of corruption snaked its way into the Order as well.

Locke smirked. He would put it down today by cutting the head off the serpent. Even if Balz had no involvement in sedition, it would send a message to everyone else.

No one in the Order was untouchable. No one.

Locke couldn't see Balz's innocence though. He shared a Link with a proven traitor, and he'd met with other Sparkers, ones who refused to embrace the new ways, in a private study in the night's small hours.

Reaching the stairs to the lower levels, Locke addressed his retinue.

"Leave me."

The Shadow Sparker followed him down the steps—so would members of his Hand, at a discreet distance—but he wanted no other Sparkers near him when he confronted Balz. The shadows lengthened as he descended, thickening, and the sense of being watched increased. The gloom threatened to swallow the flickering blue gaslight, and the temperature rose to become almost oppressive.

Locke ignored it all, focused. Darkness held no fear for him. He'd decided on an elegant solution to Balz. He had no evidence of the man's treason, and a figure of the High Sparker's standing could demand a trial, not to mention the scandal it would cause if the Conclave learned the High Sparker's lover had been involved in Kade's treachery. It would make Locke appear weak. Short-sighted.

Killing him outright appealed, but that brought its own dangers.

Reaching the Turning Room, Locke pushed the doors open. Balz and Faye stood together before the slab, heads lowered in conspiracy. They looked up in unison.

"What are you doing here?" Locke demanded. Faye stepped aside, head bowed, though she peered under her brows through eyes black as pitch.

A shadow crossed the High Sparker's face, twisting his features with hatred, resentment, before settling.

"This is my Order," Balz snapped. He took a breath, as if surprised by his tone. Then he smiled. "I did not expect you, Emperor."

"I can see you didn't," Locke replied, raising an eyebrow and grinning, though malice dripped from his voice. "I'm here to deal with you, Balz, as promised, and put an end to your insolence."

"My insolence?" he croaked, swallowing as if a sour taste flooded his mouth. "My Emperor, forgive me. I don't mean to question you."

"But you did. I told you, rasclart, that you'd do well to spend some time away from the Order, didn't I? Did you think it a joke?" Locke studied him. His skin seemed paler, his eyes duller, his features haggard. "So, you found some backbone at last? You'll need it. Everything you've shown me since I arrived here speaks volumes. The pressures of command have gotten to you, or..." He gazed at Faye, who only had eyes for the High Sparker. "...perhaps you knew what I'd think when I realised you were consorting with traitors."

"Emperor—"

Locke held up a hand, baring his teeth. "I don't care what excuses you've prepared. I've already decided. You're to join Nexes' march north. Today."

An unfortunate death on the road or a 'heroic' one in battle awaits you. A pity, but necessary. For the Empire.

"I'm no longer High Sparker?"

"*'Emperor'*," Locke snarled, his lip curling. "When you speak to me, cur, you address me as 'emperor'. You can keep the title until it finds someone worthier. Someone equipped to lead the Order as Haltveldt marches forward. Savour it. You won't have it long."

Balz gulped. "Your word is my command, Emperor."

"You might still have feelings for Faye du Gerran," Locke smiled, pointing at the woman, "but remember, she is mine. Everyone in this droking building, in this city, in this *nation* is. Remember that on your journey north." He turned to the Shadow Sparker. "We're done here."

It took Locke a moment to realise the rustling sound, like wind disturbing wet leaves, came from the Shadow Sparker. Laughing.

At least it appreciated Locke's plan.

It flowed just behind the emperor's shoulder as he left the Turning room, back into the maze of corridors beneath the university. Letting the door slam shut, Locke took a few steps forward then paused as the lamps flickered. A subtle, quick quiver, but he saw it. The oppressive heat of the underground cooled for a moment.

Then he saw flashes of orange, red and yellow. Sparkers in their bright robes, three of them, appearing in the tunnels ahead as they dropped their concealment charms. Flames of blue-green danced in their hands.

"For the Empire!" one shouted, and a weight collided with Locke from behind and forced him to the ground.

Fire streamed over his head and the Shadow Sparker glided by him, arms stretched wide. The flames arrowing their way through the tunnels turned and surged back, like petals caught in a stream's current, gaining speed until they circled around its upturned palms.

The Shadow Sparker clapped, and the flames spread into a wide curtain. They roared as they swept back from whence they came, more ferocious than before. The heat seared Locke where he lay on the ground, but he couldn't look away.

The flames surged towards the rogue Sparkers, the traitors who had dared to attack their emperor. Two had thrown up a Spark shield and cowered behind it, but the other's reaction came too late. He screamed as the blue-green fire devoured his flesh and turned his bones to ash in a matter of seconds.

Bodies lay dead behind them in the roaring flames—Emperor's Hands and other bright-robed Sparkers, loyal but too weak to make the difference. They'd failed to discover the assassination plot and had paid the ultimate price for their ineptitude.

Striding forward, the Shadow Sparker twisted a finger and the fire converged on the remaining assassins, the magic battering at their shields. Locke scrambled to his feet and gave chase. He wouldn't cower on the floor like a booted dog. He'd stare into the scum's eyes as they died if he could.

Tilting his head, the Shadow Sparker made a fist. Lightning cracked from the ceiling, crashing down on one of the Sparkers cowering behind their shield. She flew backward, head slamming into the stone wall, the crack of breaking bones echoing above the sound of the flames. She died before her corpse hit the ground, glassy eyes meeting Locke's. His lips curled into a smirk.

Heavy doors crashed behind him as Balz skittered out of the Turning Room and into the corridor, the shouts and swirling energy no doubt calling to him. Then again, Locke's old friend didn't seem so surprised. The emperor tore his eyes away and focused on the last of his attackers instead.

Once he'd been dealt with, he'd deal with Balz.

The remaining Sparker cowered behind his shield,

the Shadow Sparker looming over him like a cat trapping a mouse.

"Why?" Locke breathed, glaring down at the peon struggling to maintain his shield. Blood trickled from the Sparker's nostrils and ears, staining his gritted teeth.

"You betrayed the Order," he gasped, shoulder slumping as his shield diminished. "You betrayed the Empire with this evil."

Locke glanced at the Shadow Sparker, who had eyes only for his victim, a slim smile on its face, head cocked to the side as if it were making a study of defeat. A spider considering a fly before going in for the kill.

"No." Locke tilted his chin, meeting the Sparker's eyes as he had promised himself he would. "I make the Order and Haltveldt stronger."

The emperor made a fist, and the Shadow Sparker grinned.

A thick, black miasma smothered the ailing Sparker, who cried out in pain and dropped to his back, his shield, his Spark, his life finished in the blink of an eye. Another jet of black surged from the Shadow Sparker, an inky tendril of death, and attached itself to the stricken Sparker's face, entering through his nostrils, eyes, ears and mouth.

Locke couldn't look away. He'd never seen Evisceration performed with such speed or skill.

The victim's body convulsed with a strangled cry. The hood covering his head fell back, revealing a shock of thick, red hair. It turned white in an instant, skin fading and cracking like parchment as the Evisceration took hold.

Balz had explained it to him once, how the 'forbidden

magic' would feed upon all the energy inside the body, turn it into a husk, before disintegrating entirely if a mage proved powerful enough to do so.

This Shadow Sparker didn't drain its victim; its Spark had become a living, writhing entity, entering the rebel Sparker's body and devouring it from the inside.

Locke's eyes widened. The inky tendril left the Sparker's body, returning to the Shadow Sparker, leaving an oozing pile of slime and melted bones on the floor, bound in steaming, orange robes. Every essence of energy and life had been stripped away.

The Shadow Sparker shuddered and licked its lips. The darkness wreathed around it, the surrounding air stained darker. Locke suppressed the urge to take a step back.

It's for the greater good. We need this. And I'd be dead without them.

Returning to the present, Locke glanced over his shoulder at Balz. A moment's doubt. He could spare a moment's doubt and no more.

Locke met the Shadow Sparker's eyes. "Shield him."

Balz reacted with surprising speed, flames erupting from his palms, but the Shadow Sparker moved quicker. A shimmering field of white, tinged with black, leapt from its hands and wrapped itself around Balz, forcing him to his knees. With a gasp and squeal of frustration, the fire spluttered out. The Shadow Sparker raised a single finger, and Balz sank to his knees, fear blooming across his features. His jaws bulged. Locke's saviour had gagged him.

Such speed, such precision. If they ever decided to rule themselves... No, I've Bound them. They're mine. Mine!

Locke studied Balz, then spat on the floor. He'd planned to replace him, yes, but for the good of the Empire. Had one of his oldest friends conspired against him? His gut said yes, and, as his mother had always said, when in doubt, go with the feeling in your stones.

She had a turn of phrase to rival a sailor.

"Balz," Locke snapped, shoving his doubt into the pit of his stomach and replacing it with icy fury. "You've been with me since the beginning. The beginning, Balz. You've betrayed Haltveldt, betrayed me like no other has, and you'll pay the ultimate price. Officially, you'll have died in the crossfire of a failed assassination attempt. But in reality?" Locke bared his teeth. "Well. Be happy you're leaving here with your droking life."

Balz mumbled, his face red. Locke thought he tried to say, "Emperor..."

Faye du Gerran lurked behind Locke, eyes wide as she took in the carnage, chest rising and falling with quick breaths. Locke crooked a finger at her, and she strode into Balz's view, his skin losing any colour it still held as he wept in silence.

"Take him to the Turning Room and Bind him," Locke commanded. Faye's cracking lips split, blood running down her chin as she grinned a wide grin. "I assume you can Turn him yourself? My friend here will watch your progress. Wait for him."

Balz writhed against his bonds, face turning red, but he couldn't move, and he made no sound. Faye raised her hand, and he lifted from the ground, tears wetting his cheeks as he disappeared into the shadows.

A meeting with his worst nightmare. Just desserts.

Locke glared at the space his 'old friend' had occupied, then turned to the Shadow Sparker.

"Once he's Turned, have him meet Nexes on the march north. Faye will join him, as will a member of my Hand, a Sparker, who'll keep an eye on them and ensure there aren't any more mistakes. I want them both out of my Order, even if they're Bound. They'll deliver a message to our school. A member of the Hand will give you the details."

The Shadow Sparker inclined its head, calm after the chaos. "He will make a fine addition to our legion, Emperor."

Locke studied the weapon, raising an eyebrow. "You. You'll need a name if you're going to become my personal bodyguard after today. I can't just call you 'It'. How about Byar, after the mighty warrior and scourge of the elves?"

Byar. Yes, the citizens will like that. Make the Shadow Sparkers appear more heroic in their eyes. Perhaps we can even suggest this one is the *Byar reborn. Oh, that will do nicely.*

The Shadow Sparker met Locke's stare, eyes glittering with malice in the shadows, and shrugged.

"You honour me, Emperor, and you may call me what you wish if you continue to feed my Spark. 'Byar' is as good as any name."

Locke turned away, side-stepping the slime and charred bodies on the floor, sparing a glance for the deceased members of his Hand on the ground.

Fools. They should know better than anyone that you can't drop your guard. Not in Haltveldt. Not until I control everything and beyond.

"I'll wait outside. My Hands will see me safe topside.

No one will dare attack me again after this failure. Join me once the Turning is done, and make sure the Binding has no loopholes. Balz is the message I want delivered: 'See what happens when you cross Emperor Locke, First of his Name.'"

Byar nodded and slid away, a silent shadow of death. Balz's screams followed Locke out of the underbelly of the Order. Byar removed the gag to revel in the cries.

Locke's retinue joined him once he reached the ground floor. He whispered words to his agents, orders to root out Sparkers loyal to Balz. A few quick words about assassins set the place abuzz, a hive of activity. Despite his bold words to Byar, Locke didn't feel safe until the doors of his carriage closed behind him and the Shadow Sparker returned, confirming that Balz's sentence had been carried out. Then, and only then, did he allow himself one small sigh of relief, one moment of trembling hands, one silent prayer to Raas. Then, he pulled himself together.

He had an Empire to rule.

Locke glanced around his private quarters. Stray shafts of grey light poured in from the windows where the curtains weren't drawn. The main chamber stood empty, his wife and son asleep already. He took in the chairs and tables, the ornate mirrors, the books and ornaments, and revelled in the normalcy for a moment.

He hadn't spent a moment alone since he awoke in the morning, and it wasn't every day he experienced an attempt on his life.

Locke left Byar at the entrance to his private apartments in the palace. A guard stood watch at every door, every window, in every room except for this one and the bedrooms. Guards lurked in the gardens outside the emperor's private rooms, on the ramparts, in the halls, and a member of the Hand watched *them*.

He'd doubled security since the birth of his son and would increase it further after the attack at the Order and Balz's betrayal. Investigations would commence, of course. Questions would be levelled at higher ranking members of the Hand for not weeding out such treachery before it became a threat.

It wasn't all bad. Locke would blame foreign nations for the plot, giving Haltveldt a ready-made enemy once the Empire had taken care of the Banished.

Strength. Always strength, and there's nothing stronger than attacking from the front foot. Avastia and their elves and human sympathisers. I'll point the finger at them.

Locke moved into the bedroom, easing the doors closed behind him. His wife, Lydia, slept beside the crib, no doubt exhausted from minding the baby all day. Soon, they'd turn their attention to creating another child, another member of Locke's dynasty, but for now she could rest, recover, and raise his son.

His heir.

Locke crossed the room, and stood above the crib, smiling down at the boy who, one day, the people of Haltveldt would proclaim as Emperor Locke II. Ruler of a united Haltveldt, from the Sea of Storms to the Peaks of Eternity. Perhaps ruler of Octaria, Avastia and Velen too.

Greedy. Locke chuckled. *And foolish. One will do, and I must leave my son with someone to conquer, a nation for him to war with and secure his legacy, to ensure the continued safety of Haltveldt.*

Leaning into the crib, Locke brushed his lips against his son's forehead, studied his thick golden hair, and smiled.

"For you," he whispered, prodding his son's little hand with his thumb. The boy, still sleeping, grabbed it with all his tiny fingers and squeezed. "I do this all for you."

Pulling his thumb free, Locke sank into his armchair beside the bed and poured himself a large glass of red wine. His hand shook just a touch, an after effect from the attack. Now that he was home, he could decide who would take Balz's place as High Sparker.

His old friend's Turning—his death, as far as anyone else in Haltveldt knew—would prove unfortunate. But, like so much else, necessary.

Chapter Fifteen

To Lose a Hand

'It changed me, it did. As much as it did to the one being Turned. Felt dirty, deep inside and out, and no matter how much I scrubbed, I couldn't come clean. But... I wanted more. To do it again and again and again. I had to run, had to leave. Death will be a blessing.' - A rogue Sparker from Balz's inner circle, caught in Gallavan's Seat by the Emperor's Hands, confessing before his execution. Little did he know he'd find himself in the Turning Room... The fool should have known better.

Amico had been her name once. She used it like a cowl now, to protect her true identity. A hand of the emperor. In her heart, she knew she'd never be that person again. She had been chosen to serve Haltveldt, to serve Emperor Locke, first of his name.

Privileged. Honoured.

The Sparker, Fisher, owed himself to Locke too. They often liaised. Now, they lurked on an outcropping overlooking Adhraas from the south side, studying the Banished horde. They had been there for days as the procession made its way through the now-abandoned port town.

"Looks like that's the last of them." Fisher spat on the ground. "Stragglers, nothing more. How many would you say, in total?"

Amico studied Fisher. A shrewd man with a wicked sense of humour, and a healthy amount of loyalty to Emperor Locke and Haltveldt. He boasted a Link with two others in the capital, which meant his presence was ideal for scouting missions.

"Five hundred thousand, at least. Perhaps a little more." Amico rubbed at the side of her nose. "About two thirds of those able to fight, I'd wager."

Fisher whistled. "That's a lot of old folk and children to bring along on an invasion. Surely they'd leave them behind."

Amico shrugged. "They're barbarians. Who knows why they do anything? One thing's clear."

"And that is?"

"The Banished don't intend on going back." She pointed as the last stragglers disappeared from sight. A small party of elderly Banished helped along one even more ancient than themselves. "They intend on moving into Haltveldt permanently."

"Not if the emperor has anything to say about it," Fisher grinned.

"Or Nexes. His army marches north as we speak. The Banished are moving south and west, away from Sea's Keep and the Spring Haven-Willow road. Lucky. Almost like they're *trying* to avoid the Haltveldtian army. Send word to the capital with their numbers and intended path and get messages to Gallavan's Seat. They're heading that way."

"Lake Circa."

Amico narrowed her eyes. "What?"

"Lake Circa. It's massive, a source of water, and the Forest of Willows is close. Not a bad place to make a stand and hold, is it?"

Amico considered his words. They rang true. It had everything an army would need, never mind an entire horde—wildlife, wood, water.

"Very good. Send word."

Fisher's eyes glazed over as he communicated inside his mind, a soft smile settling on his lips as he spoke into his Link. People like Amico had no one like that. They were trained to go without, and for a good reason. If she wanted to get at a fellow like Fisher, she'd go after the Sparker he Linked with and turn the screw. Connections meant weakness.

"Done." Fisher rubbed at his arms. "Bloody cold up here, isn't it?"

He stretched a hand out and flames sprung from his fingers.

Amico rolled her eyes. "It's the sea on both sides. Wind coming in. Plus, we're in the north, so—"

Her look of exasperation saved her life. A surge of lightning plunged from the sky, heading for their position. She dove out of the way as it exploded against Fisher's skull, sending charred chunks of the Sparker in all directions, leaving just burned ground and smoke where he stood. The flash blinded Amico, and she crawled away, coughing, blinking.

Fisher had used his magic, then the bolt came.

An attack? A Sparker attack?

Amico's hand slid over the edge of the outcropping, and she almost tumbled off the cliff. Freezing, she closed her eyes, and waited for the brightness behind her eyelids to fade.

The Banished... Had they sent the lightning bolt? She gagged, the stench of cooked flesh gathering in her nostrils, and a warm liquid trickled down her face. Bits of Fisher... His blood...

A shout reached her ears, and the clatter of hooves. It came from the direction of Adhraas.

Opening her eyes, squinting through the stinging haze of light, Amico winced as riders pointed up at the funnel of smoke rising behind her. Four of them.

Not Banished.

"I need to tell the Emperor," she croaked, lights flashing in her vision. "There's more than just Banished out here, and they have the Spark. Drok!"

She staggered to her feet and stumbled forward as a sharp pain knocked the wind from her lungs, lancing through her shoulder blade and chest on the right side. Frowning, she glanced down at the silver arrowhead poking through her travelling leathers.

Numbness spread through her chest. Without thinking, she raised a finger and tapped the metal. She didn't recognise its type. It caught the sun and glittered, and her blood didn't appear to stain it.

"Pretty..."

The word didn't seem to come from her mouth, but it

did. A bizarre, detached thought, creating itself without her agreement.

She fell forward when a second arrow poked its head through her ribs, hitting her like a horse barging into her side. Amico fell on her face, blood pooling beneath her, and listened to the clatter of hooves faltering below.

The riders had dismounted and were climbing to her position. They wanted her alive.

Unable to move from her front, Amico gritted her teeth as she forced a hand toward her belt, and the herbs she kept there. Every one of the Emperor's Hands had the same fallback, just in case.

A harsh laugh came from behind, and boots slammed down beside her face, a cold blade pressed against the nape of her neck.

Amico wouldn't be able to warn her emperor, but she wouldn't talk. She'd *never* do that.

Screaming, she rammed the herbs in her mouth and swallowed, her saliva foaming as soon as the poison mixed with it.

Trembling, blood streaming from her eyes and ears, Amico tried to laugh at the riders' shouts of dismay. Mysterious killers who could use magic, dressed in armour of black and crimson with the emblem of an eye fixed to their chests, following the Banished out of their lands. They had wanted a prisoner.

When Amico's limbs stopped convulsing, they had nothing but a corpse.

Chapter Sixteen

WHERE THE WILLOWS GROW

'I'm a Sea's Keep girl myself, but if there's one other place I'd live in the whole of Haltveldt, it'd be Willow. Drugs, drink, gambling, fighting, men, women or anything that takes your fancy... It's all there, and it's my kind of town.' - Willow has a certain reputation in Haltveldt. A well-earned one.

Calene swayed with the laboured lurch of her tired mount, throwing dark looks at her companions' backs. Brina took the lead, silent and unwilling to engage, a complete change from how she'd been before they'd been separated in the Forest of Willows.

The elf had barely muttered an audible sound in three days and had gone missing for an unusual amount of time.

She wouldn't let Calene in. She'd ranged off on a couple of occasions, whenever Calene tried to question her, only to return a few hours later, sullen and quiet.

Vettigan didn't seem aware or appear to care. He slumped in his saddle, oblivious to the driving rain assaulting them through the canopy, then to the heat turning them from soaked to damp and itchy as they moved south. Any time Calene engaged him in conversation, he whispered paranoia and bile—"That elf has dark designs on us, mark my words. Why else would she take off for so long and refuse to say why? Something happened back there. You know it, I know it, Raas himself knows it"—or sought to dissuade Calene from searching for her childhood home—"There's nothing for us there but pain. Especially for you. There's no curing this. You must see that. Let's flee before it's too late! Velen... Now there's a land I'd love to see..."

The repetition started to wear on her, like itching a scab raw.

So, Calene hung back, watching the rear, though in truth they'd come across few travellers through the forest, and fewer threats. Anyone they'd met, Brina and Vettigan left the talking to her, the former melting into the trees, the latter becoming a macabre and silent spectre at Calene's shoulder, glowering at strangers with malice in his eyes.

Most people journeying north to the major cities of Sea's Keep and Gallavan's Seat found passage by boat. Anyone on the road stopped at Willow and skirted the forest, sticking to the main causeways. The lack of anyone else to talk to only increased her frustration; her jaw ached from how hard she clenched it. Calene thought she might have to start sleeping with a piece of wood jammed in her mouth to keep from grinding her teeth.

She needed a break. A break from the road, from the sulking, sullen bitterness. A moment alone, a few moments, with a drink in her hand to forget the horrors of Solitude and bring some order to her thoughts about Brina and Vettigan.

Willow presented the perfect opportunity. She could leave the other two to their personal pits of despair for a night and venture alone in the guise of searching for supplies and information. A chance to get away from Vettigan's darkness and Brina's increasingly confusing glances. She couldn't bring them with her, after all. An elf and a malignant ex-Sparker prone to outbursts of violence wouldn't suit the city.

Up ahead, Brina glanced over her shoulder, but looked away when their eyes met. They'd grown closer than ever on the road from Adhraas—talking, laughing, riding alongside one another—but since the elf's scouting trip, she'd turned cold. Shutting her out.

And yet, still protected her fiercely. Sure, she'd vanish the moment they crossed a traveller, but Calene had no doubt she watched and waited, coiled to strike. When they were alone, she refused to leave Calene's side, never allowed her off the beaten path unescorted, even to relieve herself!

At night, Brina would set up close to her, always between Calene and Vettigan, watching from the corner of her eyes as she tried to sleep. Every now and then, their eyes would meet, and Brina would open her mouth to say something, like she had words on the tip of her tongue she couldn't force out. Then she sealed her lips, scowling and looking away.

Calene yearned to reach out and touch her shoulder, to tell her she would listen if Brina would only tell her what bothered her. But every time Calene decided to, a sinking feeling in her gut made her stop, a nagging doubt tormenting her, insisting that nothing existed between her and Brina, except in her head.

Yes, she needed a break. From all of it.

Getting to Willow alone would prove tricky. Brina would no doubt try to follow, but she'd figure it out.

If it came to it, she'd use her Spark, just for a moment, and tie the elf up with bonds of air, stuff her mouth with it too, leave her and Vettigan trussed up in a ditch somewhere. Perhaps up a tree, safe and sound, off the road and out of sight. Calene let a dark chuckle escape her lips, picturing the angry, silent pair staring at her, helpless, as she hoisted them up into the branches above the road, a pair of malevolent owls, unable to hoot or flap their wings. Left there until Calene summoned the willpower to deal with them after a night or two's revelry in Willow.

Could she do it? She bit her lip. Putting aside the fact they couldn't eat or drink tied up like that, Calene still hadn't used her Spark since fleeing Solitude. The Emperor's Hand lurked everywhere, especially in the city.

And how could she trust it? That living thing inside her, with motives all its own?

Without thinking, she prodded the old Link she'd shared with Zanna and felt pure nothingness. It wasn't like grasping for an object in the dark and missing; more like stumbling forward as she tried to lean against a familiar wall that had vanished. The emptiness in her mind had a shape, a tangible absence that would remain unfilled.

Out of instinct, Calene brushed against Vettigan's Link and pulled away, shivering. She'd given it the merest of brushes, but goosebumps exploded across her skin and cold knives plunged into her stomach, the ice spreading into her chest.

Ahead, Vettigan half-turned in his saddle, then looked away, shoulders slumping. He'd felt her brush against the Link but couldn't bring himself to comment on it. To warn her away or to ask her to try again, to plunge past the layer of filth and corruption that lay on the surface and re-establish the bond that had meant so droking much to them both over the years.

Calene bit her tongue to keep from screaming. So much distance lay between her and her companions now. Too much to bridge, perhaps. A canyon of hurt dividing her and Vettigan, a valley of unspoken words keeping her from Brina.

After leaving Solitude, Calene had tried to harden her heart towards her companions, attempting to build thick walls around the torrent of emotions she felt for them both, but she couldn't. It wasn't her. Impulses drove her. They always had. Sometimes for good, often for ill, but she couldn't change.

Up ahead, Brina swayed in her saddle, hips moving from side to side. Her mind went back to when they'd travelled to Solitude, when they'd shared glances and smiles. On the cart, they'd rode in the front seat, fingertips brushing against each other's, knees and thighs touching. And when they spoke, Calene felt at ease, despite the constant warmth in her cheeks and twist in her stomach.

She recalled the elf's fingers against her thigh when she examined the slash she'd taken against the Banished. Her sudden, fierce grin when Calene made her laugh. The way her fire-red braid swayed when she walked. Those emerald eyes, so bright when—

Stop, stop, stop! That doesn't help. Not that anything's going to happen now anyway. I'd get more comfort out of a rock...

Everything had changed after the droking Forest of Willows, and Calene had no idea why. That frustrated her the most.

Road markers loomed at the roadside ahead. Calene welcomed the chance to tear her eyes from her companion's backs as the words came into view. Each time they'd passed a sign, she'd sat in her saddle a little straighter, urged her mount on a fraction more. Twenty miles had shrunk to fifteen, then ten, eight... Now it read two.

Close enough to leave the chuckle twins behind.

"Wait!" Calene cried, pulling her horse to a halt and glancing around. The road stood empty, with little sign of anyone passing this way in the last few hours, the marks in the muddy ground hardened by the sun. "We need to talk."

Brina swooped around without hesitation, trotting back to Calene like she'd expected to be given orders, or like she desperately wanted to hear her voice. Calene dismissed the notion as fanciful. Vettigan continued on a few steps until his mount seemed to run out of steam and come to a shuddering stop.

"What is it?" he called, without turning around.

"God's teeth, I'm not going to say it to your droking

back, Vettigan," Calene snapped, before drawing a breath.

He's not himself. You can't understand what he's been through, what he's still *going through. Remember that.*

Calene told herself those exact words with such frequency they'd become a mantra. She'd started saying it to calm herself down, to remind herself of the bigger picture, but godsrot if they didn't make her even angrier now.

Instead, she closed her eyes and counted to ten, hoping Vettigan would decide to stop sulking.

When Calene reached five, she heard the slow clip-clop of hooves as Vettigan's mount carried him towards their merry little party. She kept counting until she reached ten. Just in case.

"What is it?" Vettigan muttered, as she opened her eyes.

She eyed them both and grinned, hoping to start their conversation from a point of civility. Instead, Vettigan flinched from the look on her face.

Why do folk droking react like that? Raas give me strength!

The words from a conversation spoken only weeks before came back to her, from a simpler time, when none of this misfortune had befallen them. When Vettigan had still been Vettigan.

It's because your 'grin' resembles a lioness baring her teeth.

They'd spoken through their Link, as they often did, revelling in the comfort of the safe space in each other's minds.

"Do you remember that place in Seke village, Vettigan? It all seems so long ago now, doesn't it?"

Her old friend blinked, confused at her opening gambit, before a small smile spread across his lips. For a moment, despite his hard-bitten, haggard appearance, the old Vettigan revealed himself.

"Aye. The Stubborn Mule with its ornery arse of an innkeeper. If there was ever a publican and a tavern went hand-in-glove, that was it."

Calene nodded, trying to force a smile of her own. The meal they'd shared before discovering Tilo had been the last time she'd felt happy. The last time things had been normal. "Who knew what Raas had in store for us, eh?"

Vettigan chuckled. "Raas can go drok himself. Can't deny he has a sense of humour though. A twisted one."

Brina cleared her throat. "*Thiemea.* Do we really have to stop for you two to reminisce about old times? Willow is two miles away; we can be there before nightfall."

Vettigan glowered at the elf, the vestiges of the man Calene remembered sliding away behind his walls of bitterness. She sighed. They all needed a break from one another, but she couldn't leave him to his own devices when she went into the city. Like it or not, Vettigan needed a minder, and she was droked if it was going to be her.

"About that." Calene set her jaw and tilted her chin. "I'm going into Willow alone."

"You're what?" Brina breathed, voice as heavy as a mountain.

"You're leaving me with *her*?" Vettigan cried, face screwed up so tight each and every line stood out in his yellowed skin, like someone had etched a map of Haltveldt across his flesh.

"There's no point arguing with me, I've made up my mind," Calene replied, crossing her arms.

"Oh, she's 'made up her mind.'" Brina almost pouted as she glanced at Vettigan. "Isn't that nice?"

"Mother makes decisions for us all, it seems," he grumbled, squeezing the reins in his hands. "Need I remind you I've almost a century on you, girl?"

"Well, isn't it nice to see you two finally getting along?" Calene shoved a finger in Brina's face. "You're a droking elf, if you'd forgotten." She turned to Vettigan. "And the last time we came across a group of people in this Raas-forsaken land, *you* tried to kill them. Droking succeeded too. Do you think you're the wisest people to bring into a city teeming with soldiers, slavers and Janna knows what else? I certainly don't!"

"Why go there at all?" Vettigan muttered, giving her a dark glance. "Aren't you dead set on returning to your family home? Why not keep moving?"

Brina remained silent, though her eyes burned with the heat of a thousand suns.

"Because I want to know the lay of the land. Where's the Empire's armies? Are they marching north? What news from Spring Haven?" Calene held out a hand and counted on her fingers. "Food. Fresh clothes. Blankets. Fodder for the horses. Need I go on?"

"Need I remind you, you're a Sparker?" Brina asked, raising her eyebrows. "And that your eyes give you away? There might be people looking for you."

Calene had anticipated the question and schooled her voice to make it sound like she hadn't rehearsed the answer.

"There's such a thing as hoods, you know?" A little snark helped. It always helped, or so Calene told herself. "Look, we need supplies, or do you mean for us to get all the way to my parent's old home..." She could never call it her home. Never again. "...all the way to Spring Haven, or wherever the drok you're going, with just rainwater and leaves to eat? Someone has to go into Willow, and I'm the safest person. I can keep my eyes down." She pointed at Brina. "But as soon as someone catches onto the fact you're an elf, or you see a slave train, it's over. And, no offence Vettigan, but do you trust him going into a city packed with all kinds of folk? God's teeth, elf, I certainly don't!"

"No offence taken," her old friend grumbled, in a tone that suggested he had, indeed, taken offence.

Calene glared at Brina, daring her to argue, willing her to snap back at her. They needed to argue. Angry words might break the dam holding them back. Just one crack would do it, and the unspoken truths would become a wave.

"Fine." Brina scowled, throwing up her hands. Calene tried to mask her disappointment at the elf agreeing without putting up a fight. "But I'm coming as close to the city walls as I can. If you run into trouble, flee and find me. Right?"

"Ah, you really do care!" Calene turned to Vettigan. "Anything from you?"

He sighed, squeezing the bridge of his nose. "No, you're right. As much as I'd enjoy a warm fire, a mug of wine and a game of clankte, I can't trust myself in there, and you're correct not to either."

"Vettigan, look, I'm sorry, but—"

He held his palms up, the scowl he seemed to permanently wear slipping. "Calene, it's fine. Truly. I'd make the same decision in your boots."

"I'll fix you, Vettigan." She reached out and squeezed his shoulder. "You know that, right?"

He smiled, sadness tugging at the corners. "I know you'll try."

What could Calene say to that? Dismounting, and grimacing from the dead pain spreading in her glutes, she pulled her money pouch from the saddlebag, and handed the reins to Brina. Money in her pocket, hood raised, sword at her hip and, in the most desperate of situations, the Spark in her soul.

What else did she need?

"I'll go the rest of the way on foot. Raas knows my arse could do with a break from the saddle. Follow me in a while, but don't come so close the city guard can see you from the walls." She glanced at them both, one more time, eyes lingering for a touch longer on Brina's. "Try not to tear each other's droking throats out, yeah?"

With that, she strode away, the road curving into a heavily forested area. Already, her steps seemed a little lighter, and the ache in her buttocks lessened.

Following the path, the trees melted away and she smiled, finding herself at the top of a rise leading down into Willow. Travellers in groups of two and three passed beneath her, people scurrying toward the city before nightfall, and the high red walls of Willow jutted out of the plains. The first of the night-time gas lamps spluttered to life as she took in the sight of the domes and towers rearing behind the battlements. Bells rang, six times in all, the Tower of

Belti announcing the coming of evening. The setting sun shone off the golden, domed roof of the Patriarch's palace, now the home of Willow's Quorum who reported directly to Emperor Locke, headed by whoever called himself Patriarch these days.

Calene scowled at that, but otherwise she welcomed the site. She hadn't visited Willow in too long.

The echo of horse hooves made her spin, hand falling to the pommel to her sword, instincts reaching for her Spark.

Brina approached, Vettigan a ways back, leading her horse.

"I thought I told you to stay behind?" Calene snapped, taking an angry step forward.

"I know, I know," Brina replied, a surprising lack of heat in her voice. "I'm not coming, but I wanted to... I needed to..."

Something snapped inside Calene. For days, weeks—ever since she'd known the damned elf!—Brina had kept her secrets, but since the scouting trip she'd pushed her away as she thought they were growing closer. She'd had enough of it.

"Want what? Need what? Come on, out with it." Calene bared her teeth, hissing through the gaps between them. "It's always the same with you. You can criticise, get your droking opinion across when you think we should go somewhere, or I'm doing something wrong, but when you want to talk... You've barely said two droking words to me since you scouted back in the forest and, now I'm about to go out alone for a while, you're full of chat. What is it then? Come on!"

For a moment, Brina's face hardened, and Calene braced herself for a scrap. Punches could sort out issues where words couldn't. If she were honest, she welcomed it. To her surprise, the elf's expression crumpled, and she nodded. *Nodded!*

"You're right, I'm sorry."

Calene almost dropped to the mud in shock. An admission of wrongness *and* an apology! She glanced around, expecting the ground to drop away and the Riders of the Underworld to emerge on their black dogs of war, terrible trumpets signalling the end of days.

"When you come back, we'll talk. I'll tell you everything. I promise."

A promise too. Well, drok me.

Calene met her eyes. Despite the elf's words, she couldn't bring herself to believe it. "We'll see, won't we? We'll see."

"I want to kill the emperor," Brina blurted out, lifting an arm as Calene stalked away. "No, I'm *going* to kill him, and I want your help. Please."

Calene tried to stop herself laughing, she really did, but it escaped before she could trap it. Brina's scowl did nothing to wipe away the surprising amount of hurt colouring her face.

"I'm sorry," Calene insisted, grabbing Brina's hand, fingers tracing the thick calluses on the elf's palms. Neither pulled away. "You took me by surprise. Killing the Emperor. Is that all? Yeah, let's swing by Spring Haven, see the sights, kill droking Locke while we're at it. We can have it done by sunset and spend the evening carousing at the docks."

"You know it has to be done." Brina still hadn't pulled her hand free. "I have to do this."

"You *have* to? Why? Tell me."

The elf dropped her eyes. "When you return. I—"

"Promise. I know." Calene glanced at their hands, locked together. "Is that the only reason you want me to come back and stay with you? To help you kill the most powerful man in Haltveldt?"

For once, Vettigan had exercised sound judgement and kept his distance. Calene and Brina stood there, hand in hand, frowning down at their fingers, oblivious to the travellers hurrying along the road beneath them, and to the city on the horizon.

Say it. Say anything. Damn it, Brina, stop holding it all inside!

"You're a Sparker," Brina muttered, her tone hollow, "and you know the city. I... need you. For that."

Calene pulled her hand away. For a moment, the elf's fingers twitched, reaching in vain, but then she let her hand fall.

"Fair enough," Calene breathed, turning away before the tears stinging her eyes fell. "See you when I get back."

If I come back.

The thought hadn't occurred to Calene before now. Vettigan had said it. Even the Sparkers they'd met in Adhraas. Why not go it alone? What kept her in Haltveldt? She told herself her friends kept her from fleeing; saving Vettigan's soul, making...something...with Brina, and rallying the Sparkers who shared her beliefs in the old ways against the Empire.

But now? Walking away, descending the path from the forest's edge onto the road to Willow? Alone? It all didn't seem to matter as much.

Calene shook her head, tried to clear it. No. She couldn't abandon her friends. Vettigan needed her, not that he'd ever admit it, and Brina needed her too, just not in the way Calene wanted her to.

Reaching the road, Calene merged in with the travellers, pulling her hood lower over her face and hiding the sword at her hip. It wasn't illegal to carry a weapon here like it was in Protector's Watch or Prosper, but she didn't want to draw attention. Just another traveller on the road to Willow for work or fun. Maybe both.

She couldn't help herself though. Craning her neck, Calene found the shape of Brina watching from above. Then, the elf stepped back, melting into the trees. As goodbyes go, it could have gone a lot better.

Still, it could have been worse.

Willow loomed before her, the sounds of the city reaching her ears, stone walls blocking out the heavily constructed skyline. Its name had always made Calene laugh. There wasn't a green spot in the entire city, not even a single blade of grass.

Folk said it got its name from the nearby forest, though just as many argued the opposite. Whatever its origins, Willow offered many things to make up for its lack of nature. A thriving nightlife filled with drinking, gambling and music met a sprawl geared for business, both legal and illicit. Trade prospered alongside drugs and prostitution, both methods of making money working alongside each other. A merchant could close a deal over a game of clankte and a bottle of spiced rum before choosing a night of passion with any gender of their choice in the same inn. The Merchants Guild of Willow didn't believe in forcing their patrons to travel far to meet their wants and needs.

Calene hadn't visited in some time. She'd always looked forward to any excuse to visit the famous red walls and golden domes, though Order business brought her there more often than not. Rogue Sparkers, tired of their lives—more accurately, tired of the Order's dogma—often went to ground in Willow. The Merchants Guild weren't the only power there; alliances of thieves, assassins and fighters jockeyed to take their place as the city's preeminent power, and all of them had plenty to offer a Sparker who yearned for the wilder side of life.

They've competition now, what with the abolishment of the Laws and the Shadow Sparkers. The emperor's made a home for rogue Sparkers, right in the heart of the Empire, hasn't he? Droking rasclart.

Calene passed through the gate, past the guards, who only gave her the most cursory of glances as she passed. Trouble had the habit of sorting itself out within the city walls, and if they checked everyone seeking passage, the roads would be filled from morning till night with angry folk pushing and shoving their way to the front.

Glancing at a guard from beneath her hood, Calene offered a tight smile then turned away. A figure walked by, face covered by a thin, crimson veil that obscured their features. Calene kept moving, hackles rising. She'd stared whoever it was full in the face and, now she thought about it, she wasn't sure the guard hadn't seen her purple eyes either. She picked up her pace, hoping the guards would just wave her through like they'd done with every other droker so far.

"Here!" one of them called, just as Calene strode past him. "Wait! Come back so I can get a proper look at you."

Calene took a step forward, then another.

"Oi! My mate said stop! Don't take another droking step!"

Grumbles from the waiting travellers followed the second guard's orders.

Drok! Calene turned her eyes toward the darkening sky. *Raas, if I ever lay my hands on you...*

She came to a stop, and breathed in. No big trouble, she'd whisper to them. Just a Sparker on a secret mission from the Order. But then they'd ask her name, verify it with the Quorum in the Patriarch's Palace. Make her go there, probably. Someone with a Link to a Sparker in Spring Haven would tell the capital they had Calene Alpenwood visiting in Willow, and the command would quickly come to detain her. The emperor had sent Ganton, Zal and the Shadow Sparkers after her already.

Drok!

"Turn around," shouted the first guard. "No need for any trouble. Now, let's get a proper look at you."

Calene ground her teeth. Coming to Willow had been a mistake.

Chapter Seventeen

A City of Opportunity

'Willow. They add coin to our coffers, make no mistake.
Plenty of it too. But sometimes, I wonder if having them
as part of the Empire is worth the hassle.' – From the
unpublished memoirs of Emperor Edum Dazel, Locke's
father, entitled 'The Trouble with Haltveldt'.

"Gods' teeth, I said stop," the guard barked, voice like two stone blocks grinding together, "and turn around. Now!"

"Beg pardon, sir." The voice came from beside Calene. "Thought you were talking to someone else."

She blinked. They weren't talking to her! Glancing sidelong, Calene's head spun as the tension evaporated from her neck and shoulders. A veiled woman stood next to her. She couldn't see her pupils, but Calene knew the woman gave her the side eye.

Offering her a tight smile, Calene took a half-step forward.

"Don't think about going anywhere, Sparker," the woman hissed, spinning around, "or I'll let the guards know you don't want to be seen."

"She with you?" Calene heard a guard ask the veiled woman, clearly talking about her. She didn't want to turn around, but she couldn't risk running either. She just stood there, ears pricked, stomach rolling like a dinghy on the Sea of Storms.

"My sister. She came to collect me from Gallavan's Seat, to take me from the Widow's Sect. Of course, old habits die hard, and I still wear the veil."

"You still a Believer?" the guard asked, his tone taking on a cautious edge.

Maybe with good reason. The Widow's Sect, a quasi-religious order birthed in Gallavan's Seat. Only their followers knew exactly what they believed in, and only women joined. Women who kept their faces veiled, who might practice divination, necromancy, even human sacrifice. Rumours ran amok throughout Haltveldt. Superstitious folk whispered of ill fates befalling any who crossed a woman from the Widow's Sect. Most avoided them.

"Not *just* a Believer, my friend," the woman replied, her voice airy but carrying more than a hint of malicious warning. "The Widow travels with me. Always."

Silence stretched. Even the crowd of travellers bottlenecked at the gates quietened down, or so it seemed to Calene. The spot between her shoulder blades itched where the guard stared at her. Sweat from the nape of her neck dripped down her back.

She eyed the warren of streets ahead. People packed the alleys and paths, and the balconies and walkways above. In the distance, bells sounded from the Tower of Belti again.

Run. Go. You can lose yourself in the crowd and leave by another gate. None of these people will see you again.

In the distance, above the press, loomed the golden dome of the Patriarch's Palace. A reminder of where she didn't want to go. Couldn't afford to go.

"Alright, get out of here. Your sister's a braver droker than me, getting mixed up in Sect business." The guard's boots echoed as he stomped away. "Next in line. Stop droking pushing; you'll all get in…"

Fingers dug into Calene's bicep. "Come on, you heard the man. Let's get out of here, and you can tell me why a Sparker's doing a piss-poor job of avoiding notice in Willow."

"Well, the guards didn't stop me, did they?" Calene sneered, walking in step with her new friend so she didn't drag her along. She had a grip like iron!

Her Spark called to her, begged to be used. *Tie the woman up and run. Use a club of air to smack her across the back of the head and send her to sleep for a while. Anything.*

Out of instinct or panic or even plain frustration, Calene opened her Second Sight, and gasped.

The woman had the Spark too.

"Don't even think of using magic on me, mage. You might be stronger, but I fancy I'm more clever."

"You're not in the Widow's Sect," Calene half-squealed as she stumbled on the cobblestone streets, trying to keep her voice low as she banged shoulders and elbows with the people pressed around her. "You're a Sparker."

The woman glanced around, then pulled Calene into a darkened alleyway, grabbing her by the front of her robe and spinning her into the gloom. The air escaped her lungs in a rush when she slammed into the wall. The tight confines smothered the din of the city.

"Why are you disguised as one of the Widow's Sect?" Calene gasped.

"I'd rather be one of the Sect than chained to the whims of a madman," the woman snapped, lifting her veil with one hand and spitting on the ground. "But I'm neither, and I won't be a lap dog to that rasclart of an emperor again. Godsrot, I won't!"

Calene stared down at her. She had a good three or four inches on the woman. Broader across the shoulders too, but the way she carried herself... The stranger could handle a scrap, magic or no.

She spread her arms and, mindful of her lioness 'grin', fixed the most apologetic and harmless smile she could muster onto her face.

"Look, I think we've got off on the wrong foot here, yeah?" Calene nodded, like the bobbing of her head would make the woman agree with what she said. "God's teeth, think about it. You're right. I'm a Sparker, and I don't want anyone to know that. I'm no fan of the emperor, and I reckon he's no fan of mine either."

Ganton, Zal and the Shadow Sparker had proven that. Their attack in the Forest of Mists bloomed in her mind, and she raised her eyebrows.

"Actually, I know for a *fact* he ain't a fan."

The woman shoved a finger in Calene's face, her words coming quick. "You're on the run?"

"Isn't that obvious?"

The woman glanced left and right, then let Calene go. Her feet dropped to the floor, making her blink. The extra three or four inches she *thought* she had over the woman disappeared just like that.

Drok, she is tough!

The veiled Sparker crossed her arms, sleeve lifting to reveal a strange tattoo on her forearm—a cross like a spark amid overlapping circles—and tapped her foot, deep in thought.

"Alright, I'd be lying if I said we couldn't use the help, and your Spark outdoes mine by three or four times. Come with me. I'm meeting friends and we can talk there."

Peering out of the alleyway, the woman took a step forward, ready to melt into the crowd.

"Wait!" Calene cried. "I was born at night, but it wasn't last night, lady. I don't even know your droking name!"

"No, *you* wait," the woman replied, spinning around and letting her cloak part. Two shortswords hung at her hips, and her hands dropped to rest on them. "I reckon you're wise enough not to Spark out on me. It'd draw attention. But I reckon I'd have you beat in an alleyway fight, especially with that longsword you're carrying. Not ideal for city fighting. Now, I can beat your arse right here and now, or go tell a guard I've got a rogue Sparker making trouble. One thing's for certain. I don't trust you, and the best thing to do is keep you where I can see you. Understand? So, are you coming of your own free will, or what?"

My own free will? Doesn't look like I've much droking choice.

"Fine, but if we go anywhere near the Patriarch's Palace or the city guards, I'll make you wish you were never born. Everyone in Willow might see my Spark, but it'll be the last thing you *ever* see, so help me Janna." Calene fixed her cloak from where the veiled woman had ruffled it. "And I ain't going anywhere without a name."

The woman shrugged, then hid her shortswords away. "Fair enough. Maria du Gerran. Now let's go, I'm expected. Stay close."

Calene's feet followed, but her mind reeled. The odds. The chances! Maria du Gerran. She knew the woman by reputation. Rumour had it she'd single-handedly put down eight rogue Sparkers in her time, and foiled an assassination attempt on the previous High Sparker, Logan Prestar. Most thought her dead, sunk on the same ship the Order's old leader had perished on.

Calene had known her younger sister. Faye du Gerran had been her classmate at the Order's university.

"Small droking world," Calene muttered, keeping her eyes on Maria's back. "Maybe leaving Haltveldt *is* the best thing to do."

The sobbing reached Calene's ears before she saw its origin. A chorus of soft wailing, too low to hear if it came from just one set of lungs, or two, but from twenty? That made it audible enough.

More than enough.

The crowd had thinned, so Calene got a good look at the dozen cages stacked atop one another as she followed Maria into a small, near-deserted square.

Most people know this filth is here, don't they? And they don't want to see it. Like sweeping dirt under a rug...

Each cage housed an elf, females and children mostly. Calene fought the urge to embrace her Spark and set the lot free, and thanked Raas and Janna Brina hadn't tagged along. She'd have fought her way clear of Willow, killing anyone who got in her way, to bring the elves to freedom. And Calene knew she'd have helped.

It wasn't right.

Even at a distance, the stench threatened to make her gag. She hadn't realised her steps had slowed to a halt until Maria glanced over her shoulder, a quizzical look on her face.

"We're not stopping yet," she hissed, glancing around at the shadows hugging the boxy square.

The sun had set now, and night reigned. Sounds of revelry drifted in the air, though in Willow, the good times never really ended. Unless you happened to be an elf.

"Why'd we come this way?" Calene mumbled, unable to tear her eyes away from the cages.

She met the haunted stare of a woman who had more than a passing resemblance to Brina. Scabs and sores covered her skin where dirt and filth didn't. The elf bared her yellowed teeth, defiant, despite the disturbed look in her green eyes. Calene took a step towards her without thinking.

"It's a shortcut, innit?" Maria replied, frowning as

she shifted her narrow eyes between Calene and the cages. Then she raised an eyebrow. "Ah, you're an elf lover, aren't you? No harm in that, I suppose. Don't see the fascination myself but reckon all this slavery and genocide business is a bit much. I mean, we don't exterminate horses and dogs, do we? Not much difference really, except you can teach elves our language."

"What will happen with them?" Calene asked, her fingertips tingling. The Spark lay there, within reach, boiling in her stomach too. With a thought, a single command, she could pop the locks and let the elves run free.

"Look, we don't have time for this." Maria glanced back into the alleyway they'd walked down as glass echoed on stone. "They'll be sold to the nobles here or in Spring Haven, or some other city in Haltveldt. Like always. They're slaves, aren't they? Better than dead, right? And there's plenty of dead elves in Haltveldt."

"This isn't right," Calene whispered, taking another step forward. Her legs trembled as she met the caged elf's eyes. "We should..."

Up above, a cloud uncovered the moon, and its silver light hit the cages. Calene blinked. The elf's eyes were brown, not green. Her hair black, not red.

She didn't look like Brina at all. Not really.

The sores, scabs and scars worked their way across her skin, and bile rose in Calene's throat. Her fingers twitched.

"Wait a minute," Maria snarled, closing the distance and gripping Calene's wrist. "This isn't our fight. We have other targets. Other missions."

Calene shook her head. "If this isn't our fight, whose *will* it be?"

Maria winced, and opened her mouth, before another clang echoed from the alley. It wasn't glass. Metal chains made that sound.

"'Ere, what are you doing near my merchandise?"

"Come on!" Maria snapped, pulling Calene away.

She let the woman drag her along and decided not to look back. Calene didn't see the slaver approach, hatred etched into his face and a whip in his hand, didn't witness the blood of elves mix into the filth on the cage floors.

"I thought you said we were going somewhere quiet to talk?"

Calene snapped her jaw shut as they passed through the back entrance into the rowdiest tavern she'd seen in some time. The Stubborn Mule in Seke village had been the last inn she'd stopped at, and that place seemed utterly quaint compared to the bedlam she walked into.

The same strange symbol tattooed on Maria's arm had been etched into the stone by the door. What did it mean?

"I never said 'quiet'." Maria lifted her veil and flashed Calene a grin, bright orange eyes sparkling. "Welcome to the Broken Bard. It's my kind of place."

"How are we meant to talk over this?" Calene shouted, not at all worried people would overhear her. She wasn't sure how Maria could, even though they stood side-by-side.

Smoke filled the air, fumes from a couple of hundred lungs. Laughter too. The revellers roared as a full house band played a song called 'The Emperor's Lost His Milk Maid', a tune banned in Spring Haven and most of Haltveldt. Not Willow though.

Or maybe it was, and the denizens of the Broken Bard didn't give a drok. Even the bouncers standing by the front entrance grinned as they tapped feet along to the beat. One of them looked their way, and raised a hand in welcome toward Maria, who responded in kind. Then he turned his eyes on a table filled with patrons sharing a spice box, plain as day, without a care or worry in the world.

Waves of energy buffeted Calene, her Spark whispering to her about what she could do with all the joy, excitement, aggression and lust in the room. It made her head spin. Instead, she focused on the band.

It wasn't often she saw one. Solo players were more her speed, and roving bards often appeared in the remote villages and inns she and Vettigan had frequented. Now, she watched as a musician with a set of what looked like war drums accompanied two others—one with a lute, the other with a guitar—as they sang together, voices mixing into a bawdy harmony.

It was that kind of song.

"Come on," Maria yelled, pointing towards the back of the inn. "Let's get a drink before we head into the backroom. We have a permanent place to use here. Old Sagat's no fan of the Empire."

"Old Sagat?" Calene murmured, her question swallowed by the cheering crowd as the song came to an end.

She grinned despite herself. Her experiences in Willow so far hadn't been ideal, but she forgot the tension at the gate and the sorrow with the elves. The ale flying through the air helped with that. She fancied the atmosphere in the Broken Bard contained more alcohol than air. Just setting foot inside would make a person drunk. Folk slammed tankards together, played clankte, dice and cards, and took bets on any scuffles that broke out. The guards watched with raised eyebrows, ready to intervene if anyone looked on the verge of death. Maybe they'd just toss the loser outside, job done with nary any fuss.

"One, two, one-two-three-four!"

The band plunged right into another fast-paced number, one that turned Calene's smile sad. 'A Maid Goes to Spring Haven'. One of Vettigan's favourites, and one the redheaded bard back in Seke had played before her world changed forever.

"What do you want?" Maria shouted, making a drinky-drinky motion and tugging on Calene's arm.

She turned, finding herself at the bar, a giant of a man with a cleft-lip and one eye leering at her. No, not a cleft-lip. A scar, running from chin to forehead. He gave a small salute, revealing a hand with just three fingers. A veteran of war if Calene had ever seen one. Old Sagat, she presumed.

"Hi," she shouted, keeping her lioness grin under wraps. "Nice place you've got here! Got any Prosper Ale?"

"Prosper Ale?" Sagat laughed, shaking his massive head. His smile softened the harsh scar on his face, and his single eye twinkled. "Godsrot! They're shit at fighting, them lads, and even worse at brewing ale."

Maria arched an eyebrow. "Two Velen brandies, Sagat. Doubles. This is my friend's first time in the Bard so let's get her used to drinking something that isn't rat piss. Then we can work on teaching her to hide her eyes, am I right?"

"Right," Sagat agreed, leaning on the counter. "If you're

looking to blend in, those purple eyes, lovely as they are, aren't the way to do it. And I wouldn't stare with such wonder at everything if I were you."

"If these fine folks weren't all pissed out of their minds, you'd have been clocked as a...ahem...as soon as you walked in. Just like I clocked you at the gates."

"You wanting some spice with your drinks?" Sagat asked.

Calene gaped. *Spice on offer, just like that! 'Want some Velen brandies and a box of Octarian spice? No problem, ladies, coming right up!'*

Kade Besem would have suffered an instant relapse just sniffing the place as he walked in.

"Just the drinks, Sagat," Maria chuckled. "Not sure our rogue on the run could stomach a hit right now. Doesn't seem to have her wits about her."

Sagat turned away with a laugh as heat warmed Calene's cheeks. She tilted her head down and narrowed her eyes, staring at the bar. "Look, it's my first time on the run, okay? I'm new at this."

"And here you are, setting foot in one of the busiest cities in Haltveldt, bold as brass." Maria gave her a gentle shove. "At least you came across me. You'd be trying to explain yourself at the Patriarch's Palace by now if you hadn't."

Calene grinned. "The guards made you, not me. Remember?"

"Alright, alright," Maria laughed, taking the brandy from the bar as Sagat moved on to take more orders. She handed one to Calene and lifted her veil. "Anyway, you can relax here. Empire lovers don't last long at the Bard. Sagat and his crew have a way of weeding them out and…making them unwelcome, shall we say?" She raised her brandy. "Shall we toast to new friends?"

"I droking hope so," Calene muttered, downing the liquid and coughing. It burned her throat, spreading warmth to her limbs. The alcohol rose straight to her head. "Raas, that's strong! Drok me!"

"Aye, the Velens know how to make it! Another?"

"Too right," Calene laughed, shoulders relaxing a little. Maria raised two fingers to Sagat.

The other woman appeared more at ease in the inn, and much less uptight than her sister, Faye. Calene had gotten along with her well enough, but the woman had always come across as too intense for Calene's tastes. Vettigan had said it made them a pair of black kettles.

Faye had moved in the same circles as Emperor Locke and his cronies, Nexes and Balz. That made Maria's hatred of the Empire all the more interesting. Calene studied her through the veil.

"So, what brings Calene Alpenwood to Willow?"

Calene froze, eyes wide, backfooted like Maria had shield-bashed her before a killing stroke.

"Yeah, I know who you are. I remember seeing you with Faye years ago, and you look just like your mother. We should drink to her memory this round."

Drink to her…

Once, in a skirmish against the elves, Calene had found herself flat on her back in the mud, two attackers pummelling her, unable to catch her breath, her bearings. She felt the same now.

Disoriented. Vettigan had come to her rescue back then. This time, she stood alone against this woman who knew so much about her, past and present. A rogue Sparker who'd knocked her off-balance with just a few words. And a double brandy from Velen.

"You know about that?" Calene managed, tearing her tongue from the roof of her mouth.

"Aye. We know Solitude fell, and everyone there with it. We know about that huge army pouring down from Banished lands too."

"Not everyone died there," Calene whispered, as Sagat slammed another pair of brandies on the bar.

Maria grabbed her arm. "Zanna's alive?"

Calene shook her head, unable to say the words. "We met a group of Sparkers at Adhraas and stopped a group of Banished scouts from finding them. Not in the way I'd have liked, to be honest."

"Wait." Maria said and pulled Calene so close she could feel the woman's brandy-laced breath oozing from beneath her veil. "How do you know all this? You were there?"

Calene pulled her arm away and glanced around. Maria had been right. Not give a fig. They were just two more patrons at a rambunctious inn, drinking and having a fine old time of it.

Except the fine old time part...

"I went to save my mother." Calene almost mentioned Tilo, then thought better of it. "She sacrificed herself to save everyone she could. By the time I arrived, it had turned into a droking massacre on both sides. We only survived thanks to her."

Maria shoved the second brandy into Calene's hands and raised her own. "To Zanna Alpenwood then. A finer Sparker there never was."

Calene's mouth twitched, and she filled her lungs to get a grip on herself. A toast to her mother from just two women was the least she deserved but deserve it she did.

"To Zanna," Calene whispered, raising her glass. "My mother." She gasped as the liquor burned her throat, burned it good. "Another," she barked, slamming the empty on the bar.

"One more," Maria replied, nodding. "I think you need it. Then we'll have ourselves a proper talk. I'm getting the feeling you've as much to tell me as I have you."

"There's a couple of things."

Shadow Sparkers, reality-defying magic, about half a million Banished...

"Wait, you know about the droking Banished coming this way and you're all here, getting your jollies? What's wrong with you all?"

"Patriarch says there's nothing to worry about. Just a 'handful of shepherds who slipped through Solitude while the Sparkers slept'." Her tone suggested she believed it as much as Calene believed Vettigan and Brina would be best friends by the time she returned. "Plus, an army led by Nexes himself is moving from the south. Any force worth their salt won't lay siege to a city with an army bearing down on them. Reckon the Banished will find somewhere handy to defend."

"You're more right than you know." Calene bit her lip, then nodded. "From what I've seen, I don't think the Banished are here to fight at all if they can avoid it."

Two more brandies appeared, and Maria pointed at them. "Drink up, then follow me."

Calene sucked her teeth as the burn flooded her chest and turned to follow Maria. *Wish this droking inn didn't sway so much. It's like being on a boat again. That big, rickety boat with the pretty elf and...*

She staggered after the veiled woman, glaring at floorboards when they had the temerity to shift and swell under her boots. Calene had the vague awareness of the roar of the crowd growing quiet, the bardsong slipping away, and a knocking sound on a door. One rap of knuckles, followed by three quick ones. A pause, then two slow.

"Open up, it's me," Maria hissed. "Got someone with me you're all going to want to meet."

The door creaked open, and Calene came to a stop, looking up with a vacantly pleasant grin stuck to her face.

A man with glowing blue eyes frowned at her, then rage took hold of his features. Calene cocked her head.

Something about this fella...

"Calene droking Alpenwood," the 'fella' bit out, eye twitching. "Last time I saw you, you took one of my droking arms."

The memory slammed into Calene's mind, right about the moment the man's fist slammed into her face. She crashed to the floor on her back, winded and dizzy. Marc le Fondre loomed over her, his one remaining hand balled into a fist.

"Marc," she grunted, as she slid into darkness. "Still got one droker of a right..."

Chapter Eighteen

HAPPY MEETINGS

'Spring Haven, they named it. A place for new life. Safety. Well, now the rats are in the walls, and they have a name too. The Emperor's Hand. And if your home's infested with them, you're not safe anymore.' - From a letter written by Bertrand de Reyes, intercepted before it reached Faye du Gerran before his untimely death.

"Dig my grave with a silver spade..."

Singing reached Calene's ears, a voice that would see the owner's lute broken clear over his head, snapping her back from wherever her mind had fled to after Marc knocked her flat.

After a hit like that, she wondered how she still drew breath.

Running her tongue across her teeth, checking they were all still there, Calene winced at the taste of blood and the painful throbbing in her...general face area. At least they'd scraped her off the floor. Someone had plonked her onto a bed. A soft one, with a nice, comfy pillow.

Marc might only have one fist, but it's a droking big one.

"Godsrot, who's making that racket?" Calene grumbled, cradling her head in her hands. The punch to the face had seemingly evaporated the alcohol from her bloodstream, leaving her with the Raas of all hangovers.

It occurred to her too late that maybe, just maybe, she should have kept her thoughts to herself. Marc's greeting had made it clear she wasn't exactly welcome.

The singing warbled to a halt, giving Calene a moment's blessing.

"Where do you get off? Godsrot, woman, you've got some nerve."

Marc's voice. Well, at least he hadn't hit her a second time. Then again...

"Le Fondre," Calene mumbled, trying to force herself into a sitting position, "if you're going to keep singing, make sure the second one kills me, aye?"

"Maybe I should," he grumbled, with more than a little sulk to his voice. "Last time we met, you lopped my droking arm off!"

"Last time we met," Calene countered, "you were on the run from the Empire, and they sent me and Vettigan to bring you in. You're lucky the arm was all I took."

Hands grabbed her shoulders and pulled her upright, letting the pillow prop her up. Blinking, Calene gazed around the room, her vision more than a little hazy. Marc's red, round, permanently angry face swam into view, as did that of a woman with orange irises. That same spark-and-circles symbol peeked from under Marc's collar. Couldn't be a coincidence.

"And look at you now," Maria smiled, rolling her eyes. "On the run together. Well, the Order reckons Marc's dead, but no such luck for you, Alpenwood. We reached out to our contacts after Marc put you on your arse. You're supposed to be pushing up Raaswort right now, but the crew sent to do it are instead. There's a warrant out for you and Vettigan. Speaking of, is he around?"

"Why? So you can turn us *both* in?"

Calene regretted the words as soon as she said them. Not because she might piss Maria or Marc off, but because they were droking stupid. Two rogue Sparkers wouldn't go anywhere near the Empire if they could help it, let alone *help* them.

Marc aimed a fat finger at Calene. "I'd give her less shit. She's the one who went to bat for you. Me, I would have killed you without thinking twice. You were always a good little toy soldier for that rasclart, Locke."

"Look, I did what the Order asked," Calene shouted, wincing as pain shot through her temple.

Drok, she'd only had *three* Velen brandies! Doubles, yes, and a fist to the face to boot, but she'd always prided herself on her constitution.

"I wasn't the only one."

"You can hide behind that 'just following orders' rot all you want, Alpenwood, and it might ease your conscience, but I'm not the only rogue Sparker you hunted. I'm just one of the few who got away. What happened to the ones who weren't so lucky?" Marc narrowed his eyes. "And don't think I forgot how you turned your back on your own godsrotting mother."

Calene shot to her feet, throwing herself at where she thought Marc stood—the bastard room spun too much to make it an exact science—hand groping for the sword at her hip.

The *missing* sword at her hip.

"Teeth of the gods, enough!" Maria roared, shoving Calene back onto the bed and glaring at Marc. "We've all made mistakes, right? All of us. We all served the Empire through the Order, and we all received a wakeup call. Don't you regret anything you've done, Marc?"

The large man looked away, but he gave a reluctant nod. "I regret plenty."

"Now, I'm not asking you two to Link or anything," Maria continued, crossing her arms, "but can you at least agree to stop trying to kill each other?"

She stared at Calene, who stared back. Focusing made the room spin less. Maria looked like her sister—a decade older, give or take—but the elder du Gerran had a twinkle in her eye Faye never had. An angry one at the moment, but a twinkle nonetheless. Faye had always kept control of her features, her bearing, but Maria didn't seem to give a drok about all that. To her credit, the three double brandies didn't appear to affect her in the slightest.

Calene could appreciate a woman who held her liquor.

Not that I droking can. Teeth of the gods, what do the Velens put in that stuff?

"Alright," Calene agreed, wobbling to her feet, and

holding out a hand. "Let's shake on it."

"You droker!" Marc roared, face turning purple.

Maria's laughter took Calene by surprise, and, evidently, Marc too. His angry snarling spluttered out into a hurt silence.

"Shake on it. Good one." Maria slapped Marc on his shoulder and winked at Calene. "I say that to him all the time. Never fails. You took his arm about...eight years ago, was it? You'd think he'd be used to it by now."

"It was my good arm," Marc grumbled, dropping into a chair and staring sullenly at Calene. "The magic I did with that hand."

"I'll bet," Calene replied, raising an eyebrow and glancing at his crotch.

Maria laughed again, and Calene smiled at her. *At last! Someone with a droking sense of humour.*

"Wait..." Calene muttered, frowning around the room. "I thought you said you were meeting 'friends'. One person is a friend."

Maria nodded. "My other friends are out on business. Out of the city actually."

"They all have those tattoos you're both sporting?" Calene asked, pointing at Marc's sigil. "The one I saw in the tavern?"

"Maybe," Maria replied, leaning back.

"Speaking of friends..." Marc flexed his remaining fingers. "Where's Vettigan? Don't tell me he died at Solitude too."

A dull throb in Calene's jaw joined the general ache from the rest of her face. Grinding her teeth. Bad habit.

She flicked her eyes at Maria, who gave an apologetic smile. Marc's question had been less than subtle. 'Don't tell me he died at Solitude too.' She decided to let the barb slide. She'd taken his arm off after all. No reason why she couldn't answer a simple question.

"He's alive, but different. Changed. A liability, if I'm honest. It's part of why we're heading south. Looking for a way to save him."

Marc pointed at her. "Elaborate."

"In a minute," Calene muttered, testing her jaw. "You got any water, or something cold?"

Maria knelt in front of her. "Where's it hurting? He really connected with that punch."

Calene waved a hand across her entire face. "Just everywhere, really."

"I shouldn't do this," Maria muttered, glancing at Marc, "you know, in case another Sparker feels it, but I doubt anyone will pick it up."

Maria took Calene's head in her hands, and magic ran through her body. Just a trickle, but it spoke to Calene's soul as much as it did to the pain in her head. Within a second, the flicker of Spark vanished, and so did the dull ache in her skull.

The room had stopped spinning too. Blessed relief. Sparkers couldn't heal themselves. A joke from the gods, Vettigan used to say. A sick one.

"Thank you," Calene murmured, gazing into Maria's bright eyes. "Appreciate it."

"Think nothing of it." Maria groaned as she straightened up. "Now, you were telling us about Vettigan."

How much could she trust them? Marc hated her, and that didn't surprise her, but Maria treated her well. Raas knew they could have killed her several times, and the woman could have told the guards what she was before she'd even set foot in Willow.

Calene met their eyes and nodded. "Right, I'll tell you, but I want answers of my own. You two are meant to be dead, and you..." She pointed at Maria. "...keep mentioning 'we' and I don't think you're talking about the one-armed wonder here, or even your absent 'friends'. I want to know everything about this little organisation you've got working out of the Broken Bard." She tilted her chin, waiting for Marc to complain. Aggressively. Instead, he shrugged at Maria, who gave a nod. "Fine. Have you heard of the Shadow Sparkers?"

Maria shuddered, and the scowl on Marc's thick face grew deeper. "God's teeth. Wish we hadn't."

"Right." Calene agreed. "Well, me and Vettigan had an encounter with one, out by the Forest of Mists. That crew you mentioned the Order sent to kill us. We had a Banished with us. We found him in the cellar of an inn down in Seke village..."

Maria leaned back in her chair and whistled. "So, the whole of Solitude just vanished into thin air? Just like that?"

"Impossible," Marc grumbled. "Can't be true."

"Of course it's droking true!" Calene snapped, throat as dry as the Prosper Badlands after telling her story. "Teeth of the gods, Le Fondre, why would I make something like that up? Zanna made that fortress disappear. What was left of it, anyway. She saved everyone fighting on the walls. Sparkers, Banished, didn't matter. She saved them all."

"Well, I suppose your mother had some power to her. And you think old Ricken left some knowledge behind that might heal the damage done to Vettigan?"

"I have to believe it. Vettigan would search the Four Corners if he thought he could save me." Calene sighed. "Or would have done, before the Shadow Sparker droked him."

"Have you been back home?" Maria asked. "Since...?"

"No."

Marc sniffed, tossed his head and winced, stealing Calene's attention. An internal struggle, playing out across his face. Nodding, he got to his feet and held out his hand to her.

"Sounds like you've been through the Underworld itself," he muttered, head down. "I'm sorry about your mother. A fine Sparker. We'd have loved to have her on our side. I'm... I'm glad you reconnected before the end."

Calene peered up at him, then at his hand, and took it. "So am I, Marc, and thank you. So, your turn. Who's going to spill first in this little group session we're having?"

She leaned back on the bed, arms and legs crossed, tucking Marc's words about her mother away to deal with at another time. They *had* reconnected. Calene hadn't even thought about how she'd have felt if they hadn't.

But she didn't hear me tell her I loved her, did she? And she never will again.

Biting her tongue, Calene shoved the thoughts away.

"Well, fair's fair." Maria got to her feet and crossed the

room to a pitcher of water. She poured a few glasses and handed them around. Calene gulped the too-warm water, but she didn't care how it tasted. It made her gullet wet, and that was all that mattered. "We help relocate Sparkers. Ones who can't stay in Haltveldt anymore. That's why Marc here, and others in our organisation, won't take too kindly to you, but I faced down more rogue Sparkers than I care to remember in my time. So did my sister, until very recently."

"You see much of her?"

"No, not really, but she's helping with a cell down in Temekt. There's more of us than you'd think."

Calene frowned. "You don't have a Link with her?"

"A Link?" Maria cried, spluttering her water. "God's teeth, no! We were never *that* close. Besides, I wouldn't share a Link with anyone." She tapped a finger against her temple. "Having someone else living up here? No thanks. Plus, I hear it's torture when they die."

Marc sniffed and gazed into his cup. Silent. Peering into the past.

"What's your sister doing in Temekt?" Not really close to a port or anything, is it? Neither's this place, now I think about it. Suppose the Forest of Willows is handy enough to lose someone in."

"We don't just smuggle Sparkers," Maria replied, taking a drink.

"We fight against the Empire, however we can." Marc nodded at Maria. "Faye isn't really one of us, but a couple of others vouched for her. She had a change of heart, and now she's looking into some unit the emperor set up a decade or so ago in the south, just outside Spring Haven."

"Funny," Calene muttered. "Just where I'm headed."

In her story, she'd left Brina out completely, and her fracas with the slavers too. Even though they opposed the emperor, Marc probably shared the majority of Haltveldt's views on elves, and she knew Maria didn't think highly of them either.

It went without saying that Calene hadn't mentioned Brina's mission to assassinate Emperor Locke.

The others fell silent, though it didn't stop them sharing glances.

Walls must be thick here, can't hear a thing from the bar. Calene hadn't noticed it before, but then they'd all been talking without pause since she woke up. *Suppose they need 'em that way. Good for private business and all that.*

Darkness smothered the view from the window behind her, even the gas lamps dotting the street, so Calene stared at her fingernails instead. Marc and Maria wanted something. She knew that. She just had to wait for them to get to the point.

Finally, as the silence dragged into discomfort, Marc gave a shrug, mouth turning down at the corners. If Maria hadn't said she refused to share a Link with anyone, and if Calene hadn't been certain Marc had lost a Link in the past, she'd would have bet all the spice in the Broken Bard on them speaking telepathically. But then, their familiarity came from working together for so long. She'd had that with Vettigan too, and she'd forgotten.

Before the Shadow Sparker, Calene knew her old friend's thoughts even before they came through the Link, just by the look in his eyes.

"You could stay with us." Maria got to her feet and refilled their water, then dropped back into her seat, leaning forward. "If you're looking to strike a blow at the Empire, that is. We've got resources in every major city, contacts in towns and villages all over Haltveldt and abroad. Instead of chasing Sparkers down like you've done in the past, you can help set them free."

"Work for you?" Calene asked. "I suppose you'll have me living in this little room too, won't you?"

"No, your Spark's too much for that, your experience too great, much as it pains me to say," Marc said, voice still holding a fair bit of anger.

Calene had met plenty of people whose default setting had them just a finger's breadth from rage, from the moment they woke up to the second they fell asleep. She imagined it was exhausting. And she pushed away memories of Vettigan using the exact same words to describe her with a violent mental shove.

"You could do whatever you pleased, Calene, so long as you helped." Maria's orange eyes shone. "Pick your own targets, do your own research, assemble your own team. Even Vettigan, once you've healed him."

"*If* she heals him," Marc muttered under his breath.

Maria glared at him, then turned back to Calene. "Imagine it. For the first time since that Spark inside you bloomed, you'd do your own work. Not an acolyte for a splintered Order, not a tool for a tyrant. You could go where you wish, even abroad. It doesn't even change your plans. You say you're going south, back to your family home. Why not scout the area while you're there, search for this unit

Faye mentioned? You could even meet up with her, trade notes and all that. What do you say?"

Calene frowned into her mug. Doing her own thing. The concept utterly mystified her. For years, she'd followed the commands of the Order. Before that, she'd studied at the university, waking when told, eating at designated times, sleeping when the bell rang. Before that, she'd been a child, following the lead of her mother and father.

Doing her own thing.

Maria might as well have suggested she up sticks and start a new life in the Underworld.

Still, it appealed. Even now, the people around her pulled in different directions. She wanted to heal Vettigan, wanted to at least try—drok, she needed him to give her even the smallest reason to try—but he just kept talking about fleeing, begging her to come with him, without a care for what she might want. And Brina kept her around to aid her own mad quest for vengeance and nothing more. At least, that's what she'd said.

So, what do *I want? To heal Vettigan? Is that it? What have I ever wanted?*

Maria and Marc needed something from her too, that was true. From Calene the person *and* Calene the Sparker. She could achieve much for their cause with her power and experience, but they'd give her free reign. They'd even said she could go abroad if she desired, choose her own targets, strike at will.

The offer appealed. It droking did but taking them up on it meant leaving Vettigan and Brina behind. The former had no Spark and had proven ill-suited to teamwork, never mind clandestine missions, since his run in with the Shadow Sparker. And the latter... An elf, on a path to the Underworld, with or without Calene's help.

Sure, Maria said she could see to her business first, but how much did she really mean that? And what if Calene found nothing in her father's studies? Vettigan wouldn't be welcome.

Could she leave her friends behind? Were they even friends? Vettigan had been the closest thing to family once, and Brina... That elf did things to her heart.

Calene nursed her cup to keep from treading over the same well-worn ground, heading nowhere. The absence of noise nagged at her again.

"Teeth of the gods," she growled. Being put on the spot by such a reasonable and appealing offer boiled her blood. "Is it always so droking quiet in here? Last I looked, there were about two hundred people and a bloody band on the other side of those walls!"

Maria and Marc exchanged a sharp look. The unnatural quiet had escaped their notice until just then too. The one-armed man eased to his feet and leaned over Calene, glancing out the window, permanent scowl deepening.

"Can't see a thing out there."

Nodding, Maria got to her feet. "I'll go check out front, it's probably nothing. Old Sagat might have closed up for the night."

The doubt in her voice made Calene wince.

As Maria approached the door, a heavy knock sounded from the other side. Just one. No funny pattern this time. The three, and the room, held their breath.

Then the bang came again.

"Maria?" Old Sagat's strained voice echoed through the wood. "Need to settle your tab before you leave. You—"

A strangled cry interrupted his words, and Maria spun around, orange eyes wild.

"They've found us. Out the window. Now. I'll hold them off!"

Calene leapt toward the window, but Marc beat her to it, flames appearing in his hand, not caring about hiding his Spark now. The glass shattered. Behind them, the door rattled and a groan tore from the stonework surrounding it. Maria screamed. Calene spun. The woman held a barrier against the door, and her Spark shone bright with strength, but someone with more power on the other side of the wall beat at it like a hammer beating heated iron.

"Godsrot," Marc growled, pulling his head from the broken window, blue flames dancing between his fingers. "Guards down below, waiting for us to jump."

Maria dropped to one knee as the walls and door vibrated, teeth bared, cords of her neck popping, a continuous, wordless wail ripping from her lungs.

"Drok the streets!" Calene yelled. "We need to help her!"

Since Solitude, she'd shunned her Raas-given gift, the power that brought her closer to the energies of the world. She'd feared it after seeing it twisted, after watching the miasma of evil wreaking havoc above the ruined fortress, after feeling her Spark yearn to join it and embrace the all-consuming power the darkness offered. She didn't trust it and, loath as she was to admit it, she didn't trust herself either.

"What are you waiting for?" Marc yelled, flames disappearing as he added to Maria's barrier. "Rotten teeth of the gods, help us, woman! Lend us your—"

Calene's hesitation cost them.

The door blew off its hinges, taking chunks of stonework with it. It flew across the room and smashed Marc against the far wall. Calene shielded her face, pulling on the Spark just in time as debris split around her.

Maria wasn't as lucky. The blast knocked her on her back, and she lay there, dazed, staring up at the fresh cracks in the ceiling.

Calene scrambled over to her, helping Maria to her knees. She flopped around like a ragdoll, stunned, mouth opening and closing, dirt smearing her face.

Their eyes met.

"My Spark," she whispered. "Something's blocking it. Something..."

Through the dust swirling around the gaping hole in the wall, the prone body of Old Sagat leaked blood from a gaping tear in his throat. Above him, shadows crawled.

"No..." Calene growled, embracing her Spark. "Not them. Anything but them."

She might as well have tried to catch smoke. Her power lay just out of reach. They'd shielded her, and she had no weapons. Marc and Maria hadn't returned her blade.

Not that it mattered; Calene couldn't even twitch her finger.

The Empire had caught her.

A woman strode into the room, Unsparked. Calene felt no power coming from her, yet she seemed at ease in the midst of death. Dust covered her plain brown clothes, and she wiped a bloodied dagger across her cloak before sheathing it. Her dull eyes met Calene's, then she turned them on Maria and smiled. Like the rest of her, the grin proved utterly unremarkable.

"Life's funny, eh?" The woman spoke in a monotone, as if bored, but that's how they trained the Emperor's Hand to talk. They were meant to bleed into the background and leave no impression, until the moment they acted. "You know what city I came from?"

"Go drok yourself," Maria snarled, the muscles in her neck and jaw straining as she fought against her invisible restraints.

"Maybe later." The woman peered around the room, raising an eyebrow at the insensate body of Marc, flattened by the door. "Temekt city. You won't guess what I found there. Well, I should say 'who.'"

Temekt city. Calene's stomach dropped into her boots. They'd just mentioned the place, and a certain someone there.

"I don't know what you're—"

The Emperor's Hand cut Maria off. "Faye du Gerran. Your sister. What are the odds? Of course, she told us all about you." She let her eyes wander, always alert, always searching. "And your merry band acting out of Willow. After dropping her off in Spring Haven, I thought I'd make a trip up here myself."

"She's still alive?" Maria asked, desperation seeping into her voice.

The scuff of boots sounded from the back of the room.

A small noise, but it reached Calene's ears nonetheless.

"Oh, she's alive, though I reckon she won't be the way you remember her. Don't worry though. You'll be reunited soon enough, both striving to make Haltveldt a better place, all in the name of our emperor."

As she spoke, the shadows deepened, swirled and oozed into the room, rolling over Sagat's body. In slid two Shadow Sparkers, black eyes glittering in the darkness of their hoods. Calene pushed against her invisible bindings, and one of them turned its head her way. She met its stare and bared her teeth. The broken door covering Marc rattled, and the man groaned as he came to his senses.

"We'll take du Gerran with us. Kill the other two."

"No!" Calene snarled, as the Shadow Sparker slithered toward her, shadows tugging at the hem of its black cloak, tendrils curling up the walls, seeking to extinguish the gas lamps illuminating the room.

It stared down at her, face impassive, angry red fissures cracking its skin, and cocked its head.

Helpless. She felt so droking helpless. Just like she had back in the Forest of Mists when Ganton, Zal and his Shadow Sparker had attacked them, leaving their mark on Vettigan. Just as she had at Solitude, when she could do nothing to save her mother, could do nothing to keep Tilo and Arlo from falling. Since then, she'd followed her feet as she'd trudged from one place to another, going through the motions, afraid of herself, her power, and look where it had led her?

Back on her knees before a dark mage ready to end her life.

Only now she had no one to come to her rescue. No Brina. No Vettigan. No Zanna. She'd die alone.

She'd be Eviscerated like her father, on her knees with nothing but regrets to take with her into the Underworld. She didn't deserve to stand before the Gates of Eternity and enjoy her afterlife.

Frustration welled within, causing blood to pound in her ears. No. She wouldn't die like this. Her mother's sacrifice wouldn't come to nothing. She wouldn't let it. Not now, not ever.

The Shadow Sparker sneered down at her as it pulled on the dark energy inside it, the fear, death and anger in the room, the elements it needed to perform its corrupt magic.

It all spoke to Calene, a river rushing past she could plunge her hands in, and she measured the power of the Shadow before her, gauging its strength. It had plenty, but the act of shielding and binding Calene pushed it to its limits. As it pulled for more, ready to Eviscerate her, Calene swept her senses across the room and beyond.

Everything called to her. The current of negativity, yes, but more. She rejected the darkness and searched for purity. For life. And she found it.

Outside, behind another set of walls, laughter found its way to her. Fire and water. Excitement and joy. Music and delight. Calene drew from it, adding to the innate energy of her soul and her Spark, and then took more still. The humidity in the air, the combustibility of the gas in the lamps, the rich iron of spilled blood from the floor. It all built within her until her limbs trembled, her teeth rattled in her gums.

The Shadow Sparker's eyes widened and even the Emperor's Hand looked her way, a quizzical look on her face. Calene's magic still lay behind a barrier, but it built up inside her, growing. To use it...

How could she unleash it?

Whenever she used her Spark, she would open herself to it, call on it, and it would be there. Now, Calene reached for it, like pushing her hand into a jar of molasses, and came up against a barrier inside, one that bulged as she pressed. The Shadow Sparker before her staggered, gritting its teeth, a growl humming from its throat.

It took another step, raising its hand, a black cloud oozing out of its pale palm.

"No!" Calene screamed, and instead of reaching for the energy building up on the other side of the barrier, she threw off the shield, along with the mass of power that had gathered around it.

"What?" the corrupted mage hissed, staggering back. "Wait, you can't—!"

The Emperor's Hand shot forward, seizing Maria and pulling her from the room as energy rushed out of Calene in a wave, roaring in all directions, pure destruction following it. She flung backward, landing on top of the door covering Marc, and sheltered him with her body as her power slammed into the Shadow Sparkers. It disintegrated the one who'd been staring down at her. One moment it staggered backward, the next it turned to dust and echoes in the air, torn to pieces so small they could barely be seen.

The other Shadow Sparker flew into the already ruined wall, the shockwave bringing down the ceiling on it. A sundered wooden beam stove its skull like a warhammer and turned it to red paste.

"Drok!" Calene screamed, covering her head as the room crumbled, as the side of the entire building fell into the street below.

Screams reached her ears, falling stones crushing guards to death, and the clattering of hooves told her others fled on horseback into the night.

The building groaned as the initial blast settled, and silence crept back into the night.

Coughing, Calene lifted her head, peering through the dust. Debris covered the door the Emperor's Hand had escaped through, but Willow stretched out beyond the missing wall, the twinkling of a thousand gas lamps lighting the city before her.

Marc groaned, and she stared down at him. Blood oozed from a jagged cut above his eyebrow. She knew she could heal him. The Spark flowed inside her again, sweet and terrible, fire and ice, life and death, shadow and light. The Shadow Sparkers hadn't defeated her, and neither would her Spark.

It served her.

Calene took hold of the power, teeth bared, dominating it, and lay her hands on Marc, salving his wounds.

"Are you okay?" she asked, getting to her feet and heaving the door aside. She spotted her sword discarded beneath the rubble as she did.

"What did you do? It shielded you, but you just...cast it off. And that power you unleashed! I've never seen anyone do that before. Not a one!" Marc let her pull him to his feet.

The room groaned again, then tilted to the side. "Teeth of the gods, the whole building's coming down."

"We can't stay." Calene sheathed her sword and edged towards the new opening. She could use her Spark and move across the rooftops, keeping off the streets until they reached the city walls. "You're going to have to come with me. Drok, won't Vettigan be pleased with another broken soul added to our merry band?"

Marc grabbed her wrist. "Go with you? I can't. Maria's still alive. We need to rescue her."

"We?" Calene spat. "You *kidnapped* me! I came to Willow to grab a drink, some more supplies and hear the news. Nothing more. I've done two out of three, and I'm gonna call it quits."

"They have her because of you!" Marc shoved a finger in her face. "She used her Spark to heal you—"

"I never droking asked her to!"

"But she did, and now they have her. You know what they'll do to her. Torture her or worse!"

The building shifted again. Marc threw his arm out for balance. Calene grabbed it, steadying him.

"I—"

"Please," he whispered, eyes wide and shining. "Help her. There's no one else. Can you have this on your conscience? When they question her, they'll discover more names in more cities. Please..."

Spinning Calene kicked at a piece of broken wood, sending it skittering into the street, and earning a cry of alarm from below for her troubles. She couldn't leave Maria behind. The memory would dog Calene's every step until she found herself on the shores of the Underworld.

"Drok it!" she growled. She knew she couldn't leave Maria behind, but she didn't have to be happy about it. "Fine. Where do we start?"

Marc smiled. "The Patriarch's Palace. They'll take her there before heading to Spring Haven and that isn't good for a few reasons. The new Patriarch's a Sparker. A weak one, and probably would have been bounced out of the Order if it weren't for his connections, but he's no fan of the old ways."

Calene kicked something else, and this time her reward consisted of pain blooming in her foot. The Patriarch's Palace, the one place she *swore* she'd stay away from in the whole of Willow, and a middling Sparker in charge with something to prove to the world.

She laughed. What else could she do?

"Let's get droking started then," she snarled, pulling on her Spark again and skipping on air across to the rooftops.

The evening breeze swept through her hair as she landed on the other side, and she glanced at the destruction she'd caused.

Using the Spark again made her feel alive, but the damage she'd left behind... Even without using dark energies like the Shadow Sparkers, Calene had left a scar across the face of Willow. One for all to see.

I did what I had to do. Me and Marc would be dead if I hadn't, and who'd help Maria then? No one. No one at all.

She thought of her mother then. Wouldn't Zanna have said the same thing after what had happened with her father? That she'd done what she had to?

Hadn't Calene used the Spark time and time again in self-defence, because she 'had to'? What was the difference?

Turning away, Calene set her sights on the Patriarch's Palace and let her hand fall to her sword. For too long, she'd gone along with the motions, reacting when she should have been striking first, striking hard.

Now, things would change. Now, Calene Alpenwood would hit the Empire with everything she had.

Chapter Ninteen

The Cost of War

'But, I ask you, what is the Spark? We're told it's a gift from the gods, from Raas, Janna and the rest, and you can believe that if you wish. We're told of its purity, its divinity. But I've seen the horrors people have used it for. I've witnessed the corruption, and I've seen the darkness swirl in a Sparker's eyes when confronted with it. It has its own mind, and it sees all.' - From the previously unpublished works of the Sparker scholar, Greton of Willow, whose teachings formed part of the university curriculum under High Sparker Balz.

The Sparker in bright yellow robes stood before him, flickering flames of green, red, blue and orange dancing between her fingers, a loose mockery of a smile on her lips.

Nexes slumped between the ravaged remains of his grandparents. Somehow, in the sludge, their eyes remained, staring at him.

Snarling, he threw himself forward, before the mad Sparker had the chance to finish him too.

Flames engulfed him, searing his skin, but he passed through them, somehow unscathed, whole despite the pain. Swords appeared in his thin hands, twin short blades he wouldn't own until he reached adulthood. They didn't belong to him yet, but his scrawny fingers clutched them tight as he bore down on the Sparker.

Her deranged smile remained unchanged, but her robes flickered, turning black as night. Darkness invaded her purple-hued eyes and angry, crimson scars bloomed across her skin.

Just for a second, then she shifted back to the woman who'd murdered his only family.

Nexes collided with her, knocking her to the ground, and he sobbed as his twin swords buried themselves in her chest. She smiled up at him, an unflinching smile of pure madness, staring with eyes that saw too much. As he pulled the swords free, blood droplets floated around him, like the residue drifting in a different stream to the rest of the world, and he plunged into her again, weeping as the blades shuddered in her chest.

Nexes stabbed at her, just as he'd done to the Sparker who'd saved his life after the charge into the elven ranks, and her face flickered. The mage he'd murdered stared up at him, confused.

"What are you doing? He's one of yours."

Nexes stayed his hand, tears streaming down the face he had worn as a child. An elf had said those words on the battlefield, but now they came from a Shadow Sparker, its face swallowed by the darkness of its hood. Black fog surrounded it.

Snarling, Nexes charged at it, his arms a whirlwind, but his blades passed through the black cloak, finding nothing of substance. The shroud fell to the ground at his feet.

Crying out in pain, Nexes dropped his swords, their weight too much for his young arms to hold. Tallan Square had disappeared. Instead, he stood in the Cradle, the sealed stone door looming over him, the Sparker's corpse before him. Blood floated in the air like raindrops frozen in time.

Nexes approached the body and gasped.

Its face wasn't that of his grandparents' murderer, or the Sparker he'd mutilated on the battlefield.

Emperor Locke stared up at him, chest ruined, mouth slack, eyes vacant. But he wheezed a mocking laugh, one that filled Nexes' ears. Falling backward, scrambling away, he covered his head, hoping to block out the derisive sound.

"No," Nexes croaked, his voice high, shrill, childlike. "No, no, no, no!"

His last scream rang out as he bolted upright, sweat-soaked sheets sticking to him. Swinging his bare legs from the makeshift bed in his tent, Nexes staggered to the jug of wine on the table, filled a goblet, and drained it. The rich, fruity taste anchored him to reality. His arms itched, begging him to scratch with anything sharp, anything that would cut.

"Master of War?" a doubtful voice called from the entrance.

"What is it?" Nexes snapped, glaring at the guard's head peering in around the canvas flap.

"Ah, a messenger for you, sir. From the emperor."

Filling his goblet again, Nexes nodded. "Send them in."

Not a second later, a man in brown travelling clothes strolled in, his black cloak streaked with mud and soaked through. Of average height, with a face Nexes would forget as soon as he lost sight of him, the man took in the Master of War's sweaty night clothes and then the goblet. He raised an eyebrow.

Scowling, Nexes took a sip of wine. It turned into a mouthful. "You have something for me?"

The Emperor's Hand nodded. "An urgent message."

"It had better be. Make it quick. What does my emperor require of me?"

"Only that you read this." The Emperor's Hand offered him a sealed letter, which Nexes snatched away. "And that you understand his words well."

Flashing him a grin, the messenger bobbed his head and turned on his heel, merging into the night as the pavilion's entrance closed behind him.

Unsealing the letter, Nexes' eyes widened as he read, and then reread, the emperor's letter.

He understood his words. Understood them too well. But understanding didn't mean he had to welcome them.

Master of War Nexes read the update from Emperor Locke a number of times on the long march north to meet the Banished. Now, sitting in his tent, the army resting for the night, he read it again.

His nightmare the previous night plagued his mind.

They'd come more often since the 'Battle of the Black Sun', as his soldiers called it. The letter delivered by the Emperor's Hand would make things worse. Nexes had tossed them both over in his mind as they rode, sullen even by his own standards, and decided to gain more clarity regarding his discomfort. Who better to question than a Sparker?

He'd invited Mara Jura, an experienced Sparker who'd fought under his command more than once over the years, to his pavilion. As the ranking Sparker under his command, she told him the mood of the mages in his ranks—not including the Shadow Sparkers, who kept to themselves, which the others preferred—and Nexes picked her mind on the intricacies of her field. Despite his disdain for the mages, his old friend Balz aside, he never left any stone unturned.

A successful commander didn't ignore or misuse the weapons in his war chest.

But as the night drew on, the private missive from the emperor distracted him. Mara had a habit of talking without end, and Nexes didn't care for speaking for speaking's sake. The trait sickened him. It stirred the embers of his constant, deep-seated rage. These days, that furnace required little fuel. Unease affected his camp, his soldiers, his soul, and Nexes knew its origin; it seeped in from the places the fires didn't touch, the places where the shadows reigned supreme.

Flashes of the battle with the elves played in his mind, visions of his nightmare flitting between them, merging until both felt as real as a memory, abstract as a dream.

I murdered the emperor. My friend. Locke...

The skin on his forearms crawled. Not since Tallan Square had something so unmanned Nexes. Even he avoided

approaching the Shadow Sparkers during the march unless
he had to, preferring the company of regular Sparkers.
A rarity for him. His eyes betrayed him though. His gaze
wandered to the dark stain trailing behind his forces, clouds
gathering above them wherever they moved.

The rage building inside him had released during the
battle, the massacre helping him find the balance within
himself once more or so he thought. Nexes always walked
the line between ice and fire, and now doubt ate away at him.
The equilibrium he'd sought remained beyond his reach.
Regrets over these Shadow Sparkers plagued his waking and
sleeping moments.

He'd witnessed first-hand the destruction they wrought,
the madness inside their souls, the way they'd changed the
face of war forever. If more mages lost themselves to this,
honest warriors like Nexes would become obsolete.

Then came the letter. He fought the compulsion to
stare at the emperor's note again.

"Where the Spark comes from," he said, trying to focus.
"Tell me about that."

"Oh, the origins of the Spark! A fascinating subject,
indeed. There's much debate about that, Master of War, and
it's a subject I enjoy discussing."

"I thought you might, though it appears you find much
love in many areas of conversation," Nexes murmured, fold-
ing the note and placing it in his lap. He'd study it again
later. "Most Sparkers would say it came from Raas and leave
it there, isn't that right? Doesn't your order claim it's a gift
from the gods?"

Mara smiled, eyes sparkling. Nexes studied her open,

soft features and violet eyes; she didn't look like a leader, but the woman never shirked taking her place in the front lines. She had used her Spark proactively before the abolishment of the Laws. But those eyes were a shade darker than before.

Mara had picked up Evisceration with speed and relish, despite her innocent appearance.

"That's the doctrine, yes, and until recent years, it was taught that way in the Order's university."

His hand shook a little as he picked up his goblet, a tiny tremor invisible to the naked eye, but one that resulted in a stream of fiery resentment spreading through his stomach. Why could he not quiet his trembling? Nexes breathed the liquid's rich chocolate scent and filled his mouth, savouring the spiced mixture of flavours on his tongue before swallowing. The vintage was a favourite of the emperor's, and like most finery his old friend and master enjoyed, Nexes had acquired a taste for it.

He gulped down the wine, along with the lingering bitterness at the thought of Emperor Locke seeing him as nothing more than another servant. Or, worse, a slave.

Scratch, scratch, scratch.

"Tell me about that."

Mara frowned. "You've never heard it told?"

"Not from a Sparker, no. Please, indulge me."

He spoke the words like a command and, as everyone save Emperor Locke himself did, the Sparker acceded to his request.

"Well, it's said Raas travelled from his birthplace in what we now call Adhraas after a presence spoke to him in his dreams. For weeks, he journeyed to the Peaks of Eternity and climbed them in just his bare feet. The flesh on his palms and soles oozed blood by the time he found the presence inside. Whatever divine entity he discovered there healed him, and in doing so, planted the Spark in his soul. Raas, in his ultimate wisdom, called for his brothers and sisters to join him from Adhraas, and they too made the journey, though some failed, their bodies and minds too weak. Those who joined Raas—Janna, Hera, Araxaan and Bel—received the same gifts he did, and became our exalted gods, the first to learn about and wield the Spark. They passed it on to those worthy enough to follow in their footsteps. Of course, there's nothing in the Peaks of Eternity except the Banished. We'd have known otherwise."

Nexes swirled his goblet, watching the blood-red wine slosh. The Peaks of Eternity, where the Banished spent their exile. He'd heard conflicting reports of the Battle of Solitude, his own people too far away to witness it, but they'd rounded up displaced Sparkers wandering in the wilderness. They all spoke of the dark entity growing above the walls, and the presence watching from the distant mountains, before an eruption of green light destroyed the evil miasma and wiped Solitude from existence. Details of the battle varied—who struck the first blow, how many died, the number of survivors—but accounts of the black evil, so much like the darkness spreading from the Shadow Sparkers, and Solitude's final moments remained the same.

Of course, those Sparkers wouldn't tell anyone else. Shielded and bound, Nexes had tortured and executed them himself.

"Sounds grand." Nexes took another drink, thoughts

straying to the last Sparker he'd put under the blades and licked his lips. Screams and blood lived long in the memory. "And fanciful. A shepherd walking miles alone, barefoot, and climbing the tallest mountain in the continent, in a place no one visits. Utter rot. Tell me what the less fanatical believe."

"The 'less fanatical.'" Mara raised an eyebrow. "You presume I number among these?"

Nexes ignored the woman's impropriety, her assumed familiarity with him. He understood. Nexes invited the Sparker to his tent often; she would see a bond forming between them as they spoke. It was only natural, and Nexes didn't see the logic in disabusing her of the notion. Yet.

"I don't presume." Nexes let a cold smile spread across his lips. "You enjoy battle. I've seen it. I recognise it. I feel much the same. You call the Order's old ways 'doctrine', which suggests you felt enslaved by it. You've Eviscerated on the battlefield. A mere elf, true, but you used your magic to suck the essence from another soul. You fed upon it and watched as its skin withered, its hair thinned and wasted away, falling in clumps to the dirt, its organs failed and it turned to rot at your feet. More blood to add to the shit, piss and filth in the mud. I saw you smile."

Mara paled as Nexes spoke. Perhaps he *did* want to disabuse her of the foolish notion after all. He, Nexes Almor, Master of War, could never see the likes of her as a friend. Yes, her manner *did* displease him, as did all the smug faces of the mages in his camp, all of them so superior, so confident in the magic flowing in their veins, until they found themselves shielded and under his knife. They cried then, didn't they? How they begged for mercy that would never, ever come. Only the weak dealt in mercy. He leaned forward, keeping his eyes on hers, and refilled his goblet from the decanter.

"More wine?"

She hesitated, off-balance. No doubt she saw herself in a different light than her actions suggested. Her type always did.

"Please," she said.

Nexes poured her a healthy amount.

"You enjoyed it, didn't you? The death you dealt. What you did to that poor elf."

Mara shook her head, sipping at her wine. The sip turned into a gulp. "It overwhelmed me."

"What did?"

"All of it!" Darkness swirled in Mara's violet eyes. "The presence of the Shadow Sparkers, what they did... It called to me. When I saw what they did, the power they wielded. It all seemed so easy, and I lost myself in it. That elf..." She shook her head. "I swore I wouldn't do it again, *couldn't* do it again. But, in the moment, I felt such life. Such power."

Nexes leaned back, lips pursed as Mara took another gulp. "It's just another weapon, nothing more." He kept his own doubts from his words and savoured the realigning of their dynamic. "You were telling me about the Spark."

Mara blinked, mouth falling open before she closed it with a snap. Moments before, she'd appeared so comfortable, so in control of herself and the conversation. Her smiles, her slightly condescending tone as she lectured Nexes about fantasies concerning the Spark. Now she knew her place.

Really, Nexes preferred it this way. Only one person in the entirety of Haltveldt saw him as a lesser person, and it wasn't some battlefield Sparker.

He fought the urge to study his emperor's note again.

Mara cleared her throat, and Nexes nodded for her to begin, crossing his legs and running a long finger around the rim of his goblet.

"Many Sparkers, including myself, believe the Spark is the heartbeat of our world. More than that, it's the nexus point in which all realities converge, the thing that ties time and all possible realities together. All versions of the past, present and future."

Nexes laughed and licked a drop of wine from his finger. "Are you a Sparker or a theologist?"

"The 'less fanatical' believe Sparkers and theologists should be one and the same."

Nexes nodded, approving the logic in her words. "Worlds, you say? Realities? Past, present, and future? What do you mean by that?"

"I'm not sure I'm best at explaining it. Greton would be better, but he's in Spring Haven, and you'll never see him in a tent, never mind a battlefield." Mara bit her lip, eyes flicking at Nexes then away, aware of her over-familiar tone again. "You return home one night to find your other half in bed with their lover. What do you do?"

"Kill them both," Nexes answered, without hesitation.

Some acts always deserved death, betrayal one of them. The note burned in his lap.

"Well, yes..." Mara coughed, and took another gulp of her wine. "Then the world, your reality, would continue in one direction. But, say you didn't. Say you let them go. That would create a different reality."

Nexes tapped a finger against his lip. "And these realities can be created by more trivial matters?"

"Big and small, yes. They overlap, branching and expanding, but the Spark exists in all of them. The only constant. Greton believes it doesn't perceive time as we do, that it moves through all realities and time in its own moment, all of it occurring 'now', rather than before or after. The problem with that is proof."

Nexes nodded. "If the Spark doesn't come from Raas, then where does it come from? Where is it found? And the proof is hard to acquire, with the gods long gone. If they ever existed at all."

Mara shrugged. "The scriptures say Raas found the Spark in a cave at the summit of the tallest mountain in the Banished lands. Only Matrim the Mad ever journeyed to the Peaks of Eternity, and the powers that be discounted everything he ever wrote."

"What did he say?" Nexes asked, gripping his armrest with the hand not clutching his wine. "What did he find there?"

"Oh, he rambled on about the Banished, saying they weren't the simple shepherds we thought, but he never mentioned anything about a presence or a source of the Spark. He left all his notes up in Solitude somewhere before he returned to Spring Haven. Destroyed now, just like Solitude itself, or lost. Either way, it seems he was correct. About the Banished, at least."

Nexes avoided her eyes, and the questioning look in

them. Those with keener minds asked questions about the
Banished. Just whispers, and they ensured they remained
on the correct side of treason when they uttered them, but
such souls wondered just how the Banished, who Haltveldt
assured its citizens were not a threat for centuries, had managed to level a fortress defended by two hundred Sparkers.

Nexes had brought these concerns to Emperor Locke in
the days leading up to the battle, but his liege dismissed them.

*They'll believe what we tell them to believe, and the people
will want revenge. It'll blind them to everything else.*

Perhaps the lingering questions would melt away once
the battle with the Banished commenced, when Nexes handed out their punishment for entering Haltveldt and killing
Solitude's Sparkers.

It wouldn't deter the rebels so easily. Nexes' fingertips
itched as they reached for the letter in his lap. He grabbed his
goblet instead and refilled it.

*If they ever found out what we kept from them, the infor-
mation withheld at the Cradle, and how he allowed Solitude
to fall...*

No. That wouldn't happen. Not now. Unless someone
had already talked.

"Of course, the very creation of the Shadow Sparkers
proves Raas isn't a god, and the Spark isn't some divine entity, doesn't it?" Nexes changed the subject, nudging it back
where he wanted.

The Shadow Sparkers. He wanted to discuss them,
despite how they plagued his dreams, turned them to
nightmares. The way they flickered into existence, before he
murdered his emperor...

Scratch, scratch, scratch.

"What do you mean?" Mara asked, her features sharp, before she added a suitably humbled, "my lord?"

Nexes placed his goblet down and spread his hands, fixing a bland smile on his face which was anything but. "The Order's dogma says the Spark is only for good. For healing, for defence, teaching and knowledge. But tell me, when the Shadow Sparkers called on their gift, when they unleashed themselves on the battlefield, did your Spark shrink away? Did it want nothing to do with the horror inflicted on those poor elves?"

Derision dripped from Nexes' voice. He knew the answer, had seen it in the studies conducted at the university. The Sparkers, Ricken Alpenwood's acolytes, indulged themselves. And there had been others, who held the Laws and scriptures high, yet succumbed to temptation.

"I..." Mara stammered and blinked. "I-I'm not sure what you're asking, my lord."

"You know exactly what I'm asking." Nexes' voice could cut through iron. The heat in his eyes withered Mara's resolve as she stared back, breath held. "That magic inside you *yearned* for you to give in, to use it just as the Shadow Sparkers did, and you surrendered to it with great relish. It didn't take much, did it?"

"I-it's not as simple as—"

Nexes launched to his feet, throwing his goblet across the pavilion. Deep red stained the pure white canvas and dripped onto the golden sunburst rugs, his last vestiges of civility fraying at the edges. The Sparker played games with him! Her twisted words. Her condescending stare and mocking smile. Damn her!

"You're animals. All of you. Every Sparker is a weapon, and nothing more!"

Flashes of Tallan Square and his grandparents' pitiful deaths played in his mind. The light leaving the eyes of the Sparker he'd massacred on the battlefield. The unnatural filth the mages lowered themselves into without hesitation at the university. The staring eyes of his emperor, the loose, deranged smile...

"Those Shadow Sparkers are what you all want to be. What..." He thrust out a shaking finger. "...that *thing* inside you wants. The darkness, the death, it calls to it, calls to *you*, and if it were up to me, you'd suffer the same fate as the elves! You're not heroes. You're not the way the world should be! You're a plague, a pestilence. Corrupt and evil!"

Mara's face paled in the face of his onslaught, but her eyes... Darkness swirled in the bright violet there, reflecting her rotten soul.

"My lord, I don't know what I've said to offend you, but if you wish me to—"

Nexes' hands dropped to the blades attached to the belt on his waist. Even in his tent, in the middle of a camp full of the emperor's followers, Nexes wouldn't go unarmed. They were the emperor's men, after all, not his.

Nexes' fingers clenched around the gilded hilts. They stared at one another and, for a moment, Nexes almost wanted the mage to draw on her Spark and end him. Gods-rot, end it *all*.

"Are you still close to High Sparker Balz?"

Mara blinked, her mouth hanging open, confused at

the sudden, whispered question, but those eyes...

"As you know, he studied under me at the university, and we speak—"

"Get out," he whispered, but his hands remained where they were. "Now. Go!"

Mara didn't need a second invitation. Scrambling to her feet, she gave a quick bob of her head and swept out of the tent's entrance. A guard peered in, concern etched into her face—she'd have heard Nexes' shouts; they always did—then looked away again.

Nexes laughed, hands dropping to his sides, fingers already missing the feel of his weapons.

"They think I'm mad. They all do." He shook his head and dropped back into his chair. "But they haven't seen what I've seen. They don't know what I do..."

Another tremor ran through his hands. Balling them into fists, he closed his eyes and counted to five. Nexes didn't know enough about the Banished—the First People—and he always avoided a fight with an unknown enemy. The reports from Solitude made it clear they possessed some kind of magic, which meant Nexes had to rely on the Shadow Sparkers.

And you couldn't stake your life on them. Steel, determination and skill, yes. Mages, no. Life had taught him that, and now he marched his army north to face a horde of ancient magic users, with demons in his midst. You couldn't even rely on old friends...

Opening his eyes, he flicked the letter open and read it again.

'Nexes,

Our old friend Balz has betrayed us. Sparkers under his control attacked me on Order grounds. We've uncovered treason, and rumours spread of assassins from abroad in league with malcontents. He has been Turned, and poses no further threat. I send him to join you. Be sure he makes himself useful in our campaign one last time.

This disappointing turn of events has filled me with doubt. I know my own mind, my own devotion to the cause, but I'm reminded that you urged me to include our old friend Balz in our plans, that you recommended him as High Sparker.

I don't wish to doubt your judgement and loyalty, Nexes.

Emperor Locke.'

Balz. One of his oldest friends. He'd trained his mind to forget what Balz was—a Sparker, an abomination—but a person's inner nature could only remain hidden so long. You couldn't trust anyone in Haltveldt.

Nexes crumpled the letter in his hand, tears stinging his eyes. Getting to his feet, he tossed it into the fire pit at the centre of his tent. The flames made short work of it.

He turned away from his bed and left the pavilion, the night's crisp air biting at his skin. Nexes should sleep, but he feared what his mind would conjure if he did.

The darkness swirling in the eyes of Mara Jura, an old friend of the traitorous Balz. A mentor even. He trusted her like he trusted a viper in his sheets. Turning to a guard, he signalled for them to come close.

"Go to the Shadow Sparkers. Mara Jura is to be brought to me on suspicion of treason, shielded and bound. Go."

Questioning the Sparker under the knife, without her magic to bolster her, might reveal more of Balz's apparent betrayal, but it would give Nexes more than just answers.

He needed something to kill.

"Why? Why are you doing this?" Mara screamed, the cords in her neck taut, eyes bloodshot and bulging.

Nexes stared down at her tear-stained face. She didn't look so smug now, helpless and tied. He hadn't even stuck her with the blade yet. He showed her the curved knife he used to slice skin from bone and she crumpled. Proof that Sparkers were less than nothing without their magic. An honest soldier wouldn't dissolve like Mara had.

"You told me yourself," Nexes whispered, crouching so his eyes met hers. She flinched at whatever she saw in them. "Balz studied under you, and he's proven to be a traitor."

"And that's enough to question *me*?" Mara sobbed.

Shadow Sparkers lingered outside the tent, three of them, their magic shielding the mage. Nexes stared at the stocks holding Mara face-down and prone, the candlelight dimmer than it should be, but that didn't matter. Nexes pulled his mind back to his appointed task and the instrument in his hand. He found people wailed more when they couldn't see where the blade would sink next.

"It's more than enough." Nexes smiled and held the curved blade between them. "I'd encourage you to tell me everything about your role in this failed revolt. I will make it quick if you do. Sadly, it won't be painless. Sadly for you, I mean."

"Revolt?" I don't know what—"

"Yes, they all start that way, but you'll give me names, places, plans. You know, that fat pig, Bertrand de Reyes, swore on his daughter's life that he knew nothing." Nexes stood to his full height, taking in his quarry. "Needless to say, I killed her after he confessed his treason. It's only fair. He swore his false innocence on her."

"Mad," Mara sobbed. "You're droking mad! We all knew it. We just didn't know how deranged you really were!"

Nexes let the words float by him. He'd heard those before too. The traitors he put to the blade and questioning tools always called him mad. Deranged. Droked in the head and worse. Sometimes, he heard a whisper in his own mind breathing those same words, telling him to scratch when he doubted his emperor, but Nexes didn't think himself mad.

Mara knew nothing of treason. He understood that. That she had been Balz's mentor, and him a traitor, proved mere convenience.

Nexes wanted her dead, and he wanted to taste her agony, desired her blood covering his clothes and skin, the bitter taste of her on his tongue. He needed to hear her screams of mercy, her pleading, and to watch the light leave her eyes.

In this moment, with the betrayal of his friend, the suspicion of his emperor, his army marching into the unknown with untrustworthy Sparkers and the corrupt shadow in his midst, the Master of War required nothing more than to assert his dominance over a creature who thought themselves above him. To control something.

Anything.

Mara screamed as Nexes moved out of her line of sight, her neck and head straining against her bonds. Once he'd finished with her back, he'd flip the whimpering piece of pestilence over and work on her front. Make it last. Draw out her pain until the sun rose.

Reaching down, he grabbed a handful of her long hair and twisted it in his fist, smiling as her screams rose in pitch.

Nexes wrenched her neck back against the restraints, and pain filled her cries, mixing with the fear. Pulling her hair tighter, he sheared through the taut strands at the back of her head, right down to the scalp, cutting rougher as she thrashed against her restraints, as her screams became shrill.

He tossed her shorn hair to the ground in front of her, watching it float to the ground.

Less torture and more indignity. He didn't think Mara vain, but everyone had an image of themselves, captured in looking glasses and still waters, that they could gaze upon and identify with. Depriving them of that helped with the breaking, helped the pain truly bed in.

Even those who seemed weakest of spirit could prove surprisingly resilient. Nexes took his time with each and every one.

"Why?" Mara cried, grief thick on her tongue. "I've never let you down, have I? I've always fought on the frontlines, loyal to the empire. To Haltveldt!"

"Why do traitors do anything?" Nexes asked, pulling at the hem of the Sparker's bright robes and reversing the grip on his knife. He ran it through the fabric, parting it through the middle. Mara's bare shoulders heaved as she sobbed. "Money? Influence? Petty revenge? It's always the same."

He placed the tip of the blade against Mara's skin, drank in her terror, the way her skin twitched, anticipating the cut. She wanted the first one to come, just to get it over with, no matter how much she dreaded it.

"I'll give you anything you want!" Her voice switched between shrill screams and hacking sobs. Anger lay beneath the fear too. It always did. "Please. Anything!"

They always said that, right before the cutting started. Nexes shook his head. No one could give him what he wanted. Not really.

Answers to his questions came, of course, and sometimes they had truth to them, but there were always more questions. Not all of those had answers, but he'd seek them out, buy them in blood, all the same.

Nexes paused, staring at the candlelight glinting on the blade's steel.

What do I want?

He wanted to know what the First People could do, what they sought. Would Mara tell him? *Could* she? Unlikely. He wanted to be free of the Shadow Sparkers too. Relying on regular mages was bad enough. They weren't to be trusted and had too much power. These new ones—their abominable hunger, the way they twisted and perverted the world around them—disturbed him and the honest soldiers of his army. Could Mara help him be rid of them? Again, unlikely.

Nexes wanted respect. He detested the way Mara had looked at him in his tent, how she spoke to him, like he lay beneath her, an ordinary man without special powers or abilities. Someone who held his rank because of his friendship with the emperor...

Locke. His old friend. They'd plotted for years together, confided in one another, trained and became as close as brothers.

Closer.

Now the emperor questioned his judgement. *His*. Did he suspect Nexes' involvement in plots against him?

How dare he? How droking dare he!

Scratch, scratch, SCRATCH.

Nexes' vision faded, darkness flooding in from the edges as he stared at the blade, unseeing, unhearing. He'd put everything he had into serving Haltveldt, in the name of his emperor, his friend. He'd devoted himself to the man, and swam through tides of crimson to please him, had lowered himself into the filth of humanity, had waged genocide against the elven scum and just about wiped the creatures from the face of Haltveldt, all in the emperor's droking name!

And how did Locke think of him?

The emperor's words from the Cradle came back to him, when they discussed the First People's enslavement of the elves.

Slaves, yes? But we both know slaves serve a master.

Locke was Nexes' master, and a master could change his mind on their slave's worth at any moment. Discard them. Replace them.

Is that what the emperor wanted to do with him? He sent Balz to Nexes, to his death. Did Locke have plans to do away with Nexes too? Had he commanded a Shadow Sparker, or another of the Order, to ensure his Master of

War never left the battlefield?

Itch, scratch, itch.

Nexes would find out. He'd uncover any plots. Maybe Balz had conspired against him, hoping to turn the emperor against him.

And that's what it came down to. All the moving pieces in his mind swirled around one truth Nexes couldn't escape, and it tormented him.

This torture, this desire for blood, this *need* for cleansing by flaying Mara. Locke didn't trust him anymore. His own written words confirmed it. After everything Nexes had done, his emperor, his friend, doubted him. All because of Balz.

Balz. Another Sparker. Another smug, condescending elitist like the woman beneath his blade. Nexes would make her pay, would spend his anger, his loathing, his frustration on this—

Mara's scream ripped through Nexes' thoughts, pulled him back from the pits of madness yawning in his mind.

Blinking, he studied her back. The knife had sunk to the hilt, blood covering his fingertips.

"Stop!" she cried, the bench she lay on rattling. "Stop, I beg you! I've done nothing! *Nothing!*"

Nexes rested a fingertip on the pommel and leaned over. His mouth came so close to Mara's ear he could have kissed it.

"How does it feel? Knowing you have the power inside you to stop me, to turn me to nothing but a pile of oozing pus on the ground, but you can do nothing?" Her shaking stopped and she fell silent, listening to Nexes' whispered words. "I'm going to kill you, you know? And there's no reason other than because I want to. There's nothing you can tell me, no names, no places. Nothing you can give me, except for your blood. You've served your empire well."

Nexes straightened, gripped the hilt of his dagger, and pulled it free. Blood flowed along with Mara's screams.

Almost to himself, Nexes added, "And this is your reward."

As the sun broke on the horizon, Nexes staggered from the tent. His soldiers, open-mouthed, stared at him, then looked away as he swept his gaze across them. Even the Shadow Sparkers wouldn't meet his eyes.

Nexes peered through a mask of crimson, his clothes and every part of his skin covered in it. In his fingers, he held a scrap of paper.

"Did she give you names, my lord?" one of the Shadow Sparkers whispered, its thin voice carrying over the wind. It stared down at the mud. Better to sink its gaze into the filth than try to match the Master of War standing before it.

Nexes glanced at the paper and held it up. There was no ink under the blood and ichor covering it. He'd write them down later, pluck the words from the aether, fill it with the names of Sparkers in his camp. He'd question them too, his blank list ever growing.

"She did."

A laugh bubbled from his throat. She'd died before he even noticed, lost in his work. At one point, she wore her own face, then the one of the Sparker from Tallan Square. Before the end, he'd seen Locke before him, whimpering in pain as he existed between life and death.

"I'll give you the names soon, but now, we must ride. The Banished await and they must meet our vengeance." Turning, he strode away, feet squelching in his boots from the blood pooling between his toes. He raised his voice, "Strike camp. We ride!"

Sparkers. Nexes couldn't trust any of them, and neither could the emperor. He'd finish the Banished, deliver their leader's head to Locke's feet, then uncover the conspiracy at the heart of the empire. He'd regain his emperor's wavering trust.

For Haltveldt. For Locke.

Chapter Twenty

OF VENGEANCE AND FLAME

*'They don't tolerate Sparkers in Willow. Used to be worse
before Spring Haven swallowed it into Haltveldt. The
rebellious folk there placed their faith in a notion called
'science'. More reliable than magic, they said. Whatever
this 'science' used to be, it's lost in the mists of time.'* - Rener
of Kullman, the infamous war historian, spent much of
her time examining Willow's lurid, blood-filled past.

"You understand the plan, yeah?" Calene rolled
her eyes when Marc scowled. "What? Do you
get it or not?"

"Not much of a plan, is it?"

"Well, you haven't exactly come up with anything
better?"

If Marc could have folded his arms, Calene reckoned he
would have. Instead, he frowned down at his one arm, like

the sight of its asymmetry still offended him.

"It's just that, in theory, this plan isn't a plan. It's an objective. 'Get in, blend in, keep our heads down, find Maria and get out of there'. I get it. I don't even disagree. I *can't* disagree." He shook his head, jowls wobbling. "It's the 'how exactly are we going to do all that?' That's the part I don't understand!"

"God's Teeth, this is *your* droking friend, not mine!"

They fell silent, and it wasn't a comfortable one. Since the raid at the Broken Bard, Calene and Marc had kept to the rooftops, hiding in the shadows as they watched the comings and goings of the Patriarch's Palace. They'd seen the Emperor's Hand who'd confronted them entering the gates, along with a sizeable contingent of guards, not long after their fracas. They'd had Maria in tow, and they hadn't seen them leave.

Marc had wanted to press the attack right away, and Calene had asked just how long their little rebellion had lasted with such reckless thinking. Surely it wouldn't last much longer.

She'd killed two Shadow Sparkers. Disintegration and pulverising the head proved enough. Brina had decapitated the first one she'd seen, so that worked too. But Calene would bet the emperor's vault on there being more inside the palace, and regular, empire-loyal Sparkers to boot. Not to mention the squadrons of guards and Raas knew how many of the Emperor's Hand.

The thought of just walking away had crossed her mind more than once, but she blamed herself. Another one of her many failings.

Logically, she knew the Emperor's Hand had questioned Faye du Gerran for the names of the cell in Willow, as well as its location. Logically, she knew she'd stumbled into the wrong city, to the wrong inn, at the wrong moment. A small part of Calene insisted that Marc would be dead if it weren't for her, that Maria was lost without any chance of rescue, and that she'd killed two of the evil drokers already. She'd settled the account.

Despite that, she still found ways to point the finger at herself. And Marc agreed.

"She wouldn't be in the Patriarch's Palace if it weren't for you," he grumbled, flexing the fingers on his hand. "It's the least you can do."

"Aye, it is," Calene snapped, meeting his eyes. "And while I'm leading this rescue party, you follow my lead, right? If it all goes wrong, then at least we'll know who to blame."

"I already know who to blame."

"God's teeth, shut up if you don't have anything useful to say."

Calene had more of a plan in mind than what she'd told Marc. As they'd moved across the rooftops, using their Spark in short spurts, she'd sensed others in the city doing the same, with the palace as the nexus. Opening her Second Sight as she studied the walls, she saw the Spark bloom, a concentrated pocket coming from below the palace. The dungeons.

It meant, inside the palace, and close to it, they could use their Spark without drawing too much attention, but only if they were subtle about it. The thought made Calene's stomach flip.

She wasn't known for her subtlety, and Marc possessed as much as a drunken Octarian spice runner on the Spring Haven docks. After all, she'd caught him once.

Disguises were another thing. Once inside the palace, they could find them—Sparkers or guards. Marc's arm, or lack thereof, might cause a problem, but they could improvise. What Calene lacked in strategy, she made up for flying by the seat of her robes.

With disguises in hand, all they had to do was make their way to the dungeons, find Maria, and escort her out. They wouldn't even have to fight, assuming they didn't come across the Emperor's Hand or any Shadow Sparkers.

Calene explained as much to Marc, who watched with a completely blank face.

"...then we can just march her through the gates, tell them we're moving her to Spring Haven. What do you think?"

Marc rubbed the end of his nose, thoughtful, then gave up on looking measured and winced. "It's better than nothing, I'll give you that... But what if we can't find disguises? What if we *do* happen across the Emperor's Hand? What if there are more Shadow Sparkers?"

Calene smiled. "How do you feel about improvisation?"

Marc's sigh could have pulled the dead from both the Gates of Eternity and the shores of the Underworld.

"We're all going to die in there, aren't we?"

"Not if I have anything to do with it." Calene pointed at the setting sun. "We wait till that blazing bastard's gone, then we move. If we come across Shadow Sparkers, take their heads from their shoulders. Assuming you can't just obliterate them, yeah?"

Marc nodded, then shook his head. "Wait, you haven't even said how we're getting in!"

Calene spread her arms. "We're on the rooftops, aren't we? I say we use that to our advantage." She pointed at the palace's towers, at the windows lining the walls, some intriguingly close to other buildings. "A touch of air, and we're in."

"Right."

She bit her lip, eyeing his stump. "You sure you're up for this?"

Marc met her eyes, and despite an angry flash, the expected rebuke didn't arrive. "Maria's been my friend through thick and thin. After I lost..." He shook his head. "I can't leave her behind. It's a plan, Calene. A plan. I'm in."

"Good."

The sun set behind the palace, and Calene filled her lungs. Anything might go wrong, but everything could go right too.

Raas, you droker. Have my back for once, please, you utter rasclart. I'm begging you.

She prodded the memory of her connection to her mother, the vast, poorly healed wound she'd taken to feeling for like a... Like a missing limb.

You too, wherever you are. I need your help.

"Where the drok is she?"

Brina paced the outcropping, the ledge where she'd

said goodbye to Calene the day before.

Said goodbye? Hardly. You said nothing and let her wander off into that city alone. Alone!

Snarling, she kicked at a clump of grass, then kicked at it again when it had the temerity to trip her a little.

"She's fine. Probably blowing off a little steam before she gets back." Vettigan stood not too far behind, hood raised. "I don't blame her."

Brina spun around, and stalked close to the haggard, old Sparker. To his credit, he stood his ground. The two hadn't said much to each other since Calene's departure, both realising silence would keep them from each other's throats. But the longer Calene stayed away, the hotter Brina's temper grew, and confrontation would soon follow.

"You're not worried about her? God's teeth, man, you're meant to be her oldest friend!"

"Did I say I wasn't?" Vettigan snapped, once bright eyes dark in the shade. "Of course I am, but it's not like we're going to storm the gates, is it? She told us to wait, and that's what we'll do."

"What if she's in trouble?" Brina grabbed Vettigan's cloak and dragged his face closer. His breath tasted stale. "What if she's dead?"

Vettigan's features spasmed, a look of utter hatred and disgust merging into a snarl before he visibly brought himself under control. Reaching up, he gripped Brina's wrists.

"I'd feel it if she died." He eyed her hands and squeezed. Not to cause pain, but to remind her. "Now take your fingers off me, and if you grab me again, I can't promise I'll be so restrained."

Brina met his eyes. Darkness swirled within them, and hatred. Pain too, mixed with regret and self-loathing. She recognised the look well. She saw it every time she happened by a mirror or stared at her reflection in a river.

Vettigan didn't despise her, didn't hold any malice against her kind—Calene had mentioned more than once the old man's sympathetic views toward elves—but he railed against the world. Against himself. The man wanted to die, or crawl to the other side of the world and hide there until he stood before the Gates of Eternity, or the shores of the Underworld.

His love for Calene stopped him.

"You don't care if she helps you or not, do you?" Brina breathed, letting her hands fall to her sides. Vettigan's sword glinted at his hip as he shifted his cloak back into place. "You're letting her do it for her."

The old man went to spit on the ground but held himself in check again. Instead, he stared into the city.

"The Spark swells in there. I can't use it anymore, but Raas knows I can feel it. Whatever lived inside me has left its stain and changed me forever. It wants me to go into that city and drink in the energy there, create my own by any means necessary. And the moment of death excites it the most. The emotions a dying person spits out into the aether... Shame, fear, relief, excitement, anger. Love, sometimes, too. I felt it back on the road, when I killed one of the Banished. When he was about to die, his thoughts turned to his family, or maybe his sweetheart..." Vettigan sighed and pinched the bridge of his nose. "There's no helping me, no reversing this. It's better I flee, or die in a ditch, but both of those take away one of the things keeping Calene going."

Brina nodded. "Hope."

"Aye, girl. Hope." Vettigan moved to the edge of the outcropping as the last of the day's travellers moved below them, rushing into Willow before sunset. "You offer it to her too, and Raas knows I wish you'd be honest with her. It looked like things were heading that way, but whatever happened to you back there, in the forest? Ah, but that's not my business. Keeping Calene alive is, and for that she needs a mission. For now, it's fixing me. Once that fails, she'll need a new one, or a reason to keep going." He met her eyes, the darkness in his stare thick and hard. "I trust you can set aside whatever's bothering you and provide that for her?"

Mela's accusing stare floated into Brina's mind, his lip curling when he spoke about humans, the hatred plain in his face. It reflected the animosity in her soul. They'd driven her kind to the edge of extinction. But Calene wasn't like that, so why did she see the eyes of the haunted elf as he threw himself from the cliff edge every time she opened her mouth to talk to her?

She shook her head, clearing her mind.

"You said you'd feel it if she was dead. How? Isn't that Link of yours gone?"

Vettigan looked away. "Not exactly."

"Then speak to her!"

"Even if I could, I wouldn't." Vettigan's hand fell to the pommel of his sword. "The Link is there, but it's covered by the worst part of me, the corruption inside. It's like it feels the essence of the Spark there and it's trying to get at it. If I contact her, I don't know what might happen. The darkness might spread through our Link and infect her too. I wouldn't wish this on my worst enemy, let alone my only family."

"But—"

"But nothing!" Vettigan snapped, then sighed again. "Look, I want her back as much as you do. But there's nothing we can do. Let's go back to the camp. If she hasn't returned by noon, we'll head in, alright?"

Brina nodded and turned back to the city.

Noon? I don't think I can wait that long. If she isn't here by morning bell, I'm going in. Consequences be droked.

As soon as the sun plunged beneath Willow's walls, Calene turned to Marc. "Ready?"

The one-armed Sparker sighed, shook his head, then nodded. "Aye."

"In, find Maria, out. Got it?"

"You keep saying that," Marc muttered, gazing at the Patriarch's Palace, "and I might start believing it'll all be so simple."

"Believe it," Calene grinned.

Flat against a rooftop adjacent to the palace, Calene pushed herself to her feet, crouching low, and heard Marc's soft footsteps following. For a heavyset man, he knew how to move without causing a racket. She scanned her surroundings as she moved, eyeing the dark streets below.

God's teeth, it's droking great to be doing something again. Even plunging into the leopard's maw!

Thoughts of her mother melted away as soon as she got to her feet, along with the nagging urge to check on Brina and Vettigan. Action. It's what she needed, and why she came to Willow in the first place. She'd told her companions, and herself, that they needed supplies, news and rumours. Really, Calene had wanted a way to blow off steam, to throw herself headlong into a situation where she could forget, for a few blessed hours at least.

She hadn't counted on rescuing a rogue Sparker from the belly of the Patriarch's Palace, but Calene would never look a gift horse in the mouth. Du Gerran and Marc needed her help, and didn't being a Sparker mean helping those in trouble?

It used to.

Coming to the rooftop's edge, Calene held up a hand and scanned her surroundings, opening her Second Sight. Blooms of Spark in the hulking building, with its golden domes and tall towers, caught her attention, though she detected precious little from close by.

"This is it." She eyed an open window across from her, fifty feet away, the opening about ten feet above her head. Too great a distance to jump for an ordinary person, but she and Marc were hardly that. "No turning back after we cross."

"Let's get it over with," Marc grumbled. He had a sword at his hip—a thin rapier, under his cloak—and a part of Calene desperately wanted to see him fight with just his one arm. "Right?"

"Right." Calene nodded. "On my mark."

It had to be fast and nothing too extravagant, timed alongside the flashes of Spark inside the palace. She counted in her mind, her Second Sight trained on the palace, waiting, power straining to be embraced.

How had she ignored it so long? Calene's mood had suffered since shunning her gift after the events at Solitude. She felt alive again after the encounter with the Shadow Sparkers at the Broken Bard. How she *should* be.

Or was that her Spark talking?

Giving her head a quick shake, she spied what she waited for, flashes of red and blue tinged with ominous darkness. Calene didn't consider that; she hadn't the time.

Embracing her Spark, she reached out about her and pulled on the air itself, let it bear her across the divide to the palace. The city's gas lamps glowed brighter, the darkness deepening, the smells of the city both stale and fresh, fragrant and foul, in her nostrils. Wind buffered her, lifting her at her command as she flew across the gap. She squinted as the window approached all too quickly. As she passed through, she released her Spark, its loss like a dagger to the guts, and tucked her head, hitting the floorboards of the room beyond the window and coming up in a roll, sword drawn.

Marc dropped behind her, hitting the landing with as much grace as she did, rapier ready.

Dust exploded around them as they landed. Stifling a cough, Calene glanced around at the circular room. Stacks of shelves filled it, artefacts of all shapes and sizes crammed here and there without any rhyme or reason. Squinting, she could only make out their shapes, the moonlight through the window lending the room its only light. Approaching the nearest stack, Calene let out a soft whistle.

"This is pre-Empire stuff, back when Willow was the capital of the Arcread Duchy." Pulling a relic clear, and waving a hand to chase away the dust, Calene offered a narrow, metallic device to Marc. As long as her arm, the artefact had a peculiar ring on top with what looked like a crossbow trigger under a wooden shaft. It narrowed to a tube, a circular opening at its end. "Wonder if anyone remembers what this did?"

"They say the Arcread Duchy fought a bloody war against Spring Haven, holding them off even though they had few Sparkers of their own," Marc muttered, staring down the hole at the end of the tube. "Perhaps they had special weapons? It was over a thousand years ago, and a nation of constant warfare means much history is lost. Progress too. Plus, the victors are the ones who end up telling the stories."

His finger found the strange trigger and squeezed. Dust exploded in his face and Calene tried her absolute best not to laugh. She failed, the snigger escaping in a strangled choke.

"That's progress alright! A dust blower!"

Marc glared at her, eyes shining in his dirty face. He ran a finger across his cheek and frowned as it came away black. He winced as he raised it to his lips and tasted it. Barrels stood at the end of the stacks, and Marc approached one. Removing the lid, he coughed as more black powder puffed into his face.

"God's teeth, what is this stuff?" he snarled, through a hacking cough.

"Right, if you've finished playing?" Calene raised an eyebrow and tried not to laugh again. She opened her Second Sight and scanned her surroundings, finding no blooms of Spark close by, though she detected concentrated flashes deep beneath her feet. A swirl of colours, with its fair share of pulsating darkness. "See that?"

"Hard not to," Marc grumbled, setting the strange relic back where it came from amongst the other dust-ridden oddities.

"Reckon that's where we're heading. They must be questioning Maria right now."

"You're probably right. We need to get to her sooner rather than later."

"Good. Now, follow me." Calene crossed to the door and placed her hand on the handle. "I think this is going well so far."

She swung the door open and leapt back with a gasp.

"Patriarch's beard, I thought I heard a droking noise! How'd you two get in here?"

A guard in silver and gold chainmail armour stood in the doorway, one arm stretched toward the handle, the other holding a rust-coloured blade.

Calene's mouth hung open as their eyes met. She threw a thumb over her shoulder. "Captain wanted us to take an inventory."

"Which captain?" the guard asked, taking a step forward and raising his sword. "Why are you dressed like commoners?"

"Well—"

"Enough talk!" Marc growled, and a bloom of Spark caught Calene's attention.

Yelling, the guard flew forward, tendrils of air wrapped

around his waist, and plunged toward Marc. The Sparker raised his rapier, the point driving through the guard's eyeball.

Pulling his blade free, the corpse dropped to the ground, blood pooling beneath him. Marc kicked him over then bent, getting to work at unfastening the guard's clothes. He glanced up and blinked at Calene's horrified stare.

"What? You said to improvise if anything went wrong." He turned back to the corpse. "Plus, these look like they'll fit me. Didn't want to get a hole in them."

"God's teeth, you got a droking hole in *him*, didn't you?"

"We're staging a rescue, Calene. You think the guards, Sparkers and whatever else in here is just going to stand aside and let us on our merry way? There's going to be blood. Let's just hope it ain't ours."

A yell pulled Calene's attention from the pilfering Sparker, and she moved to the side, just in time. Another guard charged into the room, rust-red blade swinging. Spinning, Calene pulled her own sword free and met her attacker's, the clang ringing out and echoing down the spiral stairs outside.

Pulling her arm back, Calene's elbow slammed into a stack of shelves. Right then, she understood Maria's love of shortswords in tight spaces. Snarling, without space to manoeuvre, she ducked under another swing from the guard, and drove her knee into his midriff. Pain lanced through her leg as she connected with his chainmail, but it had the desired effect. The guard stumbled, doubled over, and Calene brought her pommel down on the back of his head, dropping him into the dust.

"You don't have to kill every droker you come across, you know?" she growled, slamming her sword into its sheath.

There's always another way.

"Sorted mine out much quicker than yours, Alpen-wood," Marc mumbled, pulling the corpse's chainmail free. "Nice colour scheme, this. Want me to turn around while you get dressed?"

"Look who's Mister Droking Sense of Humour all of a sudden." Calene thrust a finger in his face. "Listen to me—"

The rattle of metal and pounding of feet sounded from outside the room. Shouts too. Holding up a hand, Calene raced to the door and peered out. Then she pulled herself back in and slammed the door shut.

Drok!

"What is it?" Marc yelled, dropping the chainmail and scooping up his rapier. "How many?"

"Too many, and they've got a Sparker with them." Calene grabbed the strange, long relic from the shelf and jammed it under the handle. "Raas, you utter droker. When we meet..."

Calene's senses screamed, and the door rattled as the guards attempted to batter it down. Apparently, they hadn't come to talk.

CHAPTER TWENTY-ONE

OF BLOOD AND FIRE

'Seeing a Sparker let loose on regular folk is bad enough, but a Sparker on Sparker fight? You ever see one brewing, you do one thing, and one thing only. You run. God's teeth, you run and never look back.' Rus of Christof, a small backwater outside Sea's Keep, never followed his own advice. He died shepherding civilians from Prosper's Eyre Point when a Sparker from the Order confronted a rogue. The survivors built a statue for him on the site of his death.

"**W**hat are we going to do?" Marc yelled, as a booming blast shook the walls and splintered the door.

"Shields! No point hiding what we are now!" Calene replied, embracing the Spark. The world bloomed around her, the colours brighter, the smell of sulphur and blood filling her nostrils. "The Sparker on the other side isn't too strong. We can take them!"

"I'm more concerned with the rest of them making their way here," Marc growled, his Spark soaring. "And why they haven't blown the door off its hinges. Odd, no?"

Calene held up a finger. "Stay alive first, ask questions later."

A shimmering, blue light covered Marc, his shield strong. His Spark didn't match Calene's—actually, it came nowhere near—but the man had some skill in defensive magic. Calene knew that from experience.

The walls rattled again, dust filling the air. She choked as the black powder from the barrels plumed, the stench of sulphur increasing. The wooden door bulged as soldiers crashed into it.

"We don't want any undue violence," a sneering voice called, from the other side of the door. "I sense you're not simple thieves. You have the Spark. Know you're in more danger than you realise. Lower your shields and submit to arrest peacefully."

Beneath her feet, in the bowels of the palace, darkness swelled, a sliver growing into a pulse, like the miasma of evil Vettigan had released on the walls of Solitude.

"Peacefully?" Calene yelled, gritting her teeth as the wooden door splintered, the strange relic jamming the handle bending. "Is what you're doing in the dungeons of this place peaceful? I can feel the corruption from here!"

"You know what else I feel?" Marc snarled, drawing on his Spark. "This drok's Spark on the other side of the door is no threat to us."

Energy swirling in the room popped as Marc drew it into his body. Arm outstretched, he trembled with the power running through him, almost as much as the man could handle. He pulled on every essence surrounding him, and the darkness below noticed. Part of it broke off from the corruption in the depths of the building and floated upward, joining the swirling energy building inside Marc.

"Wait!" Calene yelled.

At the same time, the Sparker behind the door screamed, "No!"

Energy exploded from Marc's outstretched arm, a shockwave tinged with black flame. The stone walls cracked. His eyes widened in shock at the concussive blast as it blew the door apart, along with chunks of brick, revealing a phalanx of guards in gold and white, and a fearful-looking Sparker, pulling up his shield and dropping to the floor in unison.

The debris crushed the soldiers closest to the door and threw the others back. They bounced off the Sparker's shield and fell, moaning, to the ground.

The smell of sulphur increased.

Wiping the dust from her eyes, Calene cast about. Black flames sizzled on the barrel lids by the canisters at the door. As the dust settled, she met the fear-stricken stare of the Sparker outside.

Calene had no idea what the black powder could do, or what the ancient soldiers of the Arcreadian duchy did with it, but by the way her stomach flipped then sank into her boots, she reckoned she was about to find out.

One of the lids crumbled, and the barrel exploded in a blast of furious flame.

"Drok!" Calene yelled, throwing herself into Marc and

pulling him to the ground, adding her shield to his. "The whole room's filled with that stuff!"

Flames sprang up around the room. More explosions followed, shaking the floor and blowing apart chunks of the wall. Screams underpinned the boom as the black powder ignited around them, their eruptions of heat penetrating Calene's shield.

She gritted her teeth and covered her ears, throwing her entire focus into keeping her barrier strong. Chunks of debris from the surrounding stone, the wooden shelves, and the strange relics struck against it. The entire building quaked.

After one final, shattering boom, one last explosion of flame, the shaking came to an end. Calene raised her head from Marc's chest and met a world of fire, the fumes and dust mixing to smother her vision. It crackled and hissed around her, heat searing her skin, smoke filling her lungs, but her shield held the wildfire at bay.

"You okay?" she asked, pulling Marc upright.

He blinked, his jaw hanging loose. "Yeah. I... I didn't mean to do that. Something corrupted my Spark. I couldn't stop it!"

"I saw. We need to get out of here. Now." Calene snarled, rising into a low crouch.

Air tickled her neck and she pulled on it, then sent it out in a funnel so she could see what lay in their path.

"God's teeth," Marc whispered, crouching beside her. "They're dead. They're *all* dead."

The wall had disappeared, a pile of loose stone laying atop crushed guards, blood mixing with the dust and scorch marks. Calene sent a flow of air the other way and turned her head, following it.

Willow's gas lamps twinkled below her, the vista of gold and orange domes laid out like a carpet, the towering red walls rising in the distance.

The blast had blown the entire wall off, leaving a gaping wound and an unparalleled, and unplanned, view of the city below.

"I'm starting to see how the Arcreadian's held off Spring Haven's Sparkers for so droking long," Calene muttered. "Come on, let's—"

Above her, the ceiling groaned. A rush of dust pattered over their conjoined shield, then a chunk of stone fell.

"Move!" Marc yelled, pushing Calene ahead with his arm.

She didn't need to be told twice. Calene plunged through the flame, toward the stairs and the pile of crushed bodies, as the room collapsed behind them. Landing on her front, Marc beside her, she spun just in time to see the tower disintegrate, the floors above plunging into the palace grounds.

"Talk about making an entrance," she muttered, getting to her feet and wiping the dust off her clothes.

She gave it up as a lost cause. Glancing around, her Second Sight revealed blooms of Spark heading into the palace grounds as Sparkers fought to halt the tower's collapse. The darkness in the dungeons had vanished too, the eruption no doubt disturbing Maria's interrogation.

"Not a bad diversion, if we can get out of here in time."

The rubble shifted at her feet, and a hacking cough sounded.

"Looks like the blast didn't kill everyone," Marc growled, pulling his sword free. "Lucky him."

Calene held up a warning hand and nudged some of the rubble aside. The broken and bleeding Sparker gazed up at her through a mask of crimson, glassy-eyed. His shield had failed under the barrage of bodies and debris.

"Maria du Gerran, where is she?" Calene asked, scanning his body with her Second Sight, then meeting his eyes.

"You're...too late..." He coughed again, and blood bubbled on his lips. "The Shadow Sparker... The Turning has begun..."

"Turning?" Marc snarled, pressing the tip of his rapier against the Sparker's throat. "What Turning?"

Calene knocked the blade aside and got to her feet. "Come on. He won't tell us anything else. He's dead. Let's find Maria." Glancing over her shoulder at the star-dotted sky, she started her descent. "The only way's down, right?"

Beneath her feet, the ground trembled, then the roaring sound of destruction reached Brina's ears.

"God's teeth, what in Raas' name was that?" Vettigan cried, getting to his feet.

Together, they ran from their camp in the woods, racing toward the outcropping that overlooked Willow, and gasped.

Smoke rose from the Patriarch's Palace, obscuring the Tower of Belti behind it, and even the moon. Brina spied a chasm in one of its towers, despite the distance.

"Calene..."

The name slipped from her lips without thinking, but she knew it. That's where the woman was, in the middle of danger, at the centre of destruction. As usual.

"Raas... I think you're right." Vettigan staggered to a stop beside her. His eyes glazed over. "She's still alive."

"Speak to her."

"No! I told you, elf, no! I don't know what it would do to her."

Brina's hands balled into fists. "Fine. I'm going. Stay here. Don't try to stop me."

"I won't." Vettigan's hand snatched out and gripped Brina's. Staring into his eyes, she saw fear there. Anxiety, compassion and warmth. Reminders of the man he used to be. "Bring her back. Please."

Brina nodded and set off into a sprint. She'd scale the great, red walls of Willow, kill every soul in the palace if she had to.

Damn what Mela said! She had no intention of leaving the city unless Calene walked out beside her.

Calene's hope of the destroyed tower being an enticing distraction proved futile.

"God's teeth," she snarled, blocking a two-handed blow from a patriarch guard with her sword and forcing it into the wall. Their blades scraped across the stone, sparks exploding from the impact. "How many of you drokers are in here?"

The guard didn't have time to answer. Marc thrust his

rapier over Calene's shoulder, its point disappearing into the soldier's throat. He dropped to the floor, gurgling, sword clattering, hands trying to stall the blood evacuating his body.

"You can thank me later," Marc smiled, pushing Calene over the dying man's kicking legs.

"Just don't use your Spark, okay? It's just been guards so far, but magic will send them straight for us."

Not to mention the darkness seeping through the bricks of the Patriarch's Palace might corrupt their power again.

Calene fell into a jog, scanning her surroundings with her Second Sight, avoiding pockets of magic and moving towards where the darkness lurked. She took the lead, bearing the brunt of any guards they'd happened by, and Marc lent her support.

To be fair, it wasn't the worst arrangement. The patriarch's soldiers attacked with a forceful fury, beating at Calene's defence, and she wasn't sure Marc's one arm and thin rapier could deal with such an onslaught. The Sparker had proved adept at snaking in as Calene engaged. Together, they'd left a trail of perforated corpses in their wake.

Guilt prodded at Calene, but she pushed it aside. She'd deal with it later.

"Don't need to tell me twice," Marc grumbled, tapping her on the shoulder. "Over there. Stairs."

"Nice. Not far now."

The palace shook with another tremor, and a groan echoed through its gilded corridors and marble floors. They'd probably been so polished Calene would grimace at herself every time she glanced down, but now everything had a thin carpet of soot and brick dust. Portraits of old patriarchs, vistas of idyllic Willow, or tableaus of armies at war lined the corridors, but Calene paid them little notice. Art never grabbed her at the best of times and staging a rescue after blowing a hole in the side of a palace filled with guards, Sparkers and Raas knew what else wasn't the best of times to pick up culture.

Calene changed direction and sprinted for the stairs, then skidded to a halt as a golden-white soldier with her red-rust blade came charging up them.

Calene sailed under the blow and twisted, swiping with her blade across the back of the guard's legs. She winced at the scream of pain as her sword made purchase with the guard's hamstrings, arm shuddering as the steel bit into the soft flesh.

The woman slumped to her knees, howling with pain, as Marc ran past, smashing the pommel of his rapier into her face. She dropped to the ground, crimson rivers snaking from the tracks cutting into her legs.

Marc held out his arm and Calene took it, pulling herself to her feet. The palace rumbled again.

"Reckon the whole side of this building's gonna collapse." Marc shook his head. "That black powder's lethal."

"Gone now, and I'm not too unhappy about that. Drok me, imagine that on the battlefield?" Calene scanned the stairs and saw no sign of the Spark, or the oozing shadow, but it lurked down there somewhere. With Maria. "It's a wonder none of the emperors ever used it."

They took the stairs one at a time, creeping. They both

knew their quarry lay below, along with whatever carried out this 'Turning' the dead Sparker spoke of.

"The old patriarchs probably wanted to keep it secret, in case they went to war with Spring Haven again," Marc whispered, rapier thrust out before him. "Willow's never had the best of relationships with the capital. Been there so long they forgot what it was for, I reckon."

"Well, they knew it was dangerous. That's why they were knocking on our door instead of blowing it down." Calene narrowed her eyes. Shadows swirled at her feet, tendrils of it reaching out and snaking around her ankles. She kicked her foot at them, and they dissipated, only to gather again and slink forward. "Is it me, or is it getting darker down here?"

Marc glanced at the flickering blue lamps lining the spiral stairs as they descended into the palace's belly. Their flames blazed, as if fighting against the shadow, but knowing it would swallow them. "It's getting darker."

"Drok me."

"And there's no one down here. Listen."

Calene paused, leaning against the wall. Cold seeped into her arm, and she pulled away, damp sticking to her. Lips curling, she strained her hearing.

Silence smothered all.

It wasn't the kind of quiet of a room where people slept or sat inside their own heads, or even of an empty room.

It was an absence of sound. Like it didn't exist in the depths of the Patriarch's Palace. Like an oppressive void had replaced it and consigned all noise to oblivion.

It oozed into Calene's ears, made the voice of her thoughts hushed, and the shadows followed, crusting her tongue with their filth. She felt it crawling across her skin, looking for a way inside, like the thick tendrils of corruption that invaded Vettigan when the Shadow Sparker Eviscerated him.

"What's happened down here?" She met Marc's eyes. They shone in the gloom. "You said the current patriarch's a Sparker, albeit a weak one. How can he stand this place? He could feel this in his sleep!"

He shrugged. "Let's just get this over with. I hope Maria's still..."

"Alive?"

"Maria."

Calene nodded. Nothing more needed saying. The word 'Turning' suggested more than enough, though she didn't want to speculate out loud. Neither did Marc, it seemed.

Back at the Broken Bard, the Emperor's Hand had said Faye du Gerran still lived, but wasn't as Maria would remember her. Ice flowed through Calene's blood, freezing her heart.

They reached the bottom of the stairs and paused, peering through the preternatural gloom. The gas lamps fought a losing battle, but Calene welcomed their valiant struggle; without their pricks of blue light, complete darkness would strangle the corridor.

She opened her Second Sight, and it caused the flickering flames to bloom. It also made the shadows deeper. She let out a shuddering breath when the warm throb of a Sparker shone through the gloom.

"She's down here." Calene didn't need to whisper. The

darkness stole the volume from her voice. "Ready?"

Marc nodded. "Ready."

Squinting, Calene made out the faint shape of doors twenty paces away and pointed at them. "There's a Shadow Sparker down here. At least one. As soon as we're through there and we see Maria, shield yourself. It'll attack." Previous encounters with the monsters flashed in her mind. Lopped heads, crushed bodies, total destruction. They couldn't afford that when rescuing Maria. She could get caught in the crossfire. "One of us needs to slow it down while the other kills it."

Marc crept forward. "Spark or blade, I'll see it dead."

The darkness receded as they approached the double doors, footsteps silent on the slick stones. Dampness oozed from the cracks, turning the corridor into a cave. A creature's lair. One that fed on death.

Reaching the doors, Calene grabbed Marc's forearm and stared up at him.

"I've mentioned it before, but I'm serious. We got lucky with the Shadow Sparkers at the Broken Bard. The bricks and timber did the job for us. I've fought one before. I watched a horse trample it half to death and it didn't stop coming. Not until we droking decapitated it. So aim for the head."

Marc held her eyes for a moment. A flicker of doubt— no, fear—ran across his face, but he shrugged it off. Nodding, he took the door handle, and pulled.

The doors swung open with little resistance, revealing the Shadow Sparker's lair.

Maria hung from a tilted stone slab, arms and ankles

restrained, head lolling, but alive. Glowing red runes etched into the rock stood out around her.

The Shadow Sparker had its back to them, staring at the restrained Maria, but it didn't wear black. It dressed in robes of gold and white velvet, with a crimson conical hat, a mark of the office it held in Willow.

Turning, void eyes boring into Calene's, it grinned, the angry red cracks lining its face splitting and weeping, and raised its hands.

"God's teeth," Marc whispered, embracing his Spark. A shimmering blue shield sprung up around him. "That's the droking *patriarch*!"

Calene threw up her shields just as tendrils of corruption sprang from the Shadow Patriarch's hands and rushed at her.

Chapter Twenty-Two

Beneath the Surface

'Serve the light, serve the people. Above all, serve Raas.' - The first words from the Book of Raas.

The wave of corruption slammed into Calene, but her trembling shield held. Marc's did too, yet it wavered under the onslaught.

The patriarch's lack of strength with the Spark played into their favour but, weak as he was, his shadow still ate into their shields. Calene had faith in hers. This close, she could measure the Shadow Sparker's magical prowess and found it way below her own.

But the darkness amplified it, maybe tenfold. Made him formidable. Dangerous.

I wonder how strong I could be if I threw off my shackles... No!

The thought had popped into her head out of nowhere, and once seeded, she couldn't shake it.

Marc clenched his teeth, falling to his knees as the patriarch sent out a seemingly endless wave of shadow. Sweat beaded on the one-armed man's forehead as he held tight to his shield, unable to do anything else. The runes surrounding Maria flashed bright red as her head flopped to one side; bloody tracks ran from her ears, nostrils and mouth.

Calene's near-death experience at the hands of Ganton flashed into her mind. The destruction at Solitude, the loss of her mother. Daggers of pain plunged into her heart at the thoughts, and all jostled for space in her mind, nudging against the numb Link she'd shared with Zanna, and the sickening wound that remained of Vettigan.

If I'd only let go, if I'd only embraced my power, none of that would have happened... No, no, no!

Marc's shield pulsed, the darkness surrounding it. Devouring it.

Isn't that what my father wanted? To unlock my potential. The Laws have been abolished. There's nothing stopping me now.

Beyond her shield, the shadow called to her. Calene's Spark ran through her veins, keeping the barrier strong and leaving more to attack, but the darkness pouring from the patriarch...

She could do so much more with it. A worthier vessel.

The patriarch's void eyes locked on Calene's and grew wide.

Marc snarled, shield shrinking under the pressure of the overwhelming darkness, and Calene raised a hand.

Energy swirled around her, from all the souls in the palace, the flames licking over the stones of the collapsed tower, the fear, the adrenaline, the air rushing in from the yawning hole they'd created. Calene pulled it all in, adding it to the power inside her.

Death spoke to her too, begging her to feed. The corpses she and Marc had left in their wake, the bodies crushed by stone walls and heavy beams, the blood pouring from Maria's face, the violence in the air. It crooned to her, and hovered there, just within her grasp. Calene reached for it, hand still raised, aimed at the patriarch…

There's always another way.

Calene jerked forward, blinking tears from her eyes. The voice came from her memories, and she had spoken the words herself, but the strength of it now blew through her mind, chasing away all thoughts of darkness. The voice was Zanna's.

Calene had defeated Shadow Sparkers before. She didn't need their corrupt power to do it again.

Stepping to the side, closer to Marc, she joined her shield with his and the darkness shuddered, the air convulsing like it was screeching. Calene, raised arm vibrating, pointed at the ceiling and unleashed the energy building inside her. A fountain of light exploded from her finger and pierced the stone. The impact knocked her from her feet. The room shook, groaned. Without pausing, she directed her Spark Maria's way, covering her with a shield even as she kept hers and Marc's strong.

Above the patriarch, the ceiling collapsed.

He threw his hands above his head, obsidian tendrils reaching to hold up tonnes of stone. They pulsed, feeding on his Spark, on the essence of death, swelling as more power filled the patriarch's body. Calene watched with horror.

How much more do I have to do to kill this thing?

Then, something gave. The patriarch's body couldn't contain the energy building inside it. His skin started to bubble and blister, started to split, and the darkness oozed out, tearing him open from within. Calene ducked as a torrent of darkness rushed out from him and then the weight he'd been hefting finally tumbled, crushing him. It buried him along with his screams.

As the dust cleared, silence reigned.

Getting to her feet, patting her body for injuries, Calene looked for Marc. He stared up at her, wide-eyed.

"Getting pretty good at destroying palaces," she grinned, holding out a hand to help him up. Fingers trembling, he let her. "Let's get Maria and go. They'll be crawling all over this place like locusts after that."

The sound of shifting rubble, the fresh blooming of dust, caught her attention. The patriarch lived.

Pulling her sword free, Calene approached, Spark ready. Stones tumbled as the patriarch tried to move, but his broken limbs wouldn't allow it. They pointed at odd angles, and some were crushed flat beneath heavy stones, his blood turning the marble crimson. Void eyes rolling, the cords in his neck popping, his snarls bubbled on his lips.

In truth, he'd died, but the darkness inside refused to admit defeat.

Raising her sword, Calene brought it down across the patriarch's neck, steel ringing on stone, followed by the wet bounce of a decapitated head rolling loose.

"You just killed the Patriarch of Willow," Marc

whispered, staring down at the trembling, headless corpse. Darkness still writhed inside, until, with nowhere else to go, it dissipated.

"That thing stopped being the patriarch a long time ago." Bending, Calene wiped the ichor from her blade on the corpse's clothes, leaving a red smear across the gold and white. "Check the room for another way out. I don't fancy fighting our way through the gates. I'll get Maria."

Marc nodded, and moved away, glancing at his friend. Calene approached her, eyeing the runes with a frown. Most of them remained unknown to her, but some stood out, prickling at her memory. Calene had never seen any like it etched in stone, but she'd seen something similar scrawled on stray pieces of parchment... Using her Spark, she severed the restraints on Maria and lowered her to the ground. She cradled her head and scanned her with her Second Sight, then sighed with relief.

No sign of darkness. No major harm. Whatever the patriarch tried to do to her, it hadn't succeeded.

"Maria?" Calene wiped the blood from her face. "It's me, Calene. Marc's here too. I need you to wake up. Can you do that?"

The muscles around her mouth twitched and her eyelids flickered before opening. Maria's bright, violet eyes met Calene's, and she smiled.

"Took your droking time..."

Calene laughed, tension evaporating with it. "What did they do to you?"

"The same thing as they did to my sister. Or they tried to, at least." Sitting up with Calene's help, Maria scanned the room, frowning at the destruction and favouring the patriarch's head with a cold smile. The perpetual gloom had lifted somewhat, the lamps burning bright again. "He told me they Turned her into one of them. A Shadow Sparker. Only this pig didn't have the strength to do me. I fought, Calene. Fought so hard, and just when I nearly gave up, the palace droking exploded and distracted him."

"Ah. That might have been me. Well, Marc, really. He kind of...blew a hole in the side of the palace. And knocked a tower down in the process."

"What?"

Marc hurried over. "We'll catch up later. Need to get out of here. Sparkers are coming."

Calene shot to her feet, scanning with her Second Sight. Sure enough, figures embracing their magic moved on their location. "Drok! Did you find something?"

"Yes." Marc helped Maria to her feet, studying her like a parent examining a child after a fall. "There's a gate leading to the sewers in the far corner."

"Godsrot, we get to wade through the palace's shit. Wonderful. Better than nothing I suppose." Calene tossed her head. "Get the gate open and lead Maria out. I'll hold them off."

Nodding, Marc pulled Maria away, and Calene pulled on every essence of energy her Spark could find, save the darkness. It still called to her, encouraged thoughts in her mind, but she ignored them. Forced them away. She'd consider why the corruption sought her out with such intent at another time.

Footsteps echoed from the corridor outside, and a

metal clang sounded behind her. Tremors wracked Calene's body, made her limbs shake as power ran through her. The magic she commanded dwarfed anything she'd managed before Solitude. Always strong, she'd grown.

And it could be more...

With a snarl, she shoved the seductive whisper away.

"It's open!" Marc yelled.

Glancing over her shoulder, Calene frowned at the waiting pair. "I'll follow you. Get in!"

Figures appeared at the door and Calene unleashed a shockwave of pure Spark magic at them. Guards and Sparkers flew backwards into the corridor walls, and the entrance of the room collapsed.

She didn't stay behind to watch her handiwork, and followed her friends before the rubble buried her.

A metal drain cover rattled, disturbing a flock of nearby birds into flight. Soaking and stinking, Calene popped her head through the hole, twisting as she scanned her surroundings.

The Patriarch's Palace loomed behind her, the sky above it orange from the fire still burning in its grounds, smoke creating a grey-back haze across the horizon. Sighing, she nodded. They were close, but not close enough, and she was droked if she'd spend one more minute wading through the filth of the sewers.

Ready to give the all-clear, a figure in the shadows caught her eye. *Rotten teeth of the gods!*

Reaching down for her blade, Calene's muscles tensed,

ready to spring as the figure flowed forward, hood falling back to reveal a flash of red hair in the silver moonlight.

"Brina!"

"What is it?" Marc called, as the elf sprinted across the alleyway, footsteps silent.

"It's okay, she's a—"

Brina grabbed her under the arms and hauled Calene out of the sewer, wrapping her in a fierce embrace. For a moment, she fought against it, heat warming her cheeks, but then she melted, revelling in the closeness of their bodies.

"Calene, you *thiemea*! You fool!" Brina pushed her away, anger and relief battling across her face. "You said you'd go for information and supplies. Nothing about blowing up a palace! Or..." She frowned, staring over Calene's shoulder. "...taking a jaunt through the sewer with strangers."

"I also said I wanted you to stay outside the city." She grabbed Brina's hood and pulled it over her head. "It isn't safe!"

Brina stared at the rising smoke. "Evidently not."

"What are you doing here?"

The elf's hands twitched, as if she wanted to reach out. "You'd been gone a day, and then," she nodded at the patriarch's palace, "that happened."

"Technically, that wasn't me," Calene mumbled, a small smile fighting its way onto her lips. "So, you came to rescue me, eh?"

Brina returned the smile. Shy, but a genuine smile nonetheless. "Looks like I didn't need to."

"Everything okay, Calene?"

Maria stood beside the sewer entrance while Marc

pulled himself out.

Turning back to Brina, Calene smiled. "Give me a minute, will you?"

"I'm not leaving without you," Brina hissed, eyes flashing.

Warmth flooded Calene's stomach. Her chest too. The fierceness of Brina's words knocked something loose inside her mind. They'd spent so much time on the road in silence, speaking in half-truths, swapping loaded glances when all they both wanted was each other. Calene's ill-fortune with women, according to Vettigan, was legendary, but right then, staring into Brina's eyes, she saw the truth.

One of them had to give the other a little push. That's all. Just a nudge.

"I know you won't," Calene replied, reaching out and taking Brina's hand. The elf gasped as she stared down at it but squeezed Calene's fingers. "Please. Just give me a minute."

Nodding, Brina moved back into the shadows. Glancing around, Calene realised she'd emerged at a crossroad, an intersection of two alleyways. Direction signs stood out against the brickwork; Brina had taken the path to the South Gate, toward Spring Haven. Marc and Maria stood beneath one pointing east, away from the capital. North led back where she came. And west?

A different path altogether.

"Your friend over there," Maria murmured, standing before Calene. Dried blood crusted her face, but her eyes flashed with life. "She's an elf?"

Calene nodded.

"Explains your reaction at the cages the other night." Maria bit her lip. "I'm sorry, I took you that way. I didn't know."

"How could you?" Calene glanced over her shoulder and smiled as the moonlight reflected off Brina's bared blade. "I only realised it recently myself."

"You should come with us." Marc grinned at Calene. "Never seen someone use the Spark like you. Like a blunt instrument, but such power."

Calene laughed, the one-armed man's words so close to Vettigan's it made her nostalgic.

"Give us a moment, Marc?" Maria asked, smiling up at him.

He nodded and held his hand out to Calene, who took it. "It's been a pleasure working with you, and you have my thanks." Letting go of her hand, he placed two fingers above his heart, then to his lips. "Always."

He moved away, back to the street corner, eyes on the move, searching the darkness for threats.

"What will you do now?" Calene asked Maria.

"My sister's out there." Maria's mouth twitched, and she breathed in through her nose. "She needs my help. Even if she is a Shadow Sparker. That's not her, Calene. It isn't. But we can't stay here. You could come with us."

Calene glanced at the ground, then at the street signs, all pointing her to different paths. "I—"

"What do you want, Calene?"

The question resonated. She had choices. Four directions. Different people with different needs. But what did *she* desire?

Marc had gone back for his friend when he could have run. Brina had come looking for her. Maria wanted to save her sister, a Sparker Turned into something evil, filled with corruption. Like Vettigan, in a way.

Without realising it, Calene's trip had reminded her of what she wanted most. Friendship. Connection. She wanted Vettigan back. And, though Calene wanted to help him for his sake, more than anything she needed it for herself. She wanted to break down the barriers between her and Brina, fan the flame between them, because she wanted that relationship in her life. Now, Calene recognised the truth in the elf's mission.

The emperor had perverted the Order, had created the Shadow Sparkers.

He had to pay, but not in the way Brina planned. Two women against an empire? A suicide mission if they tried to get into Spring Haven and breach the Royal Palace. There must be another way, and they could find it together.

Calene wouldn't get what she so deeply desired by running. She wouldn't help her friends and herself by joining Maria's rebellion, even though the idea appealed. Maybe one day, once she'd seen to Vettigan, once she'd walked the path with Brina, she could find Maria again and pick up the fight to rid the Order and Empire of the corruption at its heart.

But she had to put herself first. Her friends too. They were all she had left. Maybe by sticking together, working together, as Maria and Marc did, Vettigan and Brina would see sense, would see beyond throwing their lives away.

"I'm sorry," Calene whispered. "I hope you find your sister."

"Worth a try, eh?" Maria reached up and hugged her. "I won't forget what you've done for me. If you change your mind, look for me in Protector's Watch. It's where we regroup." She pulled up her sleeve, revealing the tattoo she and Marc sported. "Look for the sign. You'll always have a place with us. May Raas favour you and your friends."

Turning on her heel, Maria melted into the shadows, Marc with her. Sighing, Calene returned to Brina, the elf falling into step beside her.

"Best get off the streets," Calene murmured, "but I'd rather not use my Spark."

"Don't worry. I like climbing. It's how I got into the city in the first place."

"Godsrot, I'm not good at hoisting myself up places without my Spark. Vettigan's not here, is he?"

Brina barked out a laugh. "Of course not! Could you imagine him scaling the red walls? Don't fret, I'll help you."

Calene bit her lip. "I hate to ask, but you didn't tear his throat out, did you? Figuratively or literally."

"Came close, but no. We came to an agreement." They reached a stack of boxes leaning against the side of the wall. "Did you get what you needed from Willow? Once we're up there, we're not turning back. It isn't safe."

A reminder. That's what she got. That she could make a difference when it mattered, for good or ill. She'd blundered into a situation bigger than her, but the strength of friendship made the difference. Calene had gone into the Patriarch's Palace, the one place she'd feared to find herself and swore she wouldn't approach, and pulled an ally, a friend, from its maw. And blown half of it up in the process. A fact that filled her with more than a little pride, truth be told.

But that wasn't her only reminder. Vettigan had stuck by her since her mother's exile, even though he never agreed with it. After the Shadow Sparker's failed Evisceration, when the darkness had swallowed his soul, he'd still tried to support her at Solitude. He'd travelled with her when he could have fled.

Brina too. The elf had proven herself on the walls, in the heat of battle, and hadn't she found them after at Adhraas? Hadn't she scaled the great droking walls of Willow at the first sign of danger?

Calene wouldn't forget it. Her trip to Willow had meant to provide her with a distraction, maybe a chance to get away, but it had delivered her a lesson. A lasting one.

"Well, I didn't get any supplies, but yeah, I think I did. No, I *know* I did."

Calene glanced around, then met Brina's eyes. She smiled and reached out, fingertips tracing the curve of her cheeks. She snatched her hand away, glad of the darkness that hid her blushing.

To her surprise, the elf just smiled. "Good. Come on."

Brina leapt up the boxes and Calene followed, leaving Willow behind, wondering if she'd ever meet Maria du Gerran and Marc le Fondre again.

She hoped so.

Chapter
Twenty-Three

Hunted

'Never underestimate an enemy with nothing to lose. It never ends well.' - Master of War Primacz, overheard before the final battle of his career, between Haltveldtian forces and elves outside Prosper. Though the elves were victorious, their good fortune didn't last long.

"Tilo? Where are you? Please?"

Arlo cast about, his shouting barely more than a whisper in the choking darkness. Waving a hand in front of his eyes did nothing to alleviate the all-encompassing gloom. Horns blared in the distance, but even they sounded muted. A memory of a noise from a lifetime ago.

"Anyone? Someone? Don't leave me here alone!"

A luminous green light flickered before him, a beacon in the deep shadow. It shone again, stronger now, dispelling the blackness of the place where he'd found himself, and he stumbled forward, drawn to it.

That's it. Keep moving. The time is drawing near.

Arlo paused. "Who are you? *What* are you?"

The green light split through the darkness, revealing the Lodestone. The shadows writhed and coiled around its pillar of illumination, but its brightness grew, forcing Arlo to shield his eyes.

Come to me. Reach out and touch the stone.

"Is Zanna there? Please, let me talk to her?" Faint laughter answered, so distant it could have been a trick of Arlo's mind, but the chill kissing his skin, making his hair stand on end, told him he'd heard it. "Is my father still alive?"

Silence.

The Lodestone flickered out, like a flame extinguished, and the shadows rolled back in.

Footsteps echoed behind him, and Arlo spun, peering through the gloom, heart hammering in his chest. He saw no one, but a weight pressed down on him, a presence full of intent and focus.

Lights flickered in the darkness, a plethora of colours fighting for his attention. Images played inside him, and he cocked his head, frowning as the brightness forced the darkness aside again. It merged into a hovering mirror, but it didn't reveal his reflection. Instead, it showed him his father and Tilo standing in a wide, stone chamber, the lodestone in its centre. He saw himself, crouching before it, hand outstretched, the luminescent green glow of the strange rock threatening to overwhelm him.

In the vision, Arlo's fingers trembled as they inched

closer, and he wanted to scream out, to stop himself, even though his purpose meant he had to. Tilo had said so, and so had the voice inside the Lodestone. So why did seeing it fill him with dread? Why did he want to scream his lungs dry? Blood pooled around Kade and Tilo's feet, and his father hunched over something, sword arm limp at his side.

Arlo took a step toward the floating mirror. His father stood right before him, back turned. He could reach out and touch him.

If he were real.

"I've never been here. Is this the future? Is my father alive?"

He received no answers.

The mirror rippled and the vision shifted, fogging over like it moved through clouds, before it settled above a great lake, a heavily wooded forest running along one side. The entire Banished people massed on a plain, warriors at the front, facing down endless rows of the Haltveldtian army. The sight took Arlo's breath.

From the height he watched them, the mass of souls stretched far into the distance on both sides. Death lingered in the air as the great blue lake turned a thick, dirty crimson, and a shadow settled over the armies. It grew and twisted, tendrils forming, and they sensed Arlo's presence. Throwing his arms across his face, the visions blinked out as the oozing black mass reached for him. He fell backward. Back into the formless darkness.

But the sense of being watched didn't leave him, nor did the faint echo of mocking laughter.

"Who are you?" Arlo cried, pulling on his Spark.

It was like trying to catch smoke.

The magic inside him slipped away, refusing to answer his call. He scrambled to his knees, tears streaming down his face, shoulders shaking. It wouldn't come to him because it wasn't there. Zanna's lessons and the instinct to draw on it remained, but the magic inside had vanished.

Arlo had never felt more alone. Never more empty.

The crunch of gravel echoed around him, and, once more, the sound of horns blared. Glancing up through wet eyes, Arlo gasped.

Formless shapes with angry red fissures running through them hovered over him, surrounding him. Watching and inching forward, oozing ever closer.

"No," Arlo whimpered, the strength flooding from his limbs. He flopped to the void-like floor, unable to even lift his head as the bright crimson rivers merged into a wall of flames. "Why?"

"Arlo!"

His eyes flew open and, beyond the treetops, a dark morning sky loomed, his memories crashing back into his mind. The heavens always looked that way now, like the dark clouds formed over the Returned army filling the Banished lands. Arlo and Tilo had travelled through a cave system for the past few days, keeping out of sight, and had taken refuge in a rock shelter when they came to its end. Tilo had insisted it wiser to rest while he judged the lay of the land.

"Arlo, come on." He clung to Tilo as the Banished shook his thin shoulders, pale face swimming into view. "We need to leave."

Horns blared again, and they were stronger and closer than in his dream.

"What is it?"

Tilo glanced around, face grim, eyes focused. "They're hunting for us. On your feet!"

"But I thought we lost them."

"A scouting party, yes," Tilo hissed, glancing around. "They will never stop. Look how many they are! We must go quickly. Be swift. They cover the plains."

Arlo struggled to his feet, his companion hauling him up more than him standing on his own. He needed the help. The pair had barely stopped moving for days and, when they had, they'd waited in the shadows, silent and alert, waiting for packs of invading soldiers to move on. Tilo hadn't closed his eyes for sleep since they'd first spied them, allowing Arlo an hour or so of rest whenever he reckoned it safe.

The sun had barely moved in the clouded sky, telling Arlo he hadn't slept for long. Twenty minutes at most.

Shaking his head, more in an attempt to shake the lingering stain of the dream from his mind, Arlo glanced to his left as he stumbled through the trees and almost dropped to the ground again, limbs refusing to move.

Tilo hadn't exaggerated when he said the army, the Returned, covered the plains.

A mass of crimson and black filled the valley from horizon to horizon, the Peak of Eternity looming ever closer behind them. Fires plumed smoke into the sky from the many camps the black-clad Returned soldiers congregated around, and crimson riders hurtled from the front lines and out into the barren, shale wastelands of the Banished territory.

"Why aren't they all moving into Haltveldt?" Arlo

muttered, unable to look away.

Tilo dropped beside him, a hand on his shoulder. "They're settling in for now. Scouting parties are scouring the forest and ranges for any of my people. It isn't wise for an army to march before it's secured its lands. Never clever to leave an enemy at your back."

A sensation tugged at Arlo. At his core, at the magic pulsating inside him. A call his inborn gift wanted to answer. *Needed* to. Arlo gasped.

"Tilo, they can use the Spark!"

Lights bloomed across the plane as his magic overlaid his vision. Zanna had called it the Second Sight, when a Sparker used their power to boost their perceptions of the world. Colours appeared brighter, sounds louder, scents easier to recognise and tease apart. And it showed him the energies underpinning life, the Spark running through it all. They hadn't used kindling for the fires in the camps. Mages in the Returned army had created them, and as Arlo's Second Sight solidified, the swirl of colours became a blanket of magic users spread out across the Banished lands.

There's so many of them!

The thought flooded his mind, and not just his. Tilo shifted beside him, and uncertainty flooded their Link.

"Sun's shadow!" Tilo hissed. "We have to leave. Now! There's another cave system nearby that will lead us to the peak. I'd hoped to reach there unseen, and I still do."

A horn sounded close by.

"Wait," Arlo insisted, studying the tallest peak.

Green tinged the air around it. Before, whenever he'd considered the Lodestone, it had comforted him, filled him with longing. Now it made his stomach flip. Arlo pulled his eyes away, blinking, ready to leave, but a change in the Returned forces caught his attention.

No, not a change. It had always been there; Arlo just hadn't recognised it. Darkness swirled beneath the bright colours, battling against them, dominating them, breaking them into pieces, scattered fragments on the field. Even the fires had it, the orange flames springing from specks of blackness.

It oozed like pus from a festering wound, seeping across the Banished lands, the grey-white shale slowly consumed by a sweeping tide of putrid darkness.

Just like the shadows in his dream.

This wasn't an absence of light. The darkness had form, a miasmic cloud of malevolence, and it wanted to grow. It tugged on Arlo's Spark, begged him to reach out to it, to accept the void into his soul, and a part of Arlo desired it.

A greater part didn't. The part that caused his skin to itch at the thought of that darkness seeping inside him, the part that whispered in the back of his mind, told him to flee, to hide, to never use his Spark again if it meant the creeping void would find him.

To his right, in the shade of the outcropping, the shadows swirled. A thin tendril slithered toward Arlo.

He acted on instinct. Embracing his Spark, Arlo sent a gust of air into the moving shadow, dispersing it like it had never existed at all.

A blast of horns followed, and alarm flooded his Link.

"What did you do?" Tilo groaned, pulling Arlo to his feet and pushing him into a run. "They know we're here!"

"How can they? I didn't—"

A lightning bolt slammed into the ground close by, near where Arlo had crouched when he used his Spark. Shale and turf exploded at the point of impact.

"Move!" Tilo cried, pulling his sword free. "Run for your life!"

"Teeth of the gods!" Arlo cried, as another lightning bolt scorched the ground, splintering a tree by the cave mouth where they'd rested. Flames erupted from the sundered trunk. "Where to?"

Tilo pointed with his sword toward the jagged and steepening mountains, black teeth rising to form the tallest peak. "That way. Listen to my voice. I'll guide you but stay ahead of me."

Another horn blared. Another shock of lightning erupted. Arlo stumbled as he sprinted, dizzy from the flashing lights, the crashing sounds, the stench of burning thick in his nostrils. His heart pumped, and his breath came in short, ragged bursts. They wanted to kill him!

An amplified voice rang out from behind. "Flush them out! Take the Sparker alive if you can!"

Horse hooves clattered behind him.

Don't look back! Tilo's voice thundered in his mind. *You have to reach the Lodestone. You have to! I'll buy you time. Go!*

But Arlo didn't listen. Glancing over his shoulder, half-falling as his frantic legs tried to bear him on, feet scrambling, Arlo came to a stop.

A lone Returned rider bore down on Tilo, who'd turned to stand his ground, sword ready. The muscled stallion heaved and snorted, as its rider charged right at the

Banished. The ground shook.

Arlo couldn't leave Tilo behind. Already he'd said goodbye to his father, lost Zanna and his new home at Solitude. Without Tilo, he had no one, nothing, except the Lodestone at the end of his path. If he ever got there.

He gritted his teeth as the Returned warrior closed the gap. *No. You can't have him! You won't!*

Raising his arms, Arlo remembered his first lessons with Zanna. They felt like an age ago, but her teachings remained strong in his mind. For hours, they'd practised in front of her fireplace, pulling the flames from it and into the palm of his hand. He focused on the flames rising from the ruined tree and drew them into his Spark. Its heat warmed his fingers to his shoulders. He released them in a roaring burst.

The ball of fire rushed past Tilo, who ducked out of the way—the Link he shared with Arlo no doubt gave him some warning—and exploded at the feet of the on-rushing horse.

The beast screeched, throwing its rider from the saddle, as the ground melted beneath its hooves. It fell into the fresh pit, bones cracking as it fell, its cries growing more frenzied as the flames cooked its flesh.

Arlo struggled against the sick feeling in his stomach, the water flooding his limbs. He'd killed. It wasn't the rider, but Arlo had still taken the life of a living creature. Only days before he'd voided his guts as he watched Tilo prepare a wild boar for their food, and now...

Tilo didn't hesitate. Rushing forward, his sword flashed before it plunged into the dark shape struggling to rise. A groan sounded, then a second swipe of the Banished's weapon cut it off and the body stilled.

Spark still embraced, Arlo stepped forward. Death called out to him. He could almost see it. Like everything else, it had its own energy, its own essence. One he could add to his power and use.

His fingers twitched and he stumbled forward another step.

"Come on!" Tilo grabbed him, snapping him from his reverie, and Arlo fumbled his connection to the Spark. It slipped away and the world returned to normal. Colours faded, sound dulled. Temptation gone. "There's more coming, and something tells me it won't be so easy next time."

Arlo's eyebrows shot up his forehead. "That was *easy*?"

The pounding of hooves thundered in time with the ground's shaking, and Arlo fell into a run at Tilo's side.

Lightning pounded around him, rending the earth and splitting stone. Even so, he glanced over his shoulder as he ran. The fire in his pit died, as did the horse's screams. Arlo wiped at his face.

He'd cry for it later. If there was a later.

"By Raas' fruits..."

Kade threw himself behind a jagged boulder as lightning danced in the dark clouds, smothering the once-blue skies. Jagged bolts hurtled to the ground, exploding into the rock and shale in the mountain pass. Trees burned, the smoke from the smouldering bark rising to the ledge he'd found on his journey through the higher passes. The going had been slow, even after his healing, but better that than try to traverse the plains.

They crawled with soldiers like the one he'd killed, the ones the Banished fled from.

Now, someone else ran. Riders thundered by on their horse below, horns blared and men shouted. Then more lightning came, crashing into the mountains as the soldiers gave chase. Kade had followed it from above, and now watched, perplexed at the sight he saw.

In the distance, a single rider rode down a Banished warrior, standing tall, sword ready, unflinching in the face of death. Then, from behind, a small figure appeared, and Kade's heart lurched into his mouth.

"Arlo?"

It *had* to be his son. Kade couldn't make out his features across the distance, but the child dressed in clothes and colours unlike those of the Banished. And a father would recognise his son anywhere, no matter the place, no matter the distance.

He scrambled to his feet, hand on his sword, but what could he do?

Nothing but watch.

The rider closed the gap on the Banished—Tilo; it had to be Tilo—sword at the ready, shale and dirt spraying from the mount's hooves. Trees exploded as more lightning lanced from the sky. Kade's vision almost failed from the shocking brightness and the tears in his eyes. He'd found his son at last.

Now he'd watch him die.

His son raised his hands. In protest? Pleading for the rider to stop?

"Arlo," Kade whispered, falling to his knees. "I've failed you."

Pain lanced in his chest. Maybe his imagination, but the beating of his heart sounded in his ears. A slow, aching beat. A heart on the verge of giving up.

Flames erupted from his son's hands. A burst of fire obliterated the ground before the horse. Tremors ran through the ground as it opened and swallowed the animal.

Stunned, elated, his heart thumping once more, Kade watched as Tilo ran forward and dispatched the unsaddled soldier before grabbing Arlo and sprinting away, flames leaping from the pit his son had created.

He scrambled to his feet, scanning the ledge where he perched, searching for a way down. And found it.

"I'm coming," Kade snarled, sprinting for the descent. "Raas' teeth, I'm coming for you, Arlo."

Horns erupted behind him and drew him to a halt. The pounding of horses' hooves followed. Beneath him, in the mountain pass, three more riders thundered by, chasing Tilo and his son.

Snarling, Kade scrambled down the slope, stones and shale cutting through his trousers and skin.

Nothing would stop him from reaching his son. Not lightning from the sky. Not murderous cavalry. Not an army filling the Banished plains.

Nothing.

"Over there!" Tilo cried, gesturing at an opening in the mountains. "That's the one we're looking for."

"And what do we do once we're in there? Fight until we can't anymore?" Arlo stumbled on the uneven ground. The cave mouth yawned ahead of them. "They can follow us, you know?"

"We'll think of something!" Tilo shouted, ducking.

An arrow slammed into the rocks beside him, and another flew past, missing Arlo's head by inches.

"Not if we die first!"

The riders had dismounted, three of them, and gave chase on foot, scrambling after them. The lightning had ended. The Returned knew their quarry had nowhere to run.

"They want us alive, or they'd have hit us by now." Tilo dropped his voice to a mutter, "They want one of us, at least."

"Well, that's reassuring," Arlo breathed, his sides hurting. He hadn't sprinted for so long in his entire life.

The incline evened out, and another volley of arrows clattered into the rocks.

Tilo shoved him forward, screaming in pain. Arlo frowned, but Tilo shoved him again. "Run until your legs ache and your lungs feel ready to burst. And when they do, keep going!"

Nodding, Arlo forced his limbs to move, forced his feet to keep purchase on the ground. The cave loomed before him, the distance closing.

Just a little further... Just... A... Little...

A cry from behind startled him. Skidding to halt, Arlo looked back.

Tilo had crashed to the ground, an arrow jutting from his shin. The projectiles, the scream of pain. They'd hit his friend, his only companion, and he'd tried to struggle on in vain.

"No! Tilo!"

He half-staggered forward, but the Banished forced himself to his feet, teeth gritted. "Go, Arlo! Go!"

Tilo unsheathed his sword, and turned, backing up, limping, as the three Returned appeared on the ridge.

Arlo glanced behind him. The cave mouth stood not ten paces away, double that for Tilo. They could still make it.

One of the warriors dropped his bow to the floor, and unsheathed a heavy mace, while another watched. He looked between Arlo and Tilo from under his hood, then strode forward, breathing hard.

Another, long blonde hair streaming in the wind, still held her bow. She nocked another arrow, aimed at Tilo, and loosed.

Arlo acted on instinct. Time slowed as his Spark erupted inside him, overlaying the world with the Second Sight. The unarmed Returned's head swivelled, void eyes glittering beneath the hood, but the boy ignored him. Commanding the elements, Arlo focused on the arrow cutting through the air, aimed at Tilo's face, and redirected it.

It all came naturally. He thought it, and it happened, like an invisible hand reached out, turned the arrow around and pushed.

Time returned to normal, and the projectile slammed into the Returned soldier who'd fired it, knocking her off her feet. A shower of blood spurted behind her as she tumbled back down the slope.

Arlo wasn't finished. Two left. With his Spark, he could take them.

Rushing backward to the cave mouth, the same invisible extension of his will grabbed Tilo and hauled him toward it, lifting the Banished from his feet. He tumbled to the ground as Arlo entered the cave, backing up slowly as the soldiers approached.

Grinning, Arlo turned to the soldiers, and flames erupted in his hands. He could end them with just a thought. Roast them from the inside. Heat rushed through his limbs, and they trembled, ready to explode.

"Enough of this!" the unarmed Returned snarled, and just like that, Arlo's Spark vanished, just as it had in his dream.

He could still sense it, the magic writhing inside him, and he could reach for it, but his fingers came back empty, like he glugged at a jar filled with water but it didn't seep into his mouth.

The Returned's hood fell back, revealing a pale, bald head with angry, red cracks surrounding its black eyes. Nodding at the remaining soldier, he smiled.

"Kill the Banished."

Mace raised, the enemy warrior flowed forward, and Tilo rose to meet him, hobbling on his injured leg, blade reverberating from the blow. Tilo tried to twist but cried out in pain as he put too much weight on his wounded limb. His opponent scored his shoulder with a glancing swipe of his mace. Tilo dropped to one knee, lashing out with his blade, forcing the Returned to parry, then scrambled forward, tackling the man and slamming him into the cave wall.

The enemy warrior slammed the pommel of his mace into Tilo's spine, who cried out but held on, rising to his feet and smashing the top of his head into the soldier's chin. Blood and a sliver of tongue sprayed from his mouth.

Snarling, Tilo's opponent shoved him away, then attacked again, steel ringing as sword met mace. Tilo pushed him back so their steel ran across stone. Sparks exploded from the rock.

"Must I do everything myself?"

Arlo gasped as darkness gathered inside the Returned mage, a black so dark it had its own form. Even though he couldn't touch the Spark, Arlo recognised the spell.

Evisceration.

The dark magic Zanna had warned him against when he drained the essence from an apple in Solitude. Tendrils of it thickened and lashed out at the two men fighting.

The Returned mage aimed to kill them both. Friend and foe.

Arlo screamed as the black tendrils of Evisceration slammed into the fighters, and the mace-wielding Returned dropped to his knees, wailing, trembling, hair shedding from his head, skin wrinkling.

Rotting from the inside, just like the apple.

But Tilo stood strong, unaffected. The inky blackness disintegrated as it touched him, and he swung to face the Returned mage.

"How can this be?" he whispered, ignoring the darkness still ravaging the body of the other Returned. "It's impossible."

A figure moving behind him caught Arlo's attention, and he half-stepped forward.

"Father?"

Kade Besem screamed as he closed the gap and drove his sword through the mage's chest, its point tearing through his sternum and releasing a gush of blood that spattered on the cave floor.

Pulling his sword free, letting the corrupt mage drop to the ground, he met Arlo's eyes, tears running down his cheeks, and smiled.

"Arlo. I've found you, at last." He held out his hand. "Come with me!"

Arlo took a step forward, almost bouncing with delight.

"I can't believe you're here!" Arlo cried, heart thudding. His father. Here! "We need to get to the summit of the Peaks of Eternity, father. Help us!"

A choking laugh bubbled from the dying mage's lips, and as the drained husk turned to mush—an oozing pool of failed flesh, rotten blood and destroyed organs—realisation dawned.

"Get back!" he cried, as the tendril of pure darkness left the ruined pile of bones and ash and slammed into the cave's roof.

Tilo crashed into Arlo, forcing him down as the cave mouth collapsed.

The dust cleared and Kade forced himself to his feet, then threw himself at the debris keeping him from his son.

More collapsed, forcing him back, but he leaped at it again, digging through chunks of rock with his fingers until they bled.

"He's right on the other side," Kade hissed, then raised his voice. "Arlo! Arlo! Can you hear me? Arlo!"

More rocks crashed down onto the pile, sending out plumes of dust. Kade coughed as it entered his lungs, choking him, but still he pulled the debris away.

He had to. His son needed him.

"I almost had you. I almost—"

"Toss aside the sword and turn around."

Kade froze, then glanced over his shoulder. A group of soldiers, ten of them, surrounded him, weapons drawn, eyeing him with care.

"You don't understand," Kade snarled, itching to get at the rocks again. "My—"

Invisible ropes wrapped around him, binding his arms to his sides, and his sword clattered to the stones. He spun around, facing the soldiers.

"He doesn't have the Spark," one of them reported, with a frown.

Another nodded. "But we felt its use from two people."

The one giving the orders raised an eyebrow at Kade, then shrugged. "Malek wanted prisoners, and we have one. Spark or no, he comes with us."

"But my s—"

Something forced its way into Kade's mouth and his eyes bulged, unable to speak, almost unable to breathe. The soldier in charge approached him, tall, lithe and dark-skinned, golden eyes devoid of humour, even life, his close-cropped hair peppered with grey. He appeared so normal, but Kade's instincts screamed at him, just like they had at the hill of dead when he'd killed the rider.

These people... Who were they?

"I'd show more respect when you meet Malek," the soldier murmured, peering into Kade's eyes. "He doesn't have my..." A cold grin spread across his face. "...humanity."

Scanning the rocks one more time, the soldier turned and walked away. Invisible ropes tugged Kade along, no matter how deep he dug his heels.

I'll find you again, Arlo. I swear it!

But the thoughts rang hollow, no matter the passion he put into them. His son stood on the other side of the rockslide, but he might as well have waited in Prosper for all Kade could do for him.

A small voice told Kade to worry about himself, but he shoved it away. His son needed him, and he had to find a way free.

Any way at all.

Chapter Twenty-Four

THAT WHICH FLOWS INSIDE

'It's not the body, nor the blood flowing in the veins, that makes a father and son. It's the heart beating inside as one, and the choices we make together.' - Words attributed to Emperor Jaen Kollar, often known as 'the Builder', on the day of his son's birth. He went down in history as one of Haltveldt's favourite rulers, as did his heir.

Arlo sat up, coughing, gasping for air. The collision with Tilo had knocked the breath from his lungs. Pushing the Banished away, he scrambled to his feet, desperate for any sign of his father. Darkness smothered his vision. Pitch black in front and behind. Without thinking, he drew on his Spark, letting out a half-laugh, half-sob when he realised he could feel it again. With the Returned mage dead, nothing could stop him. He drew on his inner energy and flames rose at his fingertips, illuminating the gloom.

Rocks were all he saw, blocking off the cave mouth. Stone and dust and nothing more, save the oozing puddle on the ground.

"Father!" Arlo cried, rushing to the rock pile, a hacking cough ripping from his throat. "I'm here! Can you hear me?"

The sound of sliding stones answered his echoing voice.

Behind him, Tilo cleared his throat. "Arlo..."

The flatness of his voice caused Arlo's stomach to drop into his boots. Turning, squinting through the dust, his neck muscles tightened and his heart hammered at what he found.

The tunnel behind them had caved in.

"No, no, no!" Arlo cried, running to the other side of the cave, searching for any openings but finding none.

"Save your breath," Tilo whispered, shaking his head. He'd snapped the arrow shaft and pulled it out, wrapped cloth around it. Blood already oozed through the material. "There's no cracks, no openings. We'll suffocate in here if we're not careful."

"Suffocate?" Arlo grabbed the front of Tilo's leather armour. "How long are you planning on staying in here? Didn't you see? My father's out there! Alone with a whole army. We need to save him!"

"How?" Tilo pointed at the cave's entrance. "The only thing stopping this whole section collapsing are the rock piles at each end. We blast them away with your Spark, the whole thing comes down."

"Don't you have your magic?" Arlo pleaded, wringing his hands. His father stood on the other side of a wall of stone. They had to do something! "Can't you use that?"

"I told you, it's too dangerous. I need to think before acting, and so do you." Tilo frowned and pulled his water-skin free. "It's a good thing we've practiced on shielding our Link, Arlo, or your emotions would send us over the edge. Calm yourself. We need cool heads here. We have to think our way out." Tilo shook the waterskin. "Empty. How about yours?"

He didn't think it possible, but Arlo's stomach plunged even lower. He didn't need to check his waterskin.

"It's empty," he muttered, wincing. He thought they'd find a brook or stream to wash in and refill.

Tilo held up a hand and narrowed his eyes as he glanced around, then smiled. "Well, not to worry. I can do something about that."

Kneeling, Tilo winced as he shuffled to the cave wall opposite the steaming pool of mush and dug his fingers into the ground, clawing out a small hole where dirt met stone. He closed his eyes, the same smile still fixed there, and sang.

The sea. It reminded Arlo of the sea. From visiting Haven Bay outside the capital, sitting on the bluffs with his father while the waves crashed below, to the infrequent times he'd visited the docks in the city. Short journeys by boat to Lira City, longer voyages to Prosper with the Widows looming above them, Haltveldt's south-western mountains gazing off across the ocean.

Tilo's soft voice rose and fell like the tide, like a gentle wave, and Arlo understood the words. The Banished begged the earth to provide him with water from a spring below, swearing to repay the gift if given. It reminded him of the words Tilo had spoken after killing the boar, but this time, he sang them. The crisp smell of salt filled the air, and the squawk of gulls echoed in his ears as they danced beneath the warm sun, and the Banished's strange magic spoke to his Spark.

He could use it, if he wanted to. Draw on it like any other type of energy. Just like he had on the mountains above where Solitude stood, when he almost lost control.

He couldn't lose control now.

The faint trickle of water reached him, and Tilo cupped his hands, still singing, as a splutter of water broke through the dirt.

We can do better than that!

Arlo wasn't sure if the thought belonged to him, or why he agreed with it with such a fierce, unshakeable confidence. His Spark told him more water ran beneath the ground, that Tilo had only tapped into a trickle, but instead of reaching out with his own magic, or drawing on his friend's like he had above Solitude, Arlo sang too.

Voice wavering at first, cracking with adolescent uncertainty, Arlo copied the same words Tilo used, matching his melody and tone, confidence growing.

Tilo threw a look over his shoulder, eyebrows raised, but the song caught him, and wouldn't let go. Panic flooded the Link they shared. Tilo didn't have the control he thought he should have, but Arlo pushed it away, building the walls high so it wouldn't interrupt him. Now he led the song, and Tilo followed, unable to stop.

This isn't right, the voice in his head whispered, but Arlo ignored that too.

The song filled him. The waves crashed about it. The

sun beat down on his upturned face, and the gulls danced, just for him.

The bottom of the cave wall where Tilo dug broke away, and water gushed through the gap, filling the hole the Banished had dug.

Still singing, Tilo scraped more of the ground away as the water continued to fill it, overflowing already, but Arlo couldn't stop. This new power thrilled him, made his blood buzz with life. He knew the melody, understood the power of his voice, the connection with the land, and how he could merge it with his Spark.

Using them together, he could do anything.

You'll drown us! Stop!

Tilo's voice boomed in his head, shocking Arlo back into the moment, back into his body. Water sloshed about his ankles, and it continued to gush from the spring he'd created.

Let go, Arlo. Let go!

His words faltered and his voice broke, losing its power. Staggering backward, Arlo slumped against the cave wall and slid to the ground, strength fleeing his body. Tilo rushed over, catching him as he tipped forward into the shin-high water, and Arlo's vision turned to night.

Flickering lights. Green, red and yellow. Voices from the void—harsh and frenzied, soft and caring, filled with sorrow and on the edge of despair.

Arlo couldn't make out the words, but they surrounded him, flowed through him, as he drifted in nothingness, ghost light playing across his vision. Panic filled him, and it only increased when the familiar weight of Tilo's Link didn't present itself. Neither did the Spark.

He tried to speak, but words wouldn't come. Arlo twisted, faster and faster, until the lights became a blur, and laughter emerged from the voices. Cold and sharp, mocking and knowing, the laughter rose and fell as the radiance blinked out, plunging Arlo into an existence of nothingness and darkness.

The laughter died, its end as abrupt as its beginning, and Arlo realised the darkness wasn't a great, vast nothing.

Shadows surrounded him.

They blotted out the flickering lights, threatening to swallow them, to devour them. Staring at them, Arlo watched as the utter blackness split into a hundred shapes, a thousand figures, and multiplied, growing further, spreading across a vast plain beside a lake of midnight. Specks of brightness battled inside the shapes, striving to break free, but the shadow beat them back.

Across the lake, bright white lights arrived, swelling as they moved to confront the darkness, but Arlo could see it wasn't the light's purpose. It only wanted to live, and not fight. To grow and find its own place in the world.

Mocking laughter. Just a hint of it, playing on the edge of his hearing, tickling it, causing the anxiety inside to swirl. A crushing sense of wrongness.

Arlo's vision spun. In the distance, looming, stood the Peaks of Eternity, its tallest point a green beacon in the corrosive darkness, but its light shone sickly, and more figures writhed beneath it, turning their backs to it as one. The Lodestone's essence tried to fall on them, but it collided against an invisible barrier, the green wisps melting away.

The laughter didn't sound then. It didn't seem aware of what Arlo witnessed, like the swirling mass beneath the Peaks of Eternity existed in a place without the Lodestone, or distant from it.

"Arlo?"

The world of shadow and the struggling light trembled.

"Arlo? Come back to me."

His vision shook, and the sound of gushing water filled his ears.

Arlo's eyes flew open. Sitting up, he spluttered and coughed, spraying Tilo with water. What happened? He recalled his father coming to their aid, then the collapse of the cave. But after that?

Relief spread through the Link as his companion eased Arlo back to the ground, his head supported by a rolled-up cloak.

"Drink," Tilo murmured. Water touched Arlo's lips, and he drank it in, dry mouth thirsting. "Easy, easy. Not too much. You've been asleep for hours."

"Hours?" Arlo croaked, pushing the waterskin away and peering around in the gloom. "You've sat in the darkness for hours?"

"I've sat by your side, listening to your breathing, trying to wake you." A flash of worry in their Link. "I couldn't feel you, in my head. You hadn't disappeared; it was like you'd gone somewhere else."

Arlo pushed himself up, head spinning, and leaned against the cave wall, forcing Tilo's weight of emotions into the corner of his mind. He didn't want to lose himself in them again. Not here, not now. Or ever, for that matter.

Holding his palm out, Arlo called on his inner energy and summoned flames.

"Ah!" he grabbed at his head with his other hand, pressing against his forehead as pain lanced through it, a chisel splitting his skull. Gritting his teeth, Arlo pushed through and the ache lessened.

Fire spluttered to life in the centre of his palm; weak, but better than nothing.

"You're in pain," Tilo gasped, holding a finger to his forehead, and grasping the boy's shoulder with his other hand. "What happened to you?"

Arlo shook his head, waiting for the twinges to disappear. He'd never felt pain when using his Spark before. Nausea built in his stomach, rushing up his gullet. For a moment, he readied himself to vomit. Grabbing the waterskin, he took another mouthful, forcing the sickness away, and pulled in a deep, steady breath.

Water.

Arlo glanced at the pool he and Tilo had created, overflowing from the crevice and filling the cave floor. The Banished had summoned just a trickle, but then Arlo...

"I used your magic." Arlo frowned. "No, not just used it. I could have drawn on it with my Spark, but I sang. Didn't I?"

Tilo gave him a careful look, then nodded. Shifting his body, he settled against the cave wall. "At least we have plenty of water."

A weak laugh escaped Arlo's mouth. "How is it possible?"

"It shouldn't be. Though I've seen plenty I thought impossible since the Lodestone gave me my purpose."

Regret and shame threatened to overload the Link, all coming from Tilo. Arlo glanced at him, the Banished seemingly unaware of the torrent of emotions flooding from him. He sat still, head bowed, staring at the cave floor. In the weak light of the fluttering flame, his stillness resembled a statue, one capturing the essence of sadness. He'd taken the bloodied cloth from his shin, and the flesh there appeared healed. Whole.

"How?" Arlo pointed at it. "Did you heal yourself?"

"You did," the Banished answered without looking up, shaking his head. "With your song."

Arlo reached out and laid a hand on his wrist.

"What is it?" he asked, as Tilo stared at him. "I can feel what you can. Tell me."

"We're trapped." he laughed, pointing at the rockslides. "We try to move either of them and the whole thing collapses. Some great purpose, eh? All I've done is led you into a dark hole to die."

"We won't die," Arlo whispered, sudden fear making his voice higher than normal. "We won't!"

"I admire your strength, Arlo. Very much." Tilo studied his fingers, twisting a piece of vine wrapped around his index finger. "I wish I had it, but I'm falling into despair. My family, my wife and daughters, my unborn son, they march into a strange land filled with people who hate them. For what? Existing? For crimes made by my people thousands of years ago that no one remembers? And I can do nothing. Nothing!"

Tilo finished in a shout, slamming his fist against the wall. Arlo didn't answer. What could he say? He could lie and say all would be well, but even at his age, Arlo knew the world didn't work that way. The Banished fled into Haltveldt, an army at their backs, and another one ahead no doubt.

"I had the chance to go to them, as we watched my people build the bridges. To walk down there, and embrace my family, never leave their sides again. What kind of man would I be if I'd left you alone here?" Tilo shook his head. "Purpose. That's what the presence inside the Lodestone told me. That I had to bring you to it. That the only way to protect my family, my people, was to do as it told me. My son..."

Arlo blinked. "You don't really talk about him."

"I know." A faint smile played on his lips, and pride trickled into the Link, but shame still chased it. "I'm a lucky man, Arlo. Every life is a blessing, each new child a gift. It discredits me that each time a child grew in Drada's belly, I wished for a boy. One that never came. But, before I left... I always wanted a boy, Arlo, and now I'll never see him, even if he survives what faces my people."

Arlo couldn't look at him. The pain thickening his words, flooding their Link, threatened to overwhelm him. A great tide rushing in, a force of nature, primal and unforgiving, ready to sweep away anything in its path. It flowed both ways, the anguish of a boy torn from his father's grasp, the agony of a father who feared he'd never stare into his child's eyes.

"I'm sure you'll see him," Arlo gasped, making a ball with his fist and digging his fingernails into his palm, just to ground himself in his own body, to remind himself of his own feelings. "I know it."

Tilo let out a low growl, then beat his fist against the cave wall. The dull thud echoed around them.

"Will I?" he snarled. "How? We're trapped here, and there's nothing we can do to help my people. They march to war. Children and the old, the sick. What will happen to them, I ask you? Every step we've taken, I've told myself I'm helping Drada and the girls, helping all of my people by getting you where you need to go. Once there, you'll stop this threat; I have to believe that. But now? In here? Slowly suffocating with nothing but water for company? I'll never see my son, Arlo. Never! I leave my family to fend for itself and how long will they last? How long *can* they last?"

As Tilo's anger built, Arlo's Spark responded. The rage wasn't aimed at him; Arlo knew that, but the emotion throbbed with energy. With it filling their Link, it filled him too, igniting the embers of the bone-deep anguish inside Arlo, and with it, the fury.

Everyone in his family but his father had shunned him. They looked down their noses at them both and treated his father like dirt for raising Arlo alone, in his own way. Enmity existed for his father too, and this shamed him, further adding to the resentment Arlo had always tried to suppress and ignore.

Why had his father sent him so far away? When he Sparked, why couldn't he learn at the university, under the Order's watch? Zanna turned out to be a brilliant teacher but look where it had led him. On the long trip to Solitude with his father, Arlo had wrestled with the question, unsatisfied with rote excuses of 'it's the best place for you' and 'it's a safe place to learn with an excellent teacher'.

So excellent she'd gotten herself exiled.

Arlo had grown to love Zanna, to understand her past, and she'd saved the lives of thousands at Solitude, if only for a while. She wasn't to know her sacrifice would ultimately be for nothing.

His father, who'd travelled through Banished lands alone, had rescued Arlo and Tilo from the Returned mage before the cave's collapse, didn't know he'd sent his son into danger. Look at what had happened when he'd attempted to make up for it. He'd raced to Solitude's walls, thrown himself into the midst of battle despite the fact he'd almost died.

Had they done all that just to prolong their deaths in the face of war and hatred?

"No..." The Spark's power made Arlo's fingers tremble. His toes curled in his boots. "You'll see your family again. You'll see your son."

His voice vibrated with the strength of the energy welling inside him, bringing him to his feet.

"And I'll see my father. Help me. Please."

Tilo nodded, eyes wide, understanding clear in his eyes. Light filled the cavern, the Spark pouring through Arlo's skin, chasing away the shadows, and the Banished sang.

His low voice wavered at first but strengthened, and the

melody warmed Arlo, surrounding him. He'd never felt the embrace of his mother, or the caress of a gentle hand on his face from anyone but his father, but the song Tilo sang gave him the feeling of basking in her love. Rune. Arlo's father whispered her name sometimes, often when he thought no one could hear. An odd name, unlike any he'd heard before, but now, with the low, fulfilling melody washing over him, Arlo closed his eyes and felt her close.

And the Spark drank in the Banished's strange magic. The same power Arlo could use too. The words washed over him, the blood thundering in his ears making them merge with the melody, but he hummed it, gave voice to it, and took that energy too, adding it to his Spark.

Alarm flooded the Link, but Tilo's voice didn't falter. Arlo's almost did, and his hold on the Spark wavered as he opened his eyes. He floated above the cave floor, just as Zanna had above Solitude, the torrent of magic swirling in his veins lifting him off the ground.

Life. Exquisite energy. Darkness and light. It swept through him in a torrent, one Arlo could only cling to by his fingertips. But hold on he did, even when the sweetness of the Spark turned to pain, like a thousand hot, tiny pins pricking his skin at once. Then daggers, driving into his temples. He grit his teeth with such force his jaw cracked. Arlo glanced at the rock piles, down at Tilo gazing up at him, the melody lost in the storm inside his head.

He flung out his arms.

"Get down!" he screamed, just as air exploded from him, spreading through the cave in a circle, a shockwave of Spark energy.

It hit Tilo, who hadn't time to react, but Arlo's instinct

took over. Before the Banished crashed into the cave wall, Arlo surrounded him with a bubble of energy, just like Zanna had with his hand back in Solitude, cushioning Tilo's impact.

The shockwave collided with the rock piles, and stones exploded left and right. Light poured in, sweet daylight, but the cave groaned. The fallen debris kept the tunnel standing, and without it...

Arlo's Spark took control. Powered by Tilo's song, and his own mimicry, it thundered through the tunnel, filling the cracks with the scattered debris. Dropping to his feet, he studied the entrance. Corpses lay about it, the ones from before, crushed and mutilated by the collapse, but his father had gone.

Taken by the Returned. With the Spark in full flow, the boot marks of many soldiers were plain to see. With this explosion of power, they'd come back to this place.

Sadness welled inside Arlo, but he pushed it away. He had to. He'd promised Tilo, and the only way to rescue his father, to see him again, and deliver the Banished people from war, was to reach the Lodestone. Tilo had said the cave would lead them to it. Arlo had to go on.

A tear ran down his cheek. His father would under-stand. Wouldn't he?

Confident the tunnel behind him would hold, Arlo used his Spark to gather the fallen rocks and pull them into the cave, blocking up the entrance. He made it a smooth wall, keeping it from falling on them once he released his power, but cutting them off from being followed. At least for now.

Soldiers might come, but they'd find corpses beside a sheer rock wall before moving on. Just as they had before.

Darkness swallowed the light, and Arlo dropped to his knees, the pain in his head overwhelming the power in his veins at last. Releasing the Spark, the world became less. He ached to touch it again, even for a moment. Just to feel it. With it, he could achieve anything.

Anything.

"By the Lodestone," Tilo whispered, scrambling to his feet and wrapping his arms around Arlo's thin shoulders. He eyed the cave's ceiling, worried it would drop at any moment. "Are you okay? I've never seen anything like that!"

"I'm..." Arlo's voice shook. His head throbbed. Grabbing his waterskin, he filled his mouth and swallowed, then did it again, the cool water burning his aching throat. "We can... We can move on..."

Tilo spun him around and met his eyes. "The voice inside the Lodestone; it told me to find and protect you above all else. I wondered why. Because of your Spark? But no. Arlo, you can use *our* magic, but you're not one of us. You're not entirely human either."

Shaking his head, coughing, Arlo frowned. Even the gloom hurt his eyes. "What do you mean? You've seen my father."

"Arlo, there was another race who could do what mine can now, ages before us. The elves. They lost their way." He smiled, tears shining in his eyes as he glanced over his shoulder at the open path. "I see it in your face. You have their blood. That's how you can use both magics. Perhaps you're the only one who can, and that's why the Lodestone wants you. That's why you were chosen." He let out a whoop and climbed to his feet. "Now we have a way!"

"An elf? No. My mother wasn't..."

My mother's name was Rune. An elven name?

Arlo stared at the water on the cave floor, his dark reflection wavering in it. The high cheek bones, the wide, large eyes. He turned his head, moving his dirty blonde hair to reveal ears not completely round. They'd changed since he'd last studied himself in a mirror. His whole face had.

Is this why father sent me away? It all makes so much sense now. The hatred from the rest of my family. I feel like such a fool.

Jigsaw pieces snapped into place in his mind. Most of the elves he'd seen were slaves. His mother had been a slave. His father's slave?

But he said he loved her, more than anything!

Arlo retched, heaving the water he'd drank from his stomach and back into the cave, tears streaming from his eyes, snot from his nose. Tilo's hand gripped his shoulder, and Arlo glanced at it, followed it till he met his friend's eyes.

"I shouldn't have spoken," he murmured, face solemn. "You didn't know."

Arlo nodded, and climbed to his feet, but staggered and fell into Tilo, sobbing. Arlo's vision spun as Tilo picked him up like he weighed nothing more than a saddlebag.

"I'll carry you, and I know a song of healing. I'll teach it to you, even though you managed to perform it on me without knowing."

Tilo's feet sloshed in the water as he moved deeper into the cave, the rocking motion and soft song he murmured lulling Arlo to sleep.

His mind needed the rest as much as his body but, as his vision turned dark, a luminous green light shone on the horizon of his mind's eye.

The Lodestone awaited, and it felt Arlo drawing near.

Chapter
Twenty-Five

The Pregnant Pause

*'There's nothing worse than sitting on the edge of battle.
Waiting. Knowing them on the other side of the field want
nothing more than your death, and knowing well you'll do
anything to stop it. The worst kind of person is them who
crave battle, and I've never met anyone thirstier for war than
Nexes Almor.'* - From the journals of Master of Education
Oldham, a staunch supporter of the old ways, and follower
of Raas. Found guilty of treason against the empire along
with Bertrand Reyes, Kade Besem and many others.

Nexes strode through Driftwood, the village
where his army camped, aiming for the ram-
shackle tavern they'd secured for his use. Basic,
but better than a tent for a change. The villagers kept to their
homes, as far from the soldiers as possible.

And the Shadow Sparkers.

Blood dripped from his fingers and clung to his clothes

as he made his way to his room. Soldiers trailed behind him, a Shadow Sparker with them.

"Any messages for me?"

As he did every time his army made camp, Nexes returned to his list. The formerly blank list, to which he added a new name each night, after the cutting. Names of mages he suspected, those who were arrogant, those who'd been close to others he'd already snuffed out. He sent his Shadow Sparkers to bring the name to him.

Rumours circulated of Sparkers going missing, but most thought they'd turned to the Shadow, or fled into the night, heads filled with doubts as they spent more time amongst the dark forces around them.

Nexes didn't care. Rumours always swirled wherever people dwelt, and there were still plenty of names to add to his list. His army had no shortage of Sparkers. For as many that 'left', more joined his ranks as his army made its way north.

"Nothing, sir," one of the soldiers replied, voice cracking. "I'm sorry, sir."

Nexes' hands balled into fists. *It's not his fault my emperor won't talk to me.* The thought didn't stop him from grinding his teeth.

"No matter," Nexes breathed, coming to a stop outside his room and meeting the eyes of the Shadow Sparker.

How he'd dearly love to put one of them to the blade.

Their stain, their corruption, infested his ranks. Every day, it grew worse, the soldiers a little more dishevelled, stubbled, haggard and grim. Sodden uniforms, stained tents, horses pushed to their limits, starved and dehydrated, some left with their saddles on all night.

A part of Nexes screamed inside his mind. The drop in standards, in discipline, was unacceptable. Drunken fights broke out between the men and women of Haltveldt, undermining the war effort, but he couldn't bring himself to stop it. A deep, paralysing hatred surged through Nexes any time he had to interact with his underlings. It had started back at the tail end of the war with the elves in the south and had only grown on the march north.

If he hadn't needed an army, Nexes would have happily watched them tear each other apart. No, he'd join in, and paint his mastery of battle across the filth-sodden ground with his people's blood.

This isn't right. It's them. The Shadow Sparkers. Remember that.

If only the voice in his head spoke the truth. If only it gave him one target to rail against, but Nexes understood the complexity of matters. His emperor's subtle accusations and continued silence, no matter the number of missives Nexes sent, by bird, Sparker or Hand, ate away at him. So did the lack of sign of collusion he found amongst the mages.

Scratch, scratch, scratch...

Silence!

The urge in his head followed his command. For now.

Nexes kept cutting at the Sparkers, kept urging them to give him the answers he needed, but which they couldn't provide. He'd continue even after they annihilated the Banished, but it rankled on him that he could find none of Balz's supporters, and that his old friend hadn't reached the army yet.

The Sparkers. Their standards had fallen too. He'd never had so many mages to call on. A group of them passed him in the corridor of the inn, all wearing their usual bright robes, though the filth clinging to them dulled their shine. They fell silent as they offered him guarded looks.

They rankled on him too, but he could never confess the true reason. Nexes would barely admit that one to himself, though his dreams tormented him with it often enough.

Shaking his head, he brought himself back to the present.

"The scouts. What do they say about the Banished?"

The soldiers and Shadow Sparker should have offered their reports before he reached the inn instead of him begging for answers like a spurned lover.

But you are, and your precious emperor has a new toy now...

"They skirted Ballorn and are heading to Lake Circa, moving fast for their numbers," the Shadow Sparker hissed, void eyes fixed on Nexes. She sniffed and licked her lips, as if she could taste and smell the corruption in the camp, or the darkness oozing from Nexes' soul. He shuddered. "Perhaps they head for Gallavan's Seat?"

"Another siege? No. Why would they? The lake gives them water, the Forest of Willows food. They're seeking to settle in before the coming winter." Nexes nodded. "But we won't let the scum. I know the land well. We'll meet them there and put an end to the barbarians. Make them pay for what they did to Solitude."

He spoke the words with such force he almost believed them. He'd tossed the issue over in his mind. What had happened there? Who really shouldered the blame? Nexes missed some detail about the First People, and it plagued him night and day.

The magic they reportedly possessed. Did the emperor know about it?

Nexes' army had passed Protector's Watch days before and picked up reinforcements, as well as more Sparkers. They'd reach Lake Circa in less than a week. He'd send more scouts to watch them, and hope they'd uncover the missing part of the puzzle that nagged him so much.

If they did possess magic, why hadn't they scoured Solitude away and attacked Haltveldt sooner? But the witness reports seemed clear. The Banished weren't what the tales of simple shepherds made them out to be. Nexes had mentioned it in his missives to the emperor, but they'd gone unanswered.

His jaw cracked with the force of his grinding teeth.

"Yes, sir," one of the soldiers barked, an eager light in her eyes. "Anything else, sir?"

"Send a slave with hot water to fill my bath, and make it quick," Nexes muttered, glaring one last time at the Shadow Sparker, "and don't disturb me, unless it's word from the emperor himself."

Flinging the door open and letting it slam behind him, Nexes stalked inside, peeling the bloodstained clothes from his skin, the material clinging as the crimson congealed. For a moment, it almost made him gag, but then images of the Sparker's final moments came back to him, when the body couldn't even scream anymore, and the light dulled in its eyes. When the soul hung between life and death but irrecoverably slipped away, never to return. The lungs rattled, sucking in the last breath, one that would do nothing for the failing organs.

Jorca Appleby. Remember that name. Remember how you enjoyed taking his life. How much you revelled in wearing his blood on your skin.

Nexes breathed in and dismissed the stained pile of clothes. The slave would clean or burn them; he didn't care.

Naked, Nexes glanced at his arms, ignoring the cold night's chill kissing his skin, and studied the thin and thick, the straight and crooked, all of the white lines tracing them. It would be warm soon. He would be clean again. The scars on his forearms fascinated, as much as they horrified, as much as they itched. Nexes let no one see them. No one. Nor did he let them know how they found themselves there.

Scratch, scratch, scratch.

Fresh, angry nicks covered small, white scars, crisscrossing the pale underside of his forearms, running from above his wrist to beneath his elbows. Nexes stared at them, as if daring them to move, daring them to wriggle like worms, to writhe, break open and bleed again. He traced them with his fingers, his nails itching to scratch them.

"What is Locke playing at?" Nexes spat, spittle landing on the scars. Shadows darkened the edges of his vision. "We're missing key details about the Banished, yet he ignores me! How dare he? How dare he!"

He plunged into the pile of clothes and pulled a dagger free, the flames of the room's braziers reflected on the steel. His fingers curled tight around the handle and he collapsed onto his double bed, beating at the pillow with one fist.

"Does he know? Has the emperor discovered some secret about them in the Cradle and he sends me to my death? Yes, just like he did at Solitude. He wants us dead, another massacre, another reason to fight his wars, but not with me. No, not this time. He thinks me a traitor. Me! A filthy traitor! Why? All I've done is support him. Always!" Head spinning, tears stinging his eyes, Nexes plunged the dagger into his pillow, pulled it out and stabbed again and again. "He wants us all dead so he can use his Shadow Sparkers. That's it. Yes, that's what he wants. I won't let him. I won't... let..."

This was the horror Nexes refused to confront until he stood alone in his tent each night, and now in a rude little room in some hinterland backwater. Emperor Locke saw men like him as obsolete. A warrior, a general, a leader on the battlefield, and loyal, but just a man. Flesh and blood, fighting with steel and muscle.

The emperor had his Shadow Sparkers now, and didn't need Nexes Almor, Master of War. If anyone led an insurgency in the heart of Haltveldt, it wasn't Balz. It wasn't Nexes either.

It was Emperor Locke Dazel himself.

He glanced down at the shredded pillow, and fell to his knees, dagger still in his hand. Treason. Nexes spoke treason. Pure and simple. He'd killed people for less and would again.

"These words are only for me, and me alone," Nexes whispered, studying his scars again.

Gripping the dagger, he sank the tip into his skin, wincing at the exquisite, terrible pain. A fresh scar. Another to remind himself of his treasonous soul, the secret words he whispered to himself in the cold reaches of the night. So many scars...

"I'm sorry, emperor. Forgive me."

He cut again and again, tears streaming down his face with each slice, each gush of blood. How much had he spilt on the march north and before that?

Every time he'd doubted his emperor. His leader. His god.

"Forgive me, forgive me, forgive me."

Itch, itch, itch.

Scratch, scratch, scratch.

A creak and splash of water disturbed him.

Looking up, bloody knife still in hand, Nexes met the eyes of the slave sent to bring him water and smiled.

An elf. A dirty, traitorous, elven whore.

"I-I'm sorry, sir," she mumbled, stepping back, heat rising from the boiling water at her feet. It covered her bare toes, but the horror she'd walked in on caused the pain not to register. "I'll get more water. I'm... Forgive me."

Nexes rose to his feet, blood streaming from the wounds in his forearm, gathering at his fingers. He pointed the dagger at the slave and took a step forward.

"You take one more step and this blade will show me the colour of your insides. Do you understand?"

She sobbed a yes, head bobbing, eyes wide.

"Look at you," Nexes snarled, stepping into the boiling water. The heat seared his skin, and he swallowed the pain, added it to the rest. "An elf. Mighty warriors." Nexes shook his head. "Scum. Obsolete. Just like everyone else without magic. You're my droking future! Don't you see that?"

The elf's limbs shook, and she stumbled back into the room's door, thudding against the wood.

Nexes held up the knife and she froze.

"I warned you. The emperor knows I did." He grinned at her, and that smile held the pain, shame, rage and madness of thousands. "No matter. You marked your card as soon as you walked in here." He ran the flat of the dagger down his arm. "No one sees this. No one."

Nexes threw himself at her, knocking her to the ground and following her down. Wrapping his hands around her neck, he squeezed, blood dripping onto her plain, white tunic, staining it. The elf kicked. She thrashed. Brought her knees into Nexes' stomach and clawed at his skin with her nails, but he held her off, staring into her face.

He wanted to see it. *Needed* to. The moment the light departed. Her movements stilled as she gasped, as her tanned skin turned purple. Nexes' face reflected back at him in her dark eyes. So clear. So perfect. Almost like he choked himself.

He couldn't look away. As the elf died, his own dumbfounded face filled his vision. Falling backward, Nexes scrambled away from the corpse, through the scalding water.

An elf. A filthy, traitorous elf. That's all. She deserved it. They all do.

Getting to his feet, legs shaking, Nexes found a robe and pulled it around himself, hiding his wounds. He stuffed the blood-stained dagger inside the ruined pillow and hid it beneath his mattress.

Approaching the room's door, he opened it, and poked his head outside, meeting the eyes of a soldier standing guard.

"The elf displeased me." Nexes pulled the door wide, revealing the corpse. The soldier's eyes twitched between the Master of War and the dead woman. "Send for another, with fresh water, and someone to remove the corpse. Now."

Nexes let the door fall shut and sat in his chair, staring into the brazier's flames. He waited for the next slave to arrive to fill his bath, mind blissfully empty.

"Another missive from the Master of War, my emperor," Byar breathed, holding out a sealed letter.

Locke eyed it. Nexes' wax seal remained intact. He turned away.

"Open it and tell me what he says."

For a Shadow Sparker, Byar wasn't all bad. Proof, if it were ever needed, that one could get used to anything. Though having the shadowy mage dog his every step felt like knowing the date of his own death and having it hovering at his shoulder.

Still, after the assassination attempt, Locke felt it only prudent to keep the Shadow Sparker around while he perused the Cradle. It may have been a safe place only a select few knew about, one where no one could reach him, but there were traitors everywhere. Balz had proven that.

He had his Hands, of course, and other mages, plenty of them Bound with oaths to serve him, but this one had a name. A personality. It made him more...human.

Not that they were, of course. In truth, the Sparkers barely were either. Nothing with so much power at their beck and call could be described as such.

The sound of wax snapping filled the air, echoing through the quiet stacks and solemn stones of the Cradle. As ever, Locke stood before the stone door, the immovable and unknowable portal looming at the back of the vault.

The place held so much knowledge, had revealed so much, yet this one door remained frustratingly closed to Locke, and it dominated his thoughts.

"The Master of War again stresses the need for more details on the...First People. And says he strives to uncover the conspiracy Balz involved himself in."

Locke rolled his eyes. Nexes knew everything about the Banished that he did, and his blathering about the conspiracy vexed him.

Rotten teeth of the gods, he's losing his nerve at the wrong time.

He meant the barb about his judgement to keep Nexes focused on the task at hand more than anything else, though he had to concede he desired to remind the Master of War of his place. An underling, a servant of the empire and its emperor.

The slight appeared to have unhinged the man, though no one could have ever labelled Nexes Almor as sane. Men of war never were.

Another problem, and one not so easily solved. Locke couldn't remove him, not now, and his Hands warned of increasingly deranged behaviour from his Master of War. An increase in interrogations and executions among their own men. Ranting at his officers. Escalating suspicion at the Sparkers.

Nexes had always walked the edge of reason. Locke knew about his past, the pain and anguish that drove him. It made him a fine Master of War and a loyal servant, but the slippery slope to madness always awaited. Nexes had hovered as close to it as possible without sliding to the bottom.

Perhaps now he bloody has. Drok it, anyway.

No matter. As long as Nexes did what he did best and destroyed the Banished, Locke could replace him later. Maybe he'd die in battle. He tapped a finger against his lip.

Now there's a thought...

"Does he say anything else?"

"Just that the enemy approaches Lake Circa, and he speculates they're about to settle there for the winter. Your forces will meet them within the week."

"Excellent."

"Do you wish to respond, sire?"

"What's the point? Mistreatment only makes a rabid dog more feral, and that's perfect before a battle." Locke clapped his hands. "What can you tell me about this door?"

He'd had Sparkers study it before, ones who lost their lives soon after. Only a select few knew of the location, and even less what lay inside, but he trusted Byar to an extent. The Binding ensured compliance. Loyalty of a kind. There'd be no need to have the Shadow Sparker killed in the near future.

"I feel nothing from it," Byar answered, his voice a flat hiss, like a viper waiting to strike.

"Is that normal?" Locke spat, fingers flexing. The door vexed him so! "This isn't the time for reticence, man."

"It isn't. Everything has an energy, an essence. A quality

the Spark can use." If Locke's temper annoyed the Shadow Sparker, he showed no sign of it, though he cocked his head, as if listening to a whisper in his ear. He did it often, and it made the small hairs on the back of Locke's neck bristle. "Yes, it's like its nature is closed to me. Blocked off somehow."

Yes? Teeth of the gods, he does *hear voices. Lunatics. I'm surrounded by lunatics.*

"Try and touch it with your Spark," Locke commanded, stepping back. "Reach out to it."

Byar nodded, the flames from the Cradle's braziers shimmering in his void eyes. He loomed before the great stone door, a towering silhouette, arms outstretched, challenging the immutable, the unconquered.

Black tendrils of writhing ink loosed from Byar's hands and Locke's breath caught in his throat. The thick coils writhed and twisted as they slammed into the stone, but they vanished. Disintegrated as soon as they made contact with it.

The door remained sealed, concealing its secrets.

Byar jerked and staggered backward, shoulders hunched.

"Well?" Locke glowered at his back, fingernails digging into the palms of his hands so they didn't grab his dagger instead. "What happened?"

Byar shook his head, then turned, fissure-lined face uncertain. "It... It says we can't touch it. That something ancient and unknown seals the door."

Despite the many braziers lining the Cradle, the air turned to ice.

"It?" Locke asked, an itch forming between his shoulder blades.

"My magic, sire."

"The Spark?"

Byar frowned, then cocked his head again. "No. I don't think it is."

Mad. They're all mad.

"Leave me. Wait outside. I'll return to my tent at nightfall." Feigning nonchalance, Locke stooped and pulled a rolled parchment from the stacks. "Might as well settle in. We'll be here until the battle is won and thoughts of assassination have settled. If you think of more concerning the door, tell me at once, Byar."

He turned to the parchment, eyes seeing through the scratchings on it. Byar hissed his goodbye and slid away.

Locke watched him go. What had he created?

The globe hung above him, the one showing all the nations surrounding them, all the potential enemies of his Haltveldt.

"A weapon," he insisted. "I've created a weapon. And attack is the best form of defence. Only a fool would believe otherwise."

Chapter Twenty-Six

FACE TO FACE

'For one side, a prisoner of war is a failure, a liability with secrets on their tongue. If they escape, a hero, one hidden from view and forgotten soon after. To the other, they're an enemy defeated, a broken thing to dominate. And, ultimately, a dead soldier walking.' - From the Annals of Beba, a text now banned in Haltveldt, written by the preeminent historian of the now-absorbed Hiberian Duchy. They switched allegiances after their capture by the Hiberian army.

K ade knelt on the ground, hands bound at the wrists behind his back. Ankles tied too. Trussed up like a pig.

The soldiers had transported him back to the plains, to the midst of the great army. They hadn't bothered to pull a hood over his head or tell him to keep his eyes fixed to the ground. Why would they? Even if Kade wriggled free, he wouldn't get far.

How he longed for it though. When they'd dragged him away from the cave, he'd kicked and screamed until they beat him. Not for sport, and they didn't seem to gain any pleasure from it. They did it just to silence him, to make him cause less of a fuss, but it wasn't the blows to his ribs, back, stomach and face that made him stop.

Kade didn't want them returning to the cave. If they did, they might discover Arlo and Tilo. He'd almost slipped up and cried out for his son before the rockslide, but the magic forced into his mouth had cut him off.

A rare slice of good fortune.

Kneeling in the middle of an army, the pinnacle of the Peaks of Eternity rearing before him, conflicting emotions warred inside Kade's mind, filling his limbs with adrenaline and dread. Arlo lived, and his son knew he did too. Kade had saved him from the strange mage, but then the cave had collapsed. If Arlo had made it this far, he had to believe he'd survive and press on.

He couldn't picture the day Arlo didn't survive. He couldn't.

Kade couldn't pull his eyes away from the Peaks of Eternity for long. Tilo and his son journeyed there, that much was clear now, and the strange army controlled it. If Kade could find his way there too...

He glanced around at the soldiers, studying them. They showed no sign of moving on in pursuit of the Banished. Winter approached, and while commanders avoided battle in the cold months, such conflicts weren't unheard of.

The camp they'd left him in appeared well-ordered, with small, pristine tents spaced evenly apart. Soldiers patrolled, black uniforms crisp as they moved, eye emblems embossed on their chests, shimmering despite the gloomy clouds. It looked like they wore leather but not as stiff.

The soldiers moved with freedom, and the unusual properties of the material suggested the element was alien to Haltveldt, or that these people had fashioned it for armour in a different way. Some wore crimson, like the soldier he'd encountered by the hill of dead. Many of these rode horses, and Kade marked them as scouts.

Their weapons puzzled Kade too. They carried familiar swords or maces sheathed to their hips and backs, and some wore bows with quivers of arrows, but they all had a narrow, crimson tube hanging from their belts, about the length of an adult's forearm.

Kade had thought them ceremonial at first, or maybe some sort of club, until a horse passed him, and refused to go any further when a crowd of soldiers in dark green armour approached. Nostrils flaring, stamping its hooves in the shale, the animal whinnied, almost on the verge of frenzy. Its handler had pulled the crimson tube from her hip and touched the end to the horse's flank. Bright light had crackled out of it, causing the beast to jump forward, pain overriding its fear.

The majority of the soldiers wore black, the scouts crimson, but those in dark green...

Kade figured the strange soldiers used the Spark. The lances of lightning from the sky had come from them but he hadn't seen their magi at first. Expecting robed figures like Haltveldt's Sparkers, or the hooded mage he'd skewered, he'd watched out for them, failing to see the facts right before him.

To a person, the men and women wearing dark green were bald, their skin cracked with angry red fissures they made no attempt to hide, their eyes black as midnight. They wore their weapons at their sides, and the other soldiers inclined their heads as they passed in their packs, the dark clouds overhead thicker wherever they walked.

Though he put that down to his imagination.

They ignored him, as they did the other soldiers, and for that he thanked Raas. Their presence made his stomach twist, made him as nervous as whenever his father summoned him to his study, be it as a child or adult.

Kade hated the sight of them almost as much as he did his old man too.

From the little interest the soldiers paid Kade, he'd begun to believe they'd forgotten all about him, or Raas himself had cast a spell of concealment over him, hiding them him view. And that suited him fine.

They'd ask questions and, with proper pressure applied, those doing the answering always broke. They'd want to know who he was, how he came to be there, why he'd fought them at the cave. Eventually, Kade would tell them.

The longer it took them to start with their questions, the longer Kade could hold out, the further Arlo could flee.

If he still lives...

Crunching shale snatched at Kade's attention. Looking up, a soldier loomed over him, the one who'd captured him at the cave.

"Malek will see you now."

Bending, the man produced a dagger and cut Kade's bonds. Pain bloomed in his limbs as blood rushed back into his extremities. He almost fell on his face. The soldier grabbed him, hand like a vice, and pulled him up, golden eyes glittering.

"I trust you understand how little point there is in you trying to run or fight?"

They'd taken his weapons, of course. Kade could use his fists and feet, but pain and weakness made his muscles watery.

Kade nodded. "None of you would put up much of a fight."

The soldier barked out a laugh. "A sense of humour. Didn't think you seemed like the type. You'll need it."

"What's your name?" Kade asked, as the soldier shoved him forward. Colours danced among the dark clouds overhead, silent lightning racing through the pall. The name of the soldier would add some normality to the situation, something Kade could work with.

"Anatol."

A name. Simple, but knowing it didn't make the soldier any more human in Kade's mind, any more knowable.

They made their way down one of the wide tracks between the identical tents, soldiers and magi passing them. The encampment resembled a town more than a temporary staging area. Smaller avenues led off the beaten path, and a rider thundered down one as Kade passed it. Beside them, a cart rolled past, pulled by horses. Obsidian-coloured rocks filled it. He frowned, not recognising them.

"Where do you come from, Anatol?"

"Malek will ask the questions. Not you."

"You don't even care to ask my name?"

"I don't. It means nothing to me." Anatol's hand gripped Kade's shoulder, steering him toward a narrow track between the tents. "You mean nothing to me, except that you may have information Malek finds useful, and your capture will elevate me in his eyes."

Shale crunched beneath Kade's boots. To his left, the flaps of a large tent opened and a soldier marched out, granting him a glance inside. More soldiers, clad in black and dark green watched a group of Banished—men, women, children of all ages, all gagged and bound—huddle on the ground. Movement in the tent to his right revealed the same.

Up ahead, a black tent emblazoned across its front with the eye emblem loomed. Larger and more detailed than the ones on the armour, red and curved up at the corners, the inner iris were yellow, and it watched Kade as he approached. He shoved the sensation away.

It's nothing more than material. A pattern, a design.

Telling himself that achieved nothing. He couldn't pull his eyes from it.

The dark clouds overhead appeared blacker above the tent, like they all gathered there, or spread from that point.

"On second thoughts." Relief buffeted Kade, Anatol's words snatching his attention from the tent. They came to a halt, a few yards away. Kade gazed around. No other tent lay close to it. The space surrounding it after so much tight regimentation yawning. "Give me your name. The information might please Malek."

Kade raised his chin, then the air exploded from his lungs when Anatol sunk his gauntleted fist into Kade's stomach.

He sank to his knees, gasping.

"I'll ask you again," Anatol repeated, looming over him. "What is your name? You were so eager to offer it before."

Kade shook his head, stomach tightening against another blow. Instead, Anatol pulled the long, crimson tube from his side and pressed it against Kade's ribs.

He trembled, his limbs shook without control, and he flopped to the ground, his back slamming against the shale. Being stabbed, having metal shoved inside his guts over and over again, had hurt more than anything he'd experienced before. It came nowhere close to this.

The pain consumed him to the point Kade couldn't even scream. His throat just refused. It closed itself off as the burning agony swept through his body, a fire within his blood searing flesh and bone. Anatol kept the tube pressed against his ribs, and the moment stretched. Kade existed within a bubble of torment, limbs spasming, mind blind to everything save the misery.

Until it stopped.

Anatol pulled the tube away and held it in front of Kade's face. He gasped, the trembling subsiding, pain fleeing into memory. He glanced at his hands, expecting to see a charred mess, but his tan skin appeared intact.

"A second. That's all. I held this against you for one second." Anatol knelt before Kade, the tube between them. "Can you imagine two? Three? What is your name?"

"Kade..." he gasped. It was just his name. Nothing more, but as soon as he gave it, he realised it would be 'nothing more' when he told this Malek about Arlo and Tilo. It would be 'nothing more' when he'd tell him anything to spare him from the pain. "Kade Besem."

Anatol got to his feet, tucking the tube away at his side. Grabbing Kade, he hauled him to his feet, straightening his clothes, wiping the dust from them. A parent fixing his wild child's appearance before meeting someone important.

"Well, Kade Besem, I hope for your sake you are more eager to answer Malek's questions. He is not as patient as I am, and why should he be? A man like him is above patience."

Holding the scruff of Kade's cloak, Anatol dragged him forward, toward the black tent with the all-seeing eye. Weakness washed through Kade's limbs.

God's teeth, a second? It lasted a day, if not a week! I have to be stronger. I need to be. I need—

Kade staggered through the entrance, Anatol beside him, gazing around. Furniture lined the space inside. Luxurious-looking chairs, a large bed with rich-coloured fabric, heavy burning braziers, and banners of war standing here and there. The permanence of the items suggested nothing of this being a temporary spot, or a fleeting engagement.

It told Kade this army had come to stay and had no intention of leaving.

In between two wide braziers, an obsidian desk lay at the rear of the tent. Behind it, sat Malek.

He wore the same black uniform as Anatol, made from the same strange, flexible, shimmering material, but his had the crimson eye emblem standing out at the shoulders. Where Anatol sported cropped dark hair and skin, and vivid golden eyes, Malek's iris merged into glittering black, and red fissures crisscrossed his bald, pale face.

Malek had magic at his command, and an army.

Impossible. Kade swallowed when Malek's void eyes met his. *Sparkers leading an army? An entire people? It's against the word of Raas! It's... It's...*

Foreign. Alien. Whatever it was, Kade realised it didn't matter. He couldn't change the fact an invading force of thousands had a mage at its head. Searching for a way to reunite with Arlo or buy his son time to reach his goal. That's all he could do.

"This is Kade Besem, my liege," Anatol announced.

Malek's onyx eyes glittered. "Besem. A minor house from Haltveldt's capital." He flowed to his feet and slid to the front of the desk. Tall and lithe, he didn't walk so much as slither, his scale-like black armour adding to the effect. A snake in human form. "You've done well, Anatol. Leave us. Oversee the obsidian collection and report to me later."

"Your will is mine, Leader. You walk and I shall follow."

Malek smiled at Kade, who wobbled when Anatol's steadying hand left him. "Polite and loyal, and not the squeamish type either. I couldn't ask for more." Malek approached, and shadows crawled in the corners of Kade's eyes, desperate to surge forward and devour him, but the firelight beat them back. Peering into his eyes, Malek whispered, "I see the effects of our Spark-baton on you. Nasty, no?"

Kade pulled his stare away. The man stared into his soul, and his inner-self wilted beneath his gaze, desperate to lay itself bare. Malek wore no...'Spark-baton' on his hip, but he commanded the Spark otherwise. Swallowing, he nodded.

"A misunderstanding."

Malek hissed, and it took Kade a moment to recognise

it as laughter. "Misunderstandings often become violent, do they not? What are you doing here in Banished lands? You are not one of them. I could tell as much the moment I laid eyes on you, even before I heard your name. A Haltveldtian nobleman, no matter how insignificant your house, alone, in these barren wastelands... A spy? Or something else?"

The slight against his name didn't rankle, though the Besem's held not insignificant power in Spring Haven. Or had, before Kade's involvement.

How do they know Besem? The soldier I fought against, back at the mound of dead. He knew, too.

Malek stood mere inches away, his scentless, warm breath in Kade's face. Could he throw himself at the man? Overpower him before he used the Spark?

And then what? Run? Through an army encampment?

No. It would solve nothing, except the continued problem of Kade's prolonged existence.

Kade opened his mouth, then winced as a weight crushed down on his shoulders, forcing him to kneel. His jaw snapped shut as his head tilted back so he stared into Malek's eyes.

The man hadn't moved, hadn't so much as crooked a finger, though the shadows writhing in the corners of the tent where the light didn't touch swirled thicker.

"Prisoners often take a while to warm up with their answers, Kade Besem, and I see strength in your soul, a vigour many others have overlooked." He reached out, and drew a fingernail down Kade's face, tracing his jaw. "Courage is a fine thing, a steel core to be commended, but you've suffered. Don't extend it. The Spark-baton hurt you? It pales into insignificance at what I can do to you. Do you believe me?"

Kade couldn't pull his eyes away this time. Malek held him in place with his power, and what could one normal man, with no magic inside them, do in the face of such mastery?

"I do."

The pressure lessened, and Kade gasped as he toppled forward, throwing his hands out to stop himself crashing face-first into the ground.

"Now, Kade Besem, what are you doing here?"

"I might ask you the same thing," Kade replied, his stomach flipping as the words tumbled out of his mouth.

Raas! I've taken leave of my senses!

Coughing, he held a hand up. "I had a dream of seeing the Banished and the Peaks of Eternity for myself. A foolish dream, my family and friends told me, but I'm a historian and our facts about this region are scarce, other than what's told in the Book of Raas." Kade didn't know where the lies came from, but they were all he had, so went with them. Why not? "I passed through Solitude a few weeks back, then hid in the forests as a whole horde of the savages appeared. I thought about fleeing, but then..." He widened his eyes and shook his head. "The explosion, the lights in the sky. I feared for my life, not knowing what happened. So, I wandered, searching for some clue, somewhere to hide until I knew it was safe."

Malek hadn't blinked. He stared at Kade, face impassive, though the fissures in his bald head seemed to glow.

"Why did you kill my soldiers?"

Kade bowed his head. "The lightning from the sky came and I panicked. When I saw one of them, I thought they hunted me and defended myself."

Malek nodded. "I can appreciate self-defence. It's my soldiers' problem you killed them. Not yours. The strong always defeat the weak; this is the way of the world." He flowed away and sat behind his desk. A force gripped Kade, pulled him forward across the carpeted floor, his knees burning as they scraped against the fabric. "Your lies are good ones. Just enough truth mixed in with them to make them believable, but you leave out key facts. My magi felt a Sparker near the cave where they found you, and you do not have the Spark in your soul, Kade Besem."

He ground his teeth, unable to move a muscle again.

"And you do?" Kade snarled. "I've never heard of a Sparker commanding an army."

Malek smiled. "I am not a commander, I am merely the Leader of the Return, and I am not a..." His mouth twisted with distaste. "...Sparker."

"But you use magic." Kade frowned, straining against his invisible restraints. "I feel it holding me. I've seen it!"

Clicking his fingers, black flames exploded from Malek's thumb. He studied them, head cocked to one side. "It came from the Spark, yes, but it is more than that now. Much more." With a sigh, he banished the fire. "I see you're not going to willingly answer me, Kade Besem, and I have little time to pull answers from you. Allow me to try a different tact. Ask me a question, just one, and I will answer it, in trade for some truth from you. Agreed?"

Kade glanced around. Questions flooded his mind, too

many, but one forced its way to the forefront of his mind, one that had plagued him since the Banished's migration. More than who this army were, or where they came from, he desired to know one thing above all.

"Why haven't you moved into Haltveldt? The Banished fled before you in fear, but you sit here with your finery, your perfectly laid out tent town, mining black rocks. Why?"

Malek laughed. "A question wrapped in an insult." He tapped a finger against his lip, eyebrow raised. "Obsidian. The rocks are a mineral called obsidian, just like the colour. We are an unimaginative type at times, no? We've no intention of invading further. Not yet. An army flees before us into the maw of another. We will allow a victor to emerge, then crush them when they are weak. Why involve ourselves in these matters when we have more pressing concerns?"

Kade shivered. The nonchalance in Malek's tone, the routine, matter-of-fact way he described the annihilation of thousands. More pressing concerns... The carts stacked with obsidian.

"You're building something, aren't you? A city?"

Malek smiled. "I said *one* question, Kade Besem, and I answered. My turn." He pursed his lips, void eyes narrowed. "Where do you wish to go?"

Kade hesitated. He hadn't expected the question. He thought Malek would press him about the Sparker his men had sensed and what happened to them, and Kade would lie again and again until Malek resorted to his magic. But this question...

"The summit of the Peaks of Eternity." It's where Arlo headed, and his son needed him. Kade didn't need to say why, just what he desired, and with this army between him and the range, he'd never get there. "That's where."

"And that's where you shall go." Getting to his feet, Malek clapped his hands. Canvas rustled, and the thump of soldiers' boots sounded behind him. "I have not been able to test one of your kind there yet, just the Banished and my possessions, and I am eager to see the results, so your desire works for us both." He glanced beyond Kade. "Take him away. Continue the questioning as you travel. Report to me your findings, and how he fares before the Lodestone."

The Lodestone? Test? Hands grabbed Kade and dragged him backward. *What is this?*

"Who are you?" Kade yelled, the soldier's inching him toward the exit, cords in his neck popping. "Tell me!"

Malek held up a hand. "Wait."

He flowed to his feet and strode toward Kade, kneeling when he reached him, onyx eyes meeting green, and smiled. Ice ages formed with that smile, a frigid grin that could never reach those haunting eyes. Malek would smile when thousands died before him. Millions.

"We are the rightful rulers of Haltveldt, Kade Besem, and I have the honour of leading our Return." He got to his feet and turned his back. "Take him away."

Something smashed into the back of Kade's head, and he saw no more.

Chapter Twenty-Seven

A Conversation Long Overdue

"As I've come to understand it, through my travels and experiments on myself and others, the Spark has a mind, its own desires. It's a living entity. The answers to where it comes from and what it wants elude me, but I know this: a mage's Spark can be changed. Turned, you might say, into a weapon. In doing so, it becomes vastly more powerful. And terrible..." - From papers discovered in Ricken Alpenwood's study, now in the possession of Emperor Locke. The basis of his studies into the Spark.

"Your family home is close?"

Calene met Brina's eyes. A small fire burned between them, but the slight warmth did little to take the edge from the night's chill. Winter spread, icy fingers scrambling for a hold on Haltveldt.

"Close enough," Calene replied, with a shrug.

They'd made slower time on their way from Willow

to Spring Haven's hinterlands, where her family estate lay. Travellers filled the roads, and Calene and her friends had agreed avoiding them was the best course of action, especially after the events in Willow.

Word would spread of rogue Sparkers freeing one of their own and leaving the Patriarch's Palace in ruins, not to mention the bodies left behind. The patriarch himself topped that list.

Brina resumed her scouting, and a touch of Vettigan's old humour returned, the flashes of darkness and malcontent brief and causing little drama. They'd given the villages and hamlets a wide berth and trekked through the wilderness. Slow going, but prudent, even if Calene's arse cheeks had complained with every bump from her horse's missteps on the uneven paths.

Sometimes, a good moaning session was in order, and Calene had never been one to turn down the opportunity.

"Do you think we'll arrive tomorrow?" Brina asked, her voice soft, a whisper on the wind.

Calene looked away. Vettigan had gone to find water, leaving the women alone. She'd talked to the elf since Willow, but they skirted around anything serious, building bridges instead.

"Talk to her," Vettigan had growled in her ear, before stalking away, waterskins in hand, "for Raas' sake. Please. If not for your own sake, then mine!"

Before Willow, Calene would have bristled at the unsolicited advice, but now she'd resolved to breach the walls of her and Brina's reticence. They both wanted to talk. *Needed* to.

Sadly for them, old habits died harder than a droking Shadow Sparker. Each woman waited for the other to take initiative, so instead, they conducted Haltveldt's most pleasantly awkward verbal dance since the dawn of time, full of loaded glances, heavy sighs, bitten lips and sentences filled with words like goose down, purely to take up space.

"We could reach it tonight, but I'm droked if I'm going there in the dark."

Brina smiled, firelight twinkling in her emerald eyes. "Didn't take you for a woman afraid of a few shadows."

"It ain't the shadows I'm afraid of." Calene swallowed. "It's the memories."

"Sorry," Brina muttered, "I didn't mean to make light of it. You've never really told me what happened there. Why going back is so hard."

"So, are we going to have this talk or not?" Calene asked, staring at Brina through the dying flames. The words came out before she had time to think. Together, they'd skirted the precipice of 'serious talk' for days, and now Calene took the plunge. "Teeth of the gods, I'm game if you are. It'll be a droking relief for Vettigan more than anything."

She'll fall silent. Grimace and glare at the flames. Keep giving me those wide-eyed stares when she thinks I'm not looking. Calene sighed and leaned back against the tree trunk behind her. *Same old, same old. Back to square droking one.*

"Alright."

Calene almost fell over. 'Alright'. A simple word. Breathed instead of spoken, but a way forward. The word, or something similar, that Calene had wanted to hear from Brina for weeks.

Then why did it sink daggers into the pits of her stomach?

"Alright?" Calene repeated, lips numb, tongue sticking to the roof of her mouth.

Now it came to it, did they really need to talk? Like, *really* talk? She'd been the one to blurt out the idea but, thinking about it, they'd gotten on fine since Willow. The barbs had lessened. The smothering tension between them all had eased, if you could count the agitation that had replaced it as an improvement.

I can live with it though, can't I? Better that than...

Brina stared at her, a slight smile on her lips. The memory of one. A shadow of humour as the internal struggle played out across Calene's face.

Vettigan always said I couldn't keep my feelings from the end of my nose. Said I was terrible with women too.

The elf shuffled a little around the fire, bringing their bodies closer.

"So, what do you want to talk about?"

Calene rolled her eyes. "Raas' teeth, you're about as good at this as I am, aren't you?"

"What do you mean?" Brina asked, ruddiness spreading across her tanned cheeks.

"Talking in general," Calene muttered.

She'd almost said 'talking to women' but thought better of it. Or worse. Who knew? She certainly didn't. At times, she fancied being direct with Brina the best course of action, then she pictured the elf's face after a full-on volley of heartfelt truths and doubted herself.

Vettigan's right. I'm droking useless. 'Be yourself,' that's what he used to say. 'Be yourself.' I suppose it can't do any harm.

She eyed Brina's profile, the flames dancing light and shadow across her face, and bit her bottom lip.

Can't it?

Brina sighed and ran her hands through her hair. "It should be easy enough for us to just...talk. About our... *Thiemea!* Why can't we?"

"Because I don't trust you."

Calene's mouth hung open. Her wide eyes met Brina's. She'd just been herself, that's all. Listened to the voice inside her head, her instinct, her gut logic, and blurted out the reason.

Last droking time I'm doing that!

But now the truth had blundered its way out into the open, did it seem so bad? Calene had spoken the truth.

"You don't trust *me*?" Brina's voice could have levelled mountains. "After everything we've been through? I saved you in the Forest of Mists. I waited for you outside of Colton when you thought I'd run. I stayed with you until Solitude, then came back to you. I even chased after you into Willow. Me, an elf! Scaling the bloody red walls, and you don't trust *me*?"

Calene spread her hands, palms raised. "Godsrot. Look, I thanked you for all of that, and droking appreciated it, but I know nothing about you. Nothing. How can I trust you? I mean, *really* trust you, when you won't tell me anything? I know you'll fight by my side, and I wouldn't ever doubt the aim of your blade, but who you are, what you want... I know as much about any of that as I did the day I met you."

Brina's scowl sent Calene's heart plummeting into her

boots. The elf grabbed a stick and stabbed at the embers, jabbing at it like the ashes had offended her in some uniquely terrible and personal way. Growling in the back of her throat, she tossed the singed wood into the terrorised flames and rounded on Calene, her face stony, emerald eyes hard.

Calene met her stare. The elf had wanted to talk. That's what she'd said. 'Alright'. Brina wanted the truth, and Calene had delivered it. They'd never move past the impasse their relationship, as friends or more, had run into without confronting it.

Simple as that.

Brina's blazing stare dropped to the ground, then flicked back. Softer now, her eyebrows still drawn together, but not in anger. With Raas as Calene's witness, the elf nodded.

Nodded.

"You're not wrong, Calene. You're not wrong." Her hands balled into fists, then opened again. Raising one finger, she waved it in front of herself, trying to conduct the correct words out of her mouth. "It's difficult. For me, I mean. I swore I'd never get close to anyone again, not even as a friend, but you... When I met... Ugh, why can't this be easier?"

"If life's taught me anything, it's that it's not a droking bowl of juicy grapes, is it?"

Brina laughed, her pitch high. Shrill almost. "That's another thing. You're so young!"

"Young?" Calene scowled. "I'm thirty-two! What's that supposed to mean?"

"Add three hundred to that and you'll have my number." Brina's eyes grew hard again. "Not to mention you're a human. A Sparker of Haltveldt. You've killed my kind."

Calene's eyes traced the thin, white scars lining Brina's face, forearms, knuckles, and the black paint running through her eye that she reapplied each morning.

"You've killed mine too."

Brina nodded. "Yes."

"So that's it then? I'm too young and a human with a dirty, murderous little soul, and you kill my kind. What else is there to talk about?"

The elf's jaw muscles bunched. "How can you fight for Haltveldt after everything they've done? It isn't a new thing, all this death. You wipe those gleaming cities away and you'll find they're built on elven bones. Did it never bother you? Ever?"

Calene breathed through her nose, the corners of her mouth curving down of their own accord as she swallowed the mountain of conflicting emotions, trying to keep them in check while she considered Brina's words. She attempted to see the situation from her point of view.

The elf liked Calene as a friend—and maybe, Calene still hoped, more—despite herself. Despite her dealings with humans, and Haltveldt specifically. To Brina and her kind, anyone who stood aside and watched as Haltveldt carried out generations of genocide were complicit in the act, and Calene had fought with the Haltveldtian army. Killed her fair share.

But hadn't she always acted in defence? Hadn't she always tried to protect those around her from the thinning number of dangerous and wild elven mages? They didn't give any quarter, and Calene had cried and screamed as friends and colleagues turned to ash before her eyes.

She could say she followed orders, but Maria du Gerran and Marc had proven Sparkers with a conscience could run away. Could fight back, even if those two had no love for the elves either.

And that's the problem isn't it? That's what Brina sees. Her kind always comes at the bottom of the pile for us when it comes to counting the reasons to hate Haltveldt. An afterthought.

"This is such a droking mess," Calene muttered, shaking her head. "I never hated elves, not like some do. The parades in the city knocked me sick. Truly. Vettigan too, before..." She grimaced, and a part of her wondered at what caused it. She had a whole lot of sourness in her life. "But I never disobeyed my commands from the Order, even though we knew the emperor gave more and more of them. I never shirked from duty on the frontline, and now I see how wrong I've been."

Brina stared into the flames. "Why?"

"Because of you." Heat exploded in Calene's cheeks, but she pushed through. "Because of the slavers we found in the forest, the elves we saved. Because I've seen the evil rotting in the heart of Haltveldt, and I don't see any way of stopping it unless it's all scrubbed away and we start again. Because my mother turned my own words back on me: 'There's always another way'. I used to say it as a stick to beat my mother with, even though she couldn't hear it most of the time, then I repeated her mistakes time and time again. Look at Haltveldt. War powers it. War and death. These Shadow Sparkers are the result of that, of us seeking out blood in every corner of the continent, and it's put us on a path to ruin. I feel it deep inside, and I'm afraid we can't droking escape it, no matter what we do."

"We can kill the emperor. Together." A fierce, wild light burned in Brina's emerald eyes. They glittered brighter than the flames of the fire. "Cut off the head of the festering snake, and the rest will wither and die."

Calene smiled at the elf and shook her head. "Will that bring your kind back?" she asked, her voice soft. "Will that stop all the duchies from re-emerging, tearing away from the empire, and plunging the entire continent into one massive, bloody battle? I don't think so. It's our nature. Not just humans. Elves too. Or maybe it's the magic inside of us."

Brina frowned, shuffled an inch closer to Calene. To be fair, the temperature had dropped, and the measly fire did little to arrest the chill.

"What do you mean?" she asked, turning to Calene, the hard planes of her face a little softer. "The Spark causes violence?"

Calene shrugged. "I don't know. God's teeth, I don't, but I've wrestled with the bloody question since Solitude. Before, I swallowed whatever the Order told us, even if it didn't wash down my throat quite right, because it came from Raas, and He gifted us this power. Now, though... If this magic inside me comes from Raas, is meant to be holy, then what in the Underworld is His purpose with the Shadow Sparkers? And why does that darkness speak to me? Since Solitude, until everything in Willow, I avoided using it. The droking stuff running through my veins scared me, Brina. Reminded me too much of my past, and then, when I had to use it in Willow, look what happened."

"You saved your friend, that's what."

"And killed a bunch of drokers in the process. Blew up half a palace. Yeah, the patriarch was a Shadow Sparker, but were they all evil? Did they all deserve it?"

Brina reached out and patted Calene's knee, movements awkward at first, like trying to comfort a beaten dog, afraid it might bite or flee.

So I'm comparing myself to a droking dog now? Teeth of the gods!

"Like you said before," Brina murmured, "they were complicit, no?"

"Then so am I. So's Vettigan." She sighed. "So was my mother."

Brina pursed her lips and gazed into the night sky. Heavy clouds gathered, but the shimmering moon broke out for just a moment before darkness swallowed it again.

"Maybe the world isn't black and white," Brina whispered, eyes still aimed at the sky but peering through it, into the past. "Maybe there aren't any heroes and villains. Just people doing what they can to survive, and others doing what they want because they can."

"I don't want to believe that." Calene twisted the ring on her finger. The only thing she had left of her family, aside from the crumbling ruin they inched toward, and that she didn't want. "It's why I have to try and save Vettigan. All this doubt about the Spark. It's inside me, Brina. Will the same thing happen to me? And if it does, is that it? Am I done for? An evil droker with nothing but violence and paranoia in my heart? And he's the only thing I've got left. Without him..."

Calene couldn't finish the thought. She flinched as Brina's fingers found hers and wrapped around them.

Brina's eyes met hers. "Not the only thing."

Calene coughed, looked away. "So, you want to know about my past then? Think you know a lot more about me than I do you."

"Let's do it this way. You tell me about your home, and I'll tell you about where I came from. Fair?"

Glancing around, she listened to the night air for a moment, almost expecting the crunch of Vettigan's boots to reach her ears. Save for the snorts and breathing of their horses, and the crackling flames of their dwindling fire, nothing disturbed the evening's quiet.

"Fair," Calene replied, nodding.

"Right." Brina nudged her with her thigh, making her budge up so the elf could lean against the tree trunk too. Calene welcomed the heat from her body, their legs leaning against one another's. "If you need to return home in order to save Vettigan, and maybe yourself in some yet-to-arrive future that may never bloody happen, what's stopping you? We could go now, get it done. What happened there?"

Calene hugged her knees, setting her chin atop them. She'd been a fool to think they could make the trip home without talking about it. She hadn't talked about it in years. At first, just to the Inquisitors and the Order because she had to, then at her mother's trial, Zanna shedding silent tears as she watched Calene detail every bloody moment. She and Vettigan had spoken of it a little, before they figured out not to approach the subject. They'd never agreed on it, given that her friend said he would have done the same, and

Calene insisted he'd deserve exile to Solitude too.

"I'd been away at the frontlines and had cycled back out." The words started before Calene realised, her tone flat, lips numb, spilling out like she purged them from her soul. "As Raas would have it, I passed my mother on the road going in the opposite direction. Father's disposition ate away at her. He'd gone on a mission for the Order he wouldn't talk about, or so he said, but there'd been tension there for a while. Anyway, I returned home, and Vettigan, who I'd already partnered with, went to Spring Haven, leaving me to see my father alone..."

Red-eyed and tear-stricken, Calene screamed at the top of her lungs, but no one came. No one would ever come.

Her father stared down at her, purple irises glittering with dark malice though his cheek muscles twitched and his mouth twisted from a slack grin to a grimace. Emaciated, his once luscious, raven hair hung in greasy tangles, clumps of it missing, the strands falling past his heavy eyebrows, all the thicker on his gaunt face.

Her father had been waiting for her when she arrived home, two weeks after she'd met her mother on the road, the house dark and empty save for him. He'd assaulted her with the Spark, knocked her senseless. On waking, she couldn't feel the Link with her mother anymore, and couldn't reach her magic. The panic exploding in her chest only increased when she found her arms and legs bound to a slab, her father standing over her, madness and grief waging war in his once-bright eyes.

He didn't seem to hear her screams, her pleading. He just stood there, head cocked to one side as if listening to a voice inside his head as he stared down at his wailing daughter, his flesh and blood.

Calene's screams ran out, her throat throbbing, raw, as if she'd swallowed a fistful of broken glass. Tears leaked from her eyes and down the side of her face, pooling in her hair.

"You could be so powerful," her father whispered, reaching out with a shaking hand. He trailed a finger across her cheek, collecting the tears. Calene tried to pull away, but a strap held her head in place too. "You have so much potential. So much..."

"Father, please," she whispered, meeting his eyes, fighting against the urge to flinch as they snapped to hers. "I-it's me! Calene! This isn't you. What... What happened? Are you sick? Please, let me go! I can help you. I can..."

He laid his hand over her mouth, pressing slightly, and shook his head. "I won't hear your excuses for not doing your best, Calene. Not anymore. I put up with them long enough, do you understand?"

Zanna had told her he hadn't been himself, but she couldn't have meant this. She'd have never left if she saw this shell of a man before her. Calene threw her mind against the connection with her mother, putting all her might into breaking through it, but what would it do?

Zanna wouldn't return home for weeks. She'd sense their Link blocked, but Calene did that from time to time anyway. For privacy, she told Zanna, but she did it most often after a spell on the frontlines, when she wept herself to sleep, trying to force the images of bloodshed and the stench of death from her mind.

Her father's hand slipped away, and Calene licked her lips.

"I'll do what I can to please you, father," she breathed, but his stare had wandered again. "I'll be the best student. I promise."

He smiled, his eyes finding hers again. "You will. Oh, you will. I'll make certain you will."

He raised a hand and pain lanced through Calene's navel, like an invisible hand reached inside her and gripped her spine, trying to pull it through her belly. Bound, her legs trembled, her arms too, and Calene faded into blissful oblivion.

Days went by, or maybe weeks.

Her father fed Calene gruel and forced water down her throat between bouts of raging tears and rants. He'd disappear from her view, throwing books against the walls and tipping tables, making her flinch and cringe, but he never touched her, never turned his temper her way.

Except for his Spark.

Occasionally, pain would overwhelm her, send her back to the blessed darkness, and she'd wake to find him kneeling beside her, begging for forgiveness, pleading for salvation. Other times, he'd stand beside her, prodding at her with his Spark as if studying her, face impassive, darkening eyes cold, deaf to her appeals for mercy.

Each time, she'd ask him the same question, and each time, he'd ignore it.

Until the last night.

"Why are you doing this to me, father?" Calene asked, wide eyes imploring, voice cracked and hoarse. "Please, remember who I am. I'm your daughter. You're hurting me. Every day, you're hurting me. Why?"

Bones stood out through stretched skin across his face and arms, clothes hanging from him, like a tall, skinny boy wearing his father's garments. A fever lit his now-black eyes, burning away inside his blood, wasting him. He cocked his head, listening to her words, face slack.

"It's not what I'm doing," he whispered, swaying on the spot. "It's what I'm not. This thing, this experiment. I can't bring myself to do it to you. I cannot. But it works! I know it does! She doesn't even understand. She came here today, raving! I had to. Had to!"

"She? Who's she? What experiment?" Calene pleaded. The most words he'd spoken to her in days, and she needed him to talk. It might bring him back to his senses. "Maybe I can help you?"

He shook his head, angry. "No, you can't. It's a matter of strength. A matter of will. It's the only way to make you strong, to make sure other Sparkers don't better you. To make sure the elves don't destroy you." He looked away, eyes wild. "Damn them, and damn those nobles who seek to command us. Us, with the Spark in our veins. Raas gave it to us! We should lead, and those mundane, unremarkable droks should follow. How dare they? How dare—"

"I don't understand," Calene half-whispered, half-sobbed. "What are you trying to do with me, poppa?"

She hadn't called him that in years, not since she stood

waist high to him. Poppa. Never father, never his name. Poppa. He trailed off, frowning, mouth moving but making no sound. He peered at her, and his face crumpled.

"Oh, Calene, what have I done?" He fell to his knees, head pressed against the slab. "I'm sick, Calene. Sick. It's inside me, and I can't get rid of it. I brought it on myself, and it won't let go. It twists my thoughts, eats away at me. I'm sorry. I'm so sorry, Raas knows that I am."

"It's okay, poppa." Calene's words tumbled out in a rush. She'd reached him. Her father still resided in this husk, wasted by sickness. She could save him if she chose the right words. "There's nothing done that can't be undone. You're just afraid for me, aren't you? You want to protect me by making me strong."

"Yes," he breathed, tears shining in his all-too-black eyes. "I need to. The world grows dark, and I fear Raas has abandoned us. I fear..."

"There's always another way, poppa," Calene interrupted, smiling as best she could. "There's always another way. Just let me go, and—"

"No." He climbed to his feet, a shadow crossing his face, wiping away the pain, the empathy and regret and sorrow, leaving nothing but chiselled stone. "There is no other way. Not in Haltveldt. People only respect strength, and you have more power than most. After tonight, none will stand in your way, no one will ever harm you. Not even me. I'm sorry, Calene, but I do what must be done. One day, you'll understand."

He raised his hand and, out of her field of vision, darkness gathered. Black thicker than shadow, an absence of light in the corner of Calene's eye.

"Poppa, please," she whispered, head still, eyes turning towards her father, unable to take him all in. "I'm your daughter."

"And that is why I do this."

"How dare you attack me?"

The scream came from behind him, from behind the door, and it crashed open. Zanna charged through, hair dishevelled, blood staining her face, a mask of fury as she took in the room. Her mouth hung open when her bright eyes fell on Calene, strapped to the slab, her father standing over her.

"Calene?" she screamed, as Ricken turned. "Teeth of the gods, Ricken, what have you done? You're not my husband! Not anymore! I don't know *what* you are."

"Mother, he's sick!" Calene screamed, straining against the bonds on her forehead, wrists and ankles. "Help him. Save him! You have—"

Ricken raised his hand, pointed it at Zanna, whose fearful, panic-stricken expression transformed into one of pure rage.

She acted with stunning speed, and Calene watched it all, strapped to the slab, helpless, powerless to stop it.

A thin thread of pure light extended from Zanna's palm, connecting her with Ricken. As it plunged into him, the shimmering white flickered, and darkness swam inside the band of magic.

Evisceration.

Calene had lost count of the times she'd witnessed an elven mage unleash it on the battlefield, could recall each and every time she'd raised her shield to ward off an attack. This time, her father reacted too late, and her mother's fury powered her Spark.

The flickering thread thickened, and Ricken sank to his knees, reaching out to Calene.

"Stop, mother! Stop! You're killing him!"

If Zanna heard Calene, she showed no sign. Teeth bared, she loomed over Ricken, palm trembling as the darkness flowed through her magic, almost swallowing the light. Calene's father turned his head, the skin withering on his face, white bone poking through the flesh, horror in his eyes. The horror of a man confronted with his crimes. The horror of a man on the precipice of death. The horror of a man whose mind flooded with the clarity of those about to perish.

"No!" Calene howled as her father's arms dropped, his muscles losing their strength. He shook, convulsed, his greasy, black hair shedding from his scalp, the remaining slithers of his skin losing their elasticity.

Helpless, Calene threw herself against the Link with her mother, but whatever Ricken had done kept her from accessing her Spark and her connection with Zanna.

Watch. She could do nothing more. Watch as her father disintegrated before her eyes, as the rapture of power, the giddy thrill of devouring life and delivering death played over Zanna's face. Watch as her mother broke the laws of the Order, the word of Raas, their god, and killed her husband, killed the father of her only child.

The pulsating light vanished with a pop. Steam rose from the pile of loose clothes and oozing pus that had once been Ricken Alpenwood. Blinking, horror overcame Zanna's rage and pleasure, and she tore her eyes away from what she'd done, rushing to Calene.

She tugged at the straps holding her and pulled her from the slab. "Let's get you out of here. Come on, Calene."

"You killed him!" she cried, kicking out at her. Zanna staggered back, shocked. Hurt. "You didn't just kill him; you Eviscerated him! Mother, do you know what you've done?"

"He attacked me, Calene," Zanna whispered, lips drained of colour, eyes blinking in shock. "Look at what he did to you. I *had* to."

Calene swung her legs from the slab. As soon as she stood up, her Spark rushed back to her like a dam had burst, filling her. So did the Link with her mother.

She staggered as a wave of emotion threatened to sweep her away, threatening to blur the line where Calene ended and Zanna began. Repulsion and shame almost overpowered her. Pride too. Fear, confusion. It slammed into her and she threw up her barriers, staunching the parts of Zanna that were bleeding through.

The remains of her father lay at her bare feet. Closing her eyes, she stepped past them, and swore she'd never look behind her again. Not at the slab, not at her father's basement study, not at his remains.

They'd fixed themselves into her memory already.

"I did what I had to," Zanna whispered. "He wasn't your father anymore. He turned on me, and what he was going to do to you..."

"He was sick," Calene snapped, eyes meeting Zanna's. Her mother flinched at what she saw there. "Sick, and you murdered him."

"Calene, he tortured you. What did you expect me to do? I'm your—"

"Don't you dare say 'mother.'" Calene trembled. The Spark flooded through her, a torrent, begging for release, but she forced it down. "You aren't my mother, because my mother would never have Eviscerated someone! My mother would never have broken the Laws. She wouldn't have defied the gods for anything, not even me, because she knew that some things are more important. There had to be another way. There's *always* another way!"

She pushed past her, toward the stairs.

"Calene! I'm sorry, but I had to! I—"

Calene slammed the door to her father's study shut so she didn't have to hear her mother's pleas, so she could sob alone. She walked until she found herself in her old room and locked it behind her. Calene curled up on her bed and wept until her eyes could take no more, until her body's trembling stopped, until the darkness outside became grey with the new morning light. She built her walls up high, as high as Solitude itself, to keep her mother out.

Then she dressed and left. The Order had to know what happened, and her mother had to answer for her crimes.

"I never went back," Calene muttered, gazing into the flames. "And other than the trial in Spring Haven, I never saw my mother again. Not until Solitude. I spoke to her one time through the Link, and told her to get droked, but I need to return. The key to healing Vettigan is in my father's study.

He had a journal, one he kept hidden. I saw him unlock it once, and I doubt anyone else could find it. All this stuff with the Shadow Sparkers. It started with him. I know it."

Brina squeezed her hand. She'd clasped her fingers the whole time Calene spoke, sitting silently, pressed side-by-side. It made the night's chill vanish as their shared heat warmed them.

"And that's why you need to save Vettigan, isn't it?" Brina murmured. "His sickness reminds you of your father, and you couldn't do anything for him."

"Yes." Tears caught in Calene's eyelashes, then trickled down her cheeks. She drew in a shuddering breath.

"You know he would have killed you, or worse."

Calene nodded. Vettigan often said the same, back in the day, and she'd react with anger. But now, after Solitude, after seeing the Shadow Sparkers, she could only accept it.

"I know. He wasn't sick; I realise that now. The Spark corrupted him, or he corrupted it, but I need to discover if there's a way back." Calene laughed. "He changed me, you know, beyond the droking obvious. I always had a lot of strength, but my Spark grew after that. He achieved part of what he wanted."

"But he couldn't carry it all out. He said so."

Calene turned to Brina. They sat so close their noses almost brushed. She stared into her eyes, the dying firelight dancing in the colour of emeralds. Years of wisdom and experience lurked inside. So close...

"Enough about me," Calene whispered, mouth dry. "What about you?"

Brina reached up and wiped the tears from Calene's

cheeks, calloused fingers brushing her skin, and she wanted nothing more than for the elf to leave her hand there, wanted to lean into the touch, but Brina pulled away. The ache of absence shot through Calene's heart.

"There isn't much to tell, and most of it I'm not proud of." Brina glanced away, a frown forming between her eyebrows. "I fought in the resistance all my life, alongside my family, or what remained of it. I had a twin. Rune."

"Rune?" Calene muttered. "Didn't—"

"Yes. Kade Besem mentioned her name. I don't know if she's the same person, not for certain, but I don't believe in coincidences, and he called me by her name." Brina shook her head, her lips tight and pale. "I thought she was dead, or as good as. Slavers captured us in an ambush, years back. A long time for a human, but not for us. It still feels like yesterday. For weeks, they kept us chained, and one night, when one of them came to me, I escaped. I followed their caravan all the way to Spring Haven, watched them cart my family into the slums there. I... I couldn't follow. Not right away. They looked like ghosts, Calene. All my people. It repulsed me. I kept myself hidden, waiting for the right time to spring them, studying the guards' movements, but I couldn't act. Everything I saw just made me rage, and we try never to act without focus. Nobles came to view the elves, like horse traders examining their new stock, and I saw Rune cry with happiness when a family bought her. Cried, Calene. She *wanted* to be a slave, so she could leave the slums."

"Kade's family..." Calene whispered.

"Maybe. She'd have been in their service for years, but that's why humans buy us, isn't it? So long as they don't mistreat us to the point of death, we last a long time. Good value."

"So, Arlo is your nephew?"

Brina stared into the flames. "A child of a noble forcing himself on his property. Nothing more."

"You don't know that." Their hands still touched, fingers still locked together. "They married, didn't they?"

Brina turned a hard stare Calene's way. "A man in a powerful position always gets what he wants, Calene, even if he tells himself it's love. For Rune, it was a way to find some comfort, some succour in slavery, but it wasn't love." She shook her head. "It couldn't be, and now she's dead like the rest of my family."

"I get that, and it's droking awful. Truly." Calene shook her head. "But we know he loved her fiercely, Brina. And look at the lengths he's gone to get his son back. Your nephew. It might have been what you say for her, but for him it was real."

"Doesn't make it right," Brina whispered, but doubt tinged her words.

Arlo's your family, and he did nothing wrong. But I can't say that. God's teeth, Brina was there at Solitude, and decided to put vengeance ahead of going after her own kin. This place...

"So, what did you do?"

Brina shrugged. "What I did best. I killed. Slavers. Nobles. Soldiers. For years, I roamed Haltveldt, taking blood owed to my people. Until..."

"Until?"

"The rivers turned into an ocean and nothing changed, so I gave up. All that death bought my people only their extinction. Haltveldt forced the elves back, inch by inch, and no amount of blood could make up for me turning my back on my family." Brina's eyes met Calene's. "That's why the emperor needs to die. It throws Haltveldt into ruin, disorder, and they deserve it. And maybe, just maybe, it gives the last of us a chance to fight back or flee in peace."

Calene bit her lip. Tears shone in Brina's eyes now, made them bright. Tears of anger, but sorrow too.

"You've been alone for so long, haven't you?" Calene murmured, reaching up to brush the fallen tears from the elf's scarred cheeks.

Brina caught her hand, held it at the wrist, and they stared at one another.

"Yes," she breathed, and let go.

Calene's fingertips tingled as they whispered against Brina's skin, the tanned flesh soft, cold.

"Getting cold." Calene's voice wavered, her tongue stuck to the roof of her mouth.

Brina leaned into her touch and Calene's fingers curled in the elf's red hair. "I don't want to be alone anymore, Calene," she breathed, grip tightening. "I'm sick of it, and it runs deep into my bones. It's all I know. Solitude and vengeance. I want something more. No, I *need* something more. Revenge isn't enough, no matter how much I tell myself it is."

Calene leaned forward, and Brina matched the movement, their lips touching, the taste of the elf rich in her mouth, on her tongue. Their tears mixed as they kissed, as their hands wandered across their bodies, and they forgot the bitter edge lingering on the night's air.

For a time, they dozed in each other's arms, the heat of their bodies warming them under their cloaks.

Calene stirred, and peered around, frowning. The moon emerged from behind the thick clouds, lower in the sky now with morning approaching.

"Hey." She nudged Brina, who woke with a smile on her lips. For a moment, Calene stared at her, drinking it in. That smile was for her. No one else. But she shook it off. Doubt nagged at her guts. "Vettigan still hasn't come back."

Brina sat up, frowning. "Can you feel him?"

"Yes. He's alive, I can tell that much."

"Then where is he?"

A high-pitched wail cut through the quiet night, answering Brina's question.

"Drok," Calene yelled, scrambling to her feet and pulling her clothes on. "It's him. I know it. Come on!"

They ran into the woods, away from their weak fire, and into the grey darkness, Calene's dread building with every step. The scream sounded again. It came from the direction of Alpenwood House.

Calene wasn't ready, but it seemed fate had chosen for her.

Chapter Twenty-Eight

HOMECOMING

'There's nothing you can trust less than a soldier at war with themselves. Whatever the outcome, the path leads to ruin.' - An excerpt from the 'Studies of the Self' by Prosper's heralded philosopher, Ol Iver II.

"Please! I stole nothing, please! Let me go!"

Calene changed direction, heading toward the voice echoing through the grey light, weaving between the trees. Brina followed, sword drawn. The shrill voice led them to a hollow Calene had explored as a child. She'd played there often, calling it her fortress, defending it from make-believe elves and enemies of Haltveldt.

The memories turned her stomach. She'd slain many an invisible elf, Velen, Avastian and Octarian, all in the name of her mighty empire, the one she'd dreamed of honouring like her parents did.

The fantasies of a girl counting down the days until she Sparked, until she could attend the University of Sparkers and live up to the reputation of the Alpenwood name. A name that held as much prestige as mud now.

"Please," the voice sobbed, hanging and drifting in the air, like a spectre haunting the woods. "Let me go. Please!"

Closer. Much nearer than before.

Vettigan, what are you doing, you old fool?

The night lifted, but the early morning remained grey. Darkness refused to clear from the sky, thick black clouds choking the fledgling light of day. Shadows writhed and shifted across a colourless, empty landscape, quiet but for the fearful sobbing echoing all around.

Calene burst through a thicket and paused as she entered the hollow from her childhood. Sword drawn, Vettigan stood hunched before a great, bent tree, its leafless fingers stretching into the endless dark. Before him, back pressed against the trunk, staring up at the human looming over him, an apple in his hands, crouched a lone elven child.

His tear-filled eyes found Calene's just as Brina rushed into the hollow.

Drok it all, Raas. Drok it all!

"*Thiemea*!" Brina growled, jerking forward.

"Wait..." Calene grabbed her forearm, the muscles tense beneath her fingers. "Please?"

Brina snatched her arm away but gave an angry toss of her head. In another moment, at a different time, the show of faith from Brina would have lifted Calene, would have helped cement the trust growing between them, but she had no time to enjoy that now.

She had to avert disaster.

"Vettigan," Calene called, taking a step forward. Her old friend's shoulders tensed, his sword arm jerking, his razor-thin blade vibrating with the subtle movement. "What's happening here?"

"Help me, please!" the elf-boy cried, reaching for Calene, tears falling when his eyes fell on Brina, a fellow elf. Confusion and relief mixed on his face. "He's going to kill me. The human is going to—"

Vettigan slashed with his sword, forcing the boy to snatch his arm back in case he lost his hand.

"This child stole from us." Vettigan's snarl filled the hollow, overpowering the gentle sobs. He didn't turn around. "Would have killed you in your sleep if I hadn't chased him away."

"I wouldn't!" the boy wailed. "Food! I just wanted food. An apple, that's all. Nothing else, nothing—"

"Silence!" Vettigan roared, raising his sword. "I saw the dagger in your hands, boy. The murder in your filthy eyes!"

Calene glanced at Brina. She'd crept forward, eyes drilling into Vettigan's back.

Drok! I don't have much time here. I need him to drop his weapon.

She brushed against their Link, and her mind staggered away from it; corruption swam across it, sinking deep into the core of him, turning his thoughts to violence and murder.

"I have no dagger!" the boy cried, pointing at his waist with his free hand. He still clutched the apple with the other. Sharp cheekbones poked through his dirty face, and his rags hung from him. The shoes on his feet were worn through and stained with blood. "Look! See?"

"I'm no fool," Vettigan growled, taking a step forward. The boy flinched. "You dropped it during the chase."

Calene inched forward, Brina to her side and a little ahead. "Vettigan, turn around."

He shook his hooded head. "No, he might attack. I have to kill him, have to protect you, Calene. You can't trust an elf."

"You used to." Words he spoke back in Seke village, when they sat eating and drinking in the Stubborn Mule in their last moments of normality came back to her. "Remember what you said about them when I asked if the war with them made you sad? 'It goes against the gods', you said. That 'they'll drive them to extinction'. Do you want more blood on your hands, Vettigan? He's just a boy."

His arm dropped a touch; his shoulders lost a little tension. "He would have killed you, Calene, and then what would I have left? Nothing. I can't have that."

Another step forward. "Let me talk to him then, if it was me he tried to kill." Calene held up a hand to the boy to stop him from protesting. "I want to know why, Vettigan. At least give me that."

Silence. It smothered the hollow as the shadows crossed the grey, washed-out trees and dirt. Brina shifted, edging closer to Vettigan, teeth bared. She wouldn't stand by and watch an elf murdered, and Calene understood. She couldn't do it herself, even if her oldest friend held the sword. If it came to it, Calene would stop Vettigan in a different way if she had to.

Her fingers dropped to the hilt of her sword and, deep in her soul, a part of her innocence and optimism fractured and split, became less.

There's always another way, right? I droking hope so.

Vettigan's arm dropped to his side. He still gripped the sword, knuckles white, but he'd lowered it.

"Fine," he whispered, glancing over his shoulder. Calene's heart ached. His yellowed, pocked skin had taken on a green tint, his once-vibrant eyes a dark and feverish cast.

I have to help him. This isn't fair.

She tore her eyes away from Vettigan and took in the elf-boy in his rags, the tears running tracks through the dirt on his face.

None of it is.

Calene almost laughed. Almost. After Solitude, as they began their journey south, she'd vowed to harden her heart. Turn it to stone. A fool's errand. The notion had lasted days, nothing more, before her emotions led her on a wild chase to save her friend, to launch a two-Sparker attack on the Patriarch's Palace in Willow, to reveal her darkest moments to Brina and, for once, allow herself to drop her guard. Now, she almost wept as her oldest friend, broken almost beyond repair, loomed over a child refugee, clinging to his only possession in the whole of Haltveldt, a half-rotten apple that he'd pilfered while Calene and Brina lay huddled beneath their blankets.

The price of expecting one happy moment in a world filled with horror and misery. The price of expecting a single, glorious, carefree moment in Haltveldt.

Drok you, Raas. Drok you. I tell you, when we meet, you'll need stronger gates in Eternity to keep me away from you. Rotten teeth of the gods, you will!

Calene forced her fingers away from the hilt of her sword and crouched, coming to the boy's level.

"What's your name?"

"Fir."

"Nice," Calene smiled. "Like the tree? I like it." The boy nodded, a small frown beneath the dirt on his face. "What are you doing in these woods, Fir?"

"Escaping from the battle. My parents told me to run. I've been alone ever since, making my way north..."

Vettigan shook his head.

"There was a battle in the south," Brina muttered. Calene stared at her. "A terrible one. I...met some elves and a survivor in the Forest of Willows."

"More elves," Vettigan growled, grip tightening on his sword. "There might be more in these woods right now. Watching us. Waiting."

"Quiet! Brina, we'll talk later about why you're only mentioning this now." To her credit, the elf looked suitably ashamed. Wiping the scowl from her face, Calene turned to Fir again, forcing a smile back onto her lips. Her droking cheeks ached with the effort of it.

"Where are you going, Fir?"

"Gallavan Forest. They said it might be safe there for us, that people from across the Sundered Sea might come. Please, I didn't mean to cause any trouble." His eyes moved to Brina. A familiar face. A sympathetic one. "I'm starving, haven't eaten for days."

"The Sundered Seas is what our people call the Avastian Sea," Brina murmured.

"And there's elves living in Avastia, isn't there?" Calene asked, turning to the elven warrior. Vettigan still stared at the child, his back and neck stiff.

"I've helped smuggle my people there before," Brina replied, nodding. "It makes sense they'd flee there."

"Are neither of you listening?" Vettigan growled, sword shaking in his tight grip. "The boy admits to stealing, and I know what I saw. The blade glinted in the moonlight, and a desperate fool makes rash decisions."

His voice dropped to a whisper for the last part, like he spoke those words to himself.

Calene ignored him and turned to the boy again. "A while ago... Well, not too long a while. Me and my friend with the sword here travelled through a forest and happened upon a starving beggar. Filthy, they were, their cloak soaked and stained, and when we spoke to them, I could hear the strain in their voice. The way it cracked, I knew it hurt them to speak to us. My friend here couldn't wait to help. Leaped from our cart, he did, with water and food in hand." Vettigan's head dropped as he listened. "You know who that beggar was, Fir?"

"No," the boy whispered, still clutching his bruised apple.

Calene pointed at Brina. "Her. An elf. We didn't know it at the time, but you know what happened next? After we moved on, leaving her behind?" Fir shook his head, and Calene stared at Vettigan's back, driving her words at him. "We were ambushed by our own kind, and Fir? They would have killed us. Almost did, but Brina, an elf, came to our rescue. She didn't need to, but she did, and she's helped us ever since. Each and every day. Isn't that right, Vettigan?"

It seemed he went to nod, but he gave an angry shake of his head instead. Darkness and evil smothered their Link when Calene brushed against it.

"Ambushes... They could be out there, in these woods, the elves. Waiting for signs of weakness. They'll come for us, mark my words, Calene. Mark my words."

Brina slid forward. A sword's length from Vettigan's back.

"I'm alone," Fir sobbed, eyeing the blade hovering in front of his nose. "All alone. There's no one else. I have no one!"

"Vettigan, if they were out there, don't you think they'd have tried to stop you from killing one of their young? What are they waiting for? The rise of the black sun?" Calene held out a hand, stretching her fingers to him. "Please, Vettigan, see sense. He's just a scared, lonely, starving boy, alone in a world desperate to kill him and his kind. Don't be like that. Don't give in to it. Godsrot, I know what's inside you. That stain's still tainting your thinking and pushes you down this droking path. If you can't stop for yourself, can't you try for me?"

His sword wavered, on the point of dropping or raising, but a branch snapped, robbing Calene of the answer.

The crack echoed around the hollow. The sound of fate. The sound of doom.

Vettigan jerked. His sword arm raised. As he moved, Brina rushed in, weapon poised and aimed for the old man's heart.

Calene drew her sword, flinging herself forward, arm

straight and true, a barrier to the steel about to pierce Vettigan's flesh. Fir watched, his mouth a perfect O, eyes just as round, shining with tears, and as Calene's blade deflected Brina's, another sound joined the ring of their steel. A child's helpless scream as a blade swooped into an overhead strike, aimed for the middle of his head.

Calene's instinct took over. Ignoring the snarl from Brina, arm vibrating from the shock of blocking her thrust, she pushed out with her Spark. She had no time to draw on the energy around her, so instead she pushed out with the power inside herself, slamming a shockwave into Vettigan. She staggered from the sudden expulsion of magic.

The blade fell from his fingers as he spiralled through the air, landing in a tangled heap on the forest floor.

Silence returned. Calene stared at Brina, the elf's face red, jaw tense, and at Vettigan, who lay stunned, eyes blinking up at the cloudy, early morning sky.

"Run," she whispered, turning to Fir. "Go, and don't stop until you find safety. Go!"

Brina took a half-step toward him as he scrambled to his feet, clutching his precious apple, leaves flying as he ran without a single glance over his shoulder.

Calene slammed her sword into her sheath, and filled her lungs with a ragged breath, then met Brina's eyes.

"I couldn't let you kill him, Brina. Not after coming so droking far. Raas, I didn't think he'd do it!"

Brina hadn't put her weapon away. Instead, she turned and scanned the woods. "That noise..."

Calene had forgotten about it. The crack of a twig or branch from the quiet woods. Shaking her head, she moved toward Vettigan who continued to stare, unmoving, though his chest rose and fell.

"He's just stunned." Goosebumps broke out across Calene's skin. Pausing, she listened.

It feels like... Drok!

"Move!"

As soon as she yelled the command, lightning lanced out of the sky, slamming into the tree Fir had cowered beneath. Calene threw herself forward, covering Vettigan with her body as another bolt surged from the heavens, splitting the tree in two. Flames erupted from the scorched trunk. Deer exploded from the thicket and galloped away in terror.

Deer? Damn you, Raas, deer stepping on twigs caused all this? Vettigan wouldn't have attacked!

Brina collided with Calene, hands covering her head as another arc of lightning slammed into the hollow.

"What is it?" she cried, pulling at Vettigan, tapping the side of his face as she tried to bring him back to his senses.

"Sparkers," Calene yelled ,above the crackle of flames and peals of thunder. "They felt my magic!"

A pause came in the assault, and Vettigan's hand shot out, grabbing Calene's.

"I'm sorry," he muttered, ashen faced. "This is all my fault, all of it. Forgive—"

"There's no time for that!" Calene snarled, climbing to her feet and pulling Vettigan up with Brina's help. "We need to run. A pause means they're coming for us. Follow me!"

Glancing left and right, Calene took off, jumping through the flames, heading in the same direction as Fir had.

"Where are we going?" Vettigan cried, as he and Brina followed.

"Home," Calene shouted over her shoulder.

She pointed through the trees. A four-storey manse loomed in the grey morning light, alone in the Spring Haven hinterlands. A low, white fence surrounded it, and the stable and barn beside it. The sight of her old home turned Calene's stomach.

"But we need to lose whoever's following us and there's only one way to do that. Stay small and out of sight. When the lightning starts again, run towards the rear of the house. I'll meet you there."

"Calene, no!" Brina shouted, grabbing her wrists. "You're not going—"

"God's teeth, this isn't a droking discussion, Brina! Get yourself and Vettigan to the house when the barrage starts, and don't you dare follow me. Either of you!"

Calene sprinted away from the thicket her friends huddled in. Her old family home offered refuge, a place to regroup while the Sparkers in the woods searched.

Shadow Sparkers, that's what they are. I know it. These aren't normal mages. What are they doing here?

Calene gulped, glancing over her shoulder, Brina's red braid fading in the gloom. She didn't have the time to turn such questions over in her mind. She pushed through the bushes, whipped by the gnarled, twisted tree branches, a part of her mind noting the diseased stink of the woods as she raced by, but she couldn't focus on it. She had to get far enough away before doubling back. She ran hard for another minute, ears straining for any noises, any sign of the Sparkers, then came to a stop, breathing hard.

"Well, here goes droking nothing," she muttered, closing her eyes and drawing a deep, steadying breath into her chest.

Focused, she reached out, searching for anything she could draw on with her Spark, and found it. She could have used her own energy again but knocking down Vettigan had taken a lot out of her, and she wanted to cause a stir. An element even further away would do the trick *and* cause a diversion. In the distance, a brook wound its way through the forest and Calene pulled on it, drawing on its unique essence, its energy, and let it explode.

Water shot up in a jet above the trees, but Calene didn't wait to admire her handiwork. Turning on her heel, she ran back the way she'd come, arcing wider than before so she'd come to her family home from the side. She still flinched when the lightning cracked from the black sky, slamming into the ground near the brook.

The energy of it throbbed through the forest, and her Spark desired it. Shaking her head, she let go of her Spark and ran, breath coming ragged as she focused on staying upright on the uneven ground. More lightning followed, further away, deeper into the woods.

"At least one droking thing's going right today," Calene panted, the building coming into view. Dark clouds hovered above it, casting deep shadows across the estate. "What's going on around here? The weather was never like this before."

Calene continued to run, unable to pull her eyes away from the manse as it grew nearer and larger. It appeared as it did in her dreams; haunted, remote, black. But this wasn't a dream. Calene lived this.

Houses were just that; buildings filled with memories,

and when abandoned they had no one to remember them. Alpenwood House seemed gripped by something ghoulish, something not just from her imagination. Thick mist tugged at the corners of it and the blackened windows were curiously intact. Like the rest of the building, in fact.

No one had lived there for a decade but, despite its macabre visage, the building appeared whole and in decent repair.

Calene's legs grew heavy, and it wasn't just from pelting through the forest.

She spared a glance over her shoulder. Seeing nothing but empty, grey fields and twisted trees, she slowed her pace and studied the route ahead.

"I hope they droking ran when I told them to. Raas damn it all!"

She turned the corner of the building, heart in her mouth, and almost sobbed. Brina and Vettigan crouched beside the wall under a dark window, peering around the corner. Relief filled both their faces as she approached.

"Nice work," Brina breathed, as Calene sagged next to them, sweat pouring from her brow, cold in the morning's chill. "If reckless."

"Hey," Calene said, between heavy breaths. "I'm a professional."

"This is professional?" Brina asked, tone drier than the Cuomo Wastelands.

"Well, as professional as it gets under the circumstances." Calene shrugged, her voice flippant, but she felt anything but. Her legs and muscles tensed, and her heart hammered in her chest.

I'm leaning against the place where my entire life changed. The place that's haunted my droking nightmares for a decade. And I'm flirting with an elf!

"What's the plan?" Vettigan asked, his dark, hooded eyes and yellowed skin grounding her a little, reminding her of the task at hand.

Shifting around so she could stare at her friends, Calene nodded. "We go in through the back, make our way down to my father's study, find his journal and lay low for a bit. If we don't draw any attention to ourselves, those Sparkers, whoever they are, should move on. From the barrage of lightning, it seems they took my diversion."

"Calene," Vettigan mumbled, "lightning. A regular Sparker wouldn't summon it. That means—"

"I know." Calene glanced left and right. "Which is why we need to be quick."

She got to her feet, stooping low, shoulder rubbing against the brickwork as she headed for the stone steps leading up to the rear door of the manse. Calene had used it more than the front entrance, rushing down the stairs and into the back field every day, even when it rained, to spend time by her oak tree.

Despite herself, she looked that way, taking in the mighty, far-reaching branches. She'd Sparked there, sitting in that tree, Zanna standing below. She'd floated down into her mother's arms. They'd held each other so tight, Calene feeling the strength of Zanna's pride with the gift inside her soul.

A gift. Raas, damn you, it's anything but a droking gift.
Calene scrubbed the tears from her eyes and took the

stairs two at a time, Vettigan stumbling by her side, Brina at the rear. They reached the door—even the back entrance seemed imposing and grand—and Calene laid her hand on the golden handle, chest tight.

"You think there's going to be something in there to save me?" Vettigan whispered, laying his hand on hers. "Truly?"

Calene met his eyes. "I have to think so, Vee. Have to, and if there isn't, I won't stop searching."

A tear trickled down his cheek, and into his scraggly beard. "All of this is my fault, Calene. Solitude, the death of your mother, today. I'm a blight. A curse."

Reaching up, she laid a hand against his cheek. Vettigan flinched, self-loathing and repulsion swimming in his eyes, but he didn't pull away. He trembled at her touch, another tear joining the one already spilled, and his shoulders shook.

"You're not a curse," Calene whispered. "You're my family, and none of this is your fault. It's the Spark's. It's the emperor's. It's Haltveldt's, and we'll fix you. I swear it on Raas' droking yellow, stinking teeth!"

She placed her hand on the handle again and took a deep breath.

"You can't expect it's unlocked, can you?" Brina hissed. "What would be the—?"

Calene pulled, and the door swung open. Darkness greeted them. She peered into it, then turned to her friends, and shrugged.

"Worth a try. Place is abandoned. Why lock it? Now, we need to get to the entry hall and take the stairs down to the study. Follow me."

She inched forward, jerking, heavy, each step a dagger to her guts, but once moving she continued to walk, and she only jumped a little when the door closed behind her, plunging them into almost complete darkness. Weak grey light from the windows formed the only illumination, a pathetic, diffuse glow that couldn't hope to fill the absence of light.

"Can't see a thing," Vettigan muttered, voice flat, like the house dulled everything.

"There's a light up ahead," Brina whispered, her better vision winning out. "Weak, but it's better than nothing."

"That's the entry hall," Calene replied, frowning, feet moving that way. She didn't need any illumination to make her way through the building. Her home. She walked it in her dreams. "But why is there any light? It wouldn't have lasted this long..."

It grew stronger, fighting through the gloom. Calene's footsteps echoed as her boots thumped on marble. The illumination flickered and shifted.

"What in Eternity is this?" Brina hissed, and the ring of steel filled the air.

Children stood in the entry hall, some of them carrying flickering candles, the light reflecting in their flat, untrusting stares.

"What are you doing in our school?" one of them asked, their voice a snarl.

"They can't be more than ten years old," Brina whispered, standing beside Calene, sword in hand. "None of them."

"School?" Calene asked, the daggers in her gut twisting.

Jigsaw pieces slammed into place in her mind. Faye du Gerran had told Maria about a place in the middle of nowhere, a secret sanctuary designed to further the emperor's illicit plans.

Her home. Her droking home!

"What school?"

"This one. The School of Shadows, our emperor named it." Another child spoke, a small, cold grin on their face. "Where we learn about how our gifts will make Haltveldt stronger."

"What gift?" Calene choked, chest so tight her shoulder blades ached.

"The Spark, of course, but not in the way the Order uses it." The child nearest Calene—a girl, pale-skinned, dark haired and pretty—raised her hand, and black flames appeared on her fingertips. "I'm the first one who's Sparked in our school. Would you like me to show you what I can do? Our teachers and their guests will be back soon. They'll be so pleased to see we have you."

Vettigan pulled his sword free and took a step forward.

"They're just children," Calene hissed, grabbing his arm. But, by Brina's stance, the elf agreed with the old man this time.

She reached out with her Spark, feeling the power in the room. The child held more strength than she should at her age, but it wasn't enough to oppose her.

"These aren't children," Vettigan snarled, tossing his head. "They're monsters. Weapons! This isn't like the elven boy, Calene. My head is clear. Destroying them would spare the people of Haltveldt misery for decades to come."

The stairs leading down to her father's study lay to their left, a few steps away, nothing more. Calene could hold them all off—only one could Spark, after all—but using her magic to keep them at bay would mean alerting the children's 'teachers', no doubt the Shadow Sparkers who'd hunted Calene in the forest.

Our teachers and their guests…

Bile filled Calene's throat. The emperor had perverted children, indoctrinated them from an early age. Shadow Sparkers as soon as their magic blossomed.

A perversion. Treason. Blasphemous…

The entry hall's door flew open, and a black-robed figure burst through, hood down, bald head and void eyes shining despite the gloom. Cracked, red fissures stood out bright against too-white skin. It raised its hands.

Calene's family home, a place once abandoned to the sickness and evil in the bricks and stone of its walls, a place now used to train Shadow Sparkers from birth, exploded into bedlam.

Chapter Twenty-Nine

PATH'S END

'Where life is exhausted, death comes.' - An old proverb spoken in Protector's Watch.

"**G**et to the stairs!" Calene yelled. "Over there. Brina, go!"

Lightning flashed outside the building, framing the Shadow Sparker standing in the doorway, hands raised. Shadows gathered around him, and rushed forward, sweeping over the children and billowing towards Calene.

She answered him, raising her own hands. A shield wall sprung up across the corridor, protecting her and her friends as they dove for the stairs. Calene had to use her Spark now. Refusal meant death. The other Sparkers would follow as soon as they felt their Shadow Sparker's power unleashed; Calene had to make it difficult for them. She had to buy her friends time.

It wasn't how she'd imagined her homecoming. For days, weeks even, she'd pictured herself arriving at a decrepit shell, taking her time picking over the ruins. Visit her room, Zanna's too, before heading down to Ricken's study. Alone at first, to confront her demons, and beat them into place. She'd locate the journal and, with it, she'd save Vettigan.

All of that had gone to drok now, but they still had to get the journal and trust Raas that they'd escape with their lives.

But how? Vettigan and Brina had headed to the study, and if Calene followed, the Shadow Sparker and the rest would follow.

I've got only one droking choice, and it ain't a pretty one.

Waves of shadow pummelled her shield. It wasn't Evisceration. She noticed that and it planted a seed of surprise in Calene's mind. Instead, the Shadow Sparker poured out dark energy in a wave, trying to overwhelm her.

It didn't appear to affect the children; they'd run to the Shadow Sparker and lurked behind him as he strode forward. Calene glanced at the ceiling...

She could bring it down on them all, open the floor, maybe, let them fall, but she'd murder the younglings. And no matter what Vettigan said, they were still children. More corrupted souls added to the emperor's tally.

No, Calene couldn't attack. Not yet.

Gritting her teeth, she turned inward, and touched the Link she shared with Vettigan, like a festering wound in her mind, thick with shadow and filth. It sickened her, but she breathed deep.

She had to. *Had* to.

Just like at Solitude, when she'd blown through Zanna's block, Calene focused her entire will on the Link, and plunged through it.

Her shield wall flickered, the shimmering blue light crumpling under the weight of the darkness, before turning a bright blue once more. The bile in Calene's throat pushed into her mouth, and she gagged, spitting on the floor. The taste lingered. It would always remain, even as a memory.

Once, Calene had fallen into a swamp, and had to wade out, disgusting, thick tendrils of unknown things clinging to her as she inched through the dense, green water, the rotten stench filling her nostrils.

Now she waded through evil, a quagmire filled with filth and darkness, a layer of corruption invading Vettigan's mind, poisonous seeping into his brain.

Tears sprang into Calene's eyes as she pushed through. Not even a second had passed, yet for Calene, a year slid by. Two. Stray thoughts assailed her, all from Vettigan's diseased memory.

The elf-boy staring at him, dagger in hand, pressed to Calene's throat.

'I'll kill her, drink her blood," Fir whispered, leering at Vettigan. "I'll kill you all...'

Riders thundering down an abandoned Adhraas road. Banished, but they didn't come in peace. Not this time. They whirled their weapons above their heads, and their pale eyes shone crimson against the black sky.

Vettigan had seen a threat at every turn, in every corner, his paranoia magnified by the darkness settled on his mind. Maybe it had been defeated, but its effects lingered, twisting him into a person he'd never been.

Protecting Calene. That's all he'd ever tried to do. What he *still* wanted to do.

Vettigan! she roared, staggering behind her shield wall as the Shadow Sparker approached, head tilted to the side, void eyes curious. *Can you hear me?*

Calene? Confusion. Shame. Joy too. Vettigan had missed using their Link. In truth, she had too. *Where are you?*

Holding this droker off! Get the journal! On the wall on the far side there's a family portrait. Behind it is a false wall; it's hollow. Tap for it and push. It should be there. Get it and leave through the back.

We're not going anywhere without you, Calene, Vettigan growled in her mind, the warmth and depth of his feeling beating the shadow back. Rising from the darkness, he was the old Vettigan, the man she remembered.

Her heart fluttered. The *real* Vettigan still existed. Hope. They still had it if they could leave this place behind them. Calene had to believe it.

We're all leaving together, for drok's sake! Now do what I asked!

Calene's relief only went so far. There was a time and place for mushy feelings, and this situation ranked as low as it got.

The Shadow Sparker approached the shield wall, black eyes glittering. The shimmering, blue barrier stood between them, but he grinned at Calene, his bloodless lips tight, dry and cracked.

Shadows swirled at his feet, a dark tide washing up

against Calene's bulwark.

"You may hold out against me," he hissed, head still tilted to the side, "even if I use Evisceration. Your defence is impressive. Sadly for you, I'm not alone. They're coming."

"Drok you," Calene spat, hands shaking. Not through strain, but through adrenaline. Bloodlust. She wanted to fight, to kill.

Vettigan had been right about one thing. The Shadow Sparkers, the adults, *they* were monsters. Nothing more. Nothing less. Creatures for exterminating. Her Spark surged, but her eyes flicked to the children, holding their candles in the gloom. Any use of her Spark would injure them—kill them, maybe—unless she...

No! Her mind reeled. Evisceration? Her? In this place? But now the idea had planted its seed...

The Shadow Sparker licked his lips. "It calls to you, doesn't it?"

"The Spark?" Calene answered, voice shaking, her desire ripe.

"No." The pale mage shook his head. "The darkness."

Her eyes fell to the shadows. The tendrils reached for her, and for a moment, for one agonising, stretching, endless moment, Calene considered dropping her shield wall, and letting it wrap around her.

Calene, we have it! Vettigan's voice roared in her mind. The Link!

She slammed her block in place, cutting herself off from her old friend's mind once more, and the shadows retreated, slithering back into the billowing fog.

The Shadow Sparker's eyes flashed. "You would make

a fine addition to our rank. Fine indeed. You don't have to come willingly, girl."

Vettigan and Brina burst into view, the elf clutching a leatherbound book, and they paused, peering past Calene.

She swallowed an order for them to keep moving and followed their fear-stricken stare beyond the Shadow Sparker, beyond the huddled children.

Three more black-robed Sparkers stood in the doorway, hoods down and faces upturned. They stepped forward, into the light, and Calene gasped.

One of them, she didn't recognise, but the other two...

Faye du Gerran leered at her, eyes sapped of colour, the beginnings of crimson cracks running down her face, and beside her stood High Sparker Balz du Regar.

The Order's leader is a droking Shadow Sparker! And Faye... Oh, Maria... How has it all come to this? How?

Like Faye, Balz wasn't as far gone as the other two mages in their party, but the tell-tale signs wracked him. His hair had turned patchy and thin, and the fissures crisscrossed his skin. And his eyes... Two black marbles shone with fever from deep, dark pits.

"Children, leave us," Balz murmured, lifting a finger. "The emperor wouldn't wish any of you harmed."

They left without hesitating, filing out into the early morning air, taking their candles with them. The shadows swelled in their absence, but hope fluttered in Calene's chest. The younglings' presence had kept her from acting, kept her from fighting. With them gone she embraced her Spark, judging the mages' power.

Calene outstripped them all individually, even with the

darkness inside them, but all of them together? She stood little chance. Reaching out, her Spark sought traces of energy, anything to even the odds.

She turned to Faye. "Faye, you remember me, don't you? We were friends, right? I met your sister. She's looking for you. We can help you."

The muscles in her face twitched. "I did not ask for this," Faye hissed, the corners of her bottom lip trembling, "but she would understand if she experienced what I have. The power, Calene. The clarity. I'll find her soon, show her the path and how to walk it."

"She'd rather die," Calene sneered. "How droking dare you, Balz. You're meant to be our leader. You're supposed to—"

"Enough of this," Balz interrupted, raising a finger and pointing at Calene, the nail as black as his robes. "Take her alive and kill the others."

The ring of steel as Vettigan and Brina released their weapons. The cries of the charge. The soft laughter of predators closing in on their prey.

They all filled the air as the shadows swirled, becoming a tsunami as all four Shadow Sparkers threw the might of their dark energy against Calene's barrier. The miasma smashed into her shield wall, and she screamed through gritted teeth, pouring her focus and power into keeping it strong.

It wasn't enough. Against two, maybe even three? She would have stood a chance of holding on. But four?

The shield faltered, flicked, then crumbled.

Calene staggered back, falling to the ground, the breath

rushing from her lungs. Vettigan thundered past, sword raised.

"No..." she whispered, reaching out to him. Against four Shadow Sparkers, her oldest friend could do nothing but die.

The shadows cleared, and the first dark mage raised his hand, smiling, aiming it at Vettigan. He unleashed an inky tendril of Evisceration that pierced into Vettigan.

And vanished.

No, not completely. The darkness lingering inside him absorbed it, like a drowning swimmer breaking the crashing waves and gasping for air before submerging again. One last breath before death.

The Shadow Sparker had no time to react. He stood, blinking in surprise, staring at his hand, as Vettigan closed the gap and drove his blade through the mage's throat. The Sparker dropped to his knees, gurgling, thick blood gushing from his mouth, eyes wide with shock.

Vettigan pulled his arm back with a twist, freeing his sword, and Brina rushed in to relieve the Shadow Sparker of its head. It bounced to a stop at Vettigan's feet.

"Do your worst!" he roared, levelling his sword at the black-robed mages. "I'll take you all to the Underworld with me!"

Calene scrambled to her feet as Vettigan charged forward. "No, wait!"

Balz lifted a finger as Vettigan reached him, and the old man froze, straining against invisible bonds.

"Evisceration may not work on you, old boy, but there are other means."

Calene's heart thundered, and she stumbled forward. Brina grabbed at her, but her flesh felt numb. Balz pulled his cloak aside, and in one smooth movement, pulled his sword from its sheath and plunged it into Vettigan's guts. The tip burst through his back. Balz twisted the blade and pulled it out again, grinning as blood showered his black robes.

Calene staggered, dropped to one knee as Vettigan slumped to the floor, the bonds holding him gone. She'd come all this way to save him, back to the place where her nightmares were born. They'd found the droking journal, the text from her father that would save him. Brina had it!

Vettigan lay on his side, blood oozing from his stomach and back, legs kicking as pain twisted inside him.

She'd failed him.

"Of all the places for this to happen..." Balz murmured, his whisper coiling into Calene's ears. "In your family home. Poetic, really. We owe dear Ricken so much. He set Haltveldt on this path. Perhaps, one day, we'll build a statue of him here, in this School of Shadows." Balz glanced at the other Shadow Sparkers. "What are you waiting for? The elf still breathes, and we can't have that."

Faye and the unnamed Sparker advanced.

"No..."

Calene met Vettigan's eyes. Felt Brina's fingers on her shoulder. Haltveldt had taken her father's experiments. If Zanna hadn't intervened, would Calene have become one of them? One of the Shadow?

Rage built inside her. Rage and anguish and shame and failure.

Rage, rage, and more droking rage.

"*No!*"

Calene screamed. The Spark exploded inside her, erupting outward, bursting through her skin, an outpouring of not just her natural energy, the life and fire of her soul, her anger and grief, the fear in her bones at the mere mention, the mere thought of her father's name, but from *everything* her Spark had gathered.

Fire, water, air and earth. The death, the blood, the darkness rooted in the mortar of her home.

It flooded out in all directions, uncontrollable, indiscriminate, wild. It hit Brina, sending her sprawling through the door and down the stairs to her father's study. It sent Vettigan's prone body sliding across the floor and into a wall, a streak of crimson in his wake. Her Spark slammed into the unnamed Sparker, into Faye, into Balz, flipping them through the air and hurling them against the walls and windows, bones cracking with the impact.

The wave crashed against the front doors, blowing them off their hinges. Bricks shattered, beams splintered, the chandelier turned to shrapnel and shards. The building groaned, creaked, then collapsed on top of the Shadow Sparkers, leaving her and Brina safe.

Calene slumped but caught herself before her face smashed into the ground, holding herself up on all fours. Shrieks from the children outside joined the cries of the Sparkers inside, the sliding, crashing stone and rock created a symphony of destruction as the front of Calene's home crumbled in on itself.

Hands grabbed her, pulling her back toward the stairs, then Brina raced by her, into the billowing dust, and emerged with Vettigan, dragging him across the ground behind her. They collapsed together, in the shelter of the doorway leading to her father's study, the place where all this death, all this darkness and shadow, had originated. Her old home groaned and shifted, walls toppling, windows shattering.

My mother was right. He had to die. If I hadn't turned her in, if I'd helped destroy all his work...

Tremors wracked the building as it creaked, landslides falling like a mountain coming apart, waterfalls of dust pouring to the ground.

Vettigan coughed, crimson splattering his lips and bearded chin, blood streaking the white. "I... I..."

He coughed again, a hacking, wet, liquid bark, and fell silent, face screwed up in pain, hands covering the hole in his guts. He couldn't speak anymore. Wouldn't. His failing body wouldn't allow it. The agony too much, the blood loss too great, the will no longer there.

"No, no, no," Calene fussed, grabbing at his shoulders, his face, peering into his dull eyes. "I won't let this happen. I can't!"

"Calene..." Brina murmured, but trailed off when Calene shot her a glare, tears blurring her vision.

"Hold on, Vettigan, I can heal this. I can. Just give me a moment!"

Empty words. Calene had delved into him already, knew the damage beyond repair. If she'd gotten to him sooner...

But even then, the blade had severed arteries, split organs, and Vettigan had spilled enough blood to kill two men already.

He grabbed at her hands, pulling them close to his chest, exposing the wound in his gut. Sobbing, Calene pulled her eyes away from it. Here, she'd lose the last family she had, in the place where her kin began and ended.

Poetic, Balz had called it. Poetic.

Calene brushed aside the wall blocking her Link with Vettigan, and plunged past the darkness seeping into his thoughts, the same corruption that had spared him a second Evisceration but couldn't change his fate. Only Raas could do that.

Raas. The yellow-teethed droker.

Don't leave me, Vee, please, Calene projected, staring into his eyes. His tears matched hers. *I can't go on alone.*

You can, girl. You can do anything.

His voice came through strong, proud and purely Vettigan, without a trace of the shadow.

I couldn't save you, Calene sobbed, and her old friend smiled through the pain.

But you did. I don't feel like one of them. I get to die feeling like myself. And maybe what you've found here will help others. Will help you. His grip tightened on her hand. *I'm sorry. For your mother, for your pain. For everything. Stay true to yourself. Remember, there's always another way, Calene.*

A tremor wracked Vettigan's body, and when it stilled his grip slackened.

No, I'm not ready to say goodbye! Calene glanced up at Brina, pleading, but the elf only stared back, her face like stone. *I'm sorry, Vettigan. I'm sorry. I should have done more. I should have—*

You did all you could and more. And you never gave up

on an old fool. Vettigan coughed, his chest rattled, and the lids of his eyes drooped. *You blessed my life by being in it. Remember me how I was before, ever your friend, and not the dark shell I became. Goodbye, Calene. Whether Eternity or the Underworld awaits, I love you.*

His last thoughts came like a whisper, a remembered caress, a tendril of smoke, drifting off into the aether. Inside her mind, Calene felt Vettigan die as his body breathed its final, ragged breath, agony gone, darkness inside defeated at last.

I love you, Vettigan. Always. The gods know I'll see you again.

Calene fell on top of him, weeping, as the Link she and Vettigan had shared since her father's death faded, shedding its layer of corruption. Her friend's personality, his bubbling emotions, tore away, leaving a wound in their place, raw and painful. The details, good and bad, slipped away, leaving only the loss.

Vettigan died, and his absence formed, palpable, inside Calene's mind. Her bones ached with it. A scream ripped out of her, tearing her throat until her voice failed and her lungs emptied.

"Damn you, Raas!" she snarled, strands of Vettigan's hair sticking to her wet face. "How could you do this to me? Haven't I suffered enough? Hadn't Vettigan?"

"Hasn't Haltveldt?"

Calene looked up at Brina's words, cracks appearing in the stony façade she'd tried to adopt. Grief leaked through the fissures. Anguish for Calene, remorse and sorrow at witnessing her naked misery. The elf reached out for her, but the sound of shifting rocks made her stop.

A cough followed by a groan of pain made them peer around the doorframe and into the destroyed entry hall.

"Someone's still alive," Brina hissed, grabbing for her sword.

Glancing at Vettigan's corpse, Calene pushed to her feet. "Let's find the droker."

She strode through the debris, streams of daylight filtering through the collapsed wall, dust drifting, searching aimlessly for a new place to settle amidst the destruction. Calene passed the crushed body of the nameless Shadow Sparker, its hand the only part not flattened by debris.

Another red stain on the emperor's ledger, a register heavy with blood.

No trace of Faye remained. Perhaps the blast had destroyed her, like it had done the Shadow Sparker in Willow. Intuition, and a life spent making war and hunting rogues for the Order, told her something else. Faye du Gerran wouldn't die so easily.

She thought of Maria and the woman's fierce love for her sister, her hope that she'd find her and that they'd fight together against Emperor Locke. Maybe they would meet again, but could it ever be so hopeful?

Balz lay in the centre of the room, near the entrance, where Calene's shockwave had thrown him. His limbs pointed at odd angles, ankles broken, wrists too. He coughed, and claret spurted from his mouth. The High Sparker didn't have long to live, if Calene didn't heal him.

She'd seen what happened to Shadow Sparkers once their bodies failed, assuming they kept their heads. The corruption inside forced them to move, to fight on, to live a mockery of existence.

Balz stared up at Calene and Brina, a sneer on his lips despite his injuries. Calene had met him on a number of occasions. Arrogant, as many of the noble born and privileged were, but he hadn't struck her as cruel, despite his close friendship with Emperor Locke and Master of War Nexes.

Embracing the Shadow had changed that, or had he been forced in that direction too?

"You're going to torture me?" he spat, bloody phlegm flying. "Is that it? Know I can't betray my emperor. It's impossible. He saw to that!"

"What do you mean?" Calene's voice came out in a slow hiss. High Sparker Balz lay before her, ruined, defeated, but she saw only the man who'd killed Vettigan. The man who'd plunged his blade into her oldest friend's guts.

It burned her pity away.

Balz flashed his teeth, bloody and broken.

"Can you make sure he doesn't use his Spark?" Brina asked, fingers brushing Calene's elbow.

"I don't think he can in his state, but I'll shield him."

A shimmering, blue bubble sprang up around him. Balz hacked out a laugh.

"Frightened of a man at death's door?"

"More about what comes after that," Calene snarled, cutting off Balz's mocking laughter.

Brina took a step forward, and drew her sword, its ring echoing out in the silence after the collapse.

"I've seen the likes of these shields before," she snarled, pointing her sword at Balz, who glared back at her. "They'll stop magic, but not a blade."

"Get away from me, you filthy beast!"

Brina pressed the point of the sword against his shoulder, and let it sink into his flesh. Balz's howls pierced Calene's brain. She should stop her. They were above torture, and what did they really need to know? But the High Sparker's face flickered to the grin he'd worn as he murdered Vettigan, and Calene said nothing.

"What's the purpose of this place?" Brina demanded, the blade two inches deep in Balz's shoulder.

"You know what we do here, Alpenwood," he snarled. "What your father tried to do to you. What he started, we perfected!"

Growling, Brina yanked the sword free and drove into his other shoulder. The screams caused Calene's vision to shake. Deep inside, her Spark reached out for the fear and anger and pain floating in the air.

"Where's the emperor then? Tell me that, *thiemea*, or so help me you'll go to the Underworld in pieces!"

Balz's screams morphed into a high-pitched laugh. "You want to go up against the emperor, is that it? You think you can stop him?" he shrieked as Brina plunged her blade deeper. "You've no chance. You won't find him, and I *can't* tell you."

Calene stared at him, realisation crystalising. *He wants to tell us. He wants revenge against the emperor just as much as we do. Whatever Locke did to him, it's stopping him. Some kind of magical binding.*

"We're no threat to him," she said. "An elf and a rogue Sparker. Not with the Shadows under his command. But if we go to ground, if we rally, we'll bring unrest to Haltveldt. He'd be safer if you just told us where to find him. Go ahead. Send us to our deaths."

Brina watched in curious silence. Balz smiled so wide his lips began to tear, but within the mania, a pinprick of insane gratitude shone through.

"The Cradle. A repository of ancient knowledge, built into the side of Haven Cliffs, across the bay from the city. Try and find him if you dare! He'll find a use for you, Alpenwood. He'll Turn you to the Shadow, and what a fine one you'll make. And you, elf..." Balz laughed, even when Brina yanked her sword free. "You'll find yourself in the slums or in a droking ditch, and even the maggots won't touch your flesh!"

Brina turned to Calene, eyes hard.

"Kill him," she whispered.

"*Me*?" Calene jerked, lips moved of their own accord like she'd left her body. "Kill *him*?"

"He doesn't deserve to live, and you know what happens to them if you don't take their heads. Do it. He killed Vettigan."

Calene's numb fingers fell to the pommel of her sword, barely able to feel it. They stayed there, unmoving, as she stared down at Balz. His broken body pinned by brick and mortar, blood oozing from myriad wounds. Wouldn't his death be on her hands anyway? Calene had created the shockwave, even if she'd been protecting herself and her friends.

Raas' word said she could, that it was permissible, and that's how she led her life. By the scriptures of her god. She'd killed with fiery blood before, like the Patriarch in Willow, but that had been survival. Self-defence.

Staring down at Balz, Calene *wanted* to kill him. She needed to take the High Sparker's head from his shoulders. For Vettigan. For whatever he and the emperor had turned her family home into. For taking her father's experiments and continuing them. For creating the Shadow Sparkers.

For the first time in her life, Calene desired nothing more than to taste blood on her blade.

"I... I can't," she murmured, hand dropping from her sword. "It's too much." Her fingers trembled. "I *need* it too much."

Brina scowled. "What are you talking about? Remember what this droker did to Vettigan!"

A hacking cough erupted from Balz. He neared death, and that meant the battle would soon begin again, once the Shadow took over.

"That's just it," Calene whispered, turning to Brina. "I can't *stop* remembering it."

Brina narrowed her eyes. She shook her head and spun, sword falling in an arc and cutting through Balz's neck. His eyes stared, unseeing, turning to glass.

The elf slid her sword back into her sheath. Calene's shoulders slumped.

"Help me with Vettigan."

She staggered away, back towards her old friend's corpse, ignoring the rubble and death.

"Help with what?" Brina called.

"I'm not leaving him here to turn to dust. We're going to bury him."

Brina caught up with her, grabbing her wrist. "What about the children out there?"

Only a few hours ago, Calene's skin had tingled whenever the elf brushed against it. She stared at Brina's wrist, then pulled her arm free.

"They're just children. They'll have run by now. Monsters for another day, I guess. Someone else's problem." The words coming from her mouth surprised Calene. Every problem was hers. That had always been how she functioned, but not now. "Are you helping me or not?"

The loss of Vettigan. The pain. It made her fires cold. Sucked the passion from her soul.

Brina peered into her eyes, concern etched in her face, then nodded. "Don't you want to go into your father's study first? Confront those memories?"

Calene glanced down the stairs, the yawning dark stretching below her, then shrugged. "No. It has nothing for me now. It never did."

Bending, she grabbed Vettigan's body under the arms. Brina caught his boots, and together they took him outside, through the darkness, into the morning light.

Calene buried him beneath the mighty oak tree. The place where she first Sparked. Some of the children watched in the distance, but they didn't approach. She ignored them.

Someone else's problem.

They'd all Spark soon, and darkness ruled them. They'd wreak havoc, but Haltveldt deserved it.

Do all the people living here deserve it too, Calene?

She shut the thought down and brushed against the fresh wound where the Link to Vettigan once lay, fresh tears stinging her eyes.

She thrust his sword into the ground, a marker for his body, and bowed her head. She almost prayed to Raas but kept the silent words to herself. Raas didn't deserve her prayers anymore.

"Did you want this?"

Brina's voice brought Calene's head up. She held her father's journal out to her. He'd drawn runes on the cover, like the ones surrounding Maria on the slab back in Willow.

"No."

Brina thrust it closer. "You may not want it now, but you will soon."

Calene reached out, wrapped her hand around the leather, and pushed it against Brina's chest, then shook her head. "What if it could have saved him?"

"Then it's just another reason to hate this diseased empire, isn't it?"

Brina tucked the journal inside her clothes, and Calene met her eyes.

"I'm coming with you. We'll kill the emperor together."

Brina placed her hand on Calene's shoulder. "Do you know anything about this Cradle?"

"No," Calene answered, shaking her head. "But we'll find it. We're not far from Haven Cliffs."

She glanced at Vettigan's sword, sticking from the ground, then at the oak tree, then at the ruined building behind her.

She walked away.

Brina followed, silent. There was no point going back to their camp for their supplies and horses; they'd be long gone by now. They'd find more on the road.

Calene walked away from her family home, from Vettigan.

This time, she wouldn't come back.

CHAPTER THIRTY

BEFORE THE LODESTONE

'To die a hero is better than to waste rage on your friends and allies. I've witnessed much, and this is ever the fate of a soldier who survives and sees too much. One need only look at Byar for proof of it...' - From Sparker Trell, who faced the First People outside Spring Haven, and helped build the Cradle. Taken from the Book of Memories, a tome shared with a select few.

Nexes rode at the head of his army, the ever-present black clouds hovering above them, stretching back to cover the entire convoy. The darkness dogged their every step, but his soldiers—Sparkers and fighters both—had stopped talking about it.

They didn't accept it. Their hooded stares spoke to that as they glared at the sky, as did the many whispered prayers to Raas. But the pall had left them so unmanned, they couldn't even speak of it anymore.

It didn't affect the Shadow Sparkers, and why should it? They moved together, their numbers swelling as other mages took to their ways on the road, ones who hadn't even been Turned, who didn't need Binding to serve the emperor and Haltveldt. They chose of their own accord, just as Emperor Locke had foreseen.

Nexes' grip tightened on his reins. He hadn't received word from his liege for weeks now and Balz had yet to arrive. Rolling his shoulders, Nexes fought to push down a wave of panic spiking in his chest. Failing to kill Balz meant failing to carry out the emperor's orders.

I can't be blamed if Balz doesn't appear, can I? The emperor shouldn't have turned him loose. He should have dealt with it himself. Sending him to me was the decision of a fool. A coward.

The wounds on his forearms itched, and the muscles in Nexes' face twitched. Treasonous thoughts came all too often now. Self-punishment would await that night, a whole day's worth.

Would another unwitting elven slave intrude on him? Thrill replaced the anxiety. Lust for blood.

The elven scum interfered with his nightly penance a pleasing amount, and Nexes silenced them before they could whisper a word of it to their kind in their filthy tongue.

He swayed in his saddle, lost in thoughts of blood. Nexes retreated there often on the road, when dark thoughts about his emperor rose from the recesses of his mind.

If only he'd reply to me. Tell me something! But he sends me into a trap, doesn't he? My own friend...

Holding the reins in one hand, Nexes scratched at his

skin under his dark blue riding jacket, breath catching when the scabs broke open.

The road climbed as they approached Lake Circa and the column continued on the beaten path, around the southern part of the body of water, to where the Banished sought to make their home on the north side. Nexes' scouts had told him of a plateau where they could make camp, one that overlooked the great lake before it wound down to the hinterlands in trickling streams.

The pounding of hooves pulled Nexes' focus. Riders raced toward him. Scouts, Niklov and Tania. Soldiers with sharp eyes and good sense. Dirt stained their uniforms, and their horses appeared gaunt, malnourished. An affliction affecting a great many in the army of Haltveldt on the march north.

"For the Empire!" Niklov saluted, pulling to stop beside Nexes. "We've spotted them!"

Nexes raised his hand, signalling to stop. The orders would be relayed down the column, and the convoy would grind to a halt.

"Where?"

"They have amassed on a plain between the northern lake and the Forest of Willows." Niklov glanced at Tania. "Their muster is...odd, sir."

Daggers of anxiety plunged into his gut. "How so?"

"They have young, old and a great number of non-combatants with them, Master of War," Tania reported, saluting, "but, for reasons we don't understand, they've split their warriors."

Nexes stared at her until she broke eye contact and looked away.

"They've moved some to protect the non-combatants in the south, Master of War." Niklov took over, clearing his throat midway when Nexes turned to him. "But the bulk of their fighters have set up in the north."

"Why?" Nexes hissed, strangling his reins.

Why did the blasted First People have so many secrets! Why did they act in such bizarre ways? Why wouldn't Locke tell him?

"Maybe they expect an assault from the north, sir?" Tania answered. Nexes stifled the urge to strike her. With her sharp, high cheekbones and wide eyes, she looked too much like an elf for his tastes.

"They think we'd take the column the long way around?" Nexes spat. "Nonsense. They're up to something. How many scouts did you see?"

"That's just it, sir," Niklov muttered, glancing at Tania again.

Why did Nexes' underlings insist on peering at each other when they spoke to him? His jaw ached from grinding his teeth. The empire knew he needed the impending battle to unleash himself before he lost control. He teetered on the edge, and many might have said he'd stumbled over it already. If any had the guts to say it to his face.

"We discovered no Banished scouts at all. They appear intent on looking to the north."

Nexes narrowed his eyes, then shrugged. "No matter. The battle will go easier for us than expected. Anything else?"

"Strange weather, sir," Tania replied, voice hushed, eyes flicking to the black clouds overhead. "Mist across the lake, working its way south."

"Fog often lies upon a body of water." Nexes showed his teeth in what some might call a smile. "Perhaps the empire's scouts are in need of re-education?"

To her credit, Tania gulped but refused to be cowed. "It's moving, Master of War, spreading over the plains. It's not..."

"Natural?" Nexes finished, pointing behind them.

Further down the trail, wisps of thick, white fog curled, creeping towards the Haltveldtian army. It spread across the south end of Lake Circa too, a blanket of cloud obscuring the water from view.

"How far is the plateau to make camp?" Nexes asked, mouth dry.

"A mile away, Master of War."

Nexes nodded.

"Return to the Banished. Watch them closely and see if you can't circle north. Find out what has them so preoccupied. Perhaps they expect an attack from Sea's Keep."

"Yes, sir," the scouts replied, snapping matching salutes. They spun their mounts around and galloped into the gathering mist.

Nexes held up his hand and urged his horse forward. He'd fought in odd weather before, they all had, but the black clouds above, the white fog below...

He shivered, cringing inside at his craven reaction. Nexes *had* lost control. He couldn't deny it. His body, his thoughts, his actions were those of a madman; the torturing of Sparkers, the endless list of 'traitors', the hunt for a conspiracy that he'd created in his mind.

"No, it's real," Nexes whispered, hands shaking on the reins. "It's all real, and I'll root it out once I've crushed the First People. I swear it!"

Nexes needed the battle, needed the release. Deep down, he knew it wouldn't sate his appetite. The Shadow Sparkers would prove how men like Nexes Almor were obsolete.

As his horse trudged forward, Nexes scratched at his scabs once more, the blood and dead skin building beneath his fingernails.

The dark clouds grew thicker. The blanket of mist swirled.

"Raas..." Kade whispered, flinching as he did. He feared a blow for speaking but, for once, no violence followed.

Malek's soldiers dragged Kade into a wide alcove inside the summit of the Peaks of Eternity, the taste of iron thick in his mouth. Everything hurt, every part of his body, even the soldiers' grip on his arms. They'd hauled him behind their horses as they returned to the mountain, and kept going when he'd stumbled, dragging him across the shale.

They'd beaten him too, for slowing them down. His captors asked no more questions and remained silent save for the grunts of exertion when sticking their fists or boots into his ribs.

Corridors ran inside the mountain, flights of steps too, leading ever upwards. Soldiers and battlemages, as Kade called them, passed this way and that through the warrens, like they'd resided inside the mountain all their lives, rather than a matter of weeks. Up they pulled him, until emerging into the chamber.

Shaped like a bowl, balconies stood on either side, one overlooking the shale-filled plains that stretched between there and Solitude, the other giving a view beyond the Peaks. A part of Kade wanted to throw off the hold of his captors and race to it, to see what hid behind the mountains, but the interior of the chamber demanded his focus.

In the room's centre, a glowing green rock stood, shining, its light flickering across the stone alcove. From its middle grew a silver-barked tree, pink and white flowers covering its thick, reaching branches, a thin carpet of petals scattered across the ground.

People filled the room. Soldiers watched lines of cowering men, women and children in rags, a harsh, red mark in the shape of an eye branded on their biceps and calves. Another line of elderly Banished stood nearby, clinging to one another.

Battlemages stood before the glowing green rock, deep in conversation. A pile of black ash lay amongst the flowers.

"What's happening here? What is that thing?"

Kade spoke without thinking but, once more, the soldiers didn't strike him.

One smirked instead. "You'll find out soon enough. Watch."

A battlemage turned and pointed at a Banished at the head of the line. The woman cried and struggled, and the Banished around her tried to pull her back as the soldiers beat them and pried her from their midst.

Their might won out, Spark-batons and armour over-powering weak fists and flesh.

They dragged the kicking, screaming woman across to the green rock, and she pleaded with them, wailing in the Banished tongue. If they understood her, it made no difference. They threw her down at the feet of the battlemage, who lifted a finger. The prisoner shot to her feet, screams suddenly louder, inching toward the glowing stone.

"What is the meaning of this?" Kade whispered, as she hovered before it, her face getting closer and closer.

Until her skin made contact with it.

Her screams became shrill, filled with pain, and the stench of seared skin filled the air. The woman couldn't move, not even her arms or legs now, and still the battle-mage kept her pressed against the rock, stroking his chin as he watched.

"He's killing her!" Kade snarled, straining against the soldiers' grip. One of them sank their fist in his stomach.

"Silence!"

The screams turned to whimpers, and the battlemage flicked a finger, allowing the woman to fall back. Kade looked away. The entire side of her face had burned away, everything blistered, bone charred to black. Soldiers picked her up and took her away without so much as looking at her.

The battlemage pointed at the other line, and the man at its head moved away, standing ready.

They're not even chained. They do this willingly. Are they slaves?

The branding suggested they were, and maybe more. Indoctrinated?

A soldier held a shortsword out to the man, who took it, then ran at the green rock, slamming the weapon down on it.

He turned to ash, floating down to join the pile, blade and all.

The battlemage turned, shaking his head, then smiled as he spotted Kade.

"Ah, the Haltveldtian!" he called, clapping his hands. "Now, this should be interesting. I fear we're learning nothing new from our current stock, as wondrous as it is to see this marvellous device in action. Bring him to me."

"I thought you were going to question me?" Kade resisted, but the soldiers pulled him along, his body too weak without food or water, and from the battering he'd taken. "You're experimenting on me?"

"You had your chance to tell us what you knew," one of the soldiers snarled. "Too late now."

"Do your worst," he snarled, glaring into the battlemage's black eyes when he came to a stop before him. "You won't hear me begging."

He clapped his hands again and laughed. "Oh, they all scream in the end when the Lodestone has its way, but I believe we will start off with some prudence in your case. No weapons. More often than not, the Lodestone disintegrates any who approaches with one, but we have only tested the First People, our workers and others from our great confederacy on it. A Haltveldtian! Now, that's something new!"

The First People aren't defenceless, fool.

The warrior Kade had fought beside the hill of dead had called them that too. The First People.

Kade glanced at the Banished. They appeared defence-less now, and this invading force seemed to know a lot more about Haltveldt's northernmost dwellers than the rest of the continent did.

Invisible hands took him, pulled him forward. Kade glared at the battlemage, who smiled back, obsidian eyes twinkling as the Lodestone's green glow reflected in them. Kade turned to it. The stench of burning flesh still hung in the air, filling his nostrils, the screams of fear and anguish still ringing in his ears.

Kade sagged, but the unseen bonds didn't let him drop. He'd failed his great quest. Arlo had come this way, but his father wouldn't be around to help him. The battlemage would throw him against the Lodestone until more ash sat amongst the pretty white and pink petals.

Tears stung his eyes. Kade wouldn't cry out. He wouldn't give his captors the satisfaction, but he wept. For his son, he cried.

The Lodestone filled his vision, and his head twisted to the side, cheek inching toward the rock.

"I'm sorry, Arlo," he whispered. "I'm so sorry."

Kade's flesh touched the surface, and cold exploded through his body. He'd expected heat. He flinched, then staggered back in surprise.

The force holding him evaporated.

Sniffing, the absence of seared flesh welcome, Kade spun around. Green light filled his vision for as far as he could see, the same glow from the stone.

"Hello?" Kade whispered, his voice echoing. "Am I alive?"

Death hadn't hurt as much as he expected. Hadn't hurt at all, really.

Protect him, a voice boomed, overpowering Kade's weak echo. It came from all directions at once, like the roar of a crowd speaking as one. *Make sure he reaches the stone or all is lost.*

"Who?" Kade shouted, spinning around. "What are you? Talk to me!"

A space amid the green opened in front of him, showing him a great lake. An army shrouded in darkness from the clouds above faced one covered in white fog, seeping from the ground below. The colours met when the armies charged at each other. Kade's instincts screamed. The side shrouded in mist had to win out. Had to.

Everything depended on it.

The vision flickered, revealing Tilo carrying Arlo along a stone passage, dirt and sweat covering them both, his son's eyes wide but somehow seeing through the rock, chest rising and falling with quick movements. Kade knew they were close, heading toward the Lodestone.

Protect him, Kade Besem, as I protect you. No matter what the Returned do to you, the Lodestone will not harm you. The vision vanished as the green light flickered. *He needs to reach the stone. Make sure he does.*

Kade fell back to the stone floor, staring into the battle-mage's eyes. Unable to move, he watched as his captor bent, and ran a black-nailed finger down his face.

"Fascinating." The mage licked his finger, like he savoured the taste. "Not so much as a scratch. What happened?"

"Nothing," Kade whispered, the visions of armies and his son swimming in his mind. The Returned. The voice called them the Returned, but returned from where? "Nothing at all."

"Lie to me all you want, Haltveldtian. My patience is vast, and my mind is curious." The Returned battlemage flicked his finger, sending Kade towards the Lodestone. "Again!"

He needs to reach the stone. Make sure he does.

The other side of Kade's face pressed against the Lodestone, but this time, he remained in the chamber, the rock neither hot nor cold, and it didn't harm him.

"Bring me some weapons," the battlemage cried, letting Kade fall to the ground again.

They could experiment on him all they wanted so long as it helped his son. Kade's eyes flicked around. Arlo and Tilo were coming. Were close. *So* close. He had to escape. Somehow, he had to escape.

But only when the time was right.

"Not much further now, Arlo. We're almost there." Tilo whispered, carrying the boy in his arms. "Purpose. We'll meet it soon. Together."

Arlo didn't answer. He couldn't. The words reached his ears, and he understood, but he'd long passed the point of responding. After clearing the cave in, Tilo had led them through a stone warren, the ceiling so low in places he had to crouch low, almost on all fours, to get through. Arlo's feet had dragged, limbs moving of their own accord, but slower, heavier which each step, his head turning in the direction of the Lodestone no matter where the winding path led.

"We used these tunnels to scout the lands, to travel without eyes on us if we had to venture close to the fortress," Tilo breathed, his words a constant stream, as if he thought his voice would keep Arlo tethered to reality. Perhaps they would. "Some of the Children used them on the migration south, but only the old and infirm. Kearn, our leader, would always preach caution. We hadn't seen any of the bright-robed mages beyond the walls in years, but he often said we had no idea what lurked in the great, stone beast. Solitude, as you call it."

Tilo lumbered on, Arlo's weight seemingly no burden to him. The green glow penetrating the rocks hovered directly ahead of them and upward, the boy's eyes fixed on it.

He'd tried looking away when he could still use his own legs, but invisible hands seemed to pull his head around, tether his vision to it. Each step brought them closer and, for a while, Arlo made good progress himself. Until he fell. He crawled, the urge to reach the Lodestone pulling him across the ragged stone ground, until his fingers bled. Knees too, the skin scraping beneath his trousers.

Arlo had screamed in rage as his limbs lost their strength and his muscles became water, begging for help.

Tilo sang to him, a song of healing, but it did nothing, as if his body shut itself down, preserving his strength for his great purpose. So, his friend carried him, and soon after, Arlo had stopped speaking. He couldn't even grunt.

Their Link kept Arlo alive, his mind able to bleed into

Tilo's and escape the shutdown of his own body, letting it rise above the sinking.

They'd feared the Link at first. How they almost lost themselves. Now, Arlo needed it.

"The Children. That's what we call ourselves, though who our father is, I know not. My people accepted many things without question, and me chief among them." Self-loathing made Tilo's voice thick. "The Keeper. That's what they called me, and many looked to me when their faith ebbed away, or they required guidance. I spent so much time before the Lodestone, kneeling in the Throat of the Gods, alone. Questions spun inside my head, but I refused to ask myself. I'd hear it whispering in my mind. Detached thoughts. Mutterings. Muir, we call it in our tongue."

Arlo's fingers twitched, desperate to reach out to Tilo. To comfort him. The whispers, he knew them all too well. A voice murmured in his head. *Arlo, Arlo, Arlo, Arlo.* Over and over. The same one he heard above Solitude. *Come to me. Come to me. Come to me.* It only stopped when Tilo spoke to him. *Help us, help us, help us.*

Another reason why Arlo's being fled to Tilo's mind. It gave him respite from a crowded brain.

Arlo's fingers wouldn't move. The tremor in his hand could have been a phantom one, a memory of movement. Despite his overwhelmed vision, and the detached voice murmuring in his head, Arlo still felt the weight of Tilo's feelings through their Link. Each step took him further away from his wife, his daughters, his unborn son. With each inch gained, realisation came too.

Tilo's head and heart spoke as one. He wouldn't come back from this. Threading their way through secret tunnels would get them to the Lodestone, into this 'Throat of the Gods', but getting them out?

An army occupied the Peaks of Eternity, the Banished lands, and they surely held the chamber Arlo needed to reach.

The Link. Arlo focused on it. He swam in it, but he didn't use it. It hadn't occurred to him. His eyes still fixed, unblinking, on the throbbing green glow above him. He sent the words he couldn't speak.

You'll see them again, Tilo. One day. You have to believe.

His friend missed his step, stumbled, crashed into the cave wall but stayed upright and avoided bringing Arlo to any harm.

"I can hear your voice inside my head!" he whispered, gazing down at him, trying to capture Arlo's attention. So close to the Lodestone, nothing could.

I can't speak, Tilo. Can't move. All I can see is the Lodestone. It's getting brighter with each step. It's like the sun, burning me, crushing me with its heat.

"It senses you, Arlo, and bends its focus on you. No one could withstand that. None of the Children could so much as touch it without pain, and many who tried simply died." Tilo shook his head. "All except me. To have its entire focus on you... It's alien. The Lodestone itself doesn't understand flesh and blood, doesn't realise we have limits. The presence inside it though. He said I would live. Even though I survived touching it, the journey it sent me on almost killed me."

The green light flickered, pulsated. It knew they spoke of it. Somehow.

It whispers to me, too, Tilo, or the presence inside does. I can't tell which anymore. It doesn't stop. Over and over. Please, keep talking to me. It keeps it away.

"You're afraid?"

Yes.

Tilo paused. Arlo's body jerked, tugging his friend forward. Fire and ice built in his chest, rage and frustration, and his legs kicked. Frowning, Tilo took a slow step forward, then another, and the spasms lessened. The impulse to move running through Arlo's body abated.

"I don't like this," Tilo muttered, shaking his head. "Any of it. The voice that told me of my purpose... It felt different to what I used to hear. More focused. Intent. Look what it's doing to you, Arlo."

What choice do we have? You've seen the Returned. Your people are walking into another battle in Haltveldt. If we can stop all this, as the Lodestone, or whatever it is, says, shouldn't we do it? If we have the power, isn't it up to us to act?

Tilo's shoulders slumped. "That's why we're still walking. You say you're afraid, but I wish I had your bravery."

Tilo, you're the most courageous person I know. Images of his father charging at the Returned mage in the cave mouth flashed in his mind, clouding out the green glow for a blessed moment. His father, who'd tracked Arlo alone through the Banished lands. *Well, second most. A close second.*

Tilo smiled. "I hope Drada speaks well of me to my son. The boy I always wanted." He hesitated, then glanced down at Arlo. "And I hope he's like you. Brave, clever, a credit to his name."

You'll tell him yourself when this is all over, Tilo. I promise.

The whispers in Arlo's mind picked up, drowning out the Banished's reply. He wanted to grind his teeth, cover his ears, close his eyes, but he couldn't. He had to lie there in Tilo's arms, paralysed, helpless, as the Lodestone's light filled his vision, its voice in his mind.

Do not be afraid, Arlo. Zanna's voice cut through it all. Zanna. His master. A comfort in the luminous green glare. *Everything will be well. Do you trust me?*

A tear trickled from the corner of his eye.

Yes.

The path led up and Tilo charged forward, legs pumping harder.

Good, Zanna replied. *Good. You are drawing close, and not before time. The end is in sight, and we need you here or else we face disaster. I believe in you, Arlo. We all do.*

Silence.

It flooded Arlo's mind, just as the green light overwhelmed his vision, smothering the cave walls, Tilo and everything else.

He bounced along with Tilo's gait, each step bringing him closer to the Lodestone. Each step bringing him closer to his purpose.

CHAPTER
Thirty-One

BETWEEN EARTH,
STONE AND WATER

'The First People never thought they could fail, their control so absolute, but wickedness dogs us all and will soon back us into a corner—human, elf, or god. I hope to Raas we remember that.' - Sparker Trell's warning, transcribed in the Book of Memories, went unheeded.

Nexes sat astride his horse, gloved hand gripping the hilt of the longsword he favoured for mounted combat. As he did during the battle with the elven scourge in the south, the Master of War would lead the charge.

His scouts reported that the Banished had cycled most of their fighters to face them, setting them up in front of the young and old, those unable to fight, but still kept a number to the north. Why, Nexes didn't know, and neither did Niklov or Tania. They'd ranged out through the night, beyond the Forest of Willows, far along the road to Adhraas, but reported the northlands quiet.

Balz hadn't arrived either, and the emperor had sent no further missives.

Nexes struck the worries from his mind, pushed away the nagging doubt about the Banished's intentions and the truth of what happened at Solitude, and dismissed the unnatural man-high fog stretching across the plains. Admittedly, he found the latter hard to accomplish; the mist proved so thick the row of mounted soldiers behind him appeared as dark, formless shapes in the haze.

None of it matters anymore. None of it. There's only the battle. There's only war.

He'd repeated the same phrase over and over since nightfall, coaxing his mind into sleep with the mantra, focusing on it when stray thoughts nagged at him. Did the Banished possess magic? If yes, what? Did the emperor seek to replace him, or implicate him in the conspiracy along with Balz?

At times, when cold reason took a hold of his mind, the Master of War couldn't deny the sense in the emperor ridding himself of his two closest friends. They knew his secrets, his vulnerabilities. In the emperor's position, Nexes would do the same.

When the doubts crept up on him during his rest, he dismissed them. Nexes couldn't help the fog, couldn't change the emperor's continued silence or apparent paranoia, and he couldn't conjure Balz or uncover the Banished horde's secrets.

The savages he *could* do something about. He could destroy them, and for now, that's all Nexes Almor wanted. To prove his continued worth to his emperor, to Haltveldt. Nothing eased the spirit better than victory.

Nothing except a blade covered in the blood of an enemy.

Squelching in the mud caught his attention. Niklov emerged from the mist, his chainmail damp with condensation. The scout drew his sleeve across his brow, soaking the material. Water dripped from his curled hair, just as it did Nexes'. The clinging cold nipped at him.

Winter approached, but the temperature had become... unnatural.

"Report," the Master of War commanded, noting Tania's absence.

"The Banished are in position. Standard defence, not suited for horse. Cavalry would overwhelm their front lines before the proper fighting starts. I see two problems though, sir. Droking major ones." Nexes raised an eyebrow at him. "Excuse the expression, sir."

The Master of War could forgive it. Already, many of his fighters were in their cups, and had been since the night before, drinking through the dark hours or taking a break to sleep before resuming. Nexes understood it, even if he'd never needed to locate his steel at the bottom of a tankard himself. Compared to dulling one's anxiety and fear, and their skill along with it, swearing wasn't so bad.

"The fog makes visibility poor," he replied, with a shrug, "but that is the same for both armies. What's your second point?"

Niklov nodded. "The ground isn't ideal for a charge, sir. I fear we'd lose a good number before we hit the front ranks. Last thing we want is falling mounts bringing down their neighbours. Or to have to pick our way past thrashing horses in this droking fog. Sorry."

Nexes rubbed at his short beard. He thought to lead the charge himself. Not because anyone expected it, even though he often did, but because he desired to unleash himself. The momentary control he had, the sudden clarity after days of teetering on the edge of madness came from a promise. The promise of blood.

Just as he had with the elves, Nexes counted down the moments before the assault, before the clash of metal, the crunch of bones and the screams of the dying filled his ears.

"How many?" Nexes asked, already knowing the estimates, but he'd leave nothing to chance.

"I'd say close to five hundred thousand in total, sir. Less than half of that are in position to fight us, and maybe three quarters of *that* are to the north."

He ground his teeth, studying the swirling mist before him. The Banished were about two miles north, and it would take time to muster before the attack and move the ranks into position. Dawn had just broken, but the mist grew thicker as the sun climbed, not thinner.

Niklov spoke sense. Even making his infantry charge in these conditions would mean carnage, and the Banished had numbers in their favour, magic or not. Nexes had thirty thousand. All fighters, including his Shadow Sparkers and regular mages. As long as the horde held no surprises, Nexes could win the day, but he'd need to use every one of his men and women wisely.

"Where is Tania?"

Niklov ducked his head a little, wiping at his brow again. "Ah, she's preparing for the battle, sir."

"Truly?" Nexes asked, meeting the man's eyes. "You wouldn't lie to me, would you?"

"Sir, it isn't my place to say."

"I'm making it your place."

Niklov twisted the reins in his hands. "You...unsettle her, sir. Yesterday, after we reported to you, she couldn't stop shaking for almost an hour."

Nexes studied the scout, face impassive. "Do I unsettle you too, Niklov?"

He swallowed. "Yes, sir."

"Good."

Turning in his saddle, he peered through the mist at the cavalry behind him, ready to charge. They'd have to change everyone's positions, pull the ranks apart, change the battle plan, but the Banished weren't moving. Nexes had time.

The sky caught his attention. Darkness hovered over his army, smothering it from above. Thick, black clouds loomed over the mist-choked plains and Lake Circa. Glaring up at the shadows, a new battle plan formed in Nexes' mind, one that could spare his cavalry and infantry from the initial charge, and perhaps weaken both his enemy in the field and the one at the heart of his empire.

"At least you've the steel to come and report to me yourself, Niklov." Nexes met his eyes. "We'll send the mages first, regular and Shadow. Bright and dark. They can break the Banished front ranks, and we'll follow their fires. Perhaps their Spark will burn this mist away. See it done."

Niklov nodded and wheeled his horse, barking out commands. Men ran to Nexes' side as his army sprang to life, requesting orders, which he gave without a second's hesitation.

The plan made sense. The mages would blaze a path for his army and bear the brunt of any Banished retaliation.

And if the savages held any surprises in reserve? The Shadow Sparkers would face those first too.

The distant crash of waves against stone reached Calene's ears long after Brina mentioned it. They'd set a steady pace since leaving the now-ruined Alpenwood House, coming across a farm with tack and horses ripe for taking.

Calene had expected more guilt after stealing the horses but the sick feeling in her stomach never arrived. Mostly, numbness lurked there, and spread to the rest of her body too. The effects of losing her Link with Vettigan, feeling his death in her mind. The choices she'd made since Solitude replayed over and over, plaguing her as she dozed in the saddle, half-awake but not fully asleep, nagging at her as she lay huddled next to Brina during the cold nights.

The path she chose to tread had resulted in Vettigan's death.

Her old friend had wanted to flee, to find a boat and leave Haltveldt behind, but Calene insisted he stay, saying she could save him because she couldn't bear to lose someone else. Not after her mother. She'd dismissed his reasons, put her own desires first.

But she hadn't committed to the path. Not really. She'd sleepwalked south, telling others what to do, like the Sparkers at Adhraas, without having any conviction herself. Calene had kept Brina close, following her while attempting to lead at the same time, causing confusion and tension in the group until Willow.

Maria du Gerran had asked her what she wanted, what Calene desired for Calene, and had given her the freedom to choose. She could have gone in any direction, picked up a new cause, or left Haltveldt, but she'd muddled on south, in the hope of curing Vettigan, and unearthing a relationship with Brina.

She and the elf had broken down the barriers between them, yes, but she'd lost Vettigan in the process. Her price to pay. Another corpse in Haltveldt's dirt, but this time, because Calene hadn't been able to let go.

After Solitude, she'd vowed to turn her heart to stone but couldn't. Another failure. If she had, she'd have let Vettigan leave. He wasn't the same man. They should never have returned to her family home, but Calene let her emotions overrule her logic.

Now, one option remained to her. The end of the path she trudged down lay in sight. To kill Emperor Locke and make him pay for the perversion of the Order of Sparkers, for what the corrupt black mages had done to Vettigan, and for the massacre at Solitude.

For Zanna's death, and the murder of so many others.

"I'm sorry, for everything," Calene murmured, as they pulled the horses to a halt.

They sat atop a hill, heavy woods beneath them and, beyond the trees, the ocean. In the past, the sound of crashing waves sounded like the whisper of freedom, a stray promise of something more, but now they slammed into Haven Cliffs with the weight of doom.

Hers, or the emperor's?

"Now's not the time for getting sentimental," Brina replied. The morning sun sparked in her determined eyes, the fresh, black paint on her face shining on her tan skin. She wore the expression of a warrior, an assassin. Calene missed the lover, the face she saw each night, when those stones beneath her skin crumbled and tenderness seeped through the cracks. "We have a job to do, and you've nothing to apologise for. You're here, aren't you?"

Calene nodded. For a while, the question of what Brina wanted with her had plagued her too. Did she want more than friendship? Companionship on the road? Or to use her as a weapon in her crusade?

The elf desired, and needed, all of those. In Brina's soul, a battle raged, just like it had in Calene's. A fight over taking a life for her, or avenging others.

She tried for both in the end.

Calene shook her head. "I should have seen sense long before. Killing the emperor. It's so clear now. All this death, all this pain. Haltveldt has to change, *needs* to, and cutting the head from the serpent will give us that chance."

"I don't care about change, Calene," Brina whispered, fingers toying with the end of her red braid. "Nothing will make Haltveldt a better place for my kind. Nothing." The elf turned to her, and Calene almost flinched at the hatred burning in her eyes. "I want to make this human pay for what he's done to me, and my family. What his line has done to all elves. And to you. Your mother. Your friends. When I sink my blade into his throat, I want him to look at me, and see it's a filthy elven savage ending his life."

"And then what?"

Brina frowned, bowed her head. "I don't know. Honestly. All I've known is war, Calene. Death. Is there anything else?"

Calene reached over and took her hand, entwining their fingers. "We'll find something. Together."

A shy smile tugged at the corner of the elf's lips. "*Thiemea. If* we survive, fool. This is the emperor we're talking about. He's hardly going to be in this Cradle alone, is he?"

Another thought that had bothered Calene. Had Brina come here to die? One last mission, doomed to failure. A release from a life of misery. Suicide in every sense, but the elf could fool herself into believing she carried out a righteous act, the odds stacked against her, but with a chance of success, no matter how slim.

Alone, as Brina planned to do it—she'd told Calene more than once, she'd walk the path in solitude if she had to—death surely waited.

"Well, that's why you have me, isn't it?" Calene smiled. "I expect we'll find Shadow Sparkers down there."

"Can you handle them?"

"Depends on how droking many."

Calene focused on her Spark. Since she'd healed Kade before Solitude and drawn on Tilo's strange magic, it had

expanded. The feats she'd accomplished when calling on it…
She'd overwhelmed the Shadow Sparkers in Willow, and at
Alpenwood House. How long could she continue to defeat
power with power?

"For as long as I can remember, since what my father
did to me, I haven't acknowledged what I am. What's inside
me. The power I have that's only grown. My father changed
me, but I can't turn a blind eye to that anymore, Brina. If
there are Shadow Sparkers down there, I'm going to make
them wish they'd never been born. Teeth of the gods, I am."

Brina nodded. "Let's get to it then. We'll leave the
horses here and make a careful approach. I'd rather reach
the emperor without burning the entire forest down to get
to him."

"Stealth's always better than causing a racket," Calene
replied, swinging down from her mount. "That's what Vettigan always said anyway."

"His death wasn't your fault." Brina traced her fingertips down Calene's cheek. "You know that, don't you? It's
the emperor's. It's Haltveldt's and those *thiemea* Shadow
Sparker's. Remember that."

Calene prodded at the space in her mind where her
Link used to sit. It still hurt to touch it, like a healing wound,
still to scar. How long before she could bear to touch it?
Would she ever?

"I'll remember it."

"Come on." Brina led her horse to a nearby tree and fastened the reins to it, an optimistic sign of success if Calene
had ever seen one. "I see a trail leading through the woods.
Be ready."

The elf walked away as Calene tied her animal to the trunk, and hesitated.

"Brina?"

The elf turned, and Calene approached her, taking her hands before kissing her, savouring the taste, enjoying the moment as the morning sun warmed their skin. For a heartbeat, maybe two, the past, present and future melted away, and the women existed together. Alone. The world quiet and distant.

Until Brina pulled away, blinking. The expression of the lover on her face, before the assassin pushed it away.

"Let's see this done. Anything it takes, you understand? Anything. We get the job done."

She turned on her heel, fingertips pulling away from Calene.

"Damn emotions," she grumbled, shoving them down as she watched Brina move away. "Drok them! Please, for the love of Raas, don't let that be our last kiss."

Calene had failed to turn her heart to stone before, but now she had to do it. As Brina said, they had to do anything to succeed. Compassion had only led to ruin so far, and if they pulled this off, if they killed the emperor and survived the Cradle, there would be time for it later.

Raas, you yellow-teethed drok, let there be a later.

Kade's head dropped.

He sat in the Lodestone chamber with the rest of the prisoners, chained to the line by his wrist. The steel cut into his skin, squeezing the bone, but numbness had smothered the pain now, and the ache in his stomach overwhelmed all.

They hadn't fed him in days.

Instead, the Returned made him watch as they sacrificed more innocent Banished, more of their own kind in the name of experiments against the Lodestone, the pile of black ash growing, the number of maimed increasing.

Kade had grown numb to the screams too.

They'd continued their tests on him. Pressing him against the Lodestone while he slept, alongside others, with a weapon in his hands, naked, fully-clothed. The battlemage carried out any idea that crossed his mind, watching all the time with his obsidian eyes, never flinching when a prisoner chained to Kade turned to embers or burned to a crisp. The stench of their seared skin still hung thick in Kade's nose. He remembered the eyes of every dead or injured Banished, as they locked gazes over the Lodestone, Kade helpless as the panic, fear, and pain built in their wild stares.

The Lodestone had no effect on him, just as it had promised, but it hadn't spoken to him again. Kade remained present during all the experiments, and the glowing green rock turned neither hot nor cold against his skin.

He gazed around the chamber. A Banished woman, cradling a child to her chest, stared at him. Many did. But while the branded prisoners from the Returned's own stock glared with barely concealed hatred, the Banished looked awestruck.

They'd lived in these mountains and knew the Lodestone. It struck Kade that they knew full well what it meant to lay a finger on it, never mind their entire bodies, and his continued survival perplexed them as much as it did anyone else.

The Returned beat him, asked him what made him different. Kade had no answers, and telling them so only made the fists, boots and Spark-batons fall with more exuberance. So Kade suffered them without speaking, though he screamed until his throat turned raw.

All the while, he clung to what the Lodestone told him. Arlo needed his help. It kept Kade alive. Kept him on the right side of sane.

A question nagged at him, flooding his mind every time the Lodestone disintegrated another prisoner or Banished. Every time it left them maimed and burned. If it could spare Kade, why didn't it do the same to everyone else? Why did it allow so many to die? Why did it cause so much needless pain?

As in everything else, Kade had no answers. In truth, he'd had precious little since leaving Spring Haven on this mad fool's quest to rescue his son. One man, a drug addict, a broken soul racked with guilt over decisions made, against an emperor's will turned into a crusade against an army of savage magic users.

He almost laughed, and would have done if he had the strength for it. *I wonder what Emperor Locke and the rest would think about this army? When the forces meet, Haltveldt will burn.*

Kade didn't care about that. Arlo. He cared for nothing else, and the help his son needed. Once he'd done as the stone wished, assuming he survived, he'd take Arlo far away, and leave Haltveldt to its fate. The entire continent could sink into the ocean. Kade wouldn't spare it a second thought.

A soldier passed in front of him and paused, his gaze sweeping the room, Spark-baton at his hip and sword in hand. They only bound Kade by his wrists. He could kick out, bring the soldier down, snatch his weapon...

He wouldn't get far. More soldiers lined the room, plus the battlemages, and what good would it do? Like the Lodestone said, he had to help Arlo. Kade needed to wait.

Movement on the other side of the chamber caught his eye, a shift in the green hue laying on the room, behind the staring Banished and near the balcony looking toward Solitude.

A part of the wall shifted. From it, carrying Arlo, Tilo emerged.

Kade's heart pounded in his chest, a cry caught in his throat along with his breath. Around him, the branded prisoners noticed, and they cried out in alarm, in surprise.

In warning.

His son had arrived. In chains, Kade could do nothing to help him.

Nothing.

Chapter Thirty-Two

FROM THE CRADLE TO THE GRAVE

'Kill or be killed. In life, there's nothing else that matters, and you always want to be the one doing the killing. Always.' - A quote attributed to Byar of Spring Haven. Many dispute the accepted history of his leadership of the resistance against the First People. The real leader's identity, like so much else, is lost to the mists of time.

"Orders, Master of War?"

Nexes stared at Niklov. Only a scout, but a capable man. One who did his job, carried it out well, and swallowed his fears. Maybe he drank himself to sleep each night, perhaps he slit the throats of dogs, but the man performed his duties a damn sight better than many others. He'd deserved his promotion to the role of Nexes' personal herald, and he could think of few compliments higher than a field promotion well-earned.

Together, they'd reordered their ranks, moving the Shadow Sparkers to the front as they marched into position and leaving their horses behind. They'd charge on foot after the hammer blow from the black mages and their uncorrupted brethren.

The hour had just passed midday, though the heavy, black clouds hid the sun from sight. With the fog still thick on the ground, it felt as far from noon as possible, like they existed in some kind of dream state, or they'd found themselves stuck between Eternity and the Underworld and the forthcoming battle would decide where they rested.

Light or darkness.

Life or death.

A thrill built in Nexes' gut, ran through his limbs. Soon, he'd unleash himself and release weeks of frustration, paranoia and hate. On the battlefield, twin swords in his hands, he'd no longer feel inadequate, antiquated. When he delivered victory for Haltveldt, securing their lands from internal threat, his emperor would smile on him, favouring him once more.

Though the menace from within wouldn't be over. No, not yet.

The conspiracy. The threat from the mages. No, I cannot think about that now. Later. Yes. Later.

On the battlefield, Nexes could reveal his madness, let it run its course, before bottling it up again. The bottle would be less full. Living would be easier. For now, it almost forced the stopper out. Nexes knew it. Felt it. The clarity of battle revealed it to him.

Beyond the mist, less than half a mile away, the Banished

waited, shouts in their guttural tongue drifting through the fog.

"Get the Shadow Sparkers ready," Nexes replied, as Niklov continued to stare at him.

"How many, sir?"

"All of them. We use them as a shield. Shadow Sparkers first, then soldiers with mage support after. Order them to Eviscerate the Banished frontlines. On my command, they advance."

Saluting, Niklov marched away towards where the Shadow Sparkers lurked. Their number had swelled on the march north. They'd numbered but twenty in the beginning, more than enough to obliterate the elven horde, but more had joined their ranks as they passed through Haltveldt, and Sparkers from Nexes' army had donned the black too. Now they boasted almost one hundred. Five times the amount that wrought genocide on the scourge in the south.

Raising his hand, Nexes turned to the army's standard bearer.

"One long blast of the horn."

She complied, the deep, echoing blow rising above the mist, settling below the black clouds above. Like a creeping shadow, the black Sparkers flowed forward. The horn's blast died. Singing took its place. Gentle voices meandered across the fog from the other side, and the mist parted before the Shadow Sparkers.

Nexes almost choked. Ranged before them, filling the horizon, stood the Banished, waiting. A throng of warriors, ready for battle. Laying eyes on them, the staggering amount of them...

Nothing could have prepared Nexes for the sight.

"Are the Shadow Sparkers doing that?" Nexes asked, searching for the bright robes of the closest Sparker.

"No," they replied, frowning. "They haven't done anything yet. It's either coincidence or..."

"The Banished are doing it," Nexes finished, shivering.

The scars on his arms itched. The doubts he'd locked away in his mind broke free. Answers at last.

From the Banished ranks, a volley of arrows loosed, disappearing into the dark clouds. They wouldn't reach the main forces, but the Shadow Sparkers...

The arrows didn't fall, and the Sparker beside Nexes laughed.

"What is it?" Nexes asked, old frustrations rising. A Master of War who could see nothing of what his forces did!

"You'll see," the Sparker responded. Nexes wanted to wipe the smug grin from their face.

Screams interrupted the singing, and the Banished front line dropped, the arrows from the sky falling among them, finding purchase among the mass of bodies. The Shadow Sparkers had snatched them from the air, turned them against their archers.

Despite himself, Nexes smiled.

"Two blasts. We follow! For Haltveldt!"

As the arrows continued to lay waste to the Banished, Nexes stayed close to his support Sparker. He thought to ask their name, then realised he really didn't care.

"Tell me when they begin their Evisceration. I want to know every detail."

Whatever secrets the Banished had, it wouldn't help them.

Nothing would.

"Can you see anything?" Brina breathed. "Any of them?"

Calene shook her head. "We can only see another Sparker when one of them uses their magic, so I'm not using mine right now, and they're not using theirs." She pointed at the black sky beyond the tall trees. "Though those clouds tell me there's some of the drokers here."

They made their way down the trail, entering the woods, and saw not a soul, the only sound the crashing of the waves. No birds, no animals.

"We're getting close to the cliff edge," Brina whispered, glancing around. "I don't like this. I feel like there's—"

Calene's Spark acted of its own accord, creating a shield over her and Brina as a thick tendril of black corruption whipped at them.

Blooms of darkness erupted around them. Snarling, she pushed out with her Spark, lifting the elf up and pushing her down the trail.

"Run!" she cried, strengthening her shield. "I'll hold them off!"

Brina raised a hand, then turned, disappearing into the woods, leaving Calene alone. Just as she'd asked her to do, but even still, her heart ached.

Whatever it takes, drok it. Whatever it takes.

Four black-robed figures emerged from the trees, hooded, silent. Obsidian serpents. Calene kept her shield strong and let her Spark reach out, searching for energy beyond her own. Earth, water, flickering flames she found. Air, and plenty of it. Death too. Creeping darkness that whispered to her, oozing from the Shadow Sparkers. She ignored that, but pulled on the rest, adding it to her Spark, feeding on the torrent of emotions colliding in her mind. Fear, anger and rage she avoided, pushing them away.

"I am Byar," one of the Shadow Sparkers murmured, his voice a hiss.

"Fancy name. Like the warrior of legend?" Calene replied, sneering. Let them talk. Delays were good. It let Brina get closer to her goal. None of the mages followed the elf, but Calene couldn't think about that now. "Either you've got some ego, or your parents had high hopes for you. Reckon they'd be disappointed if they saw you now."

Byar removed his hood, his slack smile hideous in his fissured face.

"My emperor gave me that name. A great honour, no?"

"That man wouldn't know the first thing about honour," Calene snarled, eyeing the other Shadow Sparkers. They flanked Byar. Silent. Unmoving.

"You've come to kill him?"

Calene saw no point in denying it. "Yes."

Byar took a step forward. "You could join us. Willingly. Those that do are more powerful than those Turned, a fact that rankles my brethren here. Already, the strength of your Spark outstrips any I know." His tongue snaked out, dancing over his lips. "Imagine what you could become."

Shadows crept from the dark places of the forest, gathering at the black mage's boots. Swirling. Oozing. Whispering to Calene.

"I don't think your emperor would want the person who killed his High Sparker as part of his gang, would he?"

Delay them. Keep talking. Every second brings Brina closer to that droker.

Byar laughed. "Balz is dead? I wouldn't be so sure of the emperor's ire if I were you. He might give you the job now that it's free."

Calene frowned. "Trouble in paradise, eh? Who would've thought sticking a bunch of power mad, corrupted drokers together would cause trouble?"

Byar's smile crumbled. "Enough talk. I see you won't join us, but you are much too valuable to waste. We will have to Turn you." He turned to the other mages. "Attack."

Calene didn't wait for it. Jumping backward, she lashed out with her Spark, grabbing a tree and pulling it free. Groaning, the trunk tipped, crashing toward the Shadow Sparkers.

As magic slammed into Calene's shield, a black-robed mage caught the tree with its Spark and tossed it aside, before turning their power on Calene.

She dropped to her knees. Magic battered at her. She had used the element of surprise, and it failed. *A tree, Calene? A droking tree? Why not open up the ground or hit them with everything you had? A tree?*

The Shadow Sparkers advanced on her, a barrage of darkness beating at her shield, wearing it down. Energy swirled around her, so much of it. And so much darkness.

She could use it. She could. As Byar said, imagine what she could do with it...

No!

Calene lashed out, a torrent of flame bursting from her palms, filling the woods. One of the Shadow Sparkers failed to raise their shield in time, and screamed as the flames engulfed them, but they carried on, magic pouring from them, wearing Calene down. Only their focus on their shields caused them to relent even a little.

Her fire spread around them, scorching the trees. Burning leaves tumbled, ash and embers floating past. Smoke billowed under the canopy and escaped to meet the black clouds.

Hold on, Calene. You have to hold on!

Brina raced through the woods. She heard screams behind her, and staggered, almost fell. Calene needed her. How had she left her alone? How?

She shook her head. Calene had told her to run, and she'd never met anyone as good at surviving as the Sparker. The woman who'd assaulted the Patriarch's Palace in Willow and came out alive. Who'd faced down magic and Banished warriors at Solitude. Her friend who'd killed slavers to free elves.

No, she was *more* than just a friend.

Brina bit her lip as tears stung her eyes. She could go back. Like she had on the road when they'd first met, helped her in the ambush.

No. The emperor. They had a mission, and Calene knew the risks, realised the odds.

The sounds of crashing waves grew, and Brina burst through the woods, coming right to the edge of the empty cliff. That no one followed troubled her, but Calene's magical diversion played into her favour. Spring Haven sparkled in the morning sun further along the cliffs and Brina scowled at it. Peering over the edge, she ignored the waves' assault on the resolute stone, and her breath caught in her chest.

A narrow stairway lay below her, leading into a cave built into the cliffside.

The Cradle.

Sparing one last look over her shoulder, eyes straining for any sight of Calene, for any sound of her, Brina pulled a dagger from her belt and descended.

She had a job to do.

"Who are you?" the battlemage yelled, above the cries of alarm.

Kade pulled at his chain, grabbed at the clasp, causing blood to flow from the sores on his wrist. Soldiers and mages stared at Tilo, who held Arlo in his arms, the Banished prisoners at his feet.

The Lodestone flashed, the green light brighter than before, pulsating with excitement or anticipation.

"I said, who are you?" the battlemage screamed, glancing at the Lodestone. "How did you come here?"

Tilo cocked his head to one side, as if listening to a voice only he could hear, then set Arlo on the ground. The boy teetered on his feet, wobbling like a new-born calf, uncertain and weak, and turned to face the Lodestone.

Kade gasped. His son's wide eyes had turned white, and they were fixed on the pulsating rock. He seemed utterly unaware of his surroundings and the danger he was in, of the prisoners, the battlemages, the soldiers.

Of Kade.

All he saw was the Lodestone.

The voice from the stone echoed in Kade's mind. *Protect him. Make sure he reaches the stone, or all is lost.*

"How can I protect him if I can't get free?" Kade pulled at his chain again, his useless fingers prying at the metal around his wrist. "I can't do a damned thing! Raas, help me!"

Arlo took a wobbling step forward, his limbs jerking like a puppet on a string.

"Come no closer!" the battlemage ordered. "Tell me who you are or—"

Arlo's unseeing eyes snapped to the mage, and he raised his hand.

A jet of flame poured out of it, slamming into Kade's tormenter. His screams brought the room to a standstill. Soldiers watched, paralysed with shock, as the young boy with white eyes burned the battlemage to a crisp. Tilo went to grab at him, but he fell back, like an invisible barrier had repelled him.

The movement brought life back into the room. Yelling, soldiers charged at Arlo, blazing fire pouring from his palm. Tilo leaped in the way of the nearest guard, great sword deflecting a blow, but more ran at Arlo.

Protect him. Make sure he reaches the stone, or all is lost.

Kade snarled. A soldier still stood before him, transfixed by the conflagration, his Spark-baton at his hip.

Kicking out, his boot crunched into the back of the soldier's knee, making him crash to the ground. Kade grabbed at him, pulling the Spark-baton free, and pressing it against the man's flesh. He convulsed, trembled, and still Kade held it to his skin, a part of him wanting to make the soldier pay for all the beatings he'd suffered, all the pain. Foam spluttered from the man's lips, and a cry from Tilo caught Kade's attention.

A Returned soldier lay at his feet, blood pooling, but another fought him, and a wound stood out on the Banished's thigh. Other soldiers approached Arlo, hands raised against the flames, but as soon as he stopped, they'd rush in.

Kade threw the Spark-baton aside. The soldier had dropped his sword. Kade could throw it, like he'd done at Solitude, skewer the one Tilo fought with, or one of the guards waiting for Arlo's magic to falter, but what would it accomplish? His son needed protection, had to reach the Lodestone.

More soldiers ran into the room, the screams and yells alerting them.

Kade had to act.

Baring his teeth, he grabbed the sword, and pressed his chained arm flat against the wall. Screaming, Kade brought the blade down, smashing it into the stone.

And through his flesh and bone.

Crying out, he fell to the ground, free, his hand still dangling from the chain. Blood sprayed from his stump, making the ground slick. Forcing himself to his feet, sword in hand, Kade slipped as he staggered past the Lodestone. Dizzy and weak, he fell onto it, his handless arm outstretched.

The dark clouds thickened above the Shadow Sparkers as they bore down on the Banished.

Nexes held his breath. Even without having the Spark in his veins, he knew the black-robed mages gathered their power, ready to unleash it on the horde. His stomach lurched. It would bring him victory, just as it had against the elves, but this wasn't battle. It wasn't a fight. It was the death knell for people like him. And Emperor Locke, his friend, had sounded it.

"My word!" the Sparker beside him cried, their voice shrill.

The Shadow Sparkers stumbled and came to a stop. The darkness covering them lifted just a touch. Nexes and the army following ground to a halt, and a hush washed across the plains of Lake Circa, and on the Banished too.

"What happened?" Nexes hissed, staring at the Banished. They appeared equally stunned.

"The Evisceration..." the Sparker cried. "It failed. It hit the Banished and just disappeared. Broke upon them."

The First People's secret. He'd found it. They were protected somehow, and the empire's latest, greatest weapon wouldn't work on them.

Nexes laughed.

He laughed until tears sprang in the corners of his eyes. He laughed as fire poured from the rank of Shadow Sparkers, and the Banished horde sang in response, the magical conflagration lashing against an invisible barrier and going no further.

The horde had their own magic. If the emperor had suspected, he would never have imagined it rendered his Shadow Sparkers useless. Their greatest weapon, Evisceration, useless.

"Aim your magic at the ground," Nexes cried to the Sparkers around him. "Tear it under their feet! Show these Shadow Sparkers how war is won!"

Still laughing, Nexes grabbed the horn from the standard bearer and blew three, long blasts, then tossed it into the mud and charged. Ahead, the ground exploded. Mud, limbs and blood shot in all directions as the Sparkers followed his command. The Shadow Sparkers joined them.

His line of soldiers crashed into the Banished frontlines, Nexes in the lead. He spun his twin shortswords, swinging them left, then right, opening a gap in the press of bodies as they piled around him, grunting, sweating, crying. He smashed his forehead into the pale nose of a Banished warrior, the cartilage crunching against bone, and stuck a blade through his chest. The warrior didn't fall though. The mass of bodies kept him upright as soldiers rushed in from behind, looking to fill in any gaps in their line.

The Banished sang while they fought, their faces fixed in anger, their voices one, only death silencing them. Nexes dealt it, his shortswords ideal for close-quarter fighting. The heat assailed him, the stench of dying too, but he drank it in. This was what he needed. A battle. As pure as possible in Haltveldt, and proof that Haltveldt would always need men like Nexes Almor.

Always.

Around him, the ground ruptured, throwing bodies

into the air, Haltveldtian and Banished alike. Men and women died. The Banished surged forward, and the Haltveldtians pushed back, and the blue water of Lake Circa turned crimson.

As Nexes fought and killed, he laughed. He laughed when he saw Shadow Sparkers trampled in the mud. He laughed when a Sparker exploded after drawing too much power into themselves, burning out in the most spectacular way.

The battle hung in the balance. The Banished had the numbers and had their own defensive magic, but Nexes still had the Sparkers, still had the experience, and he had nothing to lose. Behind the Banished warriors lurked the young and old, the ones unable to fight, and it added desperation to their attack.

Having something as important as that to fight for could work, for a while. But in Nexes' experience, it caused mistakes, made the stakes too high.

The entire Banished horde fought at Lake Circa, and Nexes wouldn't stop until each and every one of them rotted in the mud.

Slamming one of his blades into the mouth of an enemy, Nexes spun away, looking for his next target, his limbs moving from years of well-earned muscle memory. All around him, soldiers—men and women, warriors and mages—died by the score.

Calene pushed to her feet, refusing to falter, forcing the

Shadow Sparkers back. The burned one, still smouldering, fought on, power almost depleted. Flicking her hand, Calene sent a fist of air into the charred body, throwing it into the flames building around them.

One down!

And three to go. Her focus and will poured into maintaining her shield, Calene gripped the hilt of her sword, pulled it free and charged at a Shadow Sparker, delivering an overhead slash. The black-robed mage stumbled back, pulling its own weapon free, the blade catching in the sheath. More magic blasted into Calene, shrinking her shield, but it held. The distraction allowed her target to regain its footing. Its hood had fallen back, revealing its onyx-eyed glare. It raised its hand, and a thick tendril shot free, snaking toward Calene.

"No Evisceration!" Byar spat. "We want this one alive."

The attack didn't stop. It slammed into Calene's shield, knocking her to her knees again, the mud squelching beneath her. She pulled on the flame's heat, on the water crashing against the cliffs, but her energy flagged, and she teetered close to her limit, vast as it was.

Calene's head spun, and the heat built inside her as she continued to absorb energy into her Spark. Shoots of grass around her withered, turned brown as she stole their life, and a warning voice screamed in her mind, told her what she approached. She shoved it aside.

Brina had said they needed to do whatever it took. What if more Shadow Sparkers waited further in the woods? What if members of the Emperor's Hand lurked inside the Cradle? The elf wouldn't stand a chance, and Brina was all Calene had left.

Zanna gone. Vettigan dead. The Order of Sparkers a corrupt shell. The Empire of Haltveldt a blight on the continent.

That she'd lasted so long against four Shadow Sparkers, sending one into the flames, spoke to Calene's prowess with the Spark. Her strength. But it flagged, and that meant only one thing.

Defeat.

On her knees, dark magic battering at her, Calene raised her eyes, and met the shining darkness of the one attempting Evisceration.

How droking dare they? Calene would never let anyone try it on her again. *Never*.

Pushing to her feet, she snatched out with her Spark and absorbed a slither of the darkness assailing her. The weariness, the doubt, the worry, washed from her mind. She sent a blast of it crashing into the Shadow Sparker, who staggered back, shield obliterated.

Calene raised her hand.

A black tendril snaked out. Thin at first, but as it pushed through her skin, it grew, like the light, or the energy of the place fed it. She jerked as it squirmed from her palm, a living thing, and bile rose in her throat.

This wasn't the Spark. It was something else entirely.

The Shadow Sparker's black eyes opened wider as the others stopped their assault, watching Calene perform the darkest of evil. Once loose, she couldn't stop it. Tears stung her eyes, blurred her vision, as the inky jet of corruption oozed from her and shot right at the defenceless Shadow Sparker.

There's always another way, daughter. Please remember that.

The voice boomed in Calene's mind, coming from where her Link lay dormant with Zanna. Her mother. Impossible.

But the words chased away the darkness and, in the moment before the Evisceration landed, Calene released her Spark.

She wobbled on the spot, the black-robed mage staring at her. Weariness washed through Calene's limbs and the bile in her throat threatened vomit. She'd almost Eviscerated someone. After everything she'd seen, everything she'd done, she'd almost walked the same path as her mother, so she could come to her loved one's aid.

The mud squelched behind her, and the pommel of a sword crashed into the back of her head, knocking her into the mud.

Kade raised his hands into view. One still gripped his sword, but the other...

Where it had touched the Lodestone, the flesh had healed, leaving a stump at the end of his arm. Still gone, but at least it didn't bleed anymore. No pain either.

He looked to Arlo and Tilo and ran to them, intercepting Returned soldiers as they flooded the room. His son gazed at the Lodestone, the battlemage a smouldering ruin on the floor.

"Go, Arlo!" Kade shouted, parrying a thrust from one

of the Returned. "Touch the Lodestone. End this!"

His son didn't move. Arlo wavered on the spot. Tilo shouted something in the Banished tongue as he fought off an opponent, then grimaced, eyes glazing over as he kept up his defence.

Arlo jerked, shook his head, and the colour bled into his white eyes.

"Father!" he cried, taking a step toward Kade. "Your hand!"

Kade blocked with his sword, his stump moving to grip the hilt in two hands before letting it fall away. Instead, he swept his leg, kicking the Returned into the air and slamming his blade into his chest.

Shouts echoed from outside the chamber. More Returned ran to join the fray and, with them, the green-armoured battlemages.

"Arlo, touch the Lodestone," Kade yelled, fighting back tears. How he yearned to gather his boy up in his arms, tell him how much pride swelled in his chest. Tell him how sorry he was for sending him away and not keeping him close and fighting against what came at them. To kiss his forehead and tell him he loved him. But he couldn't. "We'll keep them away from you. Go!"

Kade dropped to his knees, frozen, snarling, sword clattering to the ground. Magic overwhelmed him. Tilo fought on, like it didn't affect him, but he couldn't stand alone.

Arlo had to touch the Lodestone while he still could.

"Father!" Arlo screamed, as the magic bloomed around him. Dark magic. To Arlo it felt like the Spark, but not exactly.

His being had flown out of the Link he shared with Tilo. The mind and body ready and willing.

In the corner of his eye, the Lodestone pulsated like it begged him to run to it. But his father, Tilo...

Returned soldiers flooded the room, ones capable of magic too. So many of them.

"I can stop them."

Arlo raised his hands and fire rushed out of them, sweeping the room. It touched his father, but Arlo raised a bubble of air around him, protecting him from the blast. Around Tilo and all the prisoners too. The magic came without thinking, without draining him. This close to the Lodestone, Arlo realised he could do anything.

Screams reached his ears, but he blocked them out. It was the Returned or his father and Tilo, and he wouldn't watch them all die so he could fulfil some purpose. The fires burned, washing over the Returned, soldiers and mages alike, and cleansed the Throat of the Gods from their evil, their corruption.

Kade covered his head as the flames rushed over him, the magic holding him still gone. The fires died, leaving death in their wake. Getting to his feet, he picked up his sword, and met Arlo's eyes.

"I'm sorry, father," Arlo murmured, looking at his hands. "You must think I'm a monster."

"No," Kade replied, taking a step forward, shaking his

head. "You're my son. Always. You've saved us. You did what you had to do."

Tilo, holding his side, blood oozing between his fingers, hobbled toward the boy, and whispered words in his tongue.

"Tilo's right," Arlo said, as if anyone could understand the Banished warrior. "More will come. I have to do this now."

Turning, Arlo walked toward the Lodestone, his footsteps echoing against the stone. He reached the glowing green rock, hands outstretched, ready to touch it.

"Arlo?" Kade called, taking a step forward.

"Yes, father?"

"I love you."

Arlo turned and smiled. "I love you too. Thank you for following me all this way."

"To Eternity and the Underworld, Arlo. Always, and you'll never need to ask."

Smiling at his father, he reached out, laid his hands on the Lodestone, and vanished.

Blood soaked Nexes' skin. His hair. His swords. The sun still hid behind the dark clouds, as if afraid to peer out and see the blood spilled beside Lake Circa, fearful of the wrath of humankind and the depravity they could sink to.

Around him, soldiers stumbled. Warriors died. Falling into the piles of dead and dying, more corpses for the worms. The ground split in places and bodies fell, the living and the deceased tumbling into the abyss. Flames spread across the battlefield, the violence snatching the singing from the Banished's tongues, their invisible barriers faltering. Lightning lanced from the sky, slamming into the sundered earth, stealing more lives.

And still more Banished came. The Haltveldtians pressed into them, crushed them, but the horde numbered so many...

But they died. Nexes dispatched another, breath ragged, and stumbled as fingers gripped his ankle.

Niklov stared up at him, a spear through his hip, a Banished body crushing him, fear, at last, naked in his eyes.

Nexes plunged his blade through the man's throat as the ground rumbled and groaned, and light danced inside the black clouds overhead.

Brina's footsteps echoed as she entered the cave, eyes growing wide as she took in the sight.

She stood on a balcony, a turning orb suspended in front of her showing the lands of Haltveldt and beyond on it. Beneath it lay stacks and stacks of books and parchment. Diadems were built into the sides of the rooms, moving figures and scenes. She recognised some.

Many showed Solitude, and the one nearest to her, close to a winding stairwell leading down from the balcony, had a single figure confronting a horde of thousands at the feet of the tallest point of the Peaks of Eternity.

A stone door pulled at Brina's eyes though.

It lay at the room's far side, dominating the entire wall. Even to an elf, it seemed ancient, like the rest of the Cradle had sprang up around it. Glowing runes, etched into the surface, burned her eyes. She walked forward, taking the stairs, unable to pull her stare away from it, unable to feel the weight of someone watching her.

The mission to kill the emperor lifted from her mind. The stone door overrode all else.

Arlo blinked and got to his feet. He floated in a void filled with luminous green, the same shade as the Lodestone, but as he stepped forward, a sound echoed, and his boots met with resistance.

"Hello?" he called, gazing around, seeing no one. "I'm here. You asked me to come, and I did. Now what?"

A laugh scratched at the edges of his hearing.

"Arlo? No, no, no. You can't be here. It's what he wanted, it's—"

Turning, Arlo found Zanna standing before him, frozen, mouth hanging open, the rest of the words refusing to come.

"What who wanted?" Arlo asked, grabbing a hold of her. She felt real, whole, looking exactly as she did when he saw her last. Bright robes, greying hair, bare feet. "What is this place? You spoke to me, didn't you?"

"No!" Zanna cried, eyes filled with horror. "Raas used—"

She froze mid-sentence. Not even her eyes moved.

"This is inside the Lodestone, Arlo. Do you like it?"

He recognised the voice. It had spoken to him often. Turning, Arlo gasped. The man wasn't what he expected.

He looked like Tilo. The same build, the same fair, curled hair and yellow eyes. The figure in the simple, white robe wore a sneer on his lips as he gazed down his nose at Arlo.

"Raas?" the boy asked, an itch between his shoulder blades.

"At your service," the man replied, the sneer not disappearing from his cold smile.

"But you look like one of the Banished!"

"Yes, I do," Raas replied, shrugging, "because I am one. Although, in my day, we called ourselves the First People, and that is what I prefer, thank you kindly."

"I thought you were a god." Arlo glanced around. He wanted to run, but Zanna still stood frozen behind him, and he saw no signs of escape from inside the Lodestone. "What's happened to Zanna?"

"I *am* a god." Raas raised an eyebrow. "A self-made one, in a world without, and I have sacrificed much to save all that is important to me. Zanna is...waiting for her turn to talk."

"You called me here."

"I did."

"Because I'm the chosen one?"

Raas' eyebrow rose higher, and he laughed, putting his hand in front of his face like a child. His laughter held a cruel edge to it. Mocking, dark and cold. Arlo had heard it before. In his visions, and before Zanna spoke.

"Chosen one?" Raas chortled, running a hand across his brow. "Come now, there is no such thing. Right time, right place. That's all you are. The sorry and sordid circumstances of your birth meant you could use both the Spark and the older magic. Humans have done an admirable job of wiping out elves, but you, due to your noble blood, were able to hide in almost plain sight. But don't mistake me, I have worked damned hard to make sure you got here. So, yes, I suppose you are chosen in a way, but not in the way you think."

Arlo took a step back, grabbing Zanna's rigid hand.

"You've used us all. Why?"

Raas turned his head to the side. "Because I am the only one able to stop what is to come, and if my people are to survive the wreckage of what the future brings, they need me out there."

Raas took a step forward.

"Your people?" Arlo asked, frowning. "The Banished?"

"The First People," Raas snapped, baring his yellowed teeth. "And yes, who else? All those who came after stole this world from us, and I was unable to stop it, or the path they put themselves on, but I can now. That is where you come in. Now, this is not going to be pleasant, but believe me, I am going to hate wearing your filthy half-elven, half-human body as much as you are going to hate staying here. At least you will have your precious Zanna, eh?"

Raas reached out and grabbed Arlo's head, and the boy's screams filled the luminous green void inside the Lodestone.

"I'm taking it away from all of them!" Raas snarled, gripping Arlo's head.

Lights exploded in his vision, and his limbs shook as the supposed god flooded his body with pure energy straight from the Lodestone.

"Every single one. Like it did to my people so long ago! When it punished us! Children should never play with their father's tools. All except my people, my kind. And with it, we will have our vengeance!"

Magic pulled Calene to her knees. Vision spinning, she gazed around, teeth bared. The three remaining Shadow Sparkers stood over her, leering down.

"This isn't ideal without the slab, but it'll do," Byar hissed, smiling at her. "My friends here have cut you off from your Spark, and I welcome the challenge of Turning one as strong as you."

Calene jerked in place. The Spark lay there, just out of grasp. Her heart hammered in her chest. As she stared up at Byar, his face flickered. In her mind, for a long moment, Ricken Alpenwood peered down at her as she lay bound to the slab in his study. Defenceless. Helpless. His face flickered again, returning to normal, the fires raging behind them back in view, the tall trees reaching into the sky, but she had been here before.

Her mother had saved her once. Brina another time. Now, she had no one but herself. Nothing but her strength of will.

Calene met Byar's eyes.

"Do your droking worst."

Nexes wrestled with a Banished warrior, swords slipping from his blood-slick hands and into the pile of corpses. Their hands locked on each other's wrists. He slammed his head into the woman's face, then did it a second time. Her hand fell away.

Grabbing at the dagger in his belt, the one he used to punish himself with, Nexes pulled it clear and sank it into the warrior's throat, her warm blood splashing his face.

Spinning, he grabbed his fallen shortswords, sticky with gore, and gazed around. The ground had stopped shaking. Lightning had stopped falling from the sky. Panicked cries reached his ears, and the Banished fell back, taking advantage of the sudden respite.

From the pile of corpses he stood on, Nexes cast around, looking for any reason why their attack had faltered.

"Sparkers!" he cried. "To me! Keep up the attack."

Only screams answered. Yells of disbelief. Weeping. He followed the sound, and found a sodden, filthy Sparker crouching among the dead.

Nexes grabbed him. "Explain yourself. Why won't you attack, man?"

"It's gone…" the Sparker sobbed. "It's droking gone! Can't you see? It's all *gone*!"

Nexes backhanded him across the face and pulled him upright. "What's gone? Speak sense."

The Sparker clutched at Nexes. "The Spark! It's gone."

Despite the battle's heat, ice cold swept over Nexes, chilling him to the bone. He let the useless Sparker fall to the ground, ignoring his weeping.

The Banished began to sing. Then, they charged.

"Drok," Nexes whispered, falling back across the piles of corpses. "Raas has forsaken us."

Calene fell forward, and the Shadow Sparkers stared at each other with alarm.

She didn't give them time to react.

Leaping to her feet, scooping her sword from the mud, she thrust it through the chest of one, bringing the other woman to her knees. She pulled it free as the mage slumped to her knees, then cleaved the Shadow's bald head from her shoulders, before moving onto the next one.

Byar fell back, sword in his hands, panic-stricken.

Calene aimed for the other, who put up no fight at all. Lips trembling, he dropped to his knees, closed his black eyes, and waited to die. Calene dispatched him, the Shadow Sparker's corpse dropping to the ground in a headless heap.

"Can't you feel it?" Byar whispered, backing up toward the flames. "It's gone. How?"

Calene paused, her hand pressing against her stomach. When the Shadow Sparkers blocked her off from her Spark, it lay just out of reach, but it still lingered there. Now, a hole existed inside her.

"Did you do this?" Calene demanded, grip tightening on the hilt.

"No, no," Byar answered, sword shaking in his hand. "I can't live without it. There's no life without the power. No point."

Turning his blade, he plunged it into his guts, sinking to his knees. Blood gushed from his mouth, and his black eyes turned blue, the darkness leaking away from them.

Calene watched. The fire in the forest burned, blocking her path to the Cradle, and to Brina. She collapsed into the mud, empty, alone, unable to reach out and feel the energy swirling around her.

Her Spark had gone.

Brina inched toward the stone door, transfixed, until she stood before it, studying it.

Instinctively, she raised her palm, and drew her blade across it, spilling blood. She pressed her hand against the stone. Warmth bloomed under the palm, and the runes glowed, until she had to close her eyes, the brightness searing her vision. Pulling her hand away, Brina shielded herself as the stone door turned into pure light.

Agony erupted in her back.

"It occurred to me," a voice whispered, as bright, white light illuminated the Cradle, "that after everything we've tried to open this damned door, I've never let one of your kind near it."

Brina dropped to her side, gasping, blood pooling under her, and stared up into the face of Emperor Locke.

"I came to...kill...you," Brina choked, the taste of iron thick in her mouth.

"I know," Locke replied, smiling. "My Shadow Sparkers told me an elf and a mage approached, so I let you enter to see what would happen. Good thing I did, eh? Well, not so good for you."

Locke knelt, and yanked Brina's head to the side. "Let's watch together. Surprises are always better with an audience, don't you think?"

The light faded, and an almost bare alcove emerged from the hue.

On the other side, sitting in a wooden chair, was an elf. She wore a simple, white robe, and as the light faded, her eyes met Brina's before fury took a hold of her features.

"How dare you?" she snarled, pointing at the emperor.

"An elf?" he mumbled, getting to his feet and letting Brina flop to the ground, life leaking out of her. "An *elf!*"

"Janna."

She strode forward, and the emperor flew back, crashing into a stack of books. She bent, cradled Brina's head, warmth radiating through her cold limbs where Janna touched.

She frowned. "Light, Raas. What have you done? This isn't going to work, you fool!"

Bright light blinded Brina, and chimes filled her ears, then wind.

Then nothing.

The Lodestone had shone bright green, filling the chamber with its light, before turning solid crimson.

Kade approached the stone, its red glow covering all. Tilo knelt beside the Banished prisoners, whispering to them, working at their chains. The branded Returned huddled together, silent.

With a pop, like the air had held its breath and finally exhaled, the light flickered out, and torches burst into life around the room, the crackle of burning filling the air. Tilo got to his feet and limped over, meeting Kade's eyes.

"I know you don't understand me all that well, but I don't like this at all," Kade murmured.

"I understand you just fine," Tilo replied.

"Then why haven't you said a word to—"

"Look!"

In front of the Lodestone, the air shimmered, and Arlo appeared, smiling.

"Ah, this is much better," he murmured, turning to the dimmed Lodestone and patting it. "You have served your purpose well."

"Arlo?" Kade whispered, taking a step forward. "Is it over?"

Tilo grabbed at his truncated arm, holding him back, eyes clouded with doubt.

"Over?" Arlo replied, grinning. "Over? No. We are only just beginning! Now, let me—"

His grin faded, a look of puzzlement washing over his face, then panic.

"Wait," he cried, spinning, grabbing the Lodestone in two hands. "Why hasn't it worked? I don't understand. Speak to me, damn you!"

"Arlo?" Kade whispered, reaching out to him.

The boy spun, rage painted across his features, just as a small, thin shape cut through the air, whistling by Kade's ear, passing between his and Tilo's heads.

The arrow slammed into Arlo's forehead, knocking him from his feet, sending his lifeless body crashing into the Lodestone, dead before his small frame hit the ground.

The scream stuck in Kade's throat until it erupted, so loud it would make the Riders of the Underworld add their voices to his grief.

He dropped to his knees, eyes fixed on Arlo's body as he crawled towards it, his heart tearing with every inch, so fixed on the corpse he didn't notice Tilo drop to the ground, limbs trembling, feet kicking, didn't see the dormant Lodestone flicker brilliant green before fading once more.

The Banished crashed into the Haltveldtian frontlines, and they buckled. Crumbled. Soldiers ignored Nexes' screams to stand firm. They'd lost their nerve. Without the Sparkers supporting them, without the black-robed mages shielding them, they saw only defeat waiting for them.

Then the ground rumbled, and lightning crashed from the sky.

It struck into the midst of the Shadow Sparkers huddled behind the Haltveldtian front row.

"Is it back?" Nexes screamed, grabbing any bright robe he could find.

"No," the Sparker whispered, face pale. "Not for me." More lightning lanced from the sky, blowing chunks out of soldiers, Haltveldtian or Banished, wherever they struck. "But it is for the Shadow Sparkers!"

The Banished's chanting changed, panicked now, and

they disengaged, falling back, as the Haltveldtian line disintegrated into chaos. Nexes scanned it.

Mages in black fought one another, tendrils of darkness flooding from their outstretched hands, lightning plummeting from the sky as they tore into one another. Stray bolts struck into the Haltveldtian lines, tossing soldiers aside like discarded, broken toys. Madness. Corrupt madness and Nexes' army had carried it from the south, brought it here to erupt at last, aimed at their fellow magi and threatening to kill them all.

"Flee!" Nexes screamed, raising his sword. "Fall back! They've lost their minds. They'll kill us all!"

Horns blared, signalling the retreat as the mad Sparkers wrought murder on each other. Nexes staggered back, memories of Tallan Square running through his mind. The day a crazed Sparker had destroyed his only family.

Now, they destroyed his army.

Turning, Nexes ran. The Shadow Sparkers promised only ruin, his instincts had always told him as much, and the man who created them had to pay, before Haltveldt burned.

Emperor Locke had ignored Nexes Almor's messages for weeks, but he'd not ignore him when Nexes plunged his dagger in the man's droking throat.

Coughing caught Calene's attention. Looking up, her heart sank when she didn't see Brina.

Byar twitched though.

Getting to her feet, sword outstretched, she approached him. As she stood over him, his eyes fluttered open.

Black once more.

Snarling, Calene shoved her sword through his shoulder, pinning him to the ground and reached out for her Spark. It didn't come.

"How are you using your magic?" Calene snarled, meeting his eyes.

Byar choked out a laugh. "The Bindings. They're gone. Whatever happened has freed us."

"Answer my droking question!" Calene growled, twisting the blade.

"Fool," Byar hissed. "The darkness doesn't come from the Spark. It's something else entirely. And now, it's the only way."

Raising her sword, she cut Byar's head away, and turned to the flames. She had to find a way into the Cradle, a way to Brina.

Then she'd leave Haltveldt well alone. Without Sparkers to protect it, those fallen to the Shadow would see it burn.

She sucked in breath when Maria du Gerran and Marc le Fondre sprang into her thoughts. They'd sworn to continue fighting the empire, and now they had no Spark. All of those standing against Emperor Locke and Haltveldt had lost their mightiest weapon, and the empire still had the Shadow Sparkers.

"Godsrot," Calene muttered, studying the flames, looking for a way through, "I can't droking leave them alone, can I?"

She knew the answer. Didn't even have to think it. But she had no magic either, nothing to call on. Calene focused inside, prodding away, searching for some sign of her Spark, anything...

And found something.

An itch in the back of her mind, lurking where her Link to Vettigan used to sit. It reminded her of running her tongue across unbrushed teeth after spending the night drinking, enamel crusted with filth.

Frowning, she reached out, and death whispered to her. Glancing around, away from the fire, darkness hovered above Byar. Without thinking, Calene reached out to it, and clicked her fingers.

Flickering black flames erupted above her hand.

Gasping, she let go of the darkness...but it lurked inside her. The residue of breaking through Vettigan's Link had left its mark, the moment of Evisceration its stain, and she'd tried to use it herself. Almost drained a life.

The shadow lay inside her. And Brina had, in her possession, the only way Calene knew to wipe it out of her body. The journal of Ricken Alpenwood.

Calene didn't have the Spark anymore, but she possessed something so much more terrifying.

Brina came to, the ache in her back gone. Sitting up, she tested her arm, rolled her shoulders.

"Calene!" she cried, jumping to her feet. "I need to find her."

"We're a long way from this Calene, girl," a voice murmured behind her.

Janna stood on a beach, a tower rising behind her. Brina glanced to the other side and saw nothing but water in every direction.

"Where are we?"

"You call it Sea's Keep, and that," she replied, pointing at the ocean, "is the Sundered Sea. We need a boat. Well, *you* need a boat."

"Why?" Brina snapped, throwing her arms up. "What are you talking about? I need to find Calene!"

Janna flowed forward and grabbed the front of Brina's leathers, lifting her from the ground. "Listen to me. Your path is not the same as your Calene's. You do not know what is at stake. Raas has erred, and it means ruin for all of us unless we stop it. And to do that, we need more of our kind. I cannot leave Haltveldt, but you can."

"Who are you?" Brina breathed, for once overwhelmed with inadequacy before the smooth-faced elf with the ancient eyes. "What are you?"

"I told you. Janna."

"*The* Janna?"

She eased Brina back to her feet and smoothed down her leathers. "Yes."

"The Janna the humans call a god? Like Raas?"

A sour expression twisted Janna's face. "The very same."

"But you're an elf!"

Janna took a step back, eyes wide in mock surprise, looking herself up and down as she spread her arms. "Well, I'll be damned, so I am!"

Brina scowled at her. "Look, you need to give me some answers, and fast. Or else I'm walking right now. How can you be *the* Janna?"

"Because my parents gave me that name," the ancient elf, the god, replied with a smirk, then held her hands up. "Listen, this isn't the time or the place, but I will tell you everything you need to know soon. First, we have a continent to save, and elves to liberate, right? Raas and I have a...complicated history, and the game he plays has been planned out *many* moves ahead. Sadly for everyone living on this Light-forsaken rock, Raas has made a mistake. A fatal one."

Brina narrowed her eyes and glanced over her shoulder at the lazy waves sloshing against the sand.

"You said I need a boat," Brina growled, meeting Janna's eyes. "I suppose you don't mean I need to sail it myself. Where do I need to go?"

"Avastia, beyond the Sundered Sea, and bring our people back with you before it is too late. Only a nation whole can fight against what's to come, and this broken Haltveldt teeters on the edge of ruin. The price of power lying in the hands of the foolish."

Brina shivered, hugged herself, and turned her back on Janna and Sea's Keep, staring out at the endless ocean without seeing.

Ruin, Janna said, but she dangled hope.

"Is Calene alive?" Brina whispered, the wind lifting her braid. She grabbed at it, tugged it.

"I don't know," Janna answered, standing beside her.

"I thought you were a god," Brina grumbled, glaring at the sand beneath her boots.

"Once, I could see the future. Once. Now it's as dark

as the shadows consuming Haltveldt. Let's hope we can lift them. We *have* to."

Hope. Brina approached the shore and knelt, wetting her hand and scrubbing the black paint from her face. Now, killing an emperor didn't seem to matter as much.

I hope I'll see you again, Calene. Please make it so.

Ricken Alpenwood's journal pressed against her chest where she kept it safe. She'd meant to force it into Calene's hands after they'd finished the emperor, a way to give her a new mission, a new task. Now she found herself half a continent away.

Turning, she stalked from the beach, towards Sea's Keep, Janna beside her. An elf, going into a human city, looking for a ship and crew to Avastia. It couldn't get any easier, could it?

"Tell me everything," Brina breathed, giving the god a sidelong look. "Everything."

Epilogue
A God's Mistake

Malek folded his arms and watched as the slaves packed the obsidian plundered from the depth of the Peaks of Eternity into bricks, brands shining in the sunlight. The Watchful Eye, a reminder to anyone who would dare think of stepping out of line. The Confederacy saw all. Knew all.

Because of its emperor.

"We captured a Sparker lurking near the canyon leading into Haltveldt, my lord."

Malek turned away from the foundations of the gateway, rubbing his chin, and nodding at Adjutant Telemens. "Did they put up much of a struggle?"

Telemens hesitated, then shook her head. "No, my lord."

"What is it?" Malek prodded, narrowing his eyes.

"They were raving, my lord, wandering through the wilderness. Lord Malek, they said they'd lost their Spark, and appeared surprised we could use any kind of magic."

"Bring them to me for questioning, Adjutant. Immediately."

Telemens snapped off a smart salute, stalking off through the camp.

Malek turned to the gateway, the one they'd built to bring through their emperor, his thoughts turning to the Haltveldtian, Kade Besem. He'd asked why they hadn't marched into Haltveldt, and Malek had answered with as much truth as he could spare. Mutual destruction of the Banished and Haltveldtian army *would* prove useful, but Malek knew the winner would still pose a threat, and for that, the Confederacy needed its emperor.

Frowning, he clicked his fingers, conjuring black flames above them. They flickered, weaker than they should, weaker than they did back home. But once he'd completed the gateway, once Malek had brought his emperor through, nothing would stand in the Confederacy's way.

For most in Haltveldt, magic came from the Lodestone. Malek and his people had studied it long enough, and come across the rare soul still capable of pulling magic from it.

For those of the Confederacy, magic came from the darkness, from where the shadows lay, and no one cast as great a shadow as the emperor.

Letting the flames die, Malek strode away toward his tent, giving the summit of the Peaks of Eternity one last look. When his emperor arrived, they'd march into Halt-veldt, and claim what belonged to them.

And no one would stop them.

No one.

THE END.

Acknowledgements

I'll try to keep this brief so the "wrap up the speech" music doesn't start playing in your heads.

To my beta readers Adrian Fletcher, Chris Hewitt, and Neen Cohen. You keep me from steering too far wrong, and tell me when I'm using drok way too much.

To Anat Eliraz for finding so many things that a writer, a publisher, an editor, three beta readers and a partridge in a pear tree couldn't find.

To Rachel Kullman. You're just totally awesome and kept me sane many, many times. Well, sane might not be the best word...

To Simone. Cuz, you're as fine an editor anyone could ask for, and your insight always elevates my words.

To Michelle for taking a chance on me in the first place, not blinking when I decided this series is four books, and for doing everything you can to get this book in front of as many eyes as possible.

And to you, readers, who have come this far. The best is ahead of us still.

David Green.

570

DAVID GREEN is a writer of the epic and the urban, the fantastical and the mysterious.

With his character-driven dark fantasy series Empire Of Ruin, or urban fantasy noir Hell In Haven starring Haven's only supernatural PI Nick Holleran, David takes readers on emotional, character-driven, action-packed thrill rides that leaves a reader needing their next fix.

Hailing from the north-west of England, David now lives in County Galway on the west coast of Ireland with his wife and train-obsessed son.

When not writing, David can be found wondering why he chooses to live in, and write about, places where it constantly rains.

Follow David everywhere.

More from Eerie River

Eerie River Publishing, is a small independant publishing house that is devoted to releasing quality dark fiction books and anthologies.

To stay up to date with all our new releases and upcoming giveaways, follow us on Facebook, Twitter, Instagram and YouTube. Sign up for our monthly newsletter and receive a free ebook Darkness Reclaimed, as our thank you gift.

https://mailchi.mp/71e45b6d5880/welcomebook

Interested in becoming a Patreon member?
Patreon membership gives you exclusive sneak peeks at upcoming books, early chapter releases, covers art as well as free ebooks and discounts on paperbacks.

https://www.patreon.com/EerieRiverPub.

Coming Soon

Shades of Night by Rachael Boucker

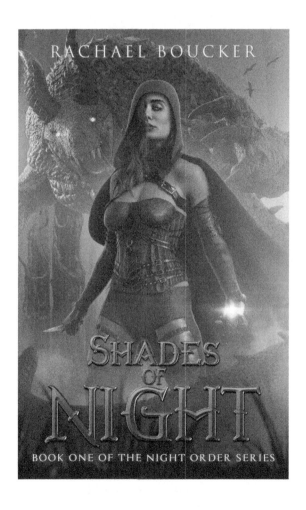

Printed in Great Britain
by Amazon

26557736R00324